TRIGGERFISH TWIST

TRIGGERFISH TWIST

A NOVEL

Tim Dorsey

WILLIAM MORROW

An Imprint of HarperCollins*Publishers*

HarperCollins books may be purchased for educational, business, or sales promotional use. For information please write: Special Markets Department, HarperCollins Publishers Inc., 10 East 53rd Street, New York, NY 10022.

FIRST EDITION

Printed on acid-free paper

Library of Congress Cataloging-in-Publication Data has been applied for.

ISBN 0-06-018571-6

02   03   04   05   06   WB/RRD   10   9   8   7   6   5   4   3   2   1

For Henry and Linda Losey

It takes a village.

—*Hillary Clinton*

It takes a village idiot.

—*Don Imus*

Acknowledgments

Appreciation is due to my agent, Nat Sobel, and my editor, Henry Ferris, for patience and understanding as I proceed in my career with the grace of a blindfolded five-year-old going at a piñata.

PROLOGUE

MY NAME IS EDITH GRABOWSKI. I'm eighty-one years old, and I had sex last night. I wanted to tell you that up front and get it out of the way because that's what all the TV people want to know. They giggle and use cute nicknames for sex when they ask. I don't think they're getting any.

I'd never been on national TV in my life before last week, and now I've been on six times in four days. In a few minutes, it'll be seven.

I'd also never been to Los Angeles. We're in the greenroom right now, but my husband, Ambrose, says it's blue. He's wrong, but I don't say anything. That's how you make a marriage last.

We're newlyweds. But you knew that already unless you've been on another planet or just come out of a coma. We were married on the *Today* show by Al Roker, because he has a notary license. They say ratings went through the roof. We're rich now, too.

One of those network hospitality ladies in a blue blazer is asking me if I'm okay again. Do I want a pillow or some juice? I tell her I'm fine. She pats my hand and smiles that stupid false smile the stewardesses give you when you're getting off the plane. You just want to smack her.

They usually want to know about the sex right after they ask how on earth we stayed alive. They still can't believe we didn't all die. What's not to believe? We just . . .

Uh-oh, here comes another woman in a blazer. This one's blond. Am I all right? Of course I'm all right! I can take care of myself.

That's how I got to be eighty-one. I'd like to see *you* make it. And don't touch me!

It's like this every time, every show. Just because I'm eighty-one, they treat me like some kind of magical little pet that can only understand four simple commands and will crap itself if they don't watch out. I'm the one who gets the most questions on camera because I say what's on my mind. Fifty years ago I was just pushy, but now I'm a "character" or a "live wire."

The networks go nuts over any story where an old person shows spunk. That's why you hear so much about Florida these days. They might as well just move their studios down there. Seems every other month one of us from the bingo hall makes the rounds of the TV shows. Last time it was that seventy-six-year-old woman from Boca Raton who bit the pit bull.

That's true. She was walking her poodle, Mr. Peepers—TV made a big deal about the name—and some lovely neighbors raising pit bulls in their backyard car-chassis farm left the gate open. Anyway, the pit bull wouldn't let go of Mr. Peepers, so she bit its ear and it ran off yelping. The way the media reacted, you'd have thought she cured cancer or invented a car that ran on tap water.

So I guess it's my turn. I don't mind telling the story again, but they always bring up the sex, like at the mere mention of it I'm going to do a handspring for them.

Or maybe: "Yippeeeeee!"

I shouldn't complain. I'm having the time of my life. I'm married to the man of my dreams. I've had a crush on Ambrose since I was seventy-eight.

They just told us to get ready here in the greenroom. They say we're about to go on. We have notecards about possible questions. About what kind of neighborhood it was.

They say it was such a quiet neighborhood. It's *always* a quiet neighborhood. Then the whole place goes berserk and everyone acts surprised. But they shouldn't. If you ask me, it's just people. Even the quietest streets are just two or three arguments away from a chain-reaction meltdown.

We can hear the audience applauding. They want the story. Can't say I blame 'em. So did *we*. I mean, me and my girlfriends— we were just trying to stay alive. We didn't see a tenth of what was going on. Same with everyone else. Things were happening all over the place. Everyone only saw a small part of the whole picture, but we were able to compare notes at the rehearsal dinner and pretty much piece it together. The entire wedding party was involved in some way. My bridesmaids were all with me, trapped as we were. Ambrose probably saw as much as anyone, riding up front in the big chase after the shootout. His best man was Jim Davenport. Poor Jim Davenport. He was such a nice, gentle man. Still is, but I don't think he's ever going to be right again. It was just one thing after another; I don't know how he held up. The ushers, Ambrose's neighbors—they saw a good bit, too. Then there was Serge. Serge had actually been Ambrose's first choice for best man, but nobody knows where he disappeared to after the gunfire started, and the explosions and all the car wrecks and the electrical transformers blowing up and strippers running naked in traffic and nearly half the city burning down.

They just gave us the one-minute signal in the greenroom.

Well, story time again. Probably the best place to start is Jim Davenport, seeing as he was in the middle of almost everything that went wrong.

Yeah, we'll start there.

And I guess we should start with the one question everyone's asking these days. Not just the TV people, but folks everywhere. They all ask the exact same thing. . . . I'll shut up now and let the narrator take over.

SO WHAT'S UP WITH FLORIDA?

Talk about a swing in reputation. Forty years ago the Sunshine State was an unthreatening View-Master reel of orange groves, alligator wrestlers, tail-walking dolphins and shuffleboard.

Near the turn of the millennium, Florida had become either romantically lawless or dangerously stupid, and often both: Casablanca without common sense, Dodge City with more weapons, the state that gave you the Miami Relatives on the evening news every night for nine straight months and changed the presidential election with a handful of confetti. Consider that two of the most famous Floridians in recent years have been Janet Reno and the Anti-Reno, Secretary of State Katherine Harris. Is there no middle genetic ground?

And yet they keep coming to Florida. People who maintain such records report that every single day, a thousand new residents move into the state. The reasons are varied. Retirement, beaches, affordable housing, growing job base, tax relief, witness protection, fugitive warrants, forfeiture laws that shelter your house if you're a Heisman trophy winner who loses a civil suit in the stabbing death of your wife, and year-round golf.

On a typical spring morning in 1997, five of those thousand new people piled into a cobalt-blue Dodge Aerostar in Logansport, Indiana. The Davenports—Jim, Martha and their three children—watched the moving van pull out of their driveway and followed it south.

A merging driver on the interstate ramp gave Jim the bird. He would have given him two birds, but he was on the phone. Jim grinned and waved and let the man pass.

Jim Davenport was like many of the other thousand people heading to Florida this day, except for one crucial difference. Of all of them, Jim was hands-down the most nonconfrontational.

Jim avoided all disagreement and didn't have the heart to say no. He loved his family and fellow man, never raised his voice or fists, and was rewarded with a lifelong, routine digestion of small doses of humiliation. The belligerent, boorish and bombastic latched onto him like strangler figs.

He was utterly content.

Then Jim moved his family to Florida, and before summer was over a most unnatural thing happened. Jim went and killed a few people.

None of this was anywhere near the horizon as the Davenports began the second day of their southern interstate migration.

The road tar at the bottom of Georgia began to soften and smell in the afternoon sun. It was a Saturday, the traffic on I-75 thick and anxious. Hondas, Mercurys, Subarus, Chevy Blazers. A blue Aerostar with Indiana tags passed the exit for the town of Tifton, SOD CAPITAL OF THE USA, and a billboard: JESUS IS LORD . . . AT BUDDY'S CATFISH EMPORIUM."

A sign marking the Florida state line stood in the distance, then the sudden appearance of palm trees growing in a precise grid. The official state welcome center rose like a mirage through heat waves off the highway. Cars accelerated for the oasis with the run-away anticipation of traffic approaching a Kuwaiti checkpoint on the border with Iraq.

They pulled into the hospitality center's angled parking slots; doors opened and children jumped out and ran around the grass in the aimless, energetic circles for which they are known. Parents stretched and rounded up staggering amounts of trash and headed for garbage cans. A large Wisconsin family in tank tops sat at a picnic table eating boloney sandwiches and generic pork rinds so they could afford a thousand-dollar day at Disney. A crack team of state workers arrived at the curb in an unmarked van and began pressure-washing some kind of human fluid off the side-walk. A stray ribbon of police tape blew across the pavement.

The Aerostar parked near the vending machines, in front of the
NO NIGHTTIME SECURITY sign.

"Who needs to go to the bathroom?" asked Jim.

Eight-year-old Melvin put down his mutant action figures and
raised a hand.

Sitting next to him with folded arms and dour outlook was
Debbie Davenport, a month shy of sweet sixteen, totally disgusted
to be in a minivan. She was also disgusted with the name Debbie.
Prior to the trip she had informed her parents that from now on
she was to be called "Drusilla."

"Debbie, you need to use the rest room?"

No reply.

Martha got out a bottle for one-year-old Nicole, cooing in her
safety seat, and Jim and little Melvin headed for the building.

Outside the rest rooms, a restless crowd gathered in front of an
eight-foot laminated map of Florida, unable to accept that they
were still hundreds of miles from the nearest theme park. They
would become even more bitter when they pulled away from the
welcome center, and the artificial grove of palms gave way to
hours of scrubland and billboards for topless doughnut shops.

Jim bought newspapers and coffee. Martha took over the driving and got back on I-75. Jim unfolded one of the papers. "Says
here authorities have discovered a tourist from Finland who lost
his luggage, passport, all his money and ID and was stranded for
eight weeks at Miami International Airport."

"Eight weeks?" said Martha. "How did he take baths?"

"Wet paper towels in the rest rooms."

"Where did he sleep?"

"Chairs at different gates each night."

"What did he eat?"

"Bagels from the American Airlines Admirals Club."

"How did he get in the Admirals Club if he didn't have ID?"

"Doesn't say."

"If he went to all that trouble, he probably could have gotten
some kind of help from the airline. I can't believe nobody noticed
him."

"I think that's the point of the story."

"What happened?"

"Kicked him out. He was last seen living at Fort Lauderdale International."

The Aerostar passed a group of police officers on the side of the highway, slowly walking eight abreast looking for something in the weeds. Jim turned the page. "They've cleared the comedian Gallagher in the Tamiami Strangler case."

"Is that a real newspaper?"

Jim turned back to the front page and pointed at the top. *Tampa Tribune.*

Martha rolled her eyes.

"Says they released an artist's sketch. Bald with mustache and long hair on the sides. Police got hundreds of calls that it looked like Gallagher. But they checked his tour schedule—he was out of state the nights of the murders."

"They actually checked him out?"

"They also checked out Gallagher's brother."

Martha looked at Jim, then back at the road.

"After clearing Gallagher, they got a tip that he has a brother who looks just like him and smashes watermelons on a circuit of low-grade comedy clubs under the name Gallagher II. But he was out of town as well."

"I hope I don't regret this move," said Martha.

Jim put his hand on hers. "You're going to love Tampa."

Jim Davenport had never planned on moving to Tampa, or even Florida for that matter. Everything he knew about the state came from the *Best Places to Live in America* magazine that now sat on the Aerostar's dashboard. Right there on page 17, across from the feature on the joy of Vermont's covered bridges, was the now famous annual ranking of the finest cities in the U.S. of A. to raise a family. And coming in at number three with a bullet—just below Seattle and San Francisco—was the shocker on the list, rocketing up from last year's 497th position: Tampa, Florida. When the magazine hit the stands, champagne corks flew in the chamber of commerce. The mayor called a press conference, and the city quickly threw together a band and fireworks at a riverfront park; the news was so big it even caused some people to get laid.

Nobody knew it was all a mistake. The magazine had recently been acquired by a German media conglomerate, which purchased the latest spelling and grammar-check software and dismissed its editors and writers, replacing them with distracted high school students in Walkman headsets. The tabular charts on the new software had baffled a student with green hair, who inadvertently moved all of Tampa's crime statistics a decimal point to the left.

JIM AND MARTHA DAVENPORT were a perfect match. She had long, flowing red hair and the patience of a firecracker. He had selective hearing.

Martha was forty-two, a year older than Jim, five-six with large hips but the perfect weight. Her lips were full, and she unconsciously favored shades of lipstick that matched her hair and freckles. Jim was five-ten with a curious physique. His frame was narrow, except for the shoulders, which were spread and bony, and he required big suits that hung all over him like a Talking Heads video.

Martha drove past the Ocala exit and checked on the kids in the rearview. Debbie was working on her sulk. Melvin wore thick glasses and read a science book, how to make a compass with a glass of water and a sewing needle. Nicole leaned forward in her safety seat, discovering her toes.

Martha set cruise control on seventy in the right lane. They entered the gravitational field of Tampa Bay. An electric-lime bullet bike shot past on the left. Another ninja bike flew by on the right, in the breakdown lane, followed by a speeding red convertible full of shirtless, tattooed rocket scientists.

Martha watched them accelerate and disappear. "They endangered our family! If I had a gun—"

"That's why you don't have a gun."

"Can we get a Suburban?"

"You know how much they cost."

"They have more armor to protect the kids. Look how the people drive here."

An Eagle Talon raced by on the right, cutting across the minivan with inches to spare. Martha hit the brakes.

"What kind of a place are we moving to?"

Jim grabbed the magazine off the dash. "Great weather, sandy beaches, beautiful state parks, historic Latin quarter, barely perceptible crime rate . . ."

They reached the city an hour before sunset. The moving van wasn't due until morning, so they had to put up. Martha drove slowly, hunched over the wheel, scanning roadside motel signs. Econo, Budget, Value, Thrift-Rite, El Rancho.

They rolled through an intersection, the gas stations on all four corners boarded up with squatters in lawn chairs selling velvet paintings, country music lawn statuary, counterfeit Beanie Babies and slightly fresh seafood. Outside a pawnshop, a homeless man and a woman in a leopard miniskirt wrestled over a VCR.

"Doesn't look safe."

Jim pointed. "There's a Motel 9."

"I don't know."

"It's a big chain," he said. "They're not going to let anything happen to us."

The Davenports checked in and unpacked. A half hour later, Jim and Martha strolled onto their second-floor motel balcony.

"See? It's beautiful!" said Jim, and they held hands as the sun set behind the Starvin' Marvin.

SHORTLY AFTER MIDNIGHT, a deep boom awakened the Davenports.

"What was that?" asked Martha, bolting up in bed.

"Thunder?" said Jim.

Martha walked to the window and peeked out the curtains. "There aren't any clouds."

TEN MINUTES AFTER midnight at the Breakers Hotel. Not the one in Palm Beach. The one in Tampa next door to Motel 9 with three cars in the lot and a flickering neon sign advertising free local calls and in-room porn.

Room 112. Mr. Rogers on TV.

"It's a beautiful day in the neighborhood, a beautiful day in the neighbor—"

Ka-boom.

A twelve-gauge blew out the picture tube of the twenty-inch Sony.

A tall blonde ran out of the bathroom with white powder across her face. "What happened?"

"I don't know. It just went off," said the man holding a sawed-off shotgun in one hand and a Schlitz in the other.

"It doesn't just go off!" yelled the blonde.

"This one did."

Dogs started barking.

"Gimme that," she said, reaching for the gun.

"No!"

"Yes!"

She jerked it out of his hands, and it went off again, blowing out the ceiling lamp. They ducked as glass fell.

More dogs barked.

"Okay, now that time it was *your* fault," said the man.

"Don't be blaming me! You're the one who can't do a simple thing like guard this asshole." She pointed at the bed and the drunk businessman who had been abducted outside a titty bar and driven around for three hours, forced to make repeated ATM with-drawals and ride in the trunk during the interspersed drug buys.

But the businessman was too tanked to be afraid. In fact, he never stopped talking, and the kidnappers began to regret their hostage selection.

"I can fix you up with a nice, clean, low-mileage Camaro," said the hostage. "No credit? *No problemo!*"

"Shut up!" screamed the woman.

The male kidnapper walked over and looked closely at the man's face. "Hey! I know him! He's the guy on TV!"

The hostage smiled. He was "Honest Al," the lying sales man-ager at Tampa Bay Motors. Twenty times a day he could be seen on local TV, banging the hood of an odometer-tampered Hyundai. "No credit? *No problemo!*"

Al became cranky. "Can I go now? I gotta be back at the lot in a few hours."

"Shut up!" screamed the woman.

"I'll give you some more money," said Al. "I have to be there by nine. Got some people coming back to look at a flood-damaged Cadillac. Except they don't know it's flood-damaged. A couple of stupid Puerto Ricans."

"Hey!" snapped the male kidnapper. "That's not very nice."

"Screw *nice*," said Al.

"Shut up!" screamed the woman.

"You guys are losers!" said Al. "I'm leaving!"

Al got up from the bed, but the woman took two quick running steps, planted her feet and slammed Al in the face with the butt of the shotgun, sending him back on the mattress with a spurting nosebleed.

"You don't have to be mean to him," said her partner.

"We're *robbing* him, you stupid fuck!"

"He's just annoying. He hasn't given us any real trouble." The man tapped a bag of cocaine over the dresser. The coke had gotten moist and wasn't coming out of the baggie well, and he tapped harder and the whole thing fell out in a big chunk and disintegrated in the carpet.

"That was all we had!" yelled the woman. She got down on her hands and knees and snorted the rug.

"You getting any?"

She raised her head. "A little."

He joined her.

"You're such an oaf, Coleman."

"You used my name."

"Yeah, it's your name. Coleman. So what?"

"He heard you."

"So?"

"So now we have to kill him."

"We're not killing shit," she said.

"I didn't hear a thing," said Al.

The woman stood up and slapped Al.

"Do you have to do that?" said Coleman.

"You're the one who wants to kill him."

"He can testify against me."

"Like I care."

"All right, let's see how you like it, *Sharon*."

"Stop it!"

"Sharon, Sharon, Sharon . . ."

"Don't push me!"

Coleman climbed on one of the beds and jumped up and down. *"Sharon, Sharon, Sharon . . ."*

The motel room door flew open. Standing against the dark parking lot: a tall, lanky man in a tropical shirt.

"What the fuck was all that shooting?"

Sharon and Coleman pointed at each other.

The man threw up his arms.

Coleman jumped down off the bed and ran up to him. "Serge! She used my name in front of the hostage!"

"You idiot!"

"Oh, I just used your name, didn't I?"

Serge looked at Sharon, nose back in the rug.

"Can I ever leave you two unsupervised? And look at the coke all over the place! Don't you know we're in the middle of the War on Drugs?"

"The War on Drugs?" said Coleman. "I think I marched against that once."

"Why don't you get high on life instead?"

"And be like you?" said Sharon. "No thanks! Wandering around the parking lot like a lunatic . . ."

"I told you! The space shuttle was visible on the south-southwest horizon at seventeen degrees for four minutes and twenty-three seconds! I can't believe you didn't want to see it!"

"Can I go now?" asked Al. "If you take me by an ATM, I can give you guys and the hooker some more money."

"Hooker?" said Sharon. *"Hooker!"*

"Mister," said Serge, "for your information, that's a coke slut."

"Hooker!" Sharon screamed. She picked up the shotgun and bashed him in the forehead again with the butt. When she did, the gun discharged, blowing out the mirror over the sink.

"I give up," said Serge. "Let's save ammo and call the police ourselves."

Dogs started barking again. This time there were sirens, too.

Serge sighed and went over to Al.

"Is he hurt?" asked Sharon.

"He's dead," said Serge.

"What?"

"Must have been the recoil from the blast. Broke his neck."

"But I only meant to hurt him."

"No good deed goes unpunished."

The dogs were getting quieter but the sirens louder.

Serge canted his head toward the window. "That's the two-minute warning. You know the drill."

The three grabbed different parts of Al by his clothing, hoisted him to hip level and shuffled out the door. They threw him in the trunk and sped away without closing the room. Serge gunned the '65 Barracuda and raced without headlights down a service alley behind Motel 9, just as two squad cars pulled into the Breakers.

Serge avoided the expressway and zigzagged across town on darkened industrial roads through the hobo-land of the underpasses.

"I hope you two are happy," said Serge. "Now I'm gonna miss the Marlins' highlights on ESPN. I think they're going all the way this year."

"No chance," said Coleman. "They'll never get past Turner's Braves."

"Will so!"

"Will not!"

"Are we going by any place we can get coke?" asked Sharon.

Serge drove to the Port of Tampa and pulled into a vacant twenty-four-hour al fresco Laundromat where all the coin slots had been pried with screwdrivers. They heaved the body out of the trunk.

Serge dragged Al by the ankles across the concrete floor.

"What are you planning?" asked Sharon.

"He was drunk, right?" said Serge.

They nodded.

Serge pulled the body up to the vending machines. "So when they do the autopsy, he'll have a high blood-alcohol content, right?"

They nodded again.

Serge laid Al on his back and spread Al's arms wide in front of a soft-drink machine. He stepped back, doing rough trigonometry in his head. He leaned down again and slid Al a few inches closer to the machine. The machine had a warning sticker: a big rectangle tipping over on a stick man with lightning bolts coming out of his head. The sticker said not to tip the machine in the event a product did not dispense.

Serge tipped it.

The machine went over with a crash and the sound of hissing soda cans. A cocktail of Pepsi, Mountain Dew and blood began to pool, only the man's fingertips sticking out from under the sides of the machine.

"There," said Serge. "Not only will we not get caught, but he'll always be remembered as a dumb-ass."

They jumped back in the car and grabbed the expressway.

"Where are we going?" asked Coleman.

"Back to the house."

"But—" said Coleman.

"But what?"

"I want to party."

"Yeah," Sharon agreed. "We want to party."

"Don't you think you've already had a pretty big night?"

"It's still early," said Sharon.

"Yeah, it's still early," said Coleman.

"Early?" said Serge. "It's getting light out."

"That's as early as it gets," said Coleman.

2

THE DAVENPORTS WERE up at first light. Jim pulleyed open the thick curtains before stepping onto the balcony. There was dew on the railing and diesel sounds from the interstate and a dozen police cars behind the motel next door. At the truck stop across the street, a line had already formed outside a Winnebago of ill repute.

The Davenports carried luggage across the parking lot.

Martha pulled up short at the Aerostar. "Someone keyed the van!"

Jim ran a finger along the scratch. "You're right."

"Is that all you're going to say?"

"You're right and I love you."

"Sometimes you make me so mad."

They climbed in the van; Jim hopped on the expressway. He threw a quarter in the automatic toll booth, but the red light didn't change. He drove through. A wino scurried from the underbrush and pulled a quarter out of the plastic basket, where he'd stuffed a rag in the coin hole.

The Davenports got off the expressway and headed into south Tampa. None of them had seen their new home yet, except in pictures. The deal was prearranged and underwritten by Jim's company, an expanding Indiana consulting firm that had asked for volunteers to move to new branch offices in Phoenix, San Antonio and Tampa. Long lines formed for Arizona and Texas. Jim wondered why he was all alone at the Florida desk.

Jim checked street signs as the van rolled down Dale Mabry Highway.

"I think we're getting close."

Drama built, everyone's face at the window. Antique malls, dry cleaners, Little League fields, 7-Elevens. Just like neighborhoods everywhere, but with lots of palm trees and azaleas.

Jim made a right. Almost there. Martha liked the sound of the street names. Barracuda Trail, Man O' War Terrace, Coral Circle. When they got to Triggerfish Lane, Jim made a left. Their mouths fell open.

Paradise.

The sun was high, the sky clear, and children played catch and rode bikes in the street. And the colors! . . . lush gardens and hedges, pastel paint schemes. Teal, turquoise, pink, peach. The houses started at the bayfront and unfolded chronologically as development had pushed inland. Clapboard bungalows from the twenties, Mediterranean stuccos from the thirties and forties, classic ranch houses of the fifties and sixties. It used to be a consistent architectural flow, but real estate in south Tampa had become so white hot that anything under two thousand square feet was bulldozed to make way for three-story trophy homes that now towered out both windows of the Aerostar. Half the places had decorative silk flags hanging over brass mailboxes. Florida Gators flags and FSU Seminoles flags. Flags with sunflowers and golf clubs and sailfish and horses. Jim pointed ahead at a light-ochre bungalow with white trim. A restoration-award flag hung from the wraparound porch.

"There she is."

Martha's eyes popped with elation, and she hugged Jim.

The moving truck was already unloading in the driveway when they pulled up in front of 888 Triggerfish. A grinning Realtor stepped down from the porch and walked to the van carrying a jumbo welcome basket of citrus jams, butters, marmalades and chewies, wrapped up in green cellophane.

"Welcome! Welcome!" The Realtor pumped Jim's hand, then Martha's. "Gonna love it here in Florida. Couldn't live anywhere else!"

Jim went out on the lawn and triumphantly pulled up the FOR SALE / SOLD! sign.

A boy on a skateboard stopped at the end of the driveway. "You bought a house on *this* street?"

The Realtor grabbed Jim by the arm. "Let's go inside."

"What did that kid mean?"

"Guess what!" said the Realtor. "The cable's already hooked up!"

Heart be still, Martha told herself as she walked between bougainvillea in terra-cotta pots atop pedestals flanking the porch steps. She stopped and turned slowly. A cedar porch swing. Three verdigris eights next to the door and a stained-glass window over it. Little fish swam in the painted glass. Triggerfish, Martha decided.

She walked inside, carrying Nicole in her car seat, and it just didn't quit. Cherry hardwood floor and a yellow brick fireplace. Jim stood in the middle of the empty living room with hands on his hips. Melvin ran upstairs and claimed the cool bedroom overlooking the porch, and Debbie sulked up the stairs and kicked him out.

Martha stopped and gazed at Jim in the center of the room. There had always been something about him. People said he reminded them of Tom Hanks, although there was little resemblance except for the eyes and slightly curly dark hair. It was a certain sympathetic quality. The disarming smile. A vulnerability that made people want to take care of him.

There was yelling upstairs.

"No fair!" shouted Melvin.

"*Life's* not fair!"

A door slammed.

Another voice from the porch: "Hellooooo, new neighbors!" Heavy panting.

Martha gave Jim a look—What can *this* be?—and opened the door.

"You must be the Davenports!"

A woman with a low center of gravity jogged in place on the welcome mat. Her sweatsuit was covered with Dalmatians. "Sorry, can't stop running. Have to keep the heart up for at least thirty minutes . . ." She tapped the stopwatch hanging from her neck and kept panting. "Saw the moving van. Your car. Had to say hello. I'm Gladys. Gladys Plant. Of the original Tampa Plants." She held out her bouncing hand for Martha to shake.

Gladys retrieved her hand and looked at the palm. "Sorry about the sweat. I'll shower and come back." She ran away.

Martha closed the door and braced it with her back. "Jeee-zus!"

"Harmless," said Jim. "Probably won't be back."

He was wrong. Gladys returned in an hour with a bottle of wine and an antique tin of homemade lemon cookies. Several excruciating hours later, the sun set over the tops of the palm trees at the end of the street. The movers in the driveway were down to just the big stuff stacked in the back of the truck, dressers, box springs. Gladys was still with them on the porch, a crowd of three on the cedar swing.

". . . So then my great-great-grandfather built the Tampa Bay Hotel for the rich Yankees coming down on his railroad . . . Churchill stayed there. And Stephen Crane. And Remington. He was a painter, you know . . ."

Jim and Martha forced smiles and pinched themselves to stay awake.

"But you don't want to hear about that . . ." said Gladys.

Thank God.

". . . You want to know about your neighbors." Gladys pointed across the street, two houses up, 907 Triggerfish. She checked her watch. "Keep your eye on the front door. Any second now . . ."

The door at 907 opened and an elegantly dressed couple emerged and got in a green LeSabre.

"The Belmonts," said Gladys. "Up close, they look like Angie Dickinson and Dean Martin, but with a lot more mileage. They like their gin. That's where they're going right now. They've got Tampa's happy-hour scene down to a science. Know every special at every bar in town, even the VFW hall and the Moose Lodge. It's actually quite remarkable."

The LeSabre drove by and Gladys waved, still talking. "See the place next door? Eight-ninety-seven?" They turned. A woman with cropped blond hair shepherded three small boys in designer tennis clothes into a sport-utility vehicle.

"Barbara Colby, soccer mom from hell. If you ask me, she's going to drive those kids up a tower with a rifle. She's compensating for a father who went insane when she was a child and forced her to start memorizing the Bible. She was up to Deuteronomy before calmer heads prevailed."

Gladys saw the looks on the Davenports' faces.

"Oh, nothing's a secret around here," she said. "Every summer the Bradfords tape newspaper up in their windows for illegal renovations, every fall Mr. Donnolly blows all his leaves into the Peabodys' yard, and every winter the Fergusons put up so many Christmas lights it smashes the power grid. Mr. Schmidt has a yard the size of a postage stamp, but he has to have the best riding mower, and he's always drunk when he's on it. The Hubbards argue *way* too loud, which is how we found out about their swinging love harness. The Rutherfords can't park in their garage because it's full of Jet Skis and mopeds and unicycles and all this stuff they buy and use just once. The Baxters claim they're Xeriscaping, but everyone knows they just don't give a damn. And we all wish the Coopers *didn't* give a damn so they'd stop with the lawn jockeys and cement mermaids. Then there's Mr. Oppenheimer. I've never even seen Mr. Oppenheimer. They say he lives in his garage, where he's been building an experimental aircraft from a kit for twelve years . . ."

Gladys pointed directly across the street at 887 Triggerfish and the man kneeling on the manicured lawn with scissors.

"Jack Terrier. His middle name is actually Russell. Can you imagine parents doing that to a child? Takes all kinds. His thing is a lawn fetish."

They stopped and watched Jack hand-prune the St. Augustine.

"He does have nice grass," said Martha. She looked around at the other yards. "Everyone else's looks so . . . *brown.*"

Gladys waved at the sky. "We're in the middle of a drought. The city's under Code Red lawn-watering restrictions. Every night at four A.M., Jack comes out in a camouflaged hunting outfit to water his yard. I kid you not."

They stopped to sip wine. Triggerfish Lane took on idyllic amber and rose hues as the sun went down. The foot traffic came out: wholesome couples jogging and riding bikes and power-walking with heart monitors.

"It's so safe," Jim marveled.

"Like the fifties," said Martha.

"*Ozzie and Harriet,*" said Gladys. "You're now living in the best part of Tampa, S.O.K."

"S.O.K.?"

"Local slang. South of Kennedy Boulevard. That's like the demilitarized zone. The Thirty-eighth Parallel . . ."

"So on the other side it's like . . . ?"

"North Korea."

A dog began barking. They looked up. A fat pit bull ran out of Jack Terrier's yard and chased a jogger three houses down the street. Then the dog stopped and lumbered back to Terrier's front yard. The jogger turned and shook a fist at Jack, but he was busy with his scissors.

"Is that his dog?" asked Martha.

Gladys nodded. "His name's Rasputin."

A Rollerblader came by, and the dog took off again. Then a couple with a twin baby stroller, who had to do a wheelie to get away.

"Isn't there a leash law?" asked Jim.

"Of course," said Gladys. "But enforcement is weak. We tried calling the police, but Jack always has the dog back in the house by the time they arrive. Cops say there's nothing they can do until it actually bites someone."

Martha noticed Jack walking across the street. "Shhhh! He's coming over here."

"Probably wants to welcome us," said Jim.

Jack stopped at the bottom of the porch steps. "Got a second?"

"Me?" asked Jim.

Terrier nodded.

"I'll be right back," Jim told Martha and Gladys.

He came down off the porch with his right hand extended. "Pleased to meet you. I'm Jim Davenport. That's my wife, Martha."

Martha smiled and waved from the porch.

"Right," said Terrier. He pointed back at the street. "Listen, is that your vehicle?"

Jim retracted his unshaken hand. "The Aerostar? Yeah, that's ours."

"Can you park it in your driveway?"

Jim looked at the driveway. The moving truck was still there.

"The driveway's full," said Jim.

"I know," said Jack. He stared at Jim. Jim began to squirm; he looked up and down Triggerfish Lane. It was one of those old streets platted extra wide, and most of the neighbors had cars in the road.

"You having a party or something?" Jim asked. "Need extra parking?"

"No."

"Am I breaking a rule?"

"No."

Jim paused. "Please don't take this the wrong way. Mind if I ask why you want me to move it?"

"I don't like it there."

"Oh." Jim looked across the street at Terrier's Audi parked at the curb. "Your car's in the street."

"I need it there."

"I see."

They stood for another awkward moment.

"So you don't want me to park in the street?" asked Jim.

"Right."

"All the time?"

"Right."

"Except when we have company. That would be okay, wouldn't it?"

"Not really."

"What about an emergency?"

Jack patted Jim on the back. "Try to keep it in the driveway, sport."

"Okay," said Jim.

Jack began walking away. "It really bothers me."

"Nice to meet you," Jim called out.

"Right." Jack looked both ways and crossed the street.

Jim went back to the porch swing.

"What did he want?" asked Martha.

"He wants us to park in the driveway."

"When?"

"All the time."

Yelling erupted across the street. Rasputin had finally gotten Jack Terrier's attention.

"Whoaaaa, doggie!" Jack held out both arms in a halt signal as Rasputin went into the squatting position. The dog froze. Jack grabbed him by the collar and dragged him across the property line into his neighbor's yard at 877.

"What about the people who live there?" Martha asked Gladys. "Doesn't Jack worry they'll see him?"

"That's Old Man Ortega's place," said Gladys. "He'd never say anything even if it did bother him. Lives there alone. Comes out to get the paper and that's about it. Pound for pound, the best neighbor on the block."

Jim and Martha nodded.

"On the other hand . . ." said Gladys, pointing three houses away at 857 Triggerfish, where cars and Jeeps and pickups sat all over the dirt yard, and a plastic flamingo drank out of a toilet on the porch. Trash spilled over the curb.

"That's the Rental House," said Gladys. "A bunch of college kids from the University of South Florida. They're majoring in dragging down our property values."

"There's a rental on the street?" Martha asked with concern.

"That's actually the *Original* Rental," said Gladys. "We now have a total of six on Triggerfish."

"Six?" said Martha.

"The same guy owns them all. It's like he has a thing for this street. And he has a knack for picking the worst tenants."

"Which ones are rentals?" asked Martha.

"That one over there, where they think chain-link fence is landscaping. And the one next to it is rented by a Latin family who built that religious Madonna grotto with rocks and bathroom caulk. And that one over there, where a couple from Knoxville liked the grotto idea so much they made their own for Tammy Wynette."

Jim stared at the students' trash pile. "I've never seen so many pizza boxes."

"It's like clockwork," said Gladys. "Every night, right after Jack comes out to water the lawn in his Delta Force outfit, the students order pizza. My guess is marijuana. That's how it works, you know. The pizza companies are in brutal competition. Backgammon Pizza guarantees delivery in thirty minutes, and Pizza Shack sends its drivers out to follow the Backgammon drivers and lure away their customers by giving out free pies, which they claim taste better. Needless to say, they tear around the neighborhood hell-bent for leather trying to make the thirty-minute deadline and catch each other."

Martha pointed at the house between the college students and Old Man Ortega. "Who lives there?"

"Mr. Grønewaldenglitz. He's an artist . . . and a renter. Half the times I've seen him, he's been wearing a welding helmet. He converted his den into an acetylene shop, where he stockpiles scrap metal from the landfill and solders it together into those whimsical creations of modern art that you're pointing at in his front yard."

"So that's what those are," said Martha.

"What's the big one supposed to be?" asked Jim.

"The cow made of fenders and umbrella skeletons?"

"No, the radar range, monkey wrenches and water faucets."

"Lady Bird Johnson."

"I think it's ugly," said Martha.

"So does everyone else," said Gladys. "We went to the zoning board, but they say it's First Amendment."

A pickup truck full of real estate signs parked in front of 867 Triggerfish. A man in jeans got out and began pounding a FOR RENT sign into the front yard between Lady Bird and a chicken-wire diorama of Gettysburg.

"Wow, Mr. Grønewaldenglitz moved out," said Gladys. "So that's what he was doing in the middle of the night."

"What else should we know about this neighborhood?" asked Martha.

"Well, do you have any pets?" asked Gladys.

"No."

"You do now. A family of opossums lives under your house. They come out at night and make the rounds of the neighborhood's pet-food bowls."

Something large and fast-moving caught the corner of Jim's eye. He turned quickly, but it was gone.

"Was that one of them?" he asked.

"Where?" said Gladys.

"Over there. I saw something big."

They looked and waited.

"There!" Jim yelled. He pointed at what seemed to be a small armored personnel carrier. "There it is again! What the hell is it?"

Gladys laughed. "That's one of our roaches."

"*That's* a roach?" said Jim.

Gladys nodded. "If you belong to the chamber of commerce, you're supposed to call 'em palmetto bugs."

"Kill it!" Martha told Jim.

"Maybe we should observe it for a while," he said. "Learn its defensive systems."

"What's are you waiting for?" said Martha. "Kill it, already!"

Jim grabbed a rake and walked across the porch.

There was sudden movement and Jim swung the rake, taking down a hanging planter.

"I forgot," said Gladys. "And they can fly."

A commercial van drove up the street. It passed the Davenport home and stopped three doors down. The van had a large magnetic sign on the side: INSULT-TO-INJURY PROCESS SERVERS. A man in white makeup and a black-and-white-striped shirt got out.

"What's that about?" asked Jim.

"A malignant version of the singing telegram," said Gladys. "For wealthy grudge-bearers: subpoenas, summonses and suits delivered with attitude . . . We usually get them on this street about once a month."

"What do they do?" asked Martha.

"Mrs. Van Fleet was served a defamation lawsuit by a barbershop quartet. Mr. Buckingham got a restraining order from a tap-dancing Shirley Temple look-alike. And Mr. Fishbine was subpoenaed by a clown who squirted him in the eye with a trick lapel flower."

The three turned to the left and watched. The mime stood at the front door, but nobody was answering because he mimed knocking on the door instead of actually knocking. Finally, someone inside noticed him through a window and opened up. The mime handed him legal papers, then did a pantomime of someone crying silently and holding on to the bars of a jail cell.

The resident grabbed a bowling trophy and began chasing the mime around the front yard. The mime ran with silly, exaggerated strides and a goofy look of alarm on his face until he was knocked cold.

3

Two A.M. The pedestrian traffic was down to a trickle at the south end of Tampa's Howard Avenue, the part of town overrun by bistros, martini bars and California cuisine. It made the young professionals feel cosmo, and they called the strip "SoHo"—South Howard—but it only increased the reek of small pond.

One of the last genuine places was a modest yellow building on a side street. Stark concrete and small windows with beer signs. The Tiny Tap tavern stood alone next to the railroad tracks and the vine-covered concrete supports of the Crosstown Expressway. There were two pool tables, some stock-car junk on the walls, lots of smoke and the loud, reassuring drone of malarkey. Tonight there was an added attraction. A leggy blonde poised with her back arched against the L-shaped bar and produced a cigarette with no intention of lighting it herself.

A young man with two beepers on his belt materialized with a flicked butane. The juke played "Indian Reservation" by Paul Revere and the Raiders. The blonde turned to the flame and lightly brushed the man's crotch with the back of her hand. His stomach fluttered. Did she do that on purpose?

Ten minutes later he was getting a hummer in the front seat of his Hummer, parked under the expressway. She came up for air. "You like to screw on coke?"

In an impressive display of prestidigitation, a wallet suddenly appeared in the man's hand. He was fishing out a hundred when she grabbed the billfold and dumped the contents in her lap. "If we get an eight-ball, we can really have some fun."

"But—" the man said, reaching for his money. She began playing the silent flute again, and his objections evaporated. "Start the car and head south on Howard," she said, then back to work. His gas-pedal leg trembled, and the Hummer lurched herky-jerky up the street. She peeked over the dashboard. "Turn here!" He ran over the curb.

"Pull into those apartments. Cut the lights but keep the engine running. I'll be right back." She jumped from the vehicle with three hundred dollars and ran for the breezeway.

"An eight-ball is only two-fifty," the man shouted after her. "Two-seventy-five tops."

"I'll get change," she yelled, and disappeared into the blackness of the apartment hallway.

The man stuck his head out the driver's window, trying to adjust his eyes. Where'd she go?

She kept running down the breezeway, right out the back of the apartments and into the next street. She spun around in the middle of the road, frantic. Headlights swung around the corner at the end of the street, and a dented Impala convertible raced up to her.

Sharon jumped in and punched Coleman in the shoulder. "You blockhead! You were supposed to be waiting!"

"Ow," said Coleman, rubbing his shoulder as he drove off. "How much we get?"

"I shouldn't give you any for being late! What if he followed me!" She bent down from the wind to light a cigarette, took a deep drag and violently exhaled out her nostrils. "I should fuckin' kill you!"

"Where'd you get that lighter?"

Sharon looked at the lighter. "What do you mean?"

"I think I recognize that lighter," said Coleman. It was an old banged-up Zippo. The paint had started to chip on some words. *Miami* and *Orange Bowl* and *1969*.

"A lighter's a lighter," said Sharon, jamming it down the tight hip pocket of her jeans.

"If that's what I think it is, we're in big trouble," said Coleman. "That looks like Serge's Super Bowl Three lighter. You haven't been getting into his *secret box*, have you?"

"Secret box? What are you guys, playing fuckin' army in the

woods? I was out of goddamn matches. He's always got a ton of matches in there. This time I found the lighter."

"You've been taking his matches, too! Oh my God, we're dead for sure!"

"Give me a break!"

"Oh, man!" said Coleman. "If you don't understand the secret box, you don't understand *anything* about Serge."

"It's a box. So what!"

"A 1905 Ybor City master cigar-maker's box," said Coleman. "Those matches are from his favorite places in Florida. Half of them have been torn down. And you've just been going through them to light cigarettes? He's going to shoot us both!"

"He's not gonna know," said Sharon. "He's got so much shit in that box I couldn't believe it. I mean just crap! Swizzle sticks, lapel pins, ticket stubs, bar coasters, ashtrays, old hotel-room keys. He's never gonna miss it."

"Oh, he'll miss it all right," said Coleman. "I've seen his ritual, packing everything away in its special place and locking the box each night in the fireproof safe under his bed . . . We are *so* dead."

"Just drive, blockhead!"

Coleman drove. He wore a T-shirt with a rum ad, cutoff shorts and dirty sneakers with no laces. He was on the pudgy side with a circular head that was a little too big for his body, and he didn't like it when Sharon called him blockhead or That Funny Round-Headed Kid. His driver's license was suspended for multiple DUIs. He opened another Schlitz.

"You're driving too slow! Step on it, you blockhead!"

"Sharon, please don't call me that."

"Fuck off, Charlie Brown!"

Sharon Rhodes, exotic, tall, high cheekbones and a full, moist mouth that caused men to let go of the controls and fly their lives into the sides of mountains. Easily the hottest stripper on Dale Mabry Highway when she got the incidental ambition to actually show up at work. She was on probation for Jet Skiing topless next to the Courtney Campbell causeway.

They pulled into a dark apartment complex behind Busch Gardens. A crescent moon peeked through the top of the Montu roller coaster. Sharon got out.

"Don't spend it all on crack this time," said Coleman. "Get some powder, too. Crack is bad for you."

"I'll get what I fuckin' want!" She put out her cigarette on the Impala's upholstery.

"Hey!"

As soon as she was out of sight, Coleman slammed the gear shift in reverse and lunged backward, spinning ninety degrees. He threw the car in drive and floored it, leaving rubber. He raced around the block and came up on the back side of the apartments just as Sharon ran into the street. She winced when she saw the Impala. "Damn."

Coleman parked at the curb and jumped out. "Nice try. I'm not letting you out of my sight."

They went back in the apartments and knocked lightly on a peeling second-floor door.

There were shuffling sounds inside, then a quiet "Who is it?"

"Sharon and Blockhead."

Coleman elbowed her.

"Don't *ever* elbow me!" She grabbed him by the hair and went to smash his head into the door, but it opened.

Their host wore an orange-and-black silk Kabuki robe, and he turned without speaking and walked back into the dark room lit only by a dozen Bic lighters. People sitting and lying on the floor, gaunt, palsied. Trash everywhere. Glass and metal pipes and spent wooden matches lying in burn marks on the carpet. A rat scampered across tufts of shredded Brillo pads. There was a TV stand, but no TV. On an empty bookcase, one of those novelty static-electric lightning globes from Spencer's Gifts. A naked, emaciated woman with deflated tits walked through the room in a trance and disappeared into the kitchen. Nobody paid attention. A stereo was going somewhere, *The Very Best of Tom Jones.*

Sharon handed money to the man in the robe, who went in another room and came back with a baggie of little butterscotch cubes.

". . . *It's not unusual to be loved by anyone . . .*"

"Let's get out of here," said Coleman. "Everyone's weird."

Sharon ignored him. She dropped to the floor and began breaking up the cubes and cramming them in a glass pipe. The naked woman walked back through the room and disappeared again. Coleman put his hands on the static-lightning globe. "Cool."

The naked woman drifted back through the room, stopped in the middle and burst into sobs. Nobody cared. Sharon flicked the Zippo, pulled hard and held the smoke. The naked woman cried louder.

Sharon exhaled a cloud. "Will someone shut that bitch up! She's pissing in my buzz!"

"That's my sister," said the man in the silk robe. He leaned down and lit his own pipe.

"Then *you* shut the cunt up!"

He wanted to slap Sharon, but he was holding his smoke. The naked woman sobbed louder.

"... *What's new pussycat? Whoa-ooo, whoa-ooo whoa-ooo . . .*"

Sharon stood up, and screamed in the woman's face. "Shut the fuck up! Shut up! Shut up! Shut up! . . ."

The sobbing got even louder.

Sharon grabbed the static globe out of Coleman's hands and bashed it over the woman's head. Glass, blood and sparks flew in the darkness; the crying stopped. The woman hit the floor.

The crack hit the robed man's bloodstream, and his dilated eyes shifted conspicuously to the pistol-grip shotgun under the couch next to Sharon's feet, telegraphing his intentions. Sharon intercepted the pass. The man jumped up and ran for the couch, but Sharon dropped and got there first. She came out with the twelve-gauge and rolled on her back just as the man was about to pounce.

"... *She's a lady. Whoa, whoa, whoa . . .*"

The man left his feet and dove for Sharon, the silk robe opening in the air like a monarch butterfly. The buckshot caught him in the stomach in midair and yanked him back the other way.

Nobody cared.

Sharon and Coleman ran out the door to the sound of air rushing through glass.

They cut across town on Twenty-second Street for the sanctuary of their crib, an Ybor City shotgun shack, one of the quaint little *casitas* built for the Cuban cigar rollers at the turn of the century that Serge had purchased for almost nothing and restored to original historic condition. Sharon was out of the car and running for the house before Coleman had the ignition off. When he came in the front door, she was already at it again on the floor with a pipe.

"Save some for me!"

Coleman plopped down on the throw rug and grabbed the pipe and was halfway through a hit when Sharon grabbed it back. She fired it up and had just started toking when he grabbed it again, and they fought back and forth for ten hectic minutes. Then it was all gone.

"We have to get some more!" Sharon yelled.

"I'm not going anywhere. That's the rock talking."

"I want more!"

"I'm too wired," said Coleman. He grabbed his face. "I've forgotten how to blink . . . I need a beer to take the edge off." He went to the fridge. Empty.

When he came back, Sharon was crawling on the floor, pawing through the rug. "I think we dropped some! Help me look!"

"We didn't drop anything. You're just really fucked up. I'm going out for beer."

It was 3:10 A.M.—ten minutes after local cutoff for alcohol sales—so Coleman picked up a sixer for seven bucks through the burglar bars of a speakeasy in a war zone off Nebraska Avenue.

He killed the first bottle on the way back to the car and stuffed the empty under the driver's seat. He placed the rest on the passenger seat, started the car and began taking in the Tampa night. He killed the second passing the football stadium and stuck that bottle under the seat as well. He drained the third circling the airport.

The beer finally counterbalanced the cocaine, and Coleman's head was full of happy pop rocks. He cruised along the waterfront on Bayshore Boulevard, the wind in his hair and the last beer in his hand. He untwisted the top.

The Rolling Stones came on the radio. Coleman loved the Stones. He cranked it up.

"I know . . . it's only rock 'n' roll . . . but I like it! . . ."

Coleman began singing along. He was having *a moment.* Everything was perfect. All the drugs were jelling, and he was in a convertible with excellent tunes. The twinkling Tampa skyline across the water seemed to be personally winking at him. Coleman decided the smartest thing to do at this point would be to drive standing up. He hit cruise control.

Coleman cranked the Stones as loud as it would go. The steering wheel was at his waist and he piloted the Impala like he was on the bridge of a ship. He had the beer in his right fist and he punched it into the night air. "Wooooooo! Stones rule! Wooooooooooo!"

He turned onto Gandy Boulevard. "Woooooooo!" He made another turn, and another.

"Woooooo!"

When he turned onto Triggerfish Lane, an empty beer bottle rolled out from under his seat and lodged beneath the brake pedal. Coleman looked down. "Uh-oh."

He tried to kick the bottle free with his foot, which made him go off the road and jump a curb. He tried to steer as he plowed across a lawn, crashing through a picket fence and into the next yard. He hit an inflatable kiddie pool full of water in front of 897 Triggerfish Lane and spun out. Coleman tumbled into the backseat. The Impala kept going. It ripped across the front yard at 887 and tore up a rosebed at 877 before hitting a metal sculpture at hip level, the top half of Lady Bird shattering the windshield and bouncing over the car. The Impala came out of the spin and stalled out in a hedge under a bedroom window, a FOR RENT sign wedged in its grille.

Coleman stuck his head up from the backseat and looked around like a groundhog. He climbed into the front and turned the key. The car started on the first try.

COLEMAN MADE IT back to Ybor City. He was a hundred yards from his home when the FOR RENT sign in the grille wiggled out of its rupture hole, and the radiator spewed antifreeze and wheezed to death. He walked the rest of the way.

When he opened the front door, Sharon was still on her hands and knees.

"Have you been at it the whole time I was gone?"

She just kept clawing at the rug.

"There's nothing there!" said Coleman. "You're stoned out of your mind!"

"Look! I found something!" Sharon held it in her palm.

"That's not crack!"

"Then what is it?"

"Some unidentifiable shit in the rug."

"I'm gonna smoke it anyway!"

Sharon stuck it in her pipe and flicked the Zippo a few times but couldn't get the substance to ignite.

"It won't light!"

"It's not crack!"

"It's the lighter. I need a better one!"

"Stop it! You're flipping me out! I thought I was coming down, but I'm not! I think I OD'd or something."

Sharon ran in the bedroom and came out with a little propane torch she had bought at a head shop. "Let's freebase it!"

She tried to get the torch going but her hands were sweaty and shaking. "Give me a hand with this thing! I think it's defective!"

"Then will you leave me alone?"

"C'mon!"

Coleman swiped the torch away from her. "We need better light." They went to the window to operate in the glow of the yellow crime lamps outside.

"I don't think you punctured the top of the propane canister. That's why nothing's coming out," said Coleman. He screwed the valve down hard on the disposable pressurized tank, and the entire odorless contents silently seeped out.

"There. That should do it." He flicked the lighter.

The fireball knocked Coleman and Sharon to the ground, and the curtains went up like gasoline-soaked toilet paper. The flames lapped at the parched ceiling boards.

"Far-fucking-out," said Sharon.

"This night just doesn't quit," said Coleman.

A minute later, fire-engine sirens.

"Cops!" Sharon yelled. They ran out the back door.

The all-wood house was gone in minutes. Then the fire started jumping roof to roof down the tight row of nineteenth-century cottages. All the firefighters could do was try to contain it. But there was a stiff wind, and embers blew to the next street, and the next. In less than an hour, three blocks were fully involved, sending flames fifty feet into the night, which drew reporters and rubberneckers on Interstate 4. The fire made it to a construction site, where a fuel tank blew on a forklift-crane, which would later get blamed for the blaze.

Coleman and Sharon regrouped behind the fire trucks. She looked at her watch and tugged on Coleman's shirt. "We can still get some more."

4

A TALL, DASHING MAN in a tuxedo sat at a poker table, discreetly peeling up corners of cards as they were dealt. He placed the cards facedown, sat back in his chair and stared across the table at his rival. In his jacket pocket was a long-empty prescription bottle.

A crowd had gathered around the table at the Seminole Bingo Palace just east of Tampa, marked by a water tower with a red arrow through it. The man in the tux calmly pushed a pile of chips to the center of the table. The crowd gasped at the boldness of the wager. They swung their gaze to his nemesis, a four-hundred-pound woman with a gray beehive smoking long brown cigarettes and petting a dachshund on her lap. All the other players had been vanquished or suffered loss of nerve as the stakes climbed. The woman straightened her rainbow pile of winnings, protected by a carefully placed perimeter of lucky stuffed animals. She made an opening between the felt monkey and octopus and pushed through a stack of chips to see his bet.

The crowd gasped again and looked back at the man in the tux. He didn't flinch. He snapped his fingers and a waiter came over with a tray. The bingo palace didn't have a liquor license, so the man in the tux lifted a carton of chocolate milk off the tray. He knew poker wasn't a game of bluffing; it was a game of intimidation. He dramatically sipped chocolate milk and squinted at the woman. He heard a voice inside his head: "I am become Death, Destroyer of Worlds." He took another sip of chocolate milk.

The woman turned her cards over. "Full house."

The man shook his head with disappointment. "All I have is two pairs . . ."

She smiled smugly and reached for the chips.

He turned his cards over. "Two pairs of aces!"

"Bastard!" She pulled her hands back and scowled and stroked the dachshund.

The man gathered up his chips, filled his tuxedo pockets and headed for the winner's window.

"Hey, stranger," the woman called out. "Who are you, anyway?"

The man in the tux turned. "Storms. Serge Storms."

Serge left the bingo hall and climbed in his Barracuda. Halfway home he heard a siren; a fire engine sped past. Then he saw the glow on the horizon.

"What the heck's burning? Must be big if I can see it this far away."

By the time Serge parked the Barracuda behind the fire trucks, he was numb. He stared at the flames with an open mouth and slowly walked up to Coleman and Sharon in the back of the crowd, then collapsed to the ground in anguish. "My house! My archives! The historic district!"

"Some careless idiot, no doubt," said Coleman.

"Where are we going to live?" said Serge. "We're homeless!"

Coleman walked over to the Impala, braced his right foot against the front bumper and yanked the FOR RENT sign from the grille. He walked back and handed the sign to Serge. "I think this place is available. Nice neighborhood. Very quiet. I just drove through it tonight."

MARTHA DAVENPORT SAT up in bed and shook Jim. He rolled over. "What is it?"

"Listen to all those sirens."

Martha got out of bed and parted the curtains. "There's some kind of big fire on the other side of town."

"You can see flames?"

"No, but there's a glow on the horizon."

"You sure it's not a sporting event?"

"At this hour?"

"What time is it anyway?" asked Jim. He grabbed his glasses off the nightstand and checked his watch. "It's almost four o'clock."

"Four o'clock?" said Martha. "I can't miss this!"

Jim sat up as Martha padded across the wood floor to the window on the other side of the room and peeked through the curtains.

"What's going on?"

"Remember what Gladys said? Jack Terrier comes out at four A.M. to water his lawn in a commando outfit."

"Honey, please get away from the window. You're acting like a nut."

"We never get out. . . . There he is! There he is!"

Jim joined Martha at the window. Across the street, a tall figure stood in a camouflaged jumpsuit and black ski mask, holding a garden hose. But the hose wasn't running. Jack Terrier wasn't moving.

"What's he doing?" asked Martha.

"Holy cow!" said Jim. "Look at the lawn! Look at *all* the lawns!"

"What happened?"

"Someone must have wiped out in a car. See? Over at 907? There's where he jumped the curb. And over there—pieces of the kiddie pool. That's where he really lost control. The doughnuts start and loop all the way across Terrier's yard and into the flowerbed next door. Then it looks like he T-boned into a hedge before driving away."

There was a horrific scream. Terrier fell to his knees crying, then went over facedown in the fresh topsoil.

"What a boob," said Martha.

"You can't help but feel for him."

"How can you say that after the way he treated you today?"

"I know, but still . . ."

"What's he doing now?"

"He's turning the water on and running around spraying everything."

"That's not going to do any good," said Martha. "The yard's shot. He should know that."

"I think he's going into shock," said Jim.

The street suddenly lit up. High beams pierced the darkness from both ends of Triggerfish as eight police cars and vans converged on the middle of the block. A helicopter swooped in with a search beam. The spotlight hit Terrier, who dropped the hose and ran in the house.

"All this over illegal lawn watering?" said Martha.

The helicopter spotlight then swung to the house next door. Car doors slammed. Officers drew guns and shielded themselves behind patrol cars. People yelled into megaphones.

"Maybe we shouldn't be so close to the window," said Jim.

More spotlights came on from the squad cars, triangulating their target, Old Man Ortega's place. A half-track arrived with federal and military agents. Then everybody sat and waited in suspense. A half hour passed. More headlights appeared at the end of the street. The agents turned with their guns. "Hold your fire!" Delivery trucks from Backgammon Pizza and Pizza Shack raced up the street, weaving between the officers and the Ortega house and pulling up in front of 837 Triggerfish, where college students were watching the drama unfold from lawn chairs.

The standoff resumed. A small bomb-squad robot on a remote-controlled dolly rolled up to the front door. It had cost the city three hundred thousand dollars and had a two-inch forged outer casing that could handle armor-piercing projectiles, extreme heat and radiation bombardment. The house's front door opened, and a small Spanish man in his underwear cursed and kicked the robot over and slammed the door shut. The robot's wheels spun in the air. They went to Plan B. Tear gas and battering rams. Old Man Ortega was dragged screaming from the house.

A LIGHT SPRINKLE FELL on south Tampa the next afternoon, which meant all the streets flooded. The storm-sewer system wouldn't work, but the city budget was strained and the money was needed to expand the mayor's office and build another football stadium.

The water was knee deep on the west end of the pre-owned yard at Tampa Bay Motors. Salesmen used canoes until the parking lot fell below flood stage. Then they switched to golf carts and rode out to inspect the damage. Most of the cars wouldn't start, carpets squished.

The top salesman at Tampa Bay Motors, Rocco Silvertone, opened the driver's door of a white Suburban. Twenty gallons of water and three fish spilled out.

JIM DAVENPORT LOVED his Martha dearly, and he always wanted to do something big for her, show her how special she was. Martha had been talking about getting a Suburban for over a year—it was her dream vehicle. But there had never been the money.

All that had changed with the promotion to Florida. Jim decided it was time. It would be a surprise.

Jim drove out to Tampa Bay Motors, the largest used-car dealership on Florida's west coast, a sprawling eighty acres on drained wetlands near the airport. Tampa Bay Motors sold everything from Yugos to BMWs and even the occasional Rolls. Everybody knew about Tampa Bay Motors. They were all over TV, ran big newspaper spreads and held a grand reopening the second Saturday of every month.

Jim saw the dealership ten blocks away. It seemed to go on forever, a sea of car roofs all the way to the bay. He figured white must have been a big color in recent model years.

Jim pulled into the lot, and a salesman zipped up in a golf cart. He greeted Jim with the warmth of twins separated at birth, shaking Jim's hand with both of his.

"Rocco Silvertone," said the salesman.

"Jim Davenport," said Jim.

"What can I do you for today?"

Jim told him.

Rocco slapped Jim on the back. "Let's take a ride." They got in the golf cart. Rocco wanted Jim to know he was his best friend. He tried to feel out whether Jim went to church regularly or liked to talk pussy. He drove with one hand and showed Jim pictures in his wallet of someone else's children.

They pulled up to a row of low-mileage Suburbans, and Jim picked out a white four-by-four with gold trim.

Rocco got the keys from the lock box and dangled them in front of Jim. "Shall we?"

They headed up Dale Mabry Highway, Rocco riding shotgun. Jim knew Rocco was riding shotgun because Rocco yelled "*Shotgun!*" as he got in the car. Jim liked the way the Suburban handled. He made a right at the first light and the windshield wipers went on.

"Did I do that?" said Jim.

"Must have hit it by accident." Rocco reached over for the wiper control, but it wouldn't turn off. He jiggled it a few times, and the wipers stopped.

"Is that a problem?" asked Jim.

"Absolutely not," said Rocco.

"It looked like it was a problem. An electrical short or something."

"That because it's so advanced. It's all controlled by computers"—Rocco pointed up—"and satellites. It's very, very modern." Rocco nodded and smiled.

Jim drove some more. He liked the Suburban. In fact, he liked it a lot. They stopped at another light and Jim turned to Rocco. "Say . . ."

Rocco had the glove compartment open and was working on something that was sparking and smoking. He popped the cover off the fuse panel and burned himself.

"Ouch!"

"What's the matter?" asked Jim.

"Nothing."

"I saw sparks. And smoke."

"That's the warning system," said Rocco. "Added safety."

"It looked like we were about to have a fire."

"That's how it's supposed to look."

"That doesn't make sense."

"Remember the Pinto?"

"Yeah?"

"They never looked like they were about to have a fire."

"So?"

"So then they'd suddenly burst into flames," said Rocco. "If you have a family, believe me you want this feature."

The wipers started again.

Rocco reached and jiggled the lever, and they stopped.

"I had a friend who owned a car like this," said Jim. "It was in a flood."

"Flood?" said Rocco, laughing heartily. "This is Florida. It's flat. And we're right on the bay; it all drains off. It's impossible to have a flood here."

"I don't know . . ."

"Don't worry. Rocco's got you covered. Everything's guaranteed. Bumper-to-bumper, five years or fifty thousand miles . . ."

Jim rode back to the showroom in the golf cart. He still wasn't sure. But he knew how much Martha wanted it. He turned to Rocco.

"Okay, how much?"

"How much do you want to pay a month?"

"I don't go by that," said Jim. "I want to know the total price."

"Oh, we can get you the total price."

"Good."

They smiled at each other. A pause.

"So?" said Jim.

"So how much do you want to pay a month?"

MARTHA WAS ON the porch swing with Nicole when a Suburban pulled into the driveway.

At first she thought it was someone lost, just turning around. Then Jim got out.

Martha couldn't stop bouncing as she test-drove around the block eight times. She returned to the driveway and gave Jim another big hug.

"It's great . . ." said Martha.

"But?"

"Well, I don't want to sound ungrateful, but I kept getting false warning lights."

"I noticed that," said Jim. "The windshield wipers activated twice on the test drive and again on the way home. But that's okay, we've got a guarantee."

"I just want to be safe driving the kids."

"You're absolutely right," said Jim. "I'll take it back and have them look at it."

Then Martha went back to gushing. She was still at it when Gladys came over with a bottle of cabernet and a covered basket of panini.

"You got a new car!"

"A new used car," said Jim.

"Same difference," said Gladys. She ran over to it. Other neighbors arrived, and they slowly circled the vehicle like a crashed UFO. Then they got bored and left. Gladys went up on the porch with Jim and Martha.

"You made a great choice," she said. "I saw a head-on between a Suburban and a Fiesta. The Suburban drove away. They hosed the people out of the Fiesta."

6

TRAFFIC ON DALE MABRY HIGHWAY honked and scattered to avoid the gold Lincoln Navigator drifting in and out of its lane.

A Datsun blared its horn and accelerated past.

The Lincoln's driver stuck his head and middle finger out the window. "Suck my dick!"

He pulled his head back in the window. "No, not you," he said in his cell-phone headset. He looked down at the map spread across the steering wheel and wandered into oncoming traffic.

A Tempo honked.

The driver's head was back out the Lincoln's window. "Hey ass-wipe! I'm working! Unlike you, I have a fuckin' job!"

"No, I'm talking to some ass-wipe," he said into his headset. "No, a *different* ass-wipe."

The driver located his position on the map, which indicated he needed to take the next right. He saw the red light ahead and cut through a corner gas station without slowing. The Navigator had a bumper sticker: MANATEES BEND PROPS.

Lance Boyle was forty-nine years old and used Grecian Formula on his pony tail and beard. He decided his beer gut was hurting his chances with the babes, so he began wearing the Untucked Barber Shirt of Denial. The radio was on, two shock jocks reading the news tag-team.

"*. . . And in Tampa, the well-known car dealer Honest Al was crushed to death . . .*"

"*He tipped a vending machine over on himself!*"

"*What a dumb-ass!*"

Lance had also sold used cars once upon a time, but now he was in real estate. It began at 2 A.M. on a Wednesday when Lance was surfing drunk for *Sex Court* on the Playboy Channel and instead found an infomercial on how to triple your income and "move out of that one-bedroom apartment." It had something to do with buying and selling houses. Lance looked around his one-bedroom apartment and called the toll-free number.

Lance didn't remember ordering the Instant Wealth Kit when the mailman delivered it three days later. But he opened it anyway, Xeroxed it, and returned the original for a full refund.

That was five years ago, and Lance had since defined his own niche. Lance was the one in a thousand who actually made wealth with the Instant Wealth Kit. He would find a checkered neighborhood and buy all the properties he could on both sides of the same street. Then he'd rent them out and wait for the houses in between to go on the market. When he finally owned enough consecutive homes, he demolished them and erected upscale town houses.

Lance was all set to begin construction on his latest complex; he just needed a few more homes. This was nail-biting time. It became a race against the clock. While waiting for those last owners to sell, Lance's tenants were busy destroying his rental houses like six-foot Formosan termites. If he completed the string of properties, it wouldn't matter. They'd all be plowed under for the town houses. But if the straight flush couldn't be assembled, Lance would have to sell off the rentals at a huge loss because of the Keith Moon wear and tear. Lance could have screened for better tenants, but the ones who were murder on the plumbing were also the best at running off home owners. Lance's current project was supposed to make him a killing.

That's how it looked on paper. The reality was something else. Turnover had hit a ceiling, and the acquisitions stalled. Meanwhile, his rentals crumbled. Lance decided to become a more active landlord.

The Lincoln pulled up to a red light. Lance waited for a break in traffic to make another right, but traffic was too heavy. Then Lance noticed all the cars had their lights on. "Oh, for the love of . . . !"

A funeral procession.

Lance used the idle time to pull a tiny metal nitroglycerin-pill tube from his pocket and snort some speed. He didn't like the idea of doing speed, because he was a staunch supporter of the War on Drugs. But this was business, and right now he needed every advantage. The funeral procession was long and slow, and Lance began punching the steering wheel. "C'mon, all these people couldn't have known this motherfucker!"

Lance finally honked and cut off one of the mourners and pulled into the procession. He turned on his headlights. There, he thought, now I don't have to worry about any more red lights. He tooted up again and began humming as he sailed through three intersections, completely forgetting what address he was looking for, then remembering at the last second when he saw the street sign. He turned sharply onto Triggerfish Lane, barely missing a white Suburban.

Jim Davenport swerved to avoid a gold Lincoln Navigator as he turned out of Triggerfish Lane and headed across town to Tampa Bay Motors. He found Rocco Silvertone at the showroom water-cooler and explained his problem.

"Oh, sure, absolutely! We can take a look at that electrical system!" said Rocco. "Anything for my old friend Jim."

Rocco walked Jim over to the service department and placed him in the care of three ex-cons wiping oil off their hands. Rocco then made his thumb and index finger into a gun and pointed it at Jim. "Call me if you need anything, big guy!" Then he left for the day.

Jim sat in the service waiting room an hour and a half, watching talking fungus on *Ricki Lake* and reading an *US* magazine article, "My Life Was a Living Hell!" by Gary Coleman.

One of the ex-cons stuck his head in the door. The car was ready. Jim thanked them and drove off the lot. No warning lights. He tested the wipers. Perfect.

He made a left turn. Someone honked. Jim looked around. Nobody. He made another left, and someone honked again. Jim realized *he* was the one honking. He looked down at the steering wheel to see where the horn was. His hands weren't near it.

Jim made a honking U-turn and headed back to the dealership. He drove around behind the showroom and made a left into the service bay.

A mechanic came out wiping his hands on a towel. "You honked?"

"No I didn't," said Jim.

The mechanic stopped wiping and gave Jim a look.

"You did something when you were working on her, and now every time I make a left, the horn honks."

"Couldn't have. I wasn't working anywhere near the horn."

"All I know is it never did it before, I bring it in here, and now it does it all the time."

"I didn't do it."

"I'm not saying you did it. I'm just telling you what the problem is."

"What do you want?"

"I want you to fix it."

"I'll have to fill out a work order."

Sally Jessy came on in the waiting room. Jim picked up *Popular Mechanics*, learning how to build a two-man submarine with hydraulic claws. An hour passed. Someone on TV began whimpering.

The mechanic stuck his head in the door. "Ready."

Jim walked up to the Suburban, opened the door and turned the wheel to the left. The horn honked.

"It's still doing it."

"Let me look at the work order." The mechanic held up a yellow sheet of paper. "Says, 'Fix horn.'" He reached through the open window and hit the horn. It honked.

"The horn works."

"I know it works," said Jim. "It goes off every time I make a left."

The mechanic was silent.

"You didn't fix it."

"The work order says fix horn."

"And?"

"The horn works."

"But I want it to stop blowing every time I turn left."

The mechanic pointed at the yellow paper. "I just go by what the work order says."

"But you're the one who wrote the work order. I told you what the problem was."

"I don't make the rules."

"I want the horn fixed."

"You want to talk to the manager?"

"I want to talk to the manager."

"Hey, Charley!" the mechanic yelled into the service bay. "Guy out here wants to talk to you!"

"What about?" said Charley, emerging from the bay wiping his hands.

"Guy says his horn don't work."

"No, that's not it—"

Charley reached in the car and hit the horn. It honked.

"Sounds fixed to me."

"It goes off every time I make a left."

"Want us to take a look at it?"

"I wanted you to look at it the first time."

Charley grabbed the yellow sheet of paper. "That's not what the work order says."

Jim bit his lip. He began speaking calmly and slowly. "The horn goes off every time I turn left, whether I hit the horn or not. I would like you to pick up tools and do repair activity so that every time I turn left, the horn does not make the horn sound in the future anymore."

"You asking us to disconnect the horn? Afraid I can't do that. Against the law."

"No, I want it fixed."

"It's already fixed."

"No it's not."

Charley reached in and hit the horn again. It honked.

"Ninety-six dollars."

"Ninety-six dollars!"

"Standard fee. Fixing horn. Says here right in the book."

"But it was never broken."

Charley squinted at Jim. "Mister, you've been arguing with me for some time now that the horn wasn't fixed. And now you tell me it was never broken to begin with. I think you're trying to pull something."

"I'm not trying to pull anything."

"I want you to start getting out your money right now."

"What about the warranty?"

"Doesn't cover unnecessary work."

"What!"

"Is there going to be trouble?"

"No, I don't want any trouble." Jim took out his checkbook.

"We don't accept personal checks."

JIM WALKED TO an ATM, came back, paid. He got in the car, put on his seat belt and turned on the radio.

Bang.

The passenger airbag went off.

Charley came out of the repair bay with a dipstick. "What was that bang?"

Jim pointed at the deployed bag. "I turned on the radio."

"The airbag's deployed."

"I know."

"You're not allowed to drive like that."

JIM DROVE HOME with his newly purchased and installed airbag. He was afraid to offend other drivers by honking at them, so each time Jim had to make a left turn, he drove an extra block and made a box of three rights instead. He got to Triggerfish Lane and pulled into the driveway.

Martha came out the front door. "You honked?"

7

SIX STUDENTS FROM the University of South Florida slouched on ratty sofas in the living room at 857 Triggerfish. *The Wizard of Oz* was on TV, no sound. The stereo was extra loud—Pink Floyd's *Dark Side of the Moon*. The only textbook in sight was under the leg of a wobbly coffee table, where residual smoke curled out the cylinder of a giant Lucite water pipe. The front door was wide open.

One of the students walked to the refrigerator and pulled the lever on the beer tap drilled through the door, refilling a large plastic stadium cup. He returned to the living room and nodded at the others; they nodded back.

"Dude."

"Dude."

"Dude."

"Dude."

The student with the fresh beer was Bernie, a freckled white kid with a huge red afro from *The Paper Chase*. His classmates, clockwise around the room from the Che Guevara poster over the Guatemalan oolite incense frog: Frankie "Slowhand" Pagnetti, wanna-be rock musician who had taken up the electric bass because it was the easiest instrument to fake and played in a very bad band consisting entirely of bass players called "No Drummer"; Chip "Memory Chip" Perkins, who had the guts of four salvaged computers spread across the kitchen table and was trying to hack into the Pentagon with a reconfigured copy of John Madden Smash-Mouth Football 6.0; Jeb "Siddhartha" Youngblood, formerly devout southern Baptist who had moved in a week ago, accidentally ate a hash brownie, became self-aware for the first time in his life and now endlessly wandered the rental house in a solipsistic daze; William "Bill the Elder" Moss, forty-two years old with twelve hundred credit hours carefully distributed among seventeen academic disciplines so as not to inadvertently precipitate graduation; Manny "Waste-oid" Wasserman, on academic suspension, scraping out the bong. They respectively majored in English, philosophy, English philosophy, French poetry, art history, and no declared major, and they all expected to land easy, high-paying jobs immediately after graduation without trying.

"Check it out!" said Waste-oid, pointing at the TV. "The movie's in perfect sync with the album. See how the heartbeat from *Dark Side* matches up with Dorothy putting her ear to the Tin Man's chest? You can't tell me that's a coincidence. Floyd planned the whole thing. They were fuckin' geniuses!" He fired up the bong.

"How did you do that again?" asked Bernie.

"You wait until the second roar of the MGM lion at the beginning of *Oz*, then start the album."

Frankie "Slowhand" Pagnetti stood next to the TV set, playing air bass along with the CD.

Bill the Elder shook his head. "Floyd's playing in *B minor.*"

Frankie looked down at his empty hands. "You're right." He made the necessary adjustments.

Bernie refilled his beer; Siddhartha sat in a corner, staring at his thumbprint and weeping.

Lance Boyle appeared in the open doorway unnoticed.

"Listening to *Dark Side* and watching *Oz*, eh?" said Lance.

The startled students turned to the door. Lance came inside and walked around the room like Dean Wormer in *Animal House*. The students stashed dope and paraphernalia behind their backs.

"Relax," said Lance. "I know you're getting fucked up in here. You got everything you need? Enough weed?" He pointed at Waste-oid, hiding the bong behind him and holding a toke.

Waste-oid nodded.

"Good, good," said Lance. "What about beer? How you fixed?" He opened the refrigerator and saw a keg with a clear tube leading to the tap in the door. "Excellent. You guys are pretty responsible."

Lance looked up at the olive army surplus parachute hanging from the ceiling, then over at the shelving system of discarded lumber and milk crates. "You must tell me who your decorator is." He went over to the stereo. "Sure this is loud enough?" He turned the volume all the way up.

"... *Kicking around on a piece of ground in your hometown* ..."

Bernie cleared his throat. "Uh, dude, I mean Mr. Boyle, about the rent ... My folks are real sick ..."

"Mine are dead," said Lance.

"Oh."

"Don't worry about the rent," said Lance. "The main thing is to make sure you're enjoying yourselves. You *are* enjoying yourselves, aren't you?"

They nodded.

"Good," said Lance. "Look, I'm in a bit of a rush—got an appointment with some new tenants. But I wanted to drop by and find out if you've been throwing any parties in here."

"Absolutely not," said Bernie.

"Then start. Say on a weeknight. This Tuesday. I'll have some kegs delivered. Any questions?"

Bernie raised his hand. "Why are you doing this?"

"That's just the kind of person I am," said Lance. "Always giving."

MARTHA DAVENPORT heard a midmorning knock at the front door.

Gladys Plant stood on the daisy welcome mat and uncovered a tray of Danish. "I still can't believe they arrested Old Man Ortega the other night. He sure didn't look like a war criminal.

Martha tasted the pastry. "The paper said he used to run a death squad in Central America. They found mass graves."

"Right under our noses on this street," said Gladys. "Makes you wonder what else we don't know about."

They heard music coming from somewhere. Martha tried to place it. "Is that *Dark Side of the Moon*?"

Suddenly, a screech of car brakes, and a beat-up '65 Barracuda skidded to the curb in front of the former Grønewaldenglitz residence and into a garbage can, scattering pork chop bones and Q-Tips. Two men and a woman got out and headed for the house.

Martha scrunched her eyebrows. "This looks less than positive."

Lance Boyle was standing on the college students' porch when he spotted his three newest tenants. He headed across the lawn with a smile and an outstretched hand.

"Who's that?" asked Martha.

"The landlord. That's the guy I've been telling you about who's buying up all the houses on the street."

"Looks like a real prince."

Lance picked through an assortment of keys and opened the front door of 867 Triggerfish, welcoming Serge, Coleman and Sharon to their new home. Lance had a really good *bad* feeling about them. The chubby one, Coleman, was drunk and promptly broke a flowerpot. The sex kitten, Sharon, never took off her dark sunglasses, fidgeting and sniffling the whole time. And Serge. Well, Serge was carrying a *Black's Law Dictionary* and an electronic stud finder.

The previous tenant, Mr. Grønewaldenglitz, had left in a hurry, in the night. Lance chuckled awkwardly as they entered the living room. "A regular fixer-upper. Lots of character . . ."

The falling-out with the previous tenant had been particularly nasty. Serge stared down at the carpet, where obscenities had been written with hydrochloric acid. Off to the side, an old bloodstain had been worked on with bleach.

Lance slid the sofa over the dirty words, revealing other words, even more vile, and slid it back.

"We want to look around," said Serge.

Before Lance could stop them, they headed for the kitchen.

"Oh, the kitchen," said Lance, putting out an arm to warn them. "I didn't really get a chance . . ."

Too late. They looked in the sink. It was the same as all the other sinks in the house—filled with concrete that had been mixed with hundreds of little metal springs from clothespins for added tensile strength, like tiny rebars. That impressed Serge.

They headed for the laundry room. Serge opened the washing machine. Full of roofing tar. Then the dryer. Five gallons of satin polyurethane outdoor deck coating, cured solid.

Serge turned to Lance. "That's a lot of rage."

Lance put up his hands in a *go figure* gesture. "People . . ." He flipped the latches on his briefcase and pulled out a contract. "If you'll just sign . . ."

Serge ignored him and headed for the master bedroom. He opened the door, completely dark. He tried the light. Nothing.

"I don't have a flashlight," said Lance.

"I do," said Serge. He pulled his sentimental halogen from a hip pocket and shone it into the room. All the windows had been nailed shut and aluminum foil Super Glued to the glass.

"What's that on the walls?" asked Coleman.

Serge shined his light on some large smears. He walked over and tested it with his fingers. Sticky.

He tasted it.

"Honey."

"Honey?" said Lance.

They headed for the master bath, making crunching noises as they walked. Serge pointed his flashlight at the floor. Hundreds of insect carcasses.

"Bees?" asked Lance.

"You're allergic to bees, aren't you?" said Serge.

"How'd you know?"

"You must not have checked this property for a while. Someone was expecting you to walk into this dark room while the bees were still alive . . ."

"Why would anyone want to hurt me?"

Lance was curious now, and he took the lead. He stepped in the master bath and went to throw the light switch, but Serge grabbed his arm.

"What's the matter?" asked Lance.

Serge pointed up at the naked lightbulb, a pool of amber liquid in the bottom of the glass. He motioned Lance out of the bathroom. Then he reached back in from around the corner, flicked the switch, and pulled his arm away fast.

A fireball blew out the doorway.

Lance turned white. "What was that?"

"They used a pinpoint diamond drill and poked a hole in the metal base of the lightbulb," said Serge, stomping out little fires on the floor. "Then they used a syringe to fill it with gasoline."

"Where'd you learn that?"

"Prison."

"They did that in prison?"

"No, we watched prison movies in prison. That was from *The Longest Yard*."

Serge headed back to the living room, and the others followed. He pulled out his stud finder and ran it along a wall. It began to ping and flash. Serge turned it off and went to manual—tapping the drywall with a two-fingered physician's thump.

"What are you doing?" asked Lance.

"Shhhhh!" said Serge, then: "This is non-load-bearing, right?"

"What are you planning?"

"Nothing." Serge went over and sat down on the couch in front of a glass-top coffee table. Lance sat down and pulled out the contract again and set it on the glass. Coleman sat down and put his feet up on the table, and the glass shattered.

Lance picked the contract out of the broken pieces. "We can sign it on our laps."

"This place gives me the creeps," said Sharon. She sniffled. "You need to drive me somewhere."

"Shut it right now or you know what happens!" said Serge.

Sharon crossed her arms in a show of defiance and marched off into the master bedroom, then realized it was dark and came out and marched somewhere else. Coleman popped his first beer of the half hour.

Serge began reading the contract. Lance uncapped a pen and held it ready. Serge was the first prospective tenant ever to read the entire contract, all twelve pages of fine print. He asked questions about every paragraph and got out his *Black's Law Dictionary* to look up words. Serge had appeared ready to sign a dozen times, and Lance kept offering the pen. But Serge would always hold up a hand to wait, then look up another word. It went on like that for an excruciating hour. Just as Lance had lost all hope and was ready to drive the pen into his own brain, Serge snatched it out of his hand and gave the contract an autograph of beautiful looping calligraphy.

Lance handed Serge the keys. "You're going to love it here."

The light in the living room began flashing on and off. Serge and Lance looked over at the light switch. Coleman was flicking it up and down.

"It works," Lance called over to him. Coleman flicked it a few more times and staggered away.

"I think his parents dropped him," said Serge. He looked down at the floor, and bent over and picked up a tiny gasket. "What's this? Part of a crack pipe?"

Sharon heard Serge from down the hall with ultrasonic addict hearing. She ran back in the room, dropped to her hands and knees at Serge's feet and finger-scraped the rug.

"Sharon! Behave!"

Lance waved good-bye, and Serge pulled a typed agenda from his pocket.

"We need to make a supply run," said Serge. "Then the games begin!"

"What the fuck are you talking about?" Sharon said from the floor.

"Don't you know what day this is?" asked Serge.

Sharon ignored him, inspecting something from the rug before deciding it was a toenail clipping and throwing it over her shoulder.

"It's June twenty-first," he said. "The solstice."

"The what?" asked Sharon.

"I can tell by the thoughtful look on your face that you've gotten it confused with the vernal equinox," said Serge. "A lot of people make that mistake. No, the solstice marks the first day of summer. And you know who invented summer, don't you?"

"Who?" asked Coleman.

"The Wham-O Corporation."

9

SERGE SCREECHED AWAY from the curb for his supply run.

Moments later, the Davenports' front door opened, and the family headed for the Suburban and their own supply run. Saturday was errand day in the Davenport household. Martha had the checklist, and Jim drove. Walgreens, Publix, Home Depot, Burdines.

"Look," said Jim. "There's a Suburban just like ours. Same color and everything."

Martha nodded. "They're popular."

"You ever get that weird feeling when you see a car exactly like yours?" asked Jim.

"What do you mean?"

"You know—you're not really paying attention, daydreaming about stuff, and you see the same car coming the other way. And for a split second you think it's *your* car, and maybe you're inside it. But then who's inside *this* car? Like a mirror universe thing. Know what I mean? Ever get that feeling?"

"We're switching to decaf."

Jim checked his watch. Twelve-thirty. "Melvin, you want a Happy Meal?"

Melvin nodded.

Jim pulled into a McDonald's, and the family started getting out. Martha looked in her purse. "We don't have enough cash."

"There's a bank next door," said Jim, getting back in the driver's seat. "You guys go on inside. I'll drive over with Nicole and be right back."

A WHITE SUBURBAN sat at the curb in front of the bank's ATM. It was in the fire lane. The driver glanced in the mirror and noticed a police car enter the parking lot and roll up behind him.

"Uh-oh." He put the vehicle in gear and pulled out of the fire lane.

Jim Davenport drove into the bank's parking lot just as the other Suburban and the police car were pulling away. "There's that same car again," he told Nicole. "It's just like ours." Jim parked in the fire lane in front of the ATM.

A tall man in sunglasses and a baseball cap sprinted out of the bank with a green canvas bag. He jumped in the Suburban's passenger seat.

"Hit it!"

"Who are you?" asked Jim.

"You're not Henry!" said the man.

Alarms started going off outside. Jim felt a gun in his ribs.

"Drive!"

Jim put the car in gear and pulled onto the highway. Nicole began crying.

"Shut that fucking kid up!"

"I'll take you wherever you want to go. You'll get away. Just don't hurt us."

The man hit Jim over the right eye with the butt of his pistol. "Shut up! . . . Goddamn Henry! This is all his fault! I have to think."

Nicole continued wailing.

"Shut that brat up or *I'll* shut her up!"

"She's just a child."

The man smacked Jim again with the gun. Blood was getting in his right eye, making it hard to see. It was happening in seconds, but adrenaline had Jim's brain on overdrive, thousands of pages of data flying through his analyzer. Nicole wailed louder.

"Shut up! Shut up! Shut up!" The man turned around in his seat and pointed his pistol at the toddler. "Shut the fuck up!"

In the nanosecond the gun swung toward his child, Jim's brain reached Option X.

"There's cocaine in the glove compartment," said Jim.

The man spun around. He opened the glove compartment and leaned over. "I don't see it."

"It's way in back," said Jim. "I hid it in case I ever get stopped."

The man was so eager, his head was practically inside the glove compartment. "I still don't see it."

"You will," said Jim. He turned on the radio.

PANDEMONIUM.

Police, TV trucks, onlookers, a sheet-covered body next to a Suburban on the edge of the highway.

Martha was hysterical, clutching Nicole hard, trying to kick the body under the sheet while cops restrained her.

Jim was at the back of a squad car, quivering, giving his version of events to a sergeant with a clipboard. A patrolman handed Jim a cup of coffee, and half of it spilled on Jim's shaking hand.

"Is he really dead?" asked Jim.

"Pretty much," said the sergeant. "Airbag broke his neck like that"—snapping his fingers.

The patrolman patted him on the back. "You did everyone a favor."

"Saved the state a lot of money," said the sergeant. "Skag McGraw was a real dirtbag."

"One less McGraw brother society has to worry about," said the patrolman.

"Brother?" asked Jim.

"Five in all," said the sergeant. "Or were. Now there's four. But I wouldn't lose any sleep. The rest are all locked away in prison and won't be getting out for a long, long time."

10

THE BARRACUDA SKIDDED to a stop on Triggerfish Lane. Serge had returned from his supply run. He unloaded hula hoops, Frisbees and giant soap-bubble wands. He unrolled a slick yellow Slip 'n Slide on the lawn behind the metal cows and the remains of Lady Bird.

Serge bounded up the front steps and into the house. He dashed from room to room. Sharon was on the couch with a vibrator and no pants.

"Where's Coleman?" he asked.

Sharon didn't look up. She pointed out the side window.

"Next door?" he asked.

She didn't respond.

"Nice talking with you."

The middle finger.

Serge crossed the lawn and ran up the steps. He stood in the open doorway of the college rental.

Two students knelt next to the turntable, turning a vinyl record slowly with their fingers. Waste-oid's ear was pressed against one of the speakers.

"What's up?" said Serge.

"Listening to 'Stairway to Heaven' backward for secret messages," said Bernie.

"Heard anything yet?" asked Serge.

Waste-oid took his head away from the speaker. "I think he just said, *'Please pass the butter, Satan.'*"

Coleman walked in from the kitchen, carrying a roll of tinfoil, a plastic scouring pad, a tube from a Windex bottle, duct tape, Saran Wrap and a rotisserie chicken.

"There you are!" said Serge.

"Don't break his concentration," said Bernie. "We've been waiting for this."

Coleman sat cross-legged on the floor and stuffed the scouring pad into the chicken.

The students gathered around and paid attention for the first time all semester.

"There's no way," Frankie whispered to Chip.

"It can't be done," said Bill.

A hush fell over the room.

Coleman was a flurry of deft motion, hands moving fast all around the chicken with unconscious muscle memory. Moments later, Coleman sat the chicken upright on a newspaper in the middle of the floor, then pulled his hands clear like a rodeo rider after tying off a calf.

"Time!" said Bernie.

Chip clicked the stopwatch button on his chronograph. "Three minutes, eighteen seconds."

"Incredible," said Waste-oid. "I wouldn't have believed it if I hadn't seen it. A bong made from a chicken."

Frankie was still skeptical. "But does it work?"

"Does it work?" said Coleman. "Pot!"

Waste-oid handed him a baggie, and Coleman began stuffing buds in the bird.

"Be careful with that stuff," said Bernie. "It's some nuclear weed."

Sharon showed up in the doorway, ragged from a night of partying, but in a very hot way. She cocked her hip and twirled a lock of blond hair with a finger. "Anyone got any coke?"

"Shhhhhhh!" said the students.

It was the first time in history her coy look had been rebuffed. She sidled up to Serge. "What's going on?"

Serge nodded toward Coleman. "He's holding court."

"I still don't think it'll work," said Frankie.

"Never count this guy out," said Serge. "He can make a delivery system out of the contents of any home in America. I've seen him do it with bicycle pumps, hot-water bottles and a souvenir coconut carved into a monkey's head."

Coleman held an unlit lighter near the chicken. "Okay, when the smoke bubbles in the water, it'll filter through the scouring pad, breaking it into thousands of even tinier bubbles. That increases the surface area of the gas in contact with the water, because the smaller bubbles have a shorter radius, which is squared and multiplied by four pi—whereas the larger bubbles have most of their volume on the interior of the sphere. The water scrubs the increased surface area, removing impurities and giving you higher THC content per airborne particulate. Hence, a smoother, more potent smoke. And now, in new chicken flavor!"

"Where'd you learn all that?" asked Bernie.

"Spent a year at Hillsborough Community College. Drugs were an incredible education. I learned all about physics, the metric system, jurisprudence, economics, agriculture, politics, pharmacology and home ec."

Sharon turned to Serge. "How come he's such a numbskull about everything else?"

"He's like a savant," said Serge. "The Rain Man of Dope."

Coleman shotgunned another beer and belched. "Enough batting practice." He grabbed the chicken and leaned over it.

"Stand clear," said Serge. "Let the doctor operate."

Coleman flicked the lighter and pulled hard. A bubbling sound came from deep inside the chicken; smoke squirted out under the drumsticks.

"Oh, man," said Chip. "He's fucked."

Finally, Coleman cut the lighter, pulled away from the chicken and inhaled deeply. He fell back in a sitting position. His face turned red and he put his hand over his mouth, but it was no use. The coughing came hard and furious, and he blew out all the smoke. The hacking went on and on. He rolled on the floor, grabbing his throat.

A student rushed up with a glass of water, but Coleman refused it. "No," he said, pushing the glass away. "Coughing gets you higher."

The fit finally subsided, and Coleman sat upright. A sugary glaze descended over his eyes.

"Uh-oh," said Serge. "Here it comes."

"How do you feel?" asked Bernie.

Coleman looked slowly around the room. *"High, stoned, hammered, bent, twisted, ripped, wrecked, wasted, trashed, annihilated, polluted, stewed, baked, fried, cooked, toasted, roasted, lit, torched, burnt, buzzed, blind, blotto, blitzed, blasted, blown, bombed, pie-eyed, glass-eyed, shit-faced, blue-faced, tight, booted up, hopped up, messed up, screwed up, goofed up, fucked up, numb, paralyzed, wired, knee-walking, wall-hugging, floating, flying, peaking, sailing, rushing, tripping, zooming, zonked . . ."*

EVERYONE WAS TRYING to console Jim Davenport. Martha drove him home after picking up a tranquilizer prescription written by a police psychiatrist. Jim sat in a daze on his porch swing, and Martha went inside to make some lemonade.

Gladys ran over from next door. "Are you all right, Jim? I just heard what happened. It's terrible!"

Martha came back on the porch with a pitcher of lemonade. There was a commotion across the street. Coleman had taken a wild tumble down the front steps of the college students' house, tearing off the side railing. The students helped him up. After they determined nothing was broken, they followed Serge next door and began playing with the Wham-O equipment.

A Florida Cable News satellite truck pulled up in front of the Davenport residence. Correspondent Blaine Crease walked up to the porch with a microphone, wanting an interview about the killing of the vicious bandit Skag McGraw.

Jim said he didn't feel like talking. Blaine begged. Jim stood his ground.

Blaine went across the street to see if any of the neighbors would agree to go on the air.

"Sure thing," said Coleman. He stepped up to the camera, and Blaine held a microphone in front of him. They began broadcasting live.

"What is your name, sir?" asked Blaine.

"Heywood."

"Heywood what?"

"Jablowmey."

Blaine faced the camera. "We're standing here with Mr. Heywood Jablowmey . . ."

Coleman and the college students began snickering in the background.

Blaine turned around. "What? What's so funny?"

Coleman and the students contained their laughter. "Nothing."

Blaine faced back to the camera. "We're speaking with a close personal friend of the man who foiled today's deadly bank robbery, Heywood Jablowmey . . ."

Coleman and the students cracked up again and were unable to stop this time.

The satellite truck drove off after the aborted interview. Serge unspooled a garden hose and took something out of a bag.

"What's that he's putting on the hose?" asked Martha.

"A Water Wiggle," said Gladys.

"A what?"

"Water Wiggle—don't you remember?" said Gladys. "They must have sold a million. A yellow plastic cone with a goofy face painted on it. You attach it to the end of a hose. It redirects the water backwards, and the cone and the hose fly like crazy all over the yard."

"What for?" asked Martha.

"For fun," said Gladys. "Just look."

Coleman stood in the middle of the yard, chugging a beer and doing a wobbly hula hoop. The Water Wiggle took an erratic course and struck Coleman in the back of the head.

"Ouch!"

But Coleman didn't think to move beyond its range.

Serge put The Lovin' Spoonful on a boom box. The students played Frisbee. Siddhartha sat next to the hedge, mollified by the soap-bubble wand.

The Water Wiggle hit Coleman again.

"Ouch!"

"*. . . Hot town, summer in the city, back of my neck gettin' dirty and gritty . . .*"

Serge went to the end of the Slip 'n Slide and paced off his approach like an Olympic long jumper. He took a few moments to mentally prepare himself, then: "Cowabunga!" He sprinted toward the yellow chute.

Coleman's face was up to the sky as he drained his beer. The Water Wiggle hit him in the head again and knocked him off balance. Serge sailed down the Slip 'n Slide on his stomach like Superman. Coleman stumbled onto the plastic tarp. They collided. Coleman was upended and landed on his clavicle; Serge's left arm got caught in Coleman's hula hoop, spinning him around and sending him off the side of the chute into the chicken-wire Gettysburg.

The Water Wiggle was still flailing in the background as the students applied ice to Coleman and untangled Serge from the snarled metal.

Gladys poured another glass of lemonade and shook her head. "Renters . . ."

A van with a magnetic sign on the side cruised slowly down the street and stopped four houses to the left.

"Who lives there?" asked Martha.

"The Sanchezes," said Gladys. "Actually, there's just one Sanchez now. Raul. They're separated. Simone recently moved out after they got hooked up to the Internet and Raul began spending eighteen hours a day at Gillian Anderson websites."

Four men with greased hair got out of the van and walked toward the house. They all wore the same black pants and sleeveless black T-shirts.

"What are they supposed to be this time?" asked Martha.

"An ersatz Sha Na Na," said Gladys. "But they're pretty good."

Mr. Sanchez answered the door. The shortest Sha Na Na handed Raul some legal papers and blew a pitch pipe. The men broke into four-part harmony.

> "Ohhhhhhhhh, you're getting a divorce, you're getting a
>   divorce, you're getting a divorce . . ."
> Bowzer: "Bow, bow, bow."
> "You wife is leaving town, no more sex for you, you don't
>   make enough money . . ."
> Bowzer: "Bow, bow, bow."
> "And you have a small pecker, tooooooooooooooo!!!!"

Raul disappeared into the house and came back seconds later firing wildly with a large revolver. He hit one Sha Na Na in the shoulder, and the singing group scattered across the lawn.

"Jesus! Did you see that!" said Martha. "He shot Bowzer!"

"I think it was just someone who was supposed to look like Bowzer," said Gladys.

Police surrounded the Sanchez homestead. It was a brief stand-off. A negotiator got on the phone with Raul, and they even had Sha Na Na apologize over loudspeakers. Since the shooting, Raul had been going through his liquor cabinet at an impressive clip, and his list of demands grew to include a lap dancer. Police sent in an undercover stripper trained in Kama Sutra and Tae Kwon Do, who quickly subdued Raul with a private dance that dislocated his hips. They stretchered him away in silent ceremony.

"You watch," said Gladys. "That'll be a rental now."

Martha looked up. "It's starting to rain."

"It'll be over in a few minutes," said Gladys. "Does this every day in the summer."

"Is that your car?" asked Martha, pointing at a blue Trans Am parked in front of the Davenport house. "It's been there since yesterday."

"No," said Gladys. "I thought it was yours."

"The Trans Am's windows are down. It's getting wet," said Martha. "We'll soon see who owns it."

They waited. Nobody came.

"That settles it," said Gladys. "It's stolen. Someone probably dumped it when they ran out of gas."

"Stolen? This neighborhood?" said Martha.

"Oh, sure," said Gladys. "We live in a grid."

"Grid?" asked Jim.

"All the streets are straight east-west and north-south like a chessboard. Easy in, easy out from the city's arteries. Criminals prefer to duck into grid neighborhoods. They avoid winding streets where they get turned around or lost or end up on a dead end. Living on a grid street puts us a whole lot closer to Tampa's scumbag element than we'd like to admit. Stolen cars get dumped here all the time. If I ever get rich, I'm moving into a serpentine neighborhood."

"I'm calling the police," said Martha. She ran down to the street, got the tag number and ran inside the house.

Martha came back out. "You were right. It's stolen. Police are sending a tow truck."

"The rain stopped," said Gladys.

"Evening!"

They turned and saw a smiling man in front of the porch, covered with chicken-wire scrapes.

"Been meaning to introduce myself. You know how it is. Work, work, work." He walked up the steps and stuck out his hand. "I'm your new neighbor. Serge. Serge Storms."

They all shook hands.

"Great neighborhood you have here. Mind if I have a seat?"

They reluctantly scooted over on the swing to make room.

"Yes, sir. Great place to raise kids. Not like some other places I've lived. I firmly believe neighbors have an obligation to each other. I mean, who can you really turn to in this unpredictable world? That's right, your neighbors! . . ."

Gladys nodded, but Martha and Jim leaned away.

"You know what makes this place so special?" asked Serge. "Front porches! It's because most of the homes are so old. They're pre-Levittown. That's where the trouble started if you ask me. The suburbs. *Parade* magazine examined the phenomenon. None of the houses had front porches. Instead, the focus shifted to the backyards, which they fenced off, shutting out their neighbors. Pretty soon, nobody knew anyone anymore. They turned inward and became self-absorbed, sacrificing the fabric of the community on a hibachi altar. But now there's talk of a new re-urbanization movement, and you know what? It smells like hope!"

A '76 Laguna screeched up the curb. The shirtless tattooed man in the driver's seat looked at the Davenport residence and leaned on the horn.

The front door flew open. Debbie ran down the porch steps and across the yard.

"Debbie, where are you going?" yelled Martha, standing up. "Who is that guy?"

Debbie jumped in the Laguna.

"I forbid you to go," yelled Martha. "Do you know what your father's been through today?"

The Laguna peeled out. Martha sat down.

"Wow!" said Serge. "I'd be completely freaked out if I was her parent! I know some guys like that. They're up to stuff you don't even want to know about. It would turn your hair white!"

Eight-year-old Melvin came out the front door wearing a baseball cap and carrying a glove and ball. He was a little small for his age, and the cap floated around his head.

"Who's this?" Serge asked cheerfully.

"Melvin," said Melvin. He tugged his dad's shirt. "Can we play catch?"

Serge jumped off the swing. "May I?"

Jim was still shaken from the day's events. He spoke quietly in a tired voice. "It's not necessary."

"It's the least," said Serge. "You know what they say—'It takes a village.'"

"I—"

"C'mon, Melvin," said Serge. "I'll teach you a spitball." The pair bounded down off the porch into the front yard.

"Shouldn't we do something?" asked Martha.

"He's just trying to be neighborly."

"I'm not sure," she said, "but I think there's something wrong with that man."

"They're playing harmlessly."

Serge rolled Melvin a grounder. "Always remember, baseball is a vicious game of intimidation. Sometimes you have to throw a little chin music."

Across the street, a professional landscaping crew relaid six pallets of St. Augustine sod in Jack Terrier's front yard. A red Ford Excursion drove up the street and turned into the driveway. The Excursion's passenger door opened and a tall boy got out wearing expensive baseball cleats. He was almost the size of a man but thinner, and he wore an immaculate home-white baseball uniform with black trim. Across the front of the jersey, in classic Yankees font: RAPTORS. On the back: BAY-WIDE DRY CLEANERS. ONE-HOUR MARTINIZING.

The boy seemed too big for Little League, because he was. His dad had doctored his birth certificate. The youth looked across the street and sneered at Melvin. "We're gonna murder you runts!"

Jack walked over to his son. His own Raptor uniform said COACH across the back. He looked across the street with the same smirk. "You hear that, Davenport? We're gonna murder you!"

"Jim, is he talking to you?" asked Martha.

"He's just a little on the competitive side."

"I don't think I like them talking to our family that way."

"You hear me, Davenport!" yelled Terrier. "You and that scrawny kid of yours—dead meat!"

"You jerk!" Martha yelled, jumping up. "You, you—"

Terrier smiled bigger. "You got some fight in ya, lady. More than I can say for your husband."

"Don't you talk about my husband that way!"

"Martha, please sit down," said Jim. "It's just trash talk. That's what sports is about."

"Then I don't think I like sports," said Martha, plopping back down and folding her arms.

Jack Terrier began smacking a fist into an open palm. His son did likewise.

Serge walked over and put his hand on Melvin's shoulder, and they watched the Terriers go inside their house laughing.

"Who was that?" asked Serge.

"Jason Terrier, star pitcher of the Raptors. His dad's the coach. We play them Friday night."

"Then we better get practicing," said Serge. "Pop fly! Go long!"

Melvin ran to the far side of the yard, and Serge reached way back and fired the ball straight up, into a streetlight, and a shower of glass fluttered to the ground.

Serge looked toward the porch and grinned. "Whoops."

Despite the inauspicious start, it was a good practice. Serge took Melvin through all the drills. They even played a little pepper.

"Serge is a cool name," said Melvin, tossing the ball. "I wish I had a cool name, too."

"Melvin does lack a certain zing," said Serge, tossing the ball back. "Let me cogitate on this a moment . . . Melvin . . . Melvin . . . hmmm . . ."

They tossed the ball back and forth a few more times.

"Wait! I got it!" said Serge. "From now on you're *Smooth M, The Gangster of Love.*"

"Cool!"

Serge got down in a catcher's crouch and punched his glove. "Runners on first and third. You gotta pitch from the stretch. And no breaking stuff. You have to get the ball to the plate in a hurry."

Jim and Martha rocked slowly on the porch swing as Melvin worked on his delivery. Before each pitch, Serge flashed a bunch of signs Melvin didn't understand; after every pitch, he leaped out of his crouch and ran to the "mound" for a conference with Melvin.

"See?" said Jim. "They're playing fine."

"He seems a little intense," said Martha.

The ballplayers called it a day. Melvin ran up the porch steps and turned around and waved.

"Bye, Serge!"

"Bye, Smooth M!"

Martha and Jim looked at each other. *"Smooth M?"*

The front door of the Terrier house opened and Jack came out in his coach's uniform. He started walking across the street.

"I'll bet he's coming over to apologize," said Jim.

"When the windchill is thirty-two in hell."

Jack stopped in front of the porch.

"Hi, neighbor," said Jim.

Jack pointed at the blue Trans Am at the curb. "Can you move your car?"

"It's not my car," said Jim.

"It's in front of your house."

"It's stolen. We just called the police—"

"See if you can move it. Okay, sport?"

Jack turned and headed back to his house.

"But it's not mine," Jim called after him.

"And try to hurry," said Terrier. "It's really bothering me."

12

SERGE A. STORMS was born in West Palm Beach during the Cuban Missile Crisis.

There were problems from the start. To say he was a hyperactive tot didn't quite capture it. When Serge was three, he covered himself head to foot in Vaseline. When he was four, he found a can of spray paint under the sink and gave every single thing in the house a pretty red stripe before his folks awoke one day.

By six, Serge appeared to have outgrown the phase. He took up hobbies—healthy stuff like collecting stamps that seemed to provide a constructive lightning rod for his focus.

It soon became clear there was too much focus. Serge was given a starter stamp kit for Christmas. Then he had to have every U.S. stamp ever issued. He refused to leave a local stamp shop until he was given one of everything. Little Serge made his body completely rigid, and his parents had to carry him out of the shop under their arms sideways like a surfboard.

Two years later, the violence began. Little things from school. At first it was overlooked because Serge was a spastic, skinny drink of water, and his victims were all bigger, stronger, well-documented bullies. The parents complained, and the teachers expressed concern, but inside they were glad that someone had finally dished it back to the little bastards. The "Serge problem" got nothing but lip service.

Eventually, however, even the most sympathetic teachers began to have second thoughts. It wasn't what he did or whom he did it to, but that he was so effective. If he had simply lost control and starting throwing punches after being picked on, well, anyone could understand that.

Serge would wait.

That was the chilling part. At an instant-gratification age when most kids have an event horizon of ten minutes, Serge would let months go by. A bully with a full foot and thirty pounds on Serge might bloody his nose before the first day of class in the fall. The next thing they knew, Christmas decorations were up and the bully had forgotten all about the incident. Heck, Serge was now even his friend, lending him cool toys, flattering him. Then it was spring. And one day the bully would finally find himself all alone, separated from the herd. His guard was down, vulnerable in some way like sitting on a toilet with gym shorts around his ankles, and then the stall door crashed open and a volleyball net flew over his head and he had the living piss kicked out of him. The victims were so shaken they refused to identify their attacker.

At the end of third grade, however, there was an incident so *Lord of the Flies* it couldn't be ignored any longer. This time, Serge hadn't been the bully's original victim. It was a boy named Joey, the scrawniest kid in class, whom Serge had befriended because he was the one who smuggled the *Mad* magazines into school. Joey's arm had been broken. The bully was suspended.

By the time suspension was over and the bully came back to class, Serge had saved up a hefty amount of allowance. It wasn't remotely a fair fight. Serge brought in hired muscle from the middle school.

A passing jogger heard the screams. They found the bully tied to stakes on a fire-ant mound behind the library. Serge was sent to juvenile assessment.

His cunning got the psychiatrists' attention. They were fascinated by the contradiction. Violence at Serge's age usually resulted from faulty impulse control. But Serge never showed rage, never an outburst. Rather, he patiently lined up an elaborate set of destructive dominoes and then set them in motion with a flick of his finger. The psychiatric community was split. They couldn't decide which drug was best to dope him to the gills.

Two decades passed. A few months before Coleman and Sharon would burn down his house, Serge was nearing his thirty-fifth birthday. He had spent much of his adulthood under a haze of psychotropic piña coladas. Those were the normal days when Serge wouldn't black out, nothing terrible happened, and the fire department didn't have to dispatch a hook-and-ladder again to peel him off the water tower.

But Serge didn't like his brain feeling so thick. He couldn't absorb knowledge, and that was important to Serge. He heard echoes from his childhood, saw bright, elusive flickers of another time, and he wanted to chase them, the melting pocket watches, persistence of memory. Serge was falling in love with the place he had taken for granted growing up, and he became a disciple of Florida history. He began traveling the state, spending entire days in the libraries of the public university system, going through arcane tomes in Special Collections. When Serge was on his meds, he would stare at a page for hours, reading the same paragraph over and over without understanding. His brain was a jug of honey. He'd start pounding his forehead on the table until they asked him to leave.

Then Serge would walk the streets and pitch his medicine in a gutter. The next day he was back at the library, begging for another chance. He was so sweet and polite he usually got it, and he pored through book after map after magazine after microfilm with encyclopedic retention. But there was a price. That night he would rob and stomp people.

He had no idea why. It was a very curious thing for Serge to watch, like he was working the levers inside a robot gone haywire in a bad 1959 science fiction movie. Sometimes it obeyed the controls; other times it ran amok in the village square.

The more Serge read and observed, the more he understood his cultural underpinnings, the social dynamic of his time and place. On a warm spring evening, he achieved absolute clarity. He saw in one broad stroke the wholesale collapse of courtesy and community. He wanted to run out in the road and wave his arms and warn the people. But if they stopped their cars, there was an even chance he'd rob and stomp them. What to do?

By the beginning of summer, Serge had worked his way around the state to Tampa Bay. He stopped taking his medicine again so he could study the library holdings at the University of South

TRIGGERFISH TWIST   87

Florida. Soon, he began teaching a course at the school. Only two problems: Serge wasn't a teacher, and the university didn't know about it. He just wandered out of the library one afternoon and into a small auditorium. A few students were using the room as a study hall. Others were goofing off altogether, watching daytime talk shows on a TV bolted to the wall over the stage. Serge couldn't have that.

He looked up at the screen. Someone was interviewing Donny Osmond about his private pain.

"You know what?" Serge yelled into the auditorium. "Fuck Donny Osmond's private pain!" He yanked the power cord out of the socket. "Jesus! What a nation of bed-wetters we've become!"

He began pacing the stage in a psychotic state, which the students mistook for professorial. He launched a disjointed, pedantic ramble about history and sociology, which further convinced the students that they had accidentally stumbled into an official part of the curriculum.

They got up to leave.

Serge started bopping up and down, playing an invisible electric organ.

"*That's the way, uh-huh, uh-huh, I like it* . . . K.C. and the Sunshine Band, the greatest musical artists to ever have come out of Florida, getting their start at T.K. Studios in Hialeah as K.C. and the Sunshine Junkanoo Band, named after the imported Bahamian music that influenced their intricate horns and percussion until their brilliance was unfairly splattered with the embarrassing stain of disco . . . *Get down tonight—yowwww!*"

Some students sat back down. This guy's wacked! Let's see what happens. Others out in the hall stuck their heads in the door—is there a class going on in here or something?

Serge resumed pacing and babbling. He kicked off his shoes and trudged across the stage like the barefoot mailmen walking the surf a century ago. He kept it up for almost an hour—the first Pan Am flights from Biscayne to Havana, Arthur Godfrey playing a ukelele in a Miami swimming pool—spitting history nonstop like an auctioneer, his fact-valve stuck open. The students loved it. Ten rivers of sweat poured down Serge's head, and he became faint. His hand felt for the arm of a chair onstage, and he fell into it like

Ted Nugent at the end of a set. A young woman threw him a towel. Serge wiped himself down, got up again and staggered to the front of the stage for the encore: nibbling cheese slices into the shapes of the state's sixty-seven counties.

The next day, the auditorium was half full. Some students cut other classes to hear what the buzz was about. Teachers were now showing up, standing along the back wall.

Serge blasted in from a side door, jumped onstage and dove into a synthesis of popular culture, local history and spiritual philosophy. He gave a manic, high-octane, hour-long presentation featuring multiple characters and voices.

The third day, the room was full. The fourth, it overflowed.

On the fifth, Serge arrived early with his antique Ybor City cigar box. He had sent one of the kids to Audio-Visual for a slide projector, and it now stood in the middle of the stage. The auditorium began to fill. Serge opened the cigar box and lovingly removed his collection of Ektachrome slides and inserted them in the projector's carousel. "Hmmm," he said to himself. "Where's my Orange Bowl lighter? Has somebody been in here? Worry about that later—you got a class to teach." He grabbed the projector's remote control in his right hand and walked to the front of the stage. The room went quiet.

"Florida, the Sunshine State—six hundred and sixty-three miles of beaches, four thousand five hundred islands, a sales tax of six percent, fifteen million people, and a five-hundred-year history that is one big real estate scam.

"The swampland come-ons didn't start in the 1920s. They go back half a millennium, all the way across the Atlantic, to the kings and queens and dukes of the Old World. The first explorers discovered that Florida was a worthless peninsula. Way too hot. No strategic value. No gold. Indians kept shooting arrows at you. But these were Europeans, and in their charming continental way they grabbed Florida just to grab it, like those shitty light-blue properties in Monopoly you only buy because you don't want your evil cousin to get them.

"Actually, the first owners found Florida wasn't worthless. It was *worse* than worthless. They poured money into forts and ag collectives, only to come back the next year and find everyone dead or insane. So they looked around Europe and said, 'How 'bout a little trade? Nice tropical real estate.' The deed to Florida started making the rounds."

Serge looked over his shoulder at the screen onstage. His thumb clicked the remote, and the projector tumbled the first slide into place.

"These are the six flags that have flown over Florida as nations passed us around like the clap. The Spanish, the French, the British, the Spanish again—the kid who has to repeat second grade for eating too much library paste—then the United States, and finally the current state flag consisting of a diagonal red cross on a white field with a circular seal depicting an Indian maiden under a sabal palm at sunrise, casting something upon the water, possibly lottery tickets."

Click.

"This is a painting of Ponce de León, a widely misunderstood man. Although he is credited as the first European to discover Florida, he is more widely known for his quixotic and most likely apocryphal search for the Fountain of Youth. A new theory has emerged. Why did Ponce explore? Anyone?"

A hand went up. "The Age of Discovery?"

"Wrong!"

"Convert the Indians to Christianity?"

"Wrong!"

"To get chicks?"

"Bingo!" said Serge. "My own take is that Ponce was suffering a classic conquistador midlife crisis. He's pushing fifty. He's done it all. But now the new guys are coming up. Cortez and De Soto. Punks! They got no respect. So there's Ponce, disillusioned with it all as his landing party begins raping and pillaging yet another Indian settlement, and Ponce is back on the beach staring out to sea, talking to himself. 'Maybe I should start working out.'"

Click.

An hour's worth of slides and lore.

Click.

"And this was taken yesterday. It's from the food court at the mall up the street. What a telling assemblage of our community. Have we just completely stopped trying? Examine how soft we've become as a people, lounging in mail-order shorts between the cheese-kabob kiosk and the Magic Wok, chewing slowly with expressions containing less verve than grazing dairy cattle. What must the rest of the world think? We've got physicists from Pakistan gladly pulling sixteen-hour shifts in our convenience stores—and *they're* made fun of by Americans like this choice specimen here on the right. I direct your attention to the middle-aged man with the tits in the tight 'One Hundred Percent Stud' T-shirt eating a chocolate-chip cookie the size of a manhole cover. . . ."

Serge turned off the projector and walked to the front of the stage.

"The shoreline of Florida has been going in and out like an accordion for millions of years. They've found pottery fifty miles offshore and shark teeth fifty miles inland. A massive jetliner crashes in six inches of water in the Everglades and vanishes beneath the muck. The first Floridians are all gone, the bloodlines wiped out forever. A thousand generations eating oysters in the same spot and tossing the shells in piles bigger than planetariums. We find an ancient circle—evidence of the first culture at the mouth of the Miami River. And we say, 'Gee. That's pretty cool. Let's put a fucking condo on it!' Have you *seen* the barrier islands from the air? They're five times taller than they are wide—these little tendrils of shifting sand covered with these ridiculous buildings. Do you know what the next decent hurricane is going to do? Are you starting to get the picture? We weren't the first here, and we won't be the last. Florida's just letting us pass through—so enjoy the ride and please pick up your trash."

The bell rang and the kids started getting up.

"Be careful," Serge admonished. "It's dumb out there."

He leaped off the stage and headed for the exit. He was mobbed. Young women slipped him their phone numbers.

The dean was among the faculty in back, and he offered Serge a prestigious chair. Serge said he was sorry, but this would have to be his last term at the university. He was being offered too much money by the private sector. The dean said he was sorry, too, but happy for Serge, and they shook hands.

The dean went back to his office and looked in his files. He began to perspire. There was nobody on the faculty by the name Serge A. Storms. He called the department of education in Tallahassee. They told him there was no teacher certified under that name at any level.

The dean panicked. He picked up the phone. Then he thought about his career. People had heard him offer Serge the chair. This could be a major embarrassment. He put the phone down. Since Serge was leaving anyway, he saw no real harm in keeping the little secret to himself. There was only one minor loose end. He also had sort of asked Serge to deliver the commencement address.

13

THREE A.M.

A Kenworth pumped diesel smoke into the north Florida air as it rolled past the official state welcome center on Interstate 75.

Four hulking men walked across the dark parking lot of the hospitality complex, toward a brown Cutlass Supreme. The largest climbed in the driver's seat and opened a wallet that wasn't his, counting money. Four hundred dollars. He threw the wallet on the dash, turned the ignition and grabbed the steering wheel tightly with two sets of tattooed knuckles. *H-A-T-E* and *H-A-T-E*. On the other side of the parking lot, in front of a sign that said NO NIGHTTIME SECURITY, a silhouette slumped in the driver's seat of a rented Chrysler Sebring. Small flames began to lap the back window of the rental.

The Cutlass pulled out of the parking lot and back onto the interstate just as the fire reached the Sebring's gas tank, and a bright orange flare went up in the night sky.

AGENT MAHONEY WORKED at the Behavioral Science Unit of the Florida Department of Law Enforcement, located in the basement of the Johnson Building, named for an indicted senator.

The unit was the state's central tracking headquarters for homicidal maniacs.

Florida was one of the few states to establish such a unit after extensive psychological profiling determined that the criminally insane prefer nice weather. Mahoney's unit was a junior version of the FBI facility at Quantico, made famous in *The Silence of the Lambs*. Mahoney had seen the movie and it made him laugh. Real-life profiling was nothing like working with a Hannibal Lecter. Most of the people he dealt with were complete morons. And there wasn't any nerve-racking mental gamesmanship, either. Law enforcement or not, this was still a government agency, which meant understaffing, chaos and catch-up. It was a two-man operation, and most of Mahoney's time was spent sifting through the avalanche of faxes, bulletins and Internet alerts from every other state about all the wack-jobs heading his way. He felt like a hockey goalie with forty-nine players firing pucks at him at the same time.

It got so bad that Mahoney finally nailed a big map of the United States on the office wall and used different-colored push-pins to track everyone. A line of blue pins marched down I-95, following a trail of pimps killed with blowguns. A line of pink pins followed the Interstate 10 corridor through the Southwest, connecting the bodies of prostitutes found in matching Samsonite. Yellow pins streamed down I-55, purple pins down I-65, red ones down I-85. A string of orange pins across the Midwest traced the ex-wives Mahoney owed alimony.

Mahoney sat down at his desk and began going through a stack of antique Florida postcards—historic hotels and restaurants and roadside attractions. He held up a hand-tinted linen card from the 1940s, the old Seminole Inn near the St. Lucie Canal, thirty miles inland from Palm Beach. He turned the card over. Handwriting in ballpoint: "Opened in 1926 as a never-realized major destination of the Seaboard Coastline railroad. The dining room was hosted by Wallis Warfield, who later became duchess of Windsor. Try the Okeechobee fried catfish. You won't be disappointed. (Only available weather permitting fishing on the lake.)" There was writing on all the cards, all recently postmarked, all from the same person. No return address. Mahoney stared at the signature. Serge.

Yelling from the next room: "Mahoney! Get in here!"

Mahoney had an erratic, long-term relationship with his boss, Lieutenant Ingersol, a sturdy, authoritative man who looked and sounded like James Earl Jones and didn't care for Mahoney or his unorthodox methods.

Ingersol was going over an expense report when Mahoney appeared in his doorway with a handful of postcards. "You wanted to see me?"

Ingersol got up and closed the door behind Mahoney and shut the venetian blinds, even though they were the only two people in the unit.

"Mahoney, what's this item on your expense report—three hundred dollars for lingerie modeling?"

"You're not going to find informants singing in the church choir."

"Disallowed!" said Ingersol, making a big swipe across the report with a red pen. He looked up and saw the postcards in Mahoney's hand. "Who are those from?"

"Serge," said Mahoney.

"What now?" asked Ingersol. "Taunts? Threats?"

Mahoney shook his head. "Travel tips."

"What?"

"Places to eat. Museums. Antique stores. Great hotel deals," said Mahoney. "Best manhunt I've ever been on."

"Well, it's over as of this minute!" said Ingersol. "This Serge thing has become an obsession with you. It's a personal vendetta, and we don't have the budget for that. Besides, I've got some real work for you. Tourist was killed last night."

"So what's new?" said Mahoney.

"At the Welcome Center."

"Ouch."

"This is a media nightmare," said Ingersol. "I can just see the British headlines."

"Any leads?"

"Nothing solid, but it has the stink of the McGraw Brothers."

"The country music group?"

"No, you putz, the bank robbers."

"I thought they were in prison?"

"Were," said Ingersol. "Got sprung two days ago from Talladega Federal."

Mahoney rubbed his chin. "Isn't that where Denny McClain did his time?"

Ingersoll nodded. "I drove through Talladega once. Passed by as a stock-car race was letting out at the speedway and got stuck in traffic. Mahoney, do you have any idea what it's like to be trapped in the Dixie boondocks at sunset with a hundred thousand rednecks all pumped up from watching NASCAR and thinking they can drive like Richard Petty on a full tank of Miller Genuine Draft?" Ingersol leaned back in his chair and stared thoughtfully out the door. "Scariest shit I ever seen in my life."

"But that's up in Alabama," said Mahoney. "The McGraws could go anywhere. What makes you think they headed to Florida?"

"Remember that botched bank job in Tampa last week? The airbag case?"

"Oh, yeah. I couldn't stop laughing."

"That was Skag McGraw, the youngest brother. Revenge is a powerful emotion. My gut tells me they're headed to the bay area. I want you to stay on top of this."

"Can I go to Tampa?"

"Not a chance," said Ingersol. "I know what you're thinking. Serge is from Tampa. You just want to take off on your own wild-goose chase."

"I swear. It'll be a fishing expedition."

"Forget it. You're going to monitor it from this office where I can keep an eye on you. Let the field agents clean up any messes."

Mahoney pointed out the door at the wall map. "I'll use green pins."

"Knock yourself out."

14

YOU COULDN'T HELP but like Jim Davenport. In addition to being agreeable, he was incredibly resilient.

He had felt terrible about killing Skag McGraw, despite the circumstances. Everyone was understanding and reassuring—his wife, the neighbors, the police and his company, who gave him a week off to rest, not so much out of compassion but because they didn't want a distracted employee running over a pedestrian on company time and getting them sued.

A week was more than enough.

Yes, Jim had taken a life, and it was against everything in his nature. He shuffled around the bottom of a funk for five days before deciding "I have a family to take care of," and he snapped out of it a second later.

Jim was more than ready when his alarm clock went off six-thirty Monday morning. He got up with the rest of the block.

Weekday mornings on Triggerfish Lane were a ballet. Lights and showers and TVs came on in sequence along the dark street. Garbage cans went down the driveways and newspapers came back up in rolling choreography. Most of the televisions were tuned to the same local morning show, *Get the Hell out of Bed, Tampa Bay!*

Jim Davenport walked through the living room tying his tie. Martha was already in the kitchen, dressed smartly, a whirling dervish. She circled the table collecting empty breakfast plates from Debbie, Melvin and Nicole. "More orange juice?"

Jim sat down with the paper. "Morning, honey."

The TV in the next room: *". . . Is too much love bad for you? Hear from the experts! . . ."*

Martha dropped the dishes in the sink and grabbed Jim's strudel as it popped from the toaster.

"Morning, dear."

All the households on Triggerfish had the same rhythms. Except one.

As he did most mornings at precisely 3 A.M., Serge screamed himself awake from another vivid nightmare involving a slaughterhouse and Mousketeers. He went into the living room brushing his teeth and turned on the three stolen TVs stacked in a pyramid. CNN, MSNBC and C-SPAN. He sat down on the couch with a clipboard and took notes.

"International observers report polling irregularities in the outlying mountainous Huizenga states, where voter turnout is close to one hundred percent as peasants arrive en masse to cast ballots in defiance of the guerrillas . . ."

Serge scribbled an urgent action item on his clipboard: *Don't take democracy for granted!*

More news, more action items. Serge watched until he felt confident he had a handle on the world, then turned up the volume to hear the sets from the kitchen while he prepared a gourmet breakfast. He flipped a southern omelet and checked his watch. "Oops." He whipped off his chef's hat and ran out the front door and stood in darkness in the middle of the lawn.

Headlights came around the corner, and a station wagon slowly rolled up the street. Serge dug in his feet and crouched. A newspaper sailed out the station wagon's window. Serge caught it on the fly and ran back inside. He spread the sections across the floor and went over them with highlighters.

Finally, Serge showered with all-natural pumice to get deep into his skin. Serge had a theory that most people's brain activity got gummed up through improperly maintained pores, and he worked diligently each morning to get his in working order. When his pores were happy, Serge was happy, and he turned the cold faucet all the way off and stood under the steaming-hot stream as long as he could stand it. Just as he was about to yell, he reversed the faucets, shivering for sixty seconds, timing himself on his diver's watch. He turned off the shower and leaped from the tub, throwing two victorious fists in the air. He was completely alive, ready for *Today.*

"DON'T YOU WANT your strudel?" asked Martha.

"Running late," said Jim, folding his paper over to the next section.

"But you have time to read the sports."

Jim knew better than to answer.

"Debbie, strudel?"

No answer.

"I'll take it, Mom," said Melvin.

"Okay, but you'll have to eat it in the car."

Martha kissed Jim good-bye, then grabbed the keys and the handle of Nicole's child seat and herded everyone out of the room.

Jim went back to his paper. "I'll read the sports if I want."

"I heard that," Martha yelled from the front door.

"I love you."

"Love you, too!"

SERGE WAS GIVING a pep talk to his porch plants when he witnessed the tightly controlled bedlam of a mother single-handedly loading three children into a Suburban. It reminded him it was time to get his own kids up.

He went back inside and slowly opened the door to Coleman's bedroom. Coleman was on top of the sheets in his BVDs, a shiny string of spit hanging from his open mouth to the pool of saliva on his pillow.

Serge quietly closed the door. "Better put that Mensa application on hold."

He checked on Sharon. She was out, too, snoring like a biker. He leaned over and made a buzzing sound near her ear. Sharon swatted insects in her sleep. He leaned closer and buzzed again. Sharon half opened one eye.

"You're an asshole!" She rolled over and covered her head with the pillow.

Serge went in the bathroom. "I'm flushing your coke!" He hit the toilet lever.

Sharon was out of bed in a flash. Coleman, who heard Serge through the wall in his sleep, arrived in the bathroom doorway the same time as Sharon, and they collided and fell down.

"Just kidding," said Serge. "You know, you guys might consider getting in some kind of program. Just a thought."

Serge marched with purpose for the kitchen table. Sharon and Coleman yawned and followed. Serge sat down and picked up his clipboard and pruned his "action items": "*Locate first edition, Islands in the Stream, enclose in protective mylar cover. Research university microfilm, Murph the Surf (legend or loser?). To Buy: used 21mm wide-angle lens w/polarizing filter for Diane Arbus–like portraits of unusual, compelling people you meet at bus stops and in public library (each one is special, has a story!). Change voter registration again: party too mean-spirited. Construct Adirondack chair for porch like one in that watercolor. Optional (if time permits): Rent ground-penetrating radar to locate network of secret 1940s organized-crime escape tunnels in Ybor City.*"

"What's with the stupid clipboard?" said Sharon.

"If you don't visualize what you want to accomplish, then you won't accomplish anything."

"That's the stupidest shit I ever heard!"

"What are you going to do today?"

Sharon lit a Marlboro and tossed the lighter on the table. "I dunno."

Serge heard a kitchen utensil rattling against glass. He turned to Coleman, eating peanut butter out of the jar with a spoon.

"Would you like an omelet instead?" asked Serge. "I can whip one up in a second. Really, no bother."

"Can you put peanut butter in an omelet?"

"It's usually better without."

"No thanks."

Serge turned. "Sharon? Omelet?"

Sharon was rubbing cocaine into her gums.

"Sorry, I forgot," said Serge. "You're on the all-blow diet."

Outside on Triggerfish Lane, twenty cars sequentially backed from driveways and accelerated down the street like a B-17 squadron rollout on an English tarmac.

Serge trotted out the door to the Barracuda, untucking his tropical shirt to cover the .38 automatic in his belt.

Jim Davenport came down the steps across the street with his briefcase and headed for his business car, a '92 Saturn.

Serge waved. "Big day ahead?"

"Huge," said Jim. "Yourself?"

Serge checked his front pocket for a spare ammo clip. "Same old same old . . ."

They waved again and got in their cars and drove off in opposite directions.

Jim made good time in morning traffic listening to the local zoo radio team. The zoo team was playing another ingenious prank, dressing up as jail prisoners and running through neighborhoods knocking on doors, asking people to saw their handcuffs off.

Jim arrived early for work. He was an eleven-year employee at Apollo Consulting. He had taken the penknife over the money clip for his tenth anniversary. Jim loved the job variety of consulting. Every week a different office, different company, different city. Jim went over their books, observed management, interviewed employees, then wrote brilliant reports that spun off unprofitable subsidiaries and pancaked steep organizational charts.

Jim was a genius at the quick sweep, coming up to speed rapidly in new surroundings and instantly zeroing in on assembly-line snags, brainless marketing campaigns and which executive was the cancer on the corporation. But Jim's real strengths were the intangibles, the stuff other consultants couldn't account for with their computer models and time-motion studies. Jim had an extra-sensitive high-gain emotional antenna and could practically see the ambient human aura in an workplace like a giant mood ring. Jim found the temperament of large groups of people working together ebbed and flowed like a single gelatinous organism. Over time, companies displayed distinct personalities. Some were sunny and optimistic, others clinically depressed. There were the giddy, the unctuous, the circumspect and the terror-stricken.

Jim targeted the dysfunctional ones for surgical fixes that paid immediate dividends to stockholders. Flex-time for working moms, beefing up human resources, production incentives. Sometimes it was as simple as a more cheerful paint scheme or getting rid of lettuce in the cafeteria salad bar once it turned brown. Jim's bosses at Apollo loved him. So did the people he interviewed—finally, someone who will listen to us! Jim believed he was making a difference.

Business exploded, and Apollo soon found it was spending way too much on travel down to the booming Tampa-Orlando corridor.

The Monday after his week off for killing Skag McGraw, Jim drove across town to the newly constructed Apollo office. He drifted through morning rush traffic on Interstate 4 with the radio on, zoo DJs running handcuffed through a day-care parking lot. Apollo Consulting had built its new branch in an expanding business park near the I-75/I-4 nexus. Jim pulled past the guard shack just as the DJs were arrested for public endangerment by Tampa police, who unhandcuffed them, then handcuffed them. Apollo had built an impressive office. There was even a handball court, the sort of thing Jim might recommend in one of his reports. Jim walked in the lobby, and a secretary told him he needed to call the home office immediately.

Jim got on the phone. "I see. I see . . ."

Apollo had just been acquired in a hostile takeover by Damocles Consulting, Inc.

The new company said it planned to keep the Florida operation—maybe even increase it—and nobody had any reason to worry.

Jim arrived for work the next day and half the staff was gone, just like that, replaced by young, sharp-looking, humorless drones from a corporate incubator in Simi Valley. Jim tried to make small talk and get to know his new colleagues, but they made him go away with a set of efficient nonverbal cues that they had picked up in a training class.

Jim's first assignment under new management was an injection-molding firm in Clearwater. He set about it the same old way, but he began getting a different vibe from the employees. Jim wasn't quite sure, but something seemed a little odd about these people. They ran away when they saw him.

Jim didn't know it, but word was out that Damocles was in the building. Jim shrugged it off and went back to the business park and wrote one of his finest reports.

The next morning, when Jim arrived at work, the receptionist told him the new office manager wanted to see him. Jim went upstairs and knocked on a mahogany door with a fresh brass nameplate.

"Come in."

Jim stuck his head inside. "You wanted to see me, Mr. Young?"

"Have a seat, Jim. And please, call me Turk."

He held up Jim's latest report. It was marked heavily with red felt-tip.

"We need to revise some things in here."

"Like what?" asked Jim.

"This stuff about employee chemistry."

"My experience has been—"

"And this section about adding positions on the assembly line . . ."

"Right, I—"

Turk scribbled some more with his red pen, then looked up. "We have to drop at least eighty jobs company-wide."

"What? That's crazy!" said Jim. "They're so understaffed now it's a safety issue. I documented it all."

Turk set the report down on his desk. "We can't use your suggestions."

"Something wrong with them?"

"No, they're perfect. But you see, these companies already know what they want to do before they call us."

"They do?"

"They do. Say a company wants to position itself for an acquisition. It's carrying too much payroll. It needs to slash X jobs to get the stock price it wants. We come in and recommend they slash X jobs and then write a report to support that conclusion."

"That must make the employees mad."

"Furious."

"Since it's already been decided, why do we get involved?"

"You've heard of going postal?"

Jim nodded.

"I don't know if you know this, but we're not really in the consulting business."

Jim was confused. "What business *are* we in?"

"The employee-violence-abatement business. The American workplace is getting too hot. Employers can no longer be whimsical with peoples' lives without having to worry about getting shot or something. Call it the decay of our culture. Our role is to allow top managers to say, 'Hey, I wanted to keep you on, but the consultants made me do it!' "

"We willingly take the blame?"

Turk smiled. "It's how we've become the biggest in the business. That and the fact that we save an incredible amount on in-house training. We have no idea how to advise these companies. We don't even know what the fuck some of them do."

"What does that say about our profession?"

"They're already saying it: Those who can't do, teach. Those who can't teach, consult."

"So my job now is—?"

"To draw fire. Like when a fighter jet dumps metallic chaff and incendiary decoys to lure away surface-to-air missiles."

"I'm chaff?"

"Chaff."

"Is that good?"

"Pays well. That's as good as it gets."

15

JOHN MILTON HAD A REALLY BAD JOB.

Everyone kept telling John this. Guys who tarred roofs in Miami in July told him. So did drainage workers in septic tanks. And the people who fixed downed power lines in the rain. And airport cavity searchers. And the team that travels as the Harlem Globetrotters' opponents. And a new *Star Trek* character without a speaking part who beams down to the hostile planet with Kirk, Spock and Bones . . . they all kept saying the same thing: "John, have you got a really bad job!"

John was a substitute teacher at a public school.

John tried to make the best of it, but it was hard to reach students when they were tampering with ankle monitors.

John lived in a tiny apartment in west Tampa that overlooked box compactors behind a Wal-Mart. It was one of those old three-story jobs that sprouted around Tampa in the fifties, powder-blue trim and the complex's name in cursive letters on the side. But the sturdy construction had far outlasted the desirability of the neighborhood, and living there had gone from modest quaintness to a decidedly dicey proposition. All vegetation was dead, soot ran halfway up the outside walls, and a row of six-hundred-dollar sedans nosed against the building, dripping oil, Prestone and brake fluid that ran to the storm drain through cigarette butts, broken beer bottles and spent phone cards. It was called "Splendid Acres."

John's wind-up alarm went off at six. If the phone call was coming, it would be in the next half hour. If it didn't, he was going back to bed. He went to his front door, checked out the peephole, unbolted and got the paper. He stood at the kitchenette munching unbuttered toast and reading a story about the new aluminum streetlights in south Florida that collapse when a driver hits them so they don't get killed, and how people in pickup trucks were hitting them on purpose, then hauling them off to sell for scrap.

The phone rang.

John arrived at Tampa High School and headed for the classroom. The principal stuck his head out his office. "John, I'd like a word."

John sat down in front of the principal's desk.

"John, we've gotten a complaint. A parent called. Did you tell a student yesterday to 'shut the hell up'?"

"What?"

"It's a simple question, and I want you to be straight with me. Did you or didn't you?"

"Yes, I did," said John. "Actually, the full quote was, 'Put the knife away, sit down and shut the hell up!'"

"John, we can't have language like that in our classrooms. We have a zero-tolerance program in place."

"This is a joke, right?"

"Zero means zero. There's going to be an investigation. Until then you're suspended."

"But what about the weapon? What about the policy against that?"

"None of the other students saw anything."

"*I* saw it."

"Because you violated the zero policy, your account must be excluded. It's all part of the program. Would you like a copy?"

John didn't answer.

The principal looked down and began doing paperwork on another matter, indicating the meeting was over.

John left the school in a fog. He went home and got out the classifieds. He picked up the phone and responded to an ad for someone to clean bedpans at the prison hospital.

They asked John what he used to do that he would apply for such a terrible job. John told them.

"Man, you had a really bad job."

They said they could see why John would have quit. John said he didn't quit; he had been suspended for swearing at an armed student. They told John they were sorry, but that made him unfit for the position.

John was undaunted. He continued working the phone for the better part of the afternoon, and persistence finally paid off. He put on his best synthetic suit and headed across town for an interview. Soon he was shaking hands with his new employers.

The next morning John walked into a gleaming office building and took off his jacket, revealing a short-sleeve dress shirt. He stepped up to a counter and removed the NEXT WINDOW PLEASE sign.

"May I help you?" asked John.

The next person in line at Consolidated Bank stepped up to John's window.

John discovered he liked being a teller. Each morning he lovingly wiped down his counter with a spray bottle and paper towels. He made sure the different-denomination bills were all pointed the same way in his drawer. He tested the chained pens and filled the lollipop bowl.

John learned the rhythms of the bank lobby. Retirees arrived in the morning, businessmen in the afternoon, sawdust-covered construction workers at lunch on Friday. The very wealthy got to skip the lines altogether and go directly to the office of the senior vice president in charge of taking millionaires to lunch.

John began to know the regular customers by name, and they trusted him enough to confide about medical conditions. He was a good listener. Some of the other clerks merely pretended to pay attention while counting money—smiling and nodding at horrible news or looking grim when the customer told a joke, but John's facial expressions were always in context.

John's appearance was also dependable. Khakis, loafers and one of the ten identical white short-sleeve dress shirts he kept hanging in his closet. He was trim, pushing fifty, with a full head of slightly oily brown hair. Efficient, content, loyal to the company, harboring no further ambition. The consummate foot soldier.

"Good morning, Mrs. Gladstone. How are you today?"

"Spastic colon."

"Sorry to hear."

"The doctors don't know what they're doing."

"No, they don't."

"It's acting up right now."

"A shame."

"You married yet?"

"Still free as a bird."

"I don't know how they're letting you get away."

"Lollipops for the grandkids?"

John was counting twenties when he saw the four older women at the back of his line. They peeked around the customers and waved at John. He smiled and waved back.

They were all widows, seventy-six to eighty-eight years old, and the tallest might make a case for five feet, if she had a new permanent. When it was their turn, they hit John's counter like it was the two-dollar window at the greyhound track.

Many of John's customers were senior citizens, and they were lonely. They tried to squeeze every last drop of human contact out of a Social Security deposit, and they could stretch transactions to astronomical lengths with a play-by-play of their last twenty-four hours on earth. The less patient clerks tried to hurry them along, but John had an endless reservoir of empathy. He never tired of discussing podiatry or extra fiber or the thankless daughter who never calls despite everything.

But the four women now standing before John were different. They had formed an investment club that was outperforming most mutual-fund managers, and they had begun popping up in newspapers and on talk shows. Edith, Edna, Eunice and Ethel. The media dubbed them "The E-Team."

They were starting to be recognized everywhere—at bars and nightclubs, and in the lines at Morrison's and Luby's, where they scraped Cool Whip off Jell-O cubes and signed autographs. They were a formidable crew at crunching numbers, and their enthusiasm for equities was only eclipsed by their rivalry for men, which often resulted in an internecine ruthlessness last witnessed on the Russian front. They spent many a day cruising up and down Dale Mabry Highway, trolling for men like spring-breaking sorority sisters. Then they dropped in the supermarket to goose the retired bag boys.

John handed the women four deposit receipts. "How's the E-Team today?"

"Rockin' and rollin'."

A door to an executive suite opened and a bank vice president walked out and headed to lunch with a distinguished gray-haired customer in a three-piece suit.

"Look!" said Edith. "It's Ambrose!"

"Who?" asked John.

"Ambrose Tarrington the Third," said Eunice. "Old money."

"A hottie," said Ethel.

"Slut," said Edith.

The women accelerated the pace of their transactions, slipped John a stock tip and hurried out the door after Ambrose.

"Where'd he go?" said Eunice.

"There he is!"

A white Bentley pulled out of the parking lot.

The woman piled in a blue Buick Regal with curb feelers and a Plexiglas love-bug shield and took off after the Bentley. They sped north on Dale Mabry Highway, four wisps of white hair at window level.

They pulled up next to Ambrose at a red light. Edith lowered her automatic window.

"Hubba hubba!"

Ambrose looked over and saw the Buick.

The light turned green and Ambrose floored it, but the Buick stayed with him for three blocks. The E-Team knelt in their seats and hung out the windows.

"Got a girlfriend?"

"Want some company?"

Ambrose rolled up his window and hit the gas. The Bentley slid into the turn lane and made a right.

"Follow him!" said Edna.

Eunice made a slow right across three lanes of honking traffic.

Ambrose thought he had gotten away and began to relax. Then he happened to glance in his rearview and saw a blue Buick a half mile back, doing ninety, weaving in and out of cars, gaining fast. Ambrose braked and made a last-second turn onto an exit ramp.

The Buick was in the far left lane and couldn't get over. Ambrose escaped.

"You did that on purpose!" Edna yelled at Eunice. "You were jealous!"

"Bite me."

"Glasses back on," said Ethel. "Doctors' orders."

They all faced forward in their seats and put on jet-black wrap-around cataract goggles.

"I hate these glasses," said Ethel. "They're so *old*-looking."

"I think they make me look fly," said Edith, "like Wesley Snipes."

Edna checked her watch. "It's still the early bird at Malio's."

"We're there," said Eunice. She went to hit the turn signal for the restaurant's exit but discovered it had been on since she didn't know when.

16

SCATTERED CLOUDS provided a break from the Florida heat, just before the traditional showers that fell across Tampa Bay every summer afternoon for fifteen minutes. Martha Davenport put on a wide-brimmed straw hat with a yellow ribbon and grabbed her basket of gardening tools. She set Nicole in her bouncy baby seat next to the flower bed.

Martha hummed and weeded under some shrubs. She made funny faces at Nicole, who giggled and bobbed in her seat.

Suddenly, something caught the corner of Martha's eye. A pit bull charging from across the street. Martha's heart skipped. She snatched Nicole from her seat and glanced toward the front door. Too far. No time. The dog was already in their yard now, full gallop.

Martha didn't know where it came from. Some prehistoric maternal genetic memory. When the dog was feet away and preparing to strike, Martha tucked Nicole under her arm like a football and hunched in a two-point stance. She let out a mighty guttural roar right in the dog's face. It startled her as much as the pit bull, who hit the brakes. Rasputin stopped and looked at her a second, then trotted back to his own yard and licked himself.

Martha went inside the house, sat down and couldn't stop shaking. She picked up the phone and called animal control.

JIM DAVENPORT DROVE home from work. When he turned onto Trig-gerfish Lane, there was a crowd in the road. An animal-control truck and lots of neighbors. Martha was in the middle of it. He recognized her screaming from the end of the block.

Jim pulled into his driveway and went down to the street.

"What do you mean you can't take the dog away!" Martha yelled at the animal-control officer.

"Take it easy," said the officer.

"I want that dog out of this neighborhood! That man doesn't properly control him! He's a dangerous menace!"

"You said he didn't bite you or your daughter?" said the officer.

"He *would* have!"

"I'm sorry. I can only give him a ticket for not having his dog on a leash. I can't do anything else until it bites someone."

"Then it'll be too late!"

Jack Terrier stepped up.

"I truly apologize for the inconvenience, officer. I don't know how he got loose. This is the first time. I swear I won't let it happen again."

Gladys Plant came out and joined the fray. "He's lying! It's always loose!"

More neighbors gathered around. Some college students. Serge and Coleman.

Martha noticed Jim's arrival. She grabbed him by the arm. "Jim! Do something!"

"I don't know what's going on."

"Jim!"

"I can only write a ticket," said the officer.

"He went for my child!" screamed Martha.

"Lower your voice, ma'am."

"He just wanted to sniff you. He was being friendly," said Jack. He looked down at Rasputin, now on a leash at his feet, addressing the dog in baby talk. "Weren't you just trying to be friendly, my little boopsie?" Rasputin wagged his tongue and rolled on his back with a half-boner.

"How revolting!" said Martha. Then, to the officer: "What the hell do we pay you for?"

"I already told you once to take it easy."

"Officer," said Jack. "Please cut her some slack. It's perfectly understandable. She misinterpreted Rasputin's playfulness. She's just being a good mom."

"Don't you fucking patronize me!" said Martha.

"Ma'am, I'll warn you one last time," said the officer.

"That monster charged my baby!"

"Rasputin is *my* baby," said Jack.

"You son of a bitch!"

"Ma'am!"

"Look, you're upsetting Rasputin," said Jack. "And it's his birthday."

"*You*—" Martha lunged for Terrier's throat, and the officer had to restrain her.

THE SILENCE WAS suffocating inside the Suburban. It was dark out when Jim and Martha approached their neighborhood.

Martha had a box of Kleenex in her lap, trying to get ink off her fingertips.

"I don't know what to say," said Jim. "I'm stunned."

"Some help you were!"

"I never thought I'd have to bail my wife out of jail."

"*Someone* had to stand up for our family!"

"But did you have to spit at the officer?"

Martha folded her arms and looked away. They turned onto Triggerfish.

Something appeared in the road.

Martha grabbed the dashboard. "Watch it!"

Jim swerved to avoid Rasputin standing in the middle of the street.

They pulled into the driveway. Jim got out and walked around and opened Martha's door, but she just sat there staring ahead, arms folded again.

"It's been a long day," he said.

She didn't budge.

Jim sighed and went inside alone.

Rasputin stood in the middle of the street, swaying his hindquarters. He watched Jim Davenport go in the house, and, a few minutes later, Martha as well.

It was quiet again. Rasputin began trotting up the street, toe-nails clicking on the pavement. On Triggerfish Lane, the night belonged to Rasputin. He was on patrol.

What's this? A squirrel? He charged. "Arrr! Arrr! Arrr! Arrr!"

The squirrel scampered up a tree.

Rasputin moved on. What's that? A cat? "Arrr! Arrr! Arrr! Arrr!"

The cat jumped on top of a car.

Who's next? Opossum? "Arrr! Arrr! Arrr! Arrr!"

It darted under the Davenports' porch.

Rasputin moseyed on down the block until he spotted something new. Ah, big game!

COLEMAN SAT ON his front porch shortly after midnight, looking around furtively as he sneaked a toke with a roach clip. It was his fourth joint since Letterman came on. Which meant munchies. That accounted for the plate of corn chips and bite-size sausages on his lap.

Coleman took another hit and got the feeling someone was watching him. He looked around but didn't see anything. He decided he was just really paranoid—good weed! Then he heard a low growl. He looked down the steps and saw Rasputin, teeth bared, saliva dripping. The dog took a step forward and snapped his teeth.

"Oh, hello," said Coleman. "One of my little nature friends."

Rasputin snapped his teeth again and barked.

"Hungry, eh?"

Coleman tossed a sausage, and Rasputin caught it in flight and swallowed.

"Wow! You must be starved!" He threw another sausage, and Rasputin wolfed it again. Then Rasputin sat down and wagged his tail.

Coleman tossed a steady stream of sausages.

"Didn't I hear earlier today that it's your birthday? . . . We gotta celebrate! Wait here."

Coleman got up to go in the house, but fell over. "Yow, good buzz." He got up again, more slowly this time, and went inside.

He came back out with a plastic Cool Whip tub, set it in front of Rasputin and filled it with beer. The dog began lapping.

"Whoa, dude. It's all about pacing yourself!"

Coleman made another trip inside and returned with a new joint and an empty toilet-paper tube. He lit the joint and took a deep hit. Then he put the tube to his mouth and held the other end over Rasputin's snout and blew him a shotgun.

"Hold it in!" said Coleman.

But apparently Rasputin wasn't paying attention. He shook his head and made little doggie coughs.

"Let's watch some tube," said Coleman. He went inside and Rasputin followed.

They caught the end of Conan. "I'm hungry again. What about you?"

Rasputin trailed Coleman into the kitchen, and Coleman opened the pantry. "See anything you like?"

The dog barked twice.

"What is it, Lassie? You say you want Chee-tos?"

Coleman dumped the entire bag in a big mixing bowl. He opened two Budweisers and emptied them into a tall plastic cup. "The key is to pour slowly at a low angle so you don't get a head." Coleman popped another can and poured it in Rasputin's Cool Whip bowl.

Rasputin followed Coleman back into the living room. Coleman set the beer and Chee-tos on the floor in front of Rasputin and turned on Nick at Nite.

Four A.M.

Serge and Sharon got in from a motel-room robbery. It was dark inside except for the TV. They talked quietly as they came in the door.

". . . You didn't have to pistol-whip him like that," said Serge.

"I didn't like the way he was looking at me," said Sharon.

"You were giving him a blow job!"

"Doesn't give him the right to leer."

"Obviously we've not going to resolve this . . ." Serge flicked on the light. "What the fuck's been going on in here?"

Coleman was passed out on the sofa and Rasputin was asleep

under the coffee table. There were separate piles of canine throw-up and Coleman throw-up.

"This is disgusting!" said Sharon.

"Wake up! Both of you!" yelled Serge.

"What? What is it?" said Coleman, slowly coming around. Rasputin awoke and hit his head on the underside of the table. He crawled out, staggered into a footstool and fell down.

"That dog has bloodshot eyes!" said Serge. He studied the mess on the floor. "You gave him Chee-tos?"

"It's what he wanted."

"No wonder he threw up. You, I expect it from. . . . What's this?"

"A lava lamp."

"I know it's a lava lamp. What's it doing on the floor?"

"So he could look at it. He got hung up on it for about an hour."

"What else did you do?" asked Serge.

Coleman look embarrassed.

"Come on," said Serge. "Out with it."

Coleman told them.

"Oh! Jesus!" Sharon exclaimed. "That's the most perverted thing I ever heard."

Coleman became defensive. "I used a glove."

"But why?" said Serge. "Why on earth would you do such a repulsive thing in the first place?"

Coleman shrugged. "It was his birthday."

17

THE CONSOLIDATED BANK BUILDING, where John Milton worked, had a row of thirty-eight glassed-in office suites running along the south wall of the first floor. Thirty-eight vice presidents.

Lights were on in all the suites except the last one, where the blinds were drawn.

There was a space between two of the blinds in the darkened suite, as if someone were peeking out, spying.

The man inside spying was Pierre Principal. He kept an eye on the sea of desks in the middle of the floor, where the account managers and phone reps worked. He watched Ambrose Tarrington III stroll across the lobby and, moments later, the E-Team rush out after him. He saw John Milton set the NEXT WINDOW PLEASE sign in his teller window and head off for lunch.

Just as John was about the walk out the front door, he got a creepy sensation. He stopped and turned around and saw the space between the two blinds on the other side of the bank. Suddenly, the blinds snapped shut.

Inside the dim executive suite, Pierre stepped back from the window. He walked around his desk and sat down, perfectly still, perspiring palms flat on top of the leather blotter. He glanced at the wall clock, ticking. The office was immaculate and well appointed, with a framed inspirational poster of a rowing crew from Yale over a big word: TEAMWORK.

Pierre Principal was the master of middle management, but at the vice presidential level the air was too thin. Pierre never wanted to be a vice president. He knew better. Vice president was one promotion too many. There was absolutely nothing to do. Literally. That's how they got you. Even if you wanted to work, you couldn't. And you lived in constant fear of being found out.

Pierre was tall, thin, defensive and bald on top with black sidewalls. Everyone said he looked like that annoying partner on *L.A. Law.* He had survived until now by staying below the company radar. He aggressively avoided any promotion into the ranks of corporate officers that always got purged with each change of administration.

So far, there had been seven administrations in Pierre's tenure, and he had gotten along famously with every one. It was his talent, his gift. More competent employees toiled for years at lower pay and station. Pierre owed his success to a single uncanny, involuntary trait. He was a human mirror. Minutes after meeting a new superior, Pierre had picked up voice inflection, figures of speech, physical mannerisms. He didn't even know he was doing it. When the bosses went out and drank too much, he drank too much. When they laughed, he laughed. On the golf course, he cursed with the best of them. When the bank had a Baptist president, Pierre felt the Pentacostal fire in his belly. When it hired a Jewish president, Pierre curiously found himself politically militant about the partitioning of Jerusalem. When a group of southerners took over the company, Pierre began eating fried okra with a paper napkin in his collar, putting on a tremendous amount of weight, developing a drawl and answering to "Buford." When an energetic group of New Yorkers supplanted the southerners, Pierre shed the weight, took taxis, talked fast and started spending weekends upstate. His superiors couldn't quite put their finger on it—they just knew they really liked this Pierre guy.

Then, disaster.

While on vacation, Pierre received an instant promotion when a long-term vice president was fired on the spot for eliminating hidden checking fees based on reckless notions of reason and fairness.

Pierre came back from Vegas to suddenly find himself near the top of the organizational chart, which wasn't the traditional pyramid but more closely resembled an hourglass. The bottom half contained the people who did all the labor and supported the top half of the hourglass, which encompassed innumerable positions of management so important and irrelevant that their work only existed in theory. The purpose of the top half of the hourglass was to eliminate jobs in the bottom half.

Pierre spent the first three days of his vice presidency in a dark office carefully assembling an anxiety attack. On the fourth day, a breakthrough. Pierre was exploring his desk drawers, taking Xanax and bending paper clips when he found a memo pad. He looked around suspiciously, then bent over and began writing. He sat back and looked it over. Professional, high-syllable count, multiple qualifiers, no point. It was more than perfect. It was safe. Pierre set the memo gently in his virgin out tray, grabbed his coat and left for the day.

The next morning, Pierre arrived at work to find the out basket empty and eight memos in his in basket. All eight replies were impressively ambiguous on multiple levels. Pierre was encouraged. He wrote another memo, this time in quadruplicate—white, blue, yellow and pink—and left for lunch.

When he got back, thirty-two memos filled his in basket.

Pierre quickly whipped off another memo, directing that he be placed on all memo lists.

The next morning, sixty-four memos bulged from his in basket, plus the pink copy of his original memo that was routed back to him per his instruction to be placed on all memo lists.

It was a new dawn. He turned on the lights, opened his blinds, and gazed out across the floor with a deep, confident breath. He noticed something on the far side of the office. Three construction workers with tool belts, wiring outlets. Pierre scurried back to his desk and scribbled a new memo, this one with a diagram and list of materials. He dropped the memo in his out basket.

The next day, Pierre watched through his window with a mixture of pride and fear as a new wall went up, sectioning off the back third of the office. Pierre decided he had finally gone too far. He dashed off another memo.

The following day, Pierre watched in awe as the wall came down.

So began Consolidated Bank's new building phase of relentless office construction and deconstruction. Studs and Sheetrock went up and down, completely new rooms mushrooming and vanishing overnight. Pierre liked what he saw. He decided that change was good, and change there would be. More walls shot from the earth with tectonic abruptness. People who sat next to each other in order to communicate found themselves sitting in the exact same spots, but suddenly in different rooms. At one point, three walls went up in successive days, forming a *U* around the phone representatives. On the fourth day, a doorless final partition went up, sealing off the work area. Employees showed up and had to be sent home. Management began looking for a scapegoat. It looked bad for Pierre.

He countered by authoring an all-eyes memo alerting the bank to an urgent work-space shortage that was unforeseen but now upon them with a vengeance, and he was roundly praised as the only vice president with any vision.

Since Pierre had so much experience with construction, the board placed him in charge of the much-needed office expansion, which resulted in the erection of the enormous new state-of-the-art Consolidated Bank Building that won civic awards and got Pierre's picture in the paper with a hard hat and gold shovel. Pierre's crowning touch: a magnificent domed atrium atop the bank that would become a downtown landmark and the logo for the bank's new stationery.

The bank's entire staff, from mail clerk to chairman of the board, was uniformly dazzled when they moved across town and walked into the new building. The president gave Pierre a stout raise and broke precedent by assigning work to a vice president. He put Pierre in charge of staff development, hoping he would do the same for personnel as he had for facilities.

Pierre wouldn't disappoint.

He proceeded under the maxim that if change was good, chaos was sublime. He decided that all employees needed to be cross-trained and reassigned to positions as removed as possible from their talents and goals. He argued it would invigorate the ranks and make the company more nimble in the equation.

The board of directors loved it. They wanted more.

Pierre gave them more.

The meetings started. Training meetings, retraining meetings, management seminars, company-direction symposiums, insensitive sensitivity sessions, and forums seeking feedback on meetings.

There were questionnaires, psychological tests, self-evaluations. Pierre was able to achieve all this without slacking off on the memos. And soon, the walls started going up and down again in the new building.

It hit a crescendo. The bank had never been so busy. It became an industrious hive of perpetual construction and demolition and hundreds of people crisscrossing the building on their way to a full day of meetings, reading memos, filling out surveys, not looking where they were going, walking into walls that weren't there the day before. Everyone was so busy, they didn't have time for any work.

And right when it was all at its feverish apex, Pierre stood in the center of the atrium with his hands on his hips, smiling proudly as two workers on ladders unfurled a giant banner over the entrance to the east wing. Everyone stopped and read the mission statement.

TO COMPLETELY FACILITATE THE NEW PARADIGM OF CUSTOMER-FOCUSED DYNAMICS, EMPLOYEE-GROWTH SYNERGY, SHAREHOLDER-EXPECTATION MODELS AND COMMUNITY-BASED LINKAGE FOR THE MAXIMUM BENEFIT OF MULTIDISCIPLINARY OBJECTIVES. BECAUSE WE HAVE BABIES, TOO.

18

JOHN MILTON was underpaid but secure. Some people need security. John was one of them. Routine made him feel snug, and if he never did anything but work as a teller, he'd be a happy man.

Then a memo went forth, and everyone was reassigned. John ended up a computer-assisted telephone account representative. John said he wanted to stay a clerk. The bank put a gun to his back. John donned a headset and took a seat in the vast matrix of telephone reps stationed on the ground floor, beneath the sparkling dome of the new Consolidated Bank Building.

They told John that because the job was computer-assisted, it would involve computers. John told them he didn't understand computers, that he was a dinosaur. They told him to evolve. They gave him till Tuesday.

John did his best. His phone manners never wavered when his CPU froze up or zapped all the data off his screen. The bank had a roving computer technician who wandered the aisles of phone reps, responding to questions.

"Please bear with me," John told a caller, hand raised for the computer tech.

"It's stuck," he told the technician.

"Hit control, alt, delete," said the tech, moving on.

"What?"

A few minutes later, John caught the technician's attention as he came back the other way.

"It's still stuck."

"Do a cold boot."

"What?"

Large sums of money began moving between unrelated accounts. The bank finally took notice when a hundred thousand dollars turned up in the file for the solitaire game that came preinstalled on John's computer.

They called him in. They said he was costing them a lot of money.

"I'd like to be a teller again, please."

They said he was too valuable.

They sent John back to his computer.

The dome high above John's desk could be seen from all over the city. It had cost a ransom, but it paid off by increasing the bank's name recognition, which remained a priority because the name changed every six months. In planning the dome, Consolidated—formerly United—would settle for nothing but the best. They hired the people who did the Hubble telescope. They did their job well. Too well. The glass was ground and polished to such a fine tolerance that between 11:45 A.M. and 12:15 P.M. each day the dome acted like a giant magnifying glass, and a concentrated beam of Florida sunlight slowly moved across the ground floor of Consolidated Bank like a cutting torch.

Employees in the penumbra of the beam could continue working with pith helmets and welder's goggles, but those in the direct path had to move. A scorched strip of carpeting was removed and a flame trench installed.

John Milton stood back from his desk as the computer technician permanently removed the solitaire game from his PC. Then John sat back down and answered the phone. He was helping a retiree balance her checkbook when his system locked up again.

"My computer's frozen."

The elderly woman didn't understand computers and expressed concern that something bad had just happened to her money.

"It's just computers. Don't worry," said John, who had just wired the woman's life savings to Mongolia.

The system remained on the fritz, and the retiree became more desperate. When it still hadn't responded after another ten minutes, the phone call turned into a crisis-line intervention.

"Oh, my God! That's all the money I have! I don't want to eat cat food again!"

"Easy," said John. "I'm here with you. I'm not going anywhere . . ."

"John!" someone yelled.

"Just a second," said John.

"John!"

"Be with you in a minute."

"Watch out!"

The beam of sunlight hit John.

Colleagues ran to him and called 911. An elementary class on a field trip was quickly hustled out of the atrium.

DESPITE PIERRE'S BEST efforts to the contrary, Consolidated Bank was able to keep humming along for about a month due to the sheer grit and pride of its workforce. Then the wheels started coming off. Productivity went into a free fall, and human errors were up a thousand percent. There was better morale in Hitler's bunker. Pierre walked into the atrium after lunch on a Friday and flew into a rage. "Who did that?" he yelled, pointing up at the wall and the large decal of Calvin and Hobbes peeing on the mission statement.

The board of directors decided enough was enough. They called Pierre in. It looked grim. The chairman laid out Pierre's blunder trail in exhaustive detail. But a curious thing happened. It slowly began to turn. The chairman crossed his leg. Pierre crossed his. A board member poured a glass of ice water from a carafe. Pierre poured his own.

"We need to think outside the box," said the chairman.

"Less is more," said Pierre.

Before they knew it, the board was wondering how they ever could have thought someone like Pierre was at fault. It would almost be like blaming themselves. But who, then, was responsible? Pierre said it was the workforce. They nodded. Of course. There was only one thing to do.

CONSOLIDATED BANK HIRED Damocles Consulting, and Jim Davenport was dispatched to the atrium in downtown Tampa. It was as impressive as he had heard.

Just after eleven o'clock, Jim was observing the phone reps and taking notes. Then something unusual started to happen. The employees began putting on dark visors and pith helmets. Was this some kind of sick joke? Were they making fun of him?

The room grew brighter until Jim had to shield his eyes. An employee ran up to him. He fell to the ground and clutched Jim's ankles. "You're the consultant, right? You have to make 'em do something about the dome! They won't listen to us! Someone's gonna end up dead!"

Three men in black suits and mirrored sunglasses grabbed the employee and dragged him off through a secret door that opened in the wall, then the door closed and more men in dark suits slid a divan and potted trees in front of it.

THE FOLLOWING MONDAY at Damocles Consulting, Mr. Young summoned Jim Davenport to his office.

"Have a seat, Jim," said Mr. Young, leaning back in his leather chair, flipping through Jim's latest report. "Apparently I didn't make myself clear during our last meeting. I'm particularly troubled by this section here called 'The Beam of Death.'"

Jim opened his mouth, but Mr. Young cut him off.

"Jim, we've decided to let Bill rewrite this report. We'll leave your name on it, of course. You'll still get credit. We want to do what's fair."

Jim paused to consider his response. He didn't know it at the time, but many years had led up to what he would say next.

"I don't think I want that report rewritten."

IT WAS JOHN Milton's first day back at work after the light-refraction incident. They had gotten him to the hospital in time, and there would be no permanent injury, just a temporary reverse Mohawk covered with an Ace bandage.

John didn't care. It was good to be back at work. He arrived early and was spraying his computer screen with Windex when they sent for him.

John timidly entered the personnel office and gave his name to the receptionist. She pointed at a conference room with an open door. "Right in there."

Pierre was already inside, reading a report. John smiled and sat down, but Pierre's face showed distress.

John became uneasy. "What's this about?"

Pierre handed John the report without speaking. It was from Damocles Consulting, and it recommended sweeping layoffs.

"We have to let you go, John."

"I'm fired?"

"Oh, absolutely not!" said Pierre. "You just can't work here anymore."

John began stammering. "I'll work harder. I'll change. I'll, I'll—"

Pierre sadly shook his head. "If it was up to me, I'd keep you on. You know I would. But we have no choice. It's those consultants. They're making us do it, *the bastards!*"

"I'M HOME!"

"Daddy!" yelled Melvin, running down the hall.

Jim set his briefcase on a table and lifted Melvin into the air.

Debbie was on the couch, watching *The Real World*.

"Hi, Debbie," said her father.

No answer.

"That's Drusilla," said Melvin.

Martha came in from the kitchen with oven mittens. "How was your day, honey?"

"Really good until I was fired."

"That's not funny."

"I know."

"You're serious?"

He nodded.

"What for?"

"They said I have a belligerent attitude."

"You? Belligerent?"

"They don't like my reports anymore."

"They can't do this! They made us move! We have a bigger mortgage, new car, kids to feed!"

Jim nodded with understanding.

"Oh, Jim. This is a really bad time. You have to go back and tell them they can't fire you right now."

"Honey, I think you need to sit down."

"How were you belligerent? This wasn't over principles, was it?"

"Not really."

"Well, was it or wasn't it?"

"Yes."

Martha became dizzy and braced herself against a window frame.

It would take something major to get Martha's mind off of what Jim had just told her, but she saw it when she looked out the window.

"I don't believe it!"

"What?"

"Come look at this!" said Martha. "That dog's loose again! And Jack is just standing there, trimming his hedge."

Martha stomped out the front door.

"Hold on," said Jim. "I'm not so sure you're thinking straight . . ."

She marched across the lawn. Jim ran after her.

"Hey, shithead!" Martha yelled across the street, not breaking stride. "I want to talk to you!"

Another near riot on Triggerfish Lane. The shouting was quite loud; curious neighbors poured into the street like a bench-clearing brawl. Since authorities weren't present, Jack didn't care to mind his manners.

"Why don't you shut your wife up and get her in the house before she embarrasses you again!"

"Me?" said Jim, pointing at himself.

"Are you going to let him insult me like that?" said Martha. "Hit him!"

"What?" said Jim.

"You're going to hit me?" said Jack. He put his hands up to

shield his face, then gave Jim a preemptive sucker punch in the nose.

"Ow! Shit!" said Jim, cupping his nose and reeling off balance.

Martha lunged at Jack again, but Gladys restrained her. More neighbors arrived.

Serge and Coleman pushed their way through the crowd.

"Excuse me," Serge said to Jack. "Do you know anything about history? The polio vaccine? The Berlin Airlift?"

"Who the fuck are you?" said Jack.

"A lot of people struggled so you can live in the land of milk and honey," said Serge.

"Get away from me, you weirdo!"

Serge stepped forward and tapped Jack in the chest with his index finger. "These people are living by the rules and you're not. That offends me."

Jack slapped Serge's finger away. "Eat shit and die!"

Serge tapped Jack's chest again. "Respect the rules."

"Yeah," said Coleman, tossing a beer can on Jack's lawn. "The rules!"

Jack screamed in falsetto. "You threw something on my lawn!" He ran and picked up the can and raced it over to the garbage.

"What's with owning a vicious dog, anyway?" said Serge. "You know what I think?" He held a thumb and index finger a half-inch apart in the international tiny-penis sign. The crowd began laughing.

Jack looked around in a fury. "To hell with all of you!"

Serge turned. "Coleman, do your thing."

Coleman lifted his right foot, displaying the bottom of his shoe. Golf spikes.

"You wouldn't," said Jack.

Coleman began shuffling across the lawn.

"No!" shouted Jack.

Coleman moonwalked.

"My grass! Stop!"

Coleman pirouetted.

"Rasputin! Kill!"

The dog stood still, Coleman tap-dancing in the background.

"I said, 'Kill!' "

Rasputin didn't move.

"What's wrong with you? Kill! I command you!"

Rasputin sat down and scratched his ear. Coleman did jumping jacks.

"You stupid mutt!" Jack kicked Rasputin in the side, and the dog yelped.

Coleman ran up to Jack and grabbed him by the arm. "Hey! Don't kick animals!"

"Get the fuck out of my face!" He shoved Coleman to the ground.

When he did, he heard a growl. He turned in time to see Rasputin lunging through the air. The dog knocked Jack over and clamped down on his right arm.

"Not me! Him!" yelled Jack. "Get off me! Let go!"

Rasputin whipped his head side to side, tearing flesh.

"He's killing me! He's gone berserk! Help!"

Gladys shook her head. "It was just a matter of time."

"A tragedy waiting to happen," said Martha.

"Somebody shoot him! Shoot this fucking thing!"

The crowd began to disperse.

"Help! Don't leave me!"

Serge and Coleman walked back to their rental house, Coleman's spikes clacking on the sidewalk.

"I didn't know you were an animal lover," said Serge.

"I'm not an extremist about it or anything, but yeah, every living thing has feelings."

"I guess I underestimated you."

"You can't just judge me when I'm fucked up."

"True, true."

19

JOHN MILTON didn't take his second firing in as many months sitting still. He had a nervous breakdown.

It wasn't one of those dramatic things where you end up crouched naked in the middle of the living room floor, shivering with the heat on full blast. It was a much slower spiral, like walking pneumonia, and John was able to maintain normal outward appearances until just before the big crash.

The following Monday, he got out the classifieds again. After a weeklong search, John took the only job available. He began working entirely on commission selling used cars at Tampa Bay Motors.

John quickly got to know the whole gang on the sales lot. Stu and Vic and Rod and Dutch and Frenchy and Rocco. Rocco Silvertone, the most aggressive used car salesman in Tampa since the untimely death of "Honest Al."

The other salesmen had an understanding. As customers strayed onto the lot, they would rotate alphabetically and take turns ambushing them. Except for Rocco. His first day on the job he announced that he would go after anything he wanted. If they didn't like it, they were free to fistfight him. Nobody objected. They let the big dog eat.

It took John Milton only a week to establish his own space at Tampa Bay Motors. At the bottom of the pecking order.

On the third Friday in June, Rocco Silvertone arrived early and hungry at the sales lot. This would be a big day—he could feel it. There was an extra bounce in his step as he headed for the sink to chase bootleg yellow jackets with a paper cone of water. Then he crumpled the cup and bounced it off John's forehead.

"Hey!" said John. "Stop it!"

"Stop it!" mocked Rocco.

The others laughed, and it encouraged Rocco to get John in a headlock.

"Let go!" said John.

"Let go!" said Rocco. John wiggled and thrashed and finally farted, which triggered more mirth until Rocco spotted a well-dressed customer and released John and headed across the showroom.

Rocco didn't know a damn thing about cars and sold them like nobody's business. What he did know was people—which ones needed approval, which ones folded under intimidation, and who wanted to hear the latest ethnic jokes. It helped that Rocco was huge and dashing, with broad shoulders that filled out his tailored suits. It was a natural athlete's build, no workout required. Rocco knew all the standard sales tricks and a few more. If he was dealing with a couple: "Please, don't let me rush you. Here, I'll leave. Take your time to discuss it privately in my office"—which he had bugged to learn the top price they would pay. Then he'd offer that price, which was bumped up four hundred dollars by the hidden "dealer prep" charge preprinted on the sales form.

Rocco could break any rule he wanted because he had the owner in his pocket. One of the first things Rocco did when he came to Tampa Bay Motors was look for the owner's weakness. It was fishing.

Rocco didn't know anything about fishing, either, but how hard could it be? He took the owner down to the Keys, and they went out on the flats. They saw a tarpon in the shallows, shiny dorsal slicing the water. The owner took out his fishing rod. Rocco took out his rifle.

The owner put down his rod as the silver fish floated by on its side with bullet holes. "Let me try that."

"Be my guest."

That afternoon, the owner pointed up at the sky.

"Look. A roseate spoonbill."

Rocco raised his rifle and fired, and the spoonbill helicoptered out of the sky and splashed next to the boat. The two men looked over the port gunwales at the scarlet carcass.

"It's beautiful," said Rocco.

"Then why'd you do that?" asked the owner.

"Wanted to get a better look."

The next Rocco fishing story had become legend. On their second trip to the Keys, the owner said he wanted to try deep-sea fishing in the Gulf Stream. Rocco rented a boat with a tuna tower, and they went out twenty miles. Soon, Rocco spotted five Cubans bobbing across the Florida Straits. He pulled alongside.

The refugees cheered the arrival of their rescuers and waved tiny, homemade American flags. The flag-waving became less enthusiastic as Rocco and the owner cast fishing lines under the raft. Rocco had heard that fish liked shadows. The pair drank beer and laughed and reeled in four fish apiece and left.

TWO WEEKS WENT by, and John Milton still hadn't sold his first car. He was living off credit cards.

An hour before lunch on a Friday, this customer comes in and asks John if he has any new Jaguars. He's real nonchalant, says he's just browsing. John gets in the golf cart and takes the guy out and shows him one in jade green, and just like that the guy pulls out his checkbook.

John rode back to the showroom on a cushion of air. This was the turning point, he told himself. No more grits for dinner.

John led the man into one of the sales offices and started on the paperwork. Rocco appeared in the doorway.

"Trevor?"

"Rocco?" said the customer.

"You two know each other?" asked John.

"Play racquetball at the club," said Rocco. "Or rather, he plays. I take a beating."

"You're holding your own," said Trevor.

"Compared to you? Are you kidding? You're a killer out there!"

Rocco turned to John. "Would you mind if I had a word with Trevor?"

"Actually, I—"

Rocco pulled a chair up next to the customer. "You can wait out in the hall. This won't take long."

John stood in the hall muttering to himself, thinking of all the comebacks he wished he had thought of in the office.

The door opened and Rocco stuck his head out. "You talking to someone out here?"

"Me?"

"Try to keep it down, okay?"

"Listen—"

Rocco closed the door.

Five minutes later, the door opened again and Trevor came out, followed by Rocco, carrying paperwork for the Jag. He patted John on the shoulder. "Thanks for the help. I'll take it from here."

"What?"

"Didn't you know? I told Trevor about this place at racquetball. Said he should come by sometime and check us out. That technically makes it my commission."

John was speechless.

Rocco punched him in the shoulder. "I owe you one."

Then Rocco and Trevor walked away chatting together, Rocco making a backhanded swing with an invisible racket.

WHEN ROCCO FINISHED the Jaguar's paperwork, it was lunchtime. Rocco sped through traffic on Dale Mabry Highway, tapping the steering wheel to the stereo. Nothing made Rocco feel better than closing a sale. Especially someone else's.

Rocco's car was a new black Corvette convertible. He'd added a hundred-watt amp, eight three-way speakers and subwoofer bazooka tube in the trunk. He was playing his theme song, "Right into the Danger Zone," by Kenny Loggins. Whenever Rocco played his theme song, he wore his green-tinted aviator sunglasses and a leather bomber jacket. On the passenger side was a set of the latest graphite-and-titanium golf clubs. They looked great in his car. And since he already had the clubs, Rocco decided he might as well take up golf. The Corvette had a single bumper sticker: NO FAT CHICKS.

Rocco sang along with the song at a red light, occasionally giving the cymbals a rimshot with a phantom drumstick. He wanted everyone to know he could pick the coolest songs. In a way, it was almost as if he were playing the music himself. Rocco felt great about Rocco. Yes, I am a Top Gun.

After every big sale, Rocco had a tradition of treating himself to a new toy at The Sharper Image. He drove over to Old Hyde Park Village, Tampa's chic, high-end shopping district with sidewalk cafés. Rocco pulled into the no-parking zone in front of The Sharper Image and stuck his CLERGY sign on the dash. He would only be a minute, so he left the top down and the stereo on full, as a service to others. Then he went inside and asked a clerk about the global-positioning wine stopper.

SERGE AND COLEMAN strolled up Howard Avenue. Serge told Coleman to stop drinking from the thirty-two-ounce bottle of Colt 45.

"But it's in a bag."

"This is a very nice place," said Serge. "We have to remember that we're guests."

"What's so great about this old village, anyway?"

"Old Hyde Park Village," corrected Serge. "It's the history. The whole area's been tastefully preserved. Everything screams class. But best of all, they've really clamped down on crime."

Serge and Coleman stopped and pressed their noses and hands against the window of The Sharper Image. "Gadgets," Serge said in a monotone. "Must have gadgets."

A salesman inside silently shooed them away from the glass.

"What's that music?" asked Serge.

" 'Right into the Danger Zone,' " said Coleman. "From *Top Gun*."

"God, I hate that song. Where's it coming from?"

They looked around the corner and saw a black Corvette.

"Nobody's in it," said Coleman.

"Look," said Serge. "The latest graphite-and-titanium clubs. I've heard wonderful things about them."

Serge removed a two iron from the bag and swished it in the air. "These are supposed to have a huge sweet spot and incredible memory in the shaft."

He carefully wrapped his fingers around the leather grip.

"Remember to keep your head down," said Coleman.

"Check," said Serge. He pulled the club back over his shoulder. ". . . *right in-to the dan-ger zone!* . . ."

Wham.

The head of the iron buried itself deep into the stereo's face-plate, and the car went silent. The outdoor tables at the café across the street stood and gave Serge an ovation. He slipped the two iron back in the bag on the passenger's seat. Then he and Coleman went up the sidewalk and pressed their hands and noses against the window at Victoria's Secret.

20

MAHONEY! GET IN HERE!"

Mahoney arrived in Ingersol's doorway with a tuna sandwich. "You wanted to see me?"

"We've got work to do." Ingersol held up a videocassette. "Agents just brought this in. Found it in the woods at the Marjorie Kinnan Rawlings house near Gainesville."

Ingersol got up from his desk and walked to the television set and stuck the tape in the VCR. A picture appeared on the TV: a burly, bearded man tied to a tree.

"What's the plot here?" asked Mahoney.

"Sound technicians were able to lift the muffled conversation in the background," said Ingersol. "That poor bastard tied to the tree is a trucker accused of selling the McGraw Brothers some bad speed."

On the screen, the McGraws paced back and forth in front of the camera, talking fast, waving pistols and rifles.

"Looks like good speed to me," said Mahoney.

"That's one of the effects of good speed," said Ingersol. "Makes you think it's bad speed."

"Where'd they get the video camera?"

"Trucker had it. Used it to make crushing videos to sell on the Internet."

"Crushing videos?"

"Narrow sexual bandwidth of the foot-fetish strain. But even the regular foot people think they're weird," said Ingersol. "A few guys get woodrows watching women's feet step on bugs and little frogs and stuff. We had a case on the east coast where one sap had it so bad he asked his wife to crush *him*. With a pickup truck no less. She was only supposed to crush him a little, and they made this plywood ramp, but something went wrong and they found him with a Dodge Ram four-by-four parked on his rib cage and his pants around his ankles."

"Why did the McGraws film an incriminating video, anyway?" asked Mahoney.

"Good speed makes you think you can make movies."

Mahoney nodded. *"Ishtar."*

"They must have been so high, they forgot about the camera and left it."

"What's happening now?" asked Mahoney, pointing at the screen.

"This is where the trucker still thinks they're just trying to scare him. And here comes the gut shot with the Marlin rifle."

The trucker doubled over, held up by the ropes tying him to the tree. A whoosh of air left his lungs.

"Now they're going to town on his legs and arms with the small-caliber stuff, and here's where the leader sticks the muzzle of his pistol in the guy's left eye and pulls the trigger."

Mahoney winced. "That was out of line."

Ingersol turned off the TV and walked back to his desk. "Their level of violence is escalating. We have to find them soon or there's going to be a major incident."

"What about the guy who killed Skag McGraw? Shouldn't we give him some sort of protection?"

"You mean Jim Davenport? Can't chance it. We still have the element of surprise. We send some baby-sitters, and the press is bound to find out. Then the McGraws will take off in another direction, and we'll never catch them."

"What if I go to Tampa myself? Undercover?"

"No way. I know you're still hung up on Serge. I'm not about to let you take off on your private agenda."

Ingersol reached in his desk and pulled out a thick file marked MCGRAWS. "Just came from the FBI." He flipped open the manila folder. "The whole family is a bunch of dangerous freaks. They've got cousins all over north Florida. Most are ex-cons or junkies or deranged from inbreeding. Five have died violently, three are back in prison, two have gone insane from untreated venereal disease, and one writes book reviews. But the McGraw Brothers are the worst of the clan. The oldest and meanest is Rufus McGraw. His rap sheet goes way back, long as your arm. A real piece of work. He started pulling a series of bank and credit-union holdups across the desert Southwest in the late seventies, never coming close to getting caught. He became known for inadequate attention to antiperspirants, and the press dubbed him 'The B.O. Bandit,' aka 'The Rank Robber,' and he was soon arrested and sent to prison." Ingersol pulled out a mug shot. "This is Sly McGraw. His thing was gas-station jobs. Always got away clean. Then the press started writing about his politeness, calling him 'The Gentleman Bandit,' 'The Courteous Crook' and 'The Mannered Malefactor,' and he was immediately picked up and sent to Leavenworth. Then there's Willie McGraw, a real scumbag, but once he got his hands on some money from a few home invasions, he started buying all these expensive suits. The press nicknamed him 'The Dapper Bandit' and 'The Sartorial Swindler,' and he was quickly apprehended."

"That's only three," said Mahoney.

"The fourth was Ed. He took forever to catch."

Mahoney rubbed his chin. "The Dapper Bandit. I remember that case. The big trial in Kansas City."

"No, Kansas City was the Debonair Duo."

"That's right," said Mahoney. "I always get them mixed up with the Courteous Crew. The Dapper Bandit used the Twinkie Defense."

"You're thinking of the Polite Posse," said Ingersol. "The Dapper Bandit used the Nintendo Defense."

"No, the Nintendo Defense was the Couch Potato Murders."

"Couch Potato?" said Ingersol. "I thought that was the Boom Box Trial."

Mahoney shook his head. "The Boom Box Seven used the Prozac Defense."

"Then which one was the Evolution Defense?"

"The Scopes Trial."

21

THE AFTERNOON WAS A SCORCHER. A hundred and five by one o'clock, 80 percent humidity. Not a single customer on the lot at Tampa Bay Motors.

Six salesmen sat around the break table playing Trivial Pursuit. Rocco stormed back in the showroom.

"What's wrong with you?" asked Vic, shuffling trivia cards. "I thought you were having a good day."

"Fuck off!" said Rocco, throwing a bent golf club in a trash can and phoning a stereo-repair shop.

The salesmen went back to their game.

"Sorry, John. Time's up," said Vic. "Answer is *Flipper*. I can't fuckin' believe you missed that one."

"Hold it," said John. "That's a flawed question. Flipper was a dolphin."

"Same thing," said Vic. "Stu. Your turn."

"It's not the same thing. The question was 'TV's famous porpoise.'"

"Right . . . Stu, your turn."

"Flipper wasn't a porpoise. I get to go again."

"Of course Flipper was a porpoise. Your turn's over. . . . Stu? . . ."

"Hold on! Flipper was *not* a porpoise. The question's bad!"

"Hey Rocco! John says Flipper wasn't a porpoise!"

Rocco turned a page in a *GQ* article. "John's a fucking wimp."

"There. It's unanimous," said Vic. "Stu, go."

"Stu, don't go," said John. "Flipper was a dolphin."

"I see bars all over the place called The Purple Porpoise," said Dutch, "and their signs have Flipper."

"Isn't it like Flippers are both dolphins *and* porpoises?" asked Rod. "But we call them porpoises so we don't confuse them with dolphins, the fish, which are now called mahimahi at restaurants so tourists won't think they're eating Flipper?"

"No, no, no!" said John. "It's finite biology. Dolphins the mammal are not porpoises the mammal and vice versa. They're mutually exclusive. Dolphins the fish just muddy the water. Stay away from them."

"John, you're the only person in the whole country who would have missed that question," said Vic. "So what are you saying? It's because you're *smarter* than everyone?"

"I just explained it," said John. "I'm taking my turn again."

"We go by the cards," said Vic. "Stu, pick a category."

John jumped up from the table and his chair fell over. He slammed down his playing pieces. "I knew Flipper was the obvious answer, but I didn't say it because I also knew for a certainty that she's not a porpoise. She was a dolphin! I don't care what the fucking cards say!"

"She?" said Rod.

"The first Flipper was a female. And *she* was a dolphin, not a porpoise!"

"John, you know we always go by the cards."

"Smooth conical teeth, not triangular and serrated!" said John. "Pronounced, cylindrical snout, not blunt!"

"What are you talking about, John?"

"I'm talking about basic ninth-grade marine biology! It's not very hard to grasp. I'm talking simple cetaceans, not a time port to the fourth dimension!"

"Cetaceans?"

"I used to be a teacher! A good one!"

"Easy, John."

"Don't you 'easy' me!"

"John, all I know is what the card says. Let's not have any trouble."

"It's that kind of attitude that gave us Hitler."

"John, what do the Nazis have to do with this?"

"Sit down, John, you know we always go by the cards."

"Yeah, John, sit down!"

"Who says the cards are right?"

"We have to go by something, John. There has to be some kind of order."

"But what if the cards are wrong? Did you ever think of that? Huh? What if the cards are wrong? And if we don't question the cards, we don't question the government! And if we don't question the government, some poor peasant in the Amazon ends up with a CIA bullet in his fucking skull!"

"John, are you on some kind of medication we should know about?"

"Calm down, John, this is just a friendly little—"

"I will not calm down! Not for some fascist board game! Is this what we fought and died for?"

"You didn't fight for shit, John! Now sit down!"

"I will *not* sit down!"

"John, it's only a game!"

"No, that's where you're wrong. It's not only a game—it's a point in time and space. It's the exact point where an individual has to stop and take a stand and say, 'I will not be boned up the ass anymore!' It's about our school system! It's about the banks! It's about exploitation! It's about Nurse Ratchett at Kash 'n' Karry on register five with her coupon cop mentality! It's—"

"Relax, John!"

"Don't tell me to relax! Did I tell you to relax that time your wife threw you out after finding you in those panties?"

"Jesus, John! Not in front of the guys!"

"Look, John, I know you've been through a lot lately. We've all been a little tense—"

"Don't you dare condescend to me, you fuck!"

"I'm a fuck? *I'm a fuck!* Why, you little cocksucker!"

"Look! A customer!"

Everyone turned. A man came through the glass doors. A sophisticated gentleman, mid-seventies, three-piece charcoal suit, briefcase. Fine jaw, firm, thin mouth, good eastern establishment bloodlines.

Everyone turned again, this time to the far side of the show-room. They watched to see what Rocco would do.

Rocco put down his magazine and got up slowly and headed for the man.

The other salesmen sagged in disappointment and went back to Trivial Pursuit.

Except John. He took off running for the front door. Rocco saw him and took off, too. But nobody had ever challenged Rocco before, and he was slow getting off the starting line. John arrived first, introducing himself and shaking hands.

Rocco stood behind him and whispered over his shoulder: "You're dead."

John smiled at the customer and jabbed his elbow into Rocco's stomach, knocking the wind out of him.

"Let's take the golf cart," said John, leading the customer out the door.

JOHN'S HANDS BEGAN to shake as he drove the golf cart. The customer had asked to see the most expensive cars on the lot. This could be the mother lode.

Once in a great while Tampa Bay Motors got in a Ferrari, an Aston Martin or maybe a Lotus, and they usually went fast. This was one of the rare times the dealership actually had a Rolls in stock, and it had remained on the lot a month, probably because of the color. A soft tangerine. It was the same color the Buccaneers football team used to wear. The Rolls had belonged to the middle linebacker, who decided to get rid of the car when the team changed to its more menacing crimson-and-pewter uniforms and he started to take a lot of grief from the interior linemen.

John and the customer exchanged business cards as the golf cart cruised across the lot. John looked down and read the fine white-satin card stock: H. AMBROSE TARRINGTON III, TARRINGTON IMPORT. There were phone numbers for offices in Tampa, New York, Beverly Hills.

"Watch out!" said the customer.

John looked up and swerved to avoid a wandering homeless

man wearing a hat full of pinwheels. The cart went up on two wheels, then slammed back down.

"Thanks, Ambrose. That was close," said John. "It's okay if I call you Ambrose, isn't it?"

The man shook his head no.

They arrived at the high-end cars, and Ambrose immediately pointed at the Rolls. "That one." He got out and walked around the car and kicked the tires. John had always thought it was just a figure of speech.

"I'll buy it," said Ambrose.

John's heart raced. He began to see little spots around his field of vision.

"But I'll need a test drive first."

"Sure thing," said John. "I'll just need to Xerox your driver's license . . ."

Ambrose stared at him. John played his own words back inside his head, and they made a clutch-grinding sound. John cringed. At the Rolls-Royce level, the license Xerox was way too gauche.

"Forget it," said John. "Wait here. I'll get the keys."

John zoomed back to the showroom in the golf cart.

He stuck his head in the secretary's office and handed her Tarrington's business card. "Call those numbers. Quick!"

"What's this about?"

"I need to verify a customer."

"What about his driver's license?"

"Do it!"

"Yes, Mr. Milton." Damn, she thought, this was a different John.

John walked briskly across the showroom to the pegboard of keys. He passed the Trivial Pursuit table.

"Dolphin!"

"Let it die, John."

He snatched a set of keys off the board and went back to the secretary's office.

She put down the phone. "Yep, they all check out. Tarrington Import. Tampa, New York, Beverly Hills."

"Yesssss!" said John, signaling touchdown. He ran out the showroom door.

"Did he just take the keys to the Rolls?" Vic asked the others.

They looked over at the pegboard. The hook for the Rolls was empty.

They all got up and went over to the window. "Lucky bastard!"

Then they looked across the showroom at Rocco, steam coming off the top of his head.

"SORRY TO KEEP you waiting, Mr. Tarrington." John handed Ambrose the keys with a conspiratorial grin. "Shall we?"

Tarrington knew his way around a Rolls. He handled it with obvious familiarity as they pulled onto the highway. John could smell the kill. Tarrington's suit was clearly tailored, probably Manhattan, East Side. And the accent: Providence? Tarrington's nostrils flared at the leather scent.

"Was Flipper a dolphin or a porpoise?"

"What?"

"We had an argument back at the dealership," said John. "Was Flipper a dolphin or a porpoise?"

"I don't know. A fish?"

"Close enough. The argument really wasn't about Flipper. It was a metaphor for individuality. When do you take the path less traveled? Know what I mean?"

Tarrington looked at John a moment, then back at the road.

"Of course you do," said John. "I felt a kinship the moment I saw you. We're a breed apart from the herd. You don't just accept what the cards say, do you?"

Tarrington opened his mouth. "I—"

"Of course not!" John exclaimed. Ambrose jumped. "I used to be a teacher. Bet you didn't know that. They don't pay teachers. Then I was a bank teller. They don't pay them either, even with all that money lying around, like they're going to miss it. They say the economy's overheating. You know what I say? Good! Let it boil over for all I care! People like you and me don't need the economy. Never have. Twenty thousand years ago there was only one job. You went out in the morning with your shitty little spear and you chased the woolly mammoths and ran from the saber-toothed tigers. That was your fucking economy! . . ."

Ambrose pulled over to the side of the road.

"What are you doing?" asked John.

"Would you mind if I drove alone?"

"You want me to get out?"

"No offense."

John stood waving on the shoulder of the road as the Rolls pulled away. "Happy trails."

WHILE JOHN WAS gone, Rocco did what any tough guy would do. He went to the owner and tattled. Not Xeroxing a license was a major infraction.

They were waiting at the front door when John walked back on the lot.

Oh, this was too good to be true, thought Rocco. No Xerox and now no *Rolls*.

The owner let John have it at a range of thirty yards. "Where's the car!"

"Everything's cool," said John. "Ambrose is just finishing up the test drive."

"Ambrose?"

"Yeah, great guy," said John.

"First you don't copy his driver's license, then you just let him drive off with a two-hundred-thousand-dollar car!"

"He said he's going to buy it."

"You're fired!"

"Fine," said John. "And one word from me, Ambrose walks. We're like this . . ." John held up two fingers together. ". . . We've made a connection."

The owner stewed as he remembered the massive markup on the Rolls. "He better buy it, or you're outta here!"

"Don't worry. It's a done deal," said John. "Just gotta dot the *i*'s."

22

IT TOOK THEM LONG ENOUGH, but Consolidated Bank's board of directors finally wised up. They had to do something about Pierre before he caused any more damage. They couldn't fire or demote him, because of all the glowing evaluations he'd received and the potential for an age-discrimination suit. So they promoted him.

Pierre was bumped up to senior vice president, the one in charge of taking top clients to lunch. Pierre boxed up his belongings, stacked them on an intraoffice trundle cart, and moved one office down.

Pierre hung the inspirational rowing poster on the new wall and took a seat behind his new desk. He stared off into space, unconsciously picking at the corner of the desk blotter. He let out a heavy breath. The previous VP had been killed in a freak spelunking accident, and nobody had cleaned out his office. Pierre started playing with a set of swinging, clacking metal balls. On the corner of the desk was one of those birds that bobs its head in a glass of water. Pierre got it bobbing, but for some reason it made him depressed, and he grabbed the bird by the neck to stop it. He noticed the twin pen holder with an engraved plate: BERT WELCH, 1989 INTERBAY BLOOD DRIVE, 3RD PLACE. He took both pens out of the holder, scribbled on a notepad, replaced them. He grabbed the sterling business-card holder and dumped Bert's cards in the wastebasket, replacing them with his own and tapping them into alignment. He leaned back in the padded leather chair and began to swivel with a rhythmic squeaking. Paranoia started its creep. Pierre got up and went over to the window and closed the blinds. He sat back down and began to swivel and squeak again in the dark.

H. AMBROSE TARRINGTON III had Sinatra on the radio. He swayed with the music as he drove down Bayshore Boulevard and pulled up the circular brick driveway of the largest mansion in town. He grabbed a Polaroid camera from his briefcase and got out of the car. He set the camera on automatic and placed it atop a stone ledge. Then he ran back and posed with the Rolls in front of the estate. He got back in the car.

THERE WAS A knock on Pierre's office door. He jumped. He ran to the blinds in terror and peeked out and felt an immediate wave of relief. He opened the door.

"Ambrose!"

"Pierre!"

Vigorous handshake.

"You free for lunch?" asked Ambrose.

"Only if I get to pay."

"If you insist."

Pierre grabbed his coat.

"Whose car?"

"Let's take the Rolls."

"What happened to the Bentley?"

"Getting up in miles."

Pierre nodded. He couldn't believe his luck. Ambrose was one of the richest men in Tampa, rumored to be worth twenty, maybe thirty million, one of the bank's top clients. Or rather, top *potential* clients. Nobody had ever quite been able to persuade Ambrose to put any of his millions in Consolidated's hands, and Pierre was now determined to change that. This might be his only shot at redemption.

Pierre knew that when dealing with a man at Ambrose's level, the trick to talking money was not to mention money. Too crude. Instead, you ate and drank and played golf and got prostitutes. Then the next day you had your people call their people.

Ambrose unlocked the Rolls, and Pierre sank into the passenger seat. "How about the club?"

"The club it is," said Ambrose.

The valet at the Palma Ceia Country Club parked the Rolls while Ambrose and Pierre cut through the men's shower room, past the polished-wood lockers, and into the men's grill with a painting of the Royal Troon golf course.

As the pair crossed the lounge, heads turned. They all knew Ambrose, and Pierre felt his stock rise. He scanned the room for his rivals. There was Nelson from Florida Fidelity, Walter from Tampa Savings, and Jacob from Chemical Bank. Pierre patted Ambrose on the shoulder and smiled back at them. He had a right to feel possessive. How many times had he been in the grill and endured their smugness as Ambrose tucked in his napkin at *their* tables?

The waiter topped off their ice water as Ambrose and Pierre flipped through burgundy menus. "I'll have the swordfish on English muffin," said Ambrose.

"The chef's salad." said Pierre "Hold the croutons. I'm on the Atkins Diet."

"Who isn't?" said the waiter, collecting the menus but thinking about the screenplay he was writing that would show everyone.

Nelson, Walter and Jacob were on their cell phones, directing secretaries to get a meeting with Ambrose.

An hour later the check came and Ambrose took out his wallet.

"Remember? On me," said Pierre, intercepting the bill.

They returned to the Rolls, and Ambrose headed across town to drop Pierre off at the bank. He took a shortcut down Triggerfish Lane. He waved out the window to Gladys Plant. Gladys waved back with pruning shears. Then he waved at Jim and Martha Davenport, sitting on their porch.

They returned unsure waves. "Do we know him?" asked Martha.

Pierre was let off at the bank and waved from the curb. "Don't be a stranger."

Ambrose checked his watch and headed over a small bridge to Davis Islands, the exclusive enclave in the bay. He pulled up the drive of a waterfront home. The real estate agent was already waiting at the front door. Fifty years old, a touch on the plump side, her natural blond hair in a seventy-dollar cut that hung down to a three-hundred-dollar mauve scarf covered with parakeets.

Ambrose came up the walkway with his briefcase. "Pleasure to meet you, Jessica."

"Call me Jessie." She opened the door.

Jessica Hollingsworth, Junior League, Tampa General charity fund-raising chairwoman and Real-Tron Ten-Million-Dollar Club member. Move this home and it was a whole new ball game. Ambrose had called her directly, which meant she wouldn't have to split the 7 percent commission with a buyer's agent. And he wanted to close immediately with cash, so she didn't have to worry about the usual tantrums during escrow. The rich were the worst! She was staring down the barrel of a $420,000 payday. She had already done the math ten ways.

Ambrose walked in, stared up at the cathedral ceiling and ruffled his eyebrows.

"Don't like the color?" said Jessica. "You can always paint. Shoot, *I'll* paint." She chuckled, then kicked herself. Too eager!

Ambrose set his briefcase on the marble coffee table. "You like martinis in the afternoon?"

"Do I like what?"

"Martinis in the afternoon," said Ambrose, walking over to the stocked wet bar and deftly shakering extra-dry cocktails. House shoppers generally weren't supposed to help themselves to the owners' liquor cabinet, but Jessica had learned long ago that all bets were off with the wealthy.

"How many olives?"

"Two," she said.

She sipped Beefeater and saw Ambrose open his briefcase and take out swim trunks. She glanced out the sliding glass doors at the pool.

"Where's the nearest bathroom?" asked Ambrose.

She pointed.

As Ambrose changed, Jessica decided she should probably say something. Ambrose reemerged from the bathroom in a Speedo.

"Uh, I'm not sure you should—"

"If I buy this place, I'll have to dump the house on Bayshore," interrupted Ambrose. He showed her the Polaroid. "I'd like you to handle it for me, if that's not an imposition."

Jessie looked at the photo: Ambrose and the Rolls in the mansion's driveway. "I know that house. *Everyone* knows that house. That's yours?"

Ambrose nodded. "I'm sorry. I interrupted you. You were saying something?"

"Don't forget sunscreen."

Ambrose floated in the deep end on a Styrofoam lounger, eyes closed, a tranquil grin on his face. Jessica sat inside reading magazines for two hours.

Ambrose finally climbed out of the pool and dried off. Jessie heard rummaging from the next room. She peeked around the corner. He was in the refrigerator. Ambrose closed the door, and Jessie jumped back before he could catch her. She heard the microwave start.

Five minutes later, Ambrose came back in the living room, barefoot, wearing a bathrobe with the owner's monograms. He sat down on the couch with a tray of snacks and propped his feet on an ottoman. He picked up the remote and clicked on the seventy-inch home theater.

"Cool. *It's a Wonderful Life*," said Ambrose. "And it's just starting."

It was getting dark outside when the movie ended. Ambrose dressed as the credits rolled. "Love the place," he said, snapping his briefcase shut and heading for the front door. "I'll sleep on it."

THE OWNER OF Tampa Bay Motors was about to call the police, but he put down the phone when the Rolls pulled onto the lot. Everyone rushed out of the showroom as Ambrose parked and got out.

John smiled with expectant eyes.

"I've changed my mind," said Ambrose. "Don't like the color."

"What?" said John.

"Clashes with the house." Ambrose produced the Polaroid.

"I know that house," said the owner of the dealership. "It's the biggest one on Bayshore. That's *yours*?"

Ambrose nodded and walked away.

The owner looked at John and pointed. "Hit the road!"

GLADYS PLANT CLIMBED up the steps of the Davenports' porch with a tray of key lime tarts.

"You can tell real key limes because they're yellow," said Gladys. "Anyone tries to sell you green key limes, they're running some kind of racket."

"Did I mention I had to call the police to tow away another stolen car?" said Martha.

"What did I tell you about the grid streets?"

"But that's two and we just moved here."

"I've had four."

A public bus stopped at the corner of Triggerfish Lane. Ambrose Tarrington III got out.

Gladys looked around the porch. "You know what this place needs? A flag." She pointed at the various pennants hanging from the neighbor's porches. College emblems, unicorns, sports teams, smiling frogs, manatees, Persian cats, bowling balls. "If you don't put something up, it looks like you don't stand for anything."

Ambrose walked by on the sidewalk and waved. He continued up three more houses, opened a picket gate and went inside the tiniest home on the street.

"I think that's the same guy who waved to us earlier," said Jim. "But he was in a Rolls-Royce."

"That's H. Ambrose Tarrington the Third," said Gladys.

"What is he, a chauffeur or something?"

"No, he's slightly insane."

"What?"

"Don't worry. Gentle as they come. One of the best neighbors on the block."

"That's what you said about Old Man Ortega before they linked him to those skeletal remains."

"He's harmless—just thinks he's a millionaire," said Gladys. "He lives in this imaginary world."

"But that was a *real* Rolls-Royce."

"No kidding," said Gladys. "He's so thoroughly convinced he's a millionaire that he convinces others. He spends all his time test-driving luxury cars, getting free meals from banks and lounging around mansions that have just gone on the market. He has this ability. He knows exactly how millionaires walk and talk. All it takes is one nice suit and a good haircut. Their greed does the rest. He showed me his business cards. He's got phone numbers in New York and Beverly Hills."

"He has offices there?" said Jim.

"No, just phone numbers," said Gladys. "It's a free Internet service."

"They don't catch on?" asked Jim.

"Not only do they not catch on, they fight over him. I brought him tea one day at his house and the phone didn't stop ringing."

"So he's a con man."

"Yes and no. He never takes anything except free food and drink. Mainly he just cons them out of quality time."

"Where'd he learn how to pretend to be a millionaire?"

"He really used to be one."

Jim pointed down the street at Ambrose's modest house.

"It's a heart-wrenching story," said Gladys. "Ambrose was born dirt poor on the edge of the Everglades. I mean no-indoor-plumbing poor. He clawed his way up and made his millions in the import business. A bunch of import outlets. Early on he married his wife, Sylvia, and they were together forty years. He never strayed. You should have known her—a real doll. About fifteen years ago, Sylvia is diagnosed with a rare lymphoma, and Ambrose's insurance company pulls some kind of crap and refuses to pay for treatment. Ambrose tried absolutely everything. Took her to specialists in Paris, Geneva, the Mayo. He started with about seven million, but what he didn't spend flying her all over the world for experimental treatment went to home health care and his team of lawyers fighting the insurance company. She went into remission twice, lasted ten years. By the time she died, they were living here. He developed a heart problem and couldn't return to work. Barely gets by on Social Security."

"So he became unstable?" asked Martha.

"He's lonely," said Gladys. "He misses his wife. He wants people to like him the way they used to when he had money, even if it's for the wrong reasons. He just wants someone to talk to. When he's out pretending, it's the high point of his day, God bless 'im."

23

THE CORPS OF SALESMEN AT Tampa Bay Motors stared sadly out the showroom window. Rocco was the only one who relished the firing of John Milton. Despite their heated differences at Trivial Pursuit, the rest of the staff watched with sorrow as John silently trudged away from the dealership for the last time, head down.

John went right past his own car in the row of employee parking slots and kept going. He reached the highway and crossed it. He began walking in earnest. Soon he had gone a mile, then two. His shirt was soaked through and pasted to his back and stomach. People drove by, stereos jackhammering. John cut behind a gyro shop and a liquor store with a bar in back. A man and woman yelled across the hood of a bumperless DeVille, then started wrestling and fell down in a silt puddle. John kept walking. He thought about his credit card balances—now twelve thousand dollars—and his car payments and rent. He had the sensation of rapid descent. He was falling off the food chain, and he looked down and saw no net. He pictured himself behind a 7-Eleven, using newspapers for blankets, fighting a bum for a mattress, then sticking up a store with a finger inside a windbreaker and getting mowed down by the G-men like Dillinger at the Biograph. He began seeing people from his life. The school principal, the bank vice president, Rocco Silvertone. Their faces showed up in an arcade at the county fair; John shot a water pistol into their mouths until their heads exploded in a rain of rubber shreds.

John cursed them all in his mind. Somewhere along the line, John stopped thinking these thoughts and began yelling them. He raised his arms to shoot the make-believe squirt guns. He kept on walking. There was a bend up ahead in the road. He went around it. John now had a new address. He was living on Crazy Street.

Being crazy was hard work. John became tired. He curled up in an alley behind a tire store.

The next morning the tire guys laughed and kicked John awake. Another big day. John began walking again. And talking, and waving his arms. He saw someone coming toward him on the sidewalk. A homeless man with a gray beard and pinwheel hat. The man was talking and waving his own arms. As they passed on the sidewalk, they nodded to each other out of professional courtesy.

John would soon get to know most of the homeless, that shadow army living out on the tattered hem of society, washing windshields, recycling aluminum and shoring up the malt liquor industry. The guy who just passed John, for instance. Ernie. Late-stage alcoholic and *über* schizophrenic. Ernie was the exception that proved the rule. He had survived since 1985 on the streets of Tampa, where life expectancy was measured in dog years.

Ernie didn't consider himself homeless. He instead liked to think of himself as the ultimate bachelor, which, in many ways, he was. Ernie had a Jesus complex. He wore sandals and a white smock and made crowns of thorns out of pipe cleaners and plastic six-pack rings. Most of the time, Ernie gently ministered to his flock. He blessed people in intersections, forgave shoppers in parking lots, and anointed the sick at the train station. Except when he was on a bender—then he was usually throwing up in the middle of a busy highway. By all rights, Ernie should have been struck and killed long ago, but drivers tend to be superstitious people, and they made an extra effort to avoid the bad luck that comes with running over a guy who looks like Christ.

Unlike most homeless people, Ernie had a nemesis. His name was Bert. He was homeless, too. Bert told himself he was a social drinker, and his society was made up of Dylan Thomas, Jack Kerouac and John Bonham. Yep, he was crazy. His flavor of madness made him believe he was the Antichrist. He shaved his skull and used a rusty razor to carve demonic stuff in his forehead.

As Christ and the Antichrist, Ernie and Bert fought pitched battles across Tampa Bay for the soul of mankind. They would tail and ambush each other on a daily basis like Inspector Clouseau and Kato, wrestling and tumbling all over town. Other times they got along quite well, playing checkers in the library, boosting each other into Dumpsters, taking turns pushing the shopping cart. When you got right down to it, they needed each other. At the end of each day, they always pooled whatever they had for quarts of Olde English.

But the Antichrist was an angry drunk. Sober, there was nobody nicer. Under the influence, however, it was another story. Something just changed in the Beast. The Messiah would go in the Circle K to get another quart, and on the way out the door, Bert would blindside him with a right hook.

The police hauled 'em in dozens of times. After a while, the cops didn't even fingerprint them anymore. They'd just throw them in the tank to dry up and tease them mercilessly—"Hey Jesus, wait till we tell your mother!" "Yo, Antichrist, who's bad now!"—the way some officers used to do before they instituted the education requirements.

John Milton would eventually learn the whole back story. But all he knew right now, as he continued his journey away from the car dealership, was that he heard a creaking noise. It sounded like a large tree branch starting to snap. John turned around. He saw the man with the pinwheel hat walking away on the sidewalk. Hanging over the sidewalk was the bough of an old oak. Another homeless man was up in the tree, perched on the branch, ready to strike.

The branch snapped.

Both men lay on their backs, groaning. John ran to help. He pulled the tree limb off their chests. The pair thanked John, then jumped each other. They fell and rolled into the gutter. Cars drove by on an otherwise pleasant afternoon. Ernie and Bert saw it differently as they tightened grips on each other's throat. The sky was blood-red, and purple lightning forked over the city. There were two moons in the sky. The earth cracked open on Dale Mabry Highway, and magma gushed out. Shopping centers burst into flames. The lava flow stopped traffic, and ten-foot winged lizards pulled people from their cars and ripped their arms off.

Suddenly, Bert jumped up from the ground, holding the pin-

wheel hat in the air like the head of his enemy. "I got it! I got it!"
He ran away.

John helped Ernie to his feet again and pulled leaves off his
shirt. Ernie asked John his name. John told him. He blessed John.
"You are the gentle one. From now on your new apostolic name
will be John."

"My name already is John."

"This is a different John."

"Oh."

Ernie bent down and stuck his thumb in the dirt. He stood back
up and pressed the thumb to John's forehead, giving him a little
Ash Wednesday action. "Now go. You have much to do."

"What do I do?"

"You will be told by the Anointed One. The Messenger who
will *reveal all.*"

"Who's the Messenger?"

Ernie pointed down the street. "You must hurry!"

John hurried. He began walking briskly. Faster. Then trotting.
Finally he was running full speed, on a mission. Only two questions. What was that mission, and who would be the one to
reveal it?

Cars blew by John on the highway. Mitsubishis, Porches, Dat-
suns and a blue Buick Regal with bug shield and curb feelers.

The E-Team was on the move. They all had coupons for the free
lunch buffet at Hot Buns, the new all-male revue in north Tampa.
Eunice pulled the Buick into the parking lot.

Twenty minutes later, Eunice pulled out of the parking lot. The
whole E-Team was mad at Edith.

"I wanted to stay!" said Edna.

"Me, too!" said Eunice.

"I can't believe we got kicked out for life!" said Ethel.

Edna glared at Edith. "Everyone knows you're not supposed to
touch the dancers."

"Or get up onstage," said Eunice.

"Big deal," said Edith. "The coleslaw was runny."

Eunice began a slow, methodical drift toward the exit ramp.
Eunice's lane changes usually took more pavement than a 747

takeoff. Unless there was another car in that lane, in which case she could be over with utter suddenness.

The exit ramp approached fast. Eunice was driving in the triangular wedge of warning stripes painted in the fork, her left wheels running over raised reflector hubs bolted to the yellow stripes, rat-a-tat-a-tat, standard operating procedure. Still plenty of time to miss the upcoming guardrail. Leaving the yellow stripes now, three-quarters of the way into the exit lane and looking good.

A low-riding Geo without a blinker shot by on the inside, taking the ramp at ninety. Eunice yanked the steering wheel left, just as they were about to crunch fenders. Everyone including Eunice clenched their eyes shut, waiting for impact. Nothing. They opened their eyes. They were back in the striped triangle again, guardrail coming up fast. No escape. They hit the guardrail end on. Driver and passenger airbags: bang-bang. Bobbing-head dolls from the rear window catapulted forward through the passenger compartment. Guardrail legs snapped off at bumper level, pow-pow-pow-pow-pow, glancing off the windshield. Curb feelers sheared off. Red and orange reflector discs from the guardrail sailed in all directions, and the horizontal aluminum rail curled away like a wood shaving. Sod and gravel slung past the windows. Four hubcaps took off independently, passing the Buick, which veered onto the wrong side of the guardrail, high up the grass embankment. They were at an angle now, leaning right as the embankment's incline increased. The Buick finally began to decelerate. Forty miles an hour. Thirty. Twenty. The women sighed with relief as the car neared a standstill. Meanwhile, the angle of the embankment had increased. Twenty degrees. Thirty. Forty. When the Buick was just about to roll to a stop, the pitch reached sixty degrees, and the Buick tilted up on its right tires and slowly creaked over for a soft landing on its roof.

Everything was still. The four woman looked around at each other hanging upside down in their seat-belt harnesses.

"This reminds me of *The Poseidon Adventure*," said Edith.

"Shut up," said Eunice.

"At least it's over," said Ethel.

The Department of Transportation had done a fine job landscaping the interchange. The grass was smooth and mowed, still wet with dew. The Buick had just been waxed.

There was a lurch. The women stopped talking.

Another lurch.

The car began sliding down the embankment on its roof.

Edith looked out the window at the grass going by inches above her head.

"Shit."

The Buick picked up velocity again, tobogganing down the embankment. Ten, fifteen, twenty miles an hour, speeding for the retention pond choked with hyacinths, reeds and cattails growing to improbable heights due to nutrient-rich fertilizer runoff. The Buick slammed into the cattails, flipping back upright and landing fifteen yards out in the pond. All was still again.

"Look on the bright side," said Eunice. "Nothing else can go wrong."

They began sinking. Swamp water squirted in the rivet holes at the base of the firewall. The women watched water and minnows swirl on the floorboards.

"Remember how Shelley Winters held her breath in *The Poseidon Adventure*?"

"Shut up!"

Suddenly, it stopped, a foot of water in the car.

"There's got to be a morning after . . ."

"I'm warning you!"

"Maybe we should climb on the roof and get someone's attention."

Eunice tried her door, but the cattails were thick and tight against the car. It wouldn't budge. "Try yours."

The other three pushed on their own doors. Negative.

"Don't worry," said Edna. "Help must be on the way. Probably a hundred people saw us go down. And we're in the middle of a big city."

"My window's working," said Eunice. She crawled out and climbed on the roof.

The rest of the E-Team looked up as they heard her footsteps.

"Can you see anything?" asked Edna.

"No. The cattails are too tall. But I hear something."

Police and fire rescue had gotten thirty-two cell-phone calls about a vehicle going off the highway. Trucks with flashing lights responded immediately.

Unfortunately for the E-Team, the Geo that had cut them off on the ramp had been running from police, and it failed to negotiate the turn at the bottom of the exit, spinning off the shoulder and wedging nosedown in the edge of the pond. Police cuffed the driver; a city tow truck winched the Geo out of the water. Everyone drove away.

It was quiet again.

"I think they left," said Eunice, climbing back in the window. "Shit."

24

FLOODLIGHTS LIT UP the Palma Ceia Little League complex in south Tampa.

Parents stood in the bleachers and cheered as the Raptors ran from the dugout and fanned out across the field in gleaming white uniforms and satin warm-up jackets. Then the team's four-man coaching staff ran onto the field. Head Coach Jack Terrier waved to the crowd with his good arm, his other dressed in a sling from pit-bull punctures.

On the other side of the diamond, the visiting team huddled in the dugout. Two weeks earlier, the team's original coach had been sent to prison for securities fraud and absconding with the team's uniform fund. The coaches of the other five teams quickly responded to the civic crisis by snatching up all the best players from the local talent pool. The leftovers, a platoon of underweight, spastic, nearsighted children, were delegated by default to the coachless sixth team. Problem solved. The coaches could count on at least one automatic win every fifth game. But they still needed a warm, adult body to sit on the last team's bench, for insurance purposes.

Jim Davenport arrived to drop Melvin off for baseball practice. The other coaches summarily drafted him. Jim told them he was swamped with work. They told him to think of the children.

"What about uniforms?" asked Jim.

Sorry, they said. The former coach needed the money for jewelry and personal electronics. Jim decided to buy the uniforms himself. He went to the sporting-goods store.

"I'm on a really tight budget. Give me anything you have."

"We got some factory seconds and sample runs, but I don't think you—"

"I'll take 'em."

The Raptors had been warming up for five minutes when there was a second roar. The parents in the visitors' bleachers stood and cheered as their children took the field. The cheering dribbled off into puzzlement as the players ran to their positions in mismatched T-shirts, the team's new name in a different typeface on each jersey: TEST PATTERN.

The public-address system crackled. "Please rise . . ." Everyone stood at attention for the national anthem.

"Coming through! Coming through!" Coleman balanced a tray of nachos and wobbled up the steps of the aluminum bleachers wearing a rainbow afro wig under a beer helmet.

Serge was already standing on the top row, hand over his heart, and he gave Coleman a look of disapproval.

"What's wrong?" asked Coleman.

Everyone was silent in the stands. Serge made a head motion toward the flagpole.

"What?"

Serge glanced down at the hand over his heart.

"What are you trying to say?"

"Fucking national anthem!"

Parents turned around.

The music ended and everyone sat back down. Coleman took the beer tubes out of his mouth. "Nacho?"

"I'm on a diet," said Serge.

"You don't need to diet."

"I'm not doing it because I need to. I doing it just to prove I can. I haven't had anything solid for three days."

"Is it working?"

"Hard to tell. But I'm dizzy all the time, so I guess that's something."

Serge leaned toward the family on his left. "Politics!"

The family looked at him.

"Little League," said Serge, pointing at the field. "It's all politics!"

The family moved to a lower row.

"What's *their* problem?" said Coleman.

"Pressures of modern society," said Serge. "People like that need to learn how to kick back."

Jason Terrier led off the Raptor half of the first with a home run, and the floodgates opened. Nine more runs before the end of the frame.

The Test Patterns came to bat. Jason took the mound and struck out the side with high heat, the Raptor bleachers erupting in cheers each time a child was sent back to the bench. "Way to go, son!" Coach Terrier patted Jason on the back as he came off the field.

Everyone scrambled for the concession stand.

The Test Patterns took the field again.

Coleman pointed down at the diamond. "Where's the rest of our coaches?"

"It's just Jim," said Serge.

"But the other team has parents in the first- and third-base coaches' boxes. That's a clear edge."

"You're right," said Serge. They got up and began bounding down the bleachers toward the dugout, Coleman grabbing people's shoulders to stay upright.

"I don't know," Jim told them.

"Think of the children," said Serge.

Jim finally relented, but said Coleman's beer helmet would have to go. The Test Patterns were trailing seventeen–zip in the bottom of the second inning when Serge and Coleman ran onto the field and took up positions in the first-base coach's box.

"You're supposed to be on the third-base side," said Serge. "One coach per box."

"But I want someone to talk to."

The first batter came up and Serge and Coleman crouched next to each other with their hands on their knees.

Coleman: "*Hey, batter, batter, batter. Hey, batter, batter, batter. Swing!*"

Serge elbowed him. "That's *our* batter!"

Coleman thought a second. "How come they don't chatter in the pros?"

"All the fame and money," said Serge. "They forget the fundamentals."

Serge clapped his hands and shouted encouragement to the batter. "Okay! Big inning! Let's put some Louisville on the ol' horsehide!"

The boy struck out and tripped on his way back to the bench. Serge helped him up and patted him on the back. "Way to look alive! Way to take that called third strike!"

The next batter struck out.

"Way to hustle! That's the spirit! Good eye! There's still plenty of time to come back!"

The third batter struck out to complete the inning.

"Okay, that ends the rally," said Serge, clapping hard. "Still a lot of innings left! It ain't over till it's over!"

It was twenty-nine to nothing by the middle of the third, but the Raptors weren't finished. Jason had a no-hitter going, and Coach Terrier wanted to break the local record of fifty-two runs. He directed his players to turn up the aggression. They stole and bunted and hit-and-ran. They slid with cleats high.

The Test Patterns' second baseman was taken out of a double play in a nasty collision. Serge and Coleman ran out and helped the boy off the field. The Raptor bleachers began singing.

"Na-na, na-na-na-na, hey hey-ay, good-bye! . . ."

Coach Terrier got his record, fifty-three-to-zero in the middle of the sixth. Just one more out and Jason would also have his no-hitter. It was up to Percy, the smallest player batting in the ninth position. He adjusted his owl glasses and choked up on the bat almost to the label. Jason's fastball was still working, and he sizzled one high inside to brush Percy off the plate. Percy never saw the ball. It hit the end of his bat handle and bounced in front of the plate, rolling slowly down the third-base line. The third baseman charged for the ball. Percy stood frozen in the batter's box, surprised he had made contact for the first time in his life.

"Run!" yelled Serge.

"Run!" yelled Coleman.

Percy ran.

The third baseman made a great off-balance throw, but Percy beat it to first by a full step.

"Safe!" said the umpire.

The no-hitter was dead.

The Raptor bleachers booed. Debris flew onto the field. Hot dogs and batteries and ice cubes. Coach Terrier stormed out of the dugout. He twisted his cap around and got nose to nose with the ump. He screamed in his face. He kicked dirt on his shoes. He began mocking him, acting like he was blind and walking with a cane. The bleachers threw popcorn and chanted.

"Bull-shit, bull-shit . . ."

Serge and Coleman stood nonchalantly in the first-base box.

"What an absolutely pathetic display of citizenship," said Serge.

The umpire stood his ground and told Terrier to get back in the dugout or he was tossed. Jason had begun crying on the mound.

Melvin Davenport was the next batter. Coach Terrier went back and stood on the top step of the dugout, signaling urgently to Jason. "Hit him!" Jason nodded.

Serge saw the exchange, but it was too late. Jason threw a fastball into the batter's box without a windup. Melvin partially ducked, and the ball ricocheted off the oversized batting helmet swimming around on Melvin's head.

Melvin ran to first base. Serge came out of the coach's box and knelt in the orange dirt. He grabbed Melvin by the shoulders: "You okay, son?"

"Never even felt it, Serge!" said Melvin. "High five!" Melvin put up his hand for Serge to slap. Serge gave him the high five, but it was without enthusiasm. His mind was elsewhere. Across the diamond, Coach Terrier gave Jason a thumbs-up.

Serge returned to the coach's box. He became a statue, eyes locked in tunnel vision on the other dugout.

"Uh-oh," said Coleman. "I've seen that look before."

25

TWO A.M., THE DOORBELL RANG AT 887 TRIGGERFISH LANE.

Jack Terrier came down the stairs rubbing his eyes. "Who can it be at this hour?" He looked out the window but didn't see anyone. He was just about to close the curtain when he noticed something flicker.

"What the hell?"

He quickly opened the front door and began stomping the flaming paper bag on his welcome mat. When the fire was out, Jack raised his leg to look at the bottom of his slipper.

"Son of a bitch!"

A twig snapped. He looked up. "What the—"

Then he saw stars.

WHEN JACK TERRIER came to, he was in a familiar place. His mouth was taped shut and he was tied securely to a chair sitting on the pitcher's mound. The Little League field was dark, but he could make out two figures standing in front of him. A tall one and a shorter, plumper model to his left. They wore panty-hose masks and T-shirts with something written in indelible ink.

TEST PATTERN AVENGERS.

The tall one had a gun, and the fat one had a beer.

"You know why I love baseball?" said the tall one. "Because it's a game of history, that's why." He unrolled a spool of outdoor

extension cord, plugged it in at the concession stand and ran it
back out to the pitcher's mound.

"You know who played right here on this field? Palma Ceia Little League? . . . What? Not even a guess? I'm disappointed in you.
It was the one and only Wade Boggs!"

The plump one killed his beer. "You ought to listen to the man.
He knows all kinds of cool stuff." Burp.

The tall one disappeared into the dugout and came back carrying a large electric machine and a paper sack. Jack recognized the
device. He had one in his own garage. A pressure washer.

"All the greats played in this town during spring training, back
when you had access to the players and could get so close to the
action you could smell the rosin bag. Not like today's antiseptic
spring-training mini-stadiums. They played at the old Al Lopez
Park, named for Tampa's patron saint of baseball. And you know
what they did to that park? Huh? Do ya?" The tall one suddenly
grabbed Jack by the throat. "They knocked it down for a football
parking lot!"

The chubby one grabbed his partner by the arm. "Easy, easy. He
didn't do it."

"You're right. Sorry." He stepped back. Then he reached down
and took something out of the paper sack and attached it to the
end of the pressure washer.

"These washers are amazing," said Serge. "You know they gen-
erate fifty to a hundred times the pressure of a regular garden
hose?"

When everything was all hooked up, the tall one took a step
back. "This is for the children."

He turned on the pressure washer.

TWO POLICE OFFICERS arrived at the Little League field shortly after
dawn.

They froze in horror when they saw the pitcher's mound. A
Water Wiggle whipped violently on the end of the pressure
washer, occasionally striking the corpse in the chair with a meat-
tenderizing thud.

They cut the power to the pressure washer and ran to the mound, but it was far too late. One of the officers picked up the Water Wiggle and turned it over to look at its face. It had the regular crossed eyes and goofy smile, but someone had added fangs dripping blood.

26

MAHONEY! GET IN HERE!"

Mahoney appeared in Ingersol's doorway with a box of push-pins. "You called for me, Lieutenant?"

Ingersol held up some pages from Mahoney's investigative notebook. "What the hell is this stuff?"

Mahoney bent forward and squinted. "That's my doodling."

"This is some pretty sick shit. I don't even know what half of it is." Ingersol set the notebook down and turned to a page covered with flaming chariots, winged swordsmen, seven-eyed goats' heads, crucifixes, 666's, tongues of fire and race cars.

"Mahoney, do you belong to some kind of doomsday cult you're not telling me about?"

"No."

"I don't want to come to work and find out you've poisoned a bunch of people with Kool-Aid so you could catch the next comet to the Resurrection."

"That's crazy stuff," said Mahoney. "I've just been getting into the Book of Revelations."

"Revelations?"

"Powerful writing. And it's starting to come true."

"You're not reading this on state time, are you?"

"It has law-enforcement relevance. When Armageddon breaks out, we could be looking at some serious overtime."

Ingersol sat back in his chair and paused for effect. "Mahoney, you know the department is cracking down on doodling. Last year it cost us something like ten thousand man-hours."

Mahoney nodded.

"But I'm going to overlook it this time because you've been pro-
ductive and because the crackdown was mainly aimed at the guys
drawing all those breasts and bearded clams." Ingersol shook his
head. "Mahoney, what's wrong with men?"

"That's the big question on the street."

"Got anything new for me today?"

"The McGraws struck again. Take a look at this." Mahoney
handed him a file of crime-scene photos.

"Holy Jesus!" said Ingersol.

"That used to be a biker with the Riders of Eternal Doom. Sold
them some bad mescaline . . ."

". . . which was actually *good* mescaline?"

"Right. And then they knocked him unconscious and backed
their car up on him."

"Looks like they patched out on his face."

"Looks that way," said Mahoney.

"What about our informants?"

"I'm beating the bushes, but nobody's dropped the dime, and
the McGraws don't have a consistent M.O."

"M.O.? This isn't *The Rockford Files*. Speak English!"

"Modus operandi."

"That's Latin."

"Method of operation."

"Witnesses?"

"Just a few vague encounters, fuzzy descriptions, stale memo-
ries."

"Sounds like your marriages."

"Good one, sir."

"Mahoney, I don't like you. You know that."

"I don't like you, either."

"Then we have a lot in common. We should get along fine."

"Sir, they're getting awfully close to Tampa. If only I could—"

"Forget about it. I know you and this Serge thing! You've been
completely obsessed with the case for three years now."

"Four," said Mahoney. "But it seems like only yesterday . . ."

"No! Not a fade-out!" said the lieutenant. "Don't you *dare* do
a fade-out!"

"You want to forget, but the nightmares won't let you . . ."

"God! I hate it when you do a fade-out!"

"Yes, it's all coming back to me now . . ."

MAHONEY WAS A rookie, working undercover, when he hooked up with a crew just off a string of successful society robberies from Boynton to Palm Beach. Silent auctions, charity balls, foundation galas. They were pros and they hit fast and hard, only taking the best stuff. Flawless jewels, precision watches, expensive artwork, stuffed mushrooms. Everyone set up surveillance on Alligator Alley and the Tamiami Trail, expecting the gang to make for the Gulf Coast and more easy pickings.

They were headed for the Gulf all right, but only Mahoney guessed the right road. The gang avoided the usual routes across the bottom of the state, instead heading into the Everglades from West Palm Beach, past Lion Country Safari and into sugarcane country with the migrant trucks and prison work vans.

It was a hot Monday. The gang had struck three more times over the weekend.

Mahoney picked up on something the others missed. All the scores were at the most historic venues in town when more lucrative targets sat nearby. The Biltmore, White Hall, Vizcaya. People got roughed up, folding tables tossed, but none of the antique fixtures received as much as a smudge. And there was a stray thread that didn't make any sense. After the Palm Beach job, the gang was spotted at the old island post office; one of them ran inside and took a photo of the giant portrait collage over the door—a kind of *Sgt. Pepper's* cover of the island's history. Henry Flagler, John F. Kennedy, Marjorie Merriweather Post, architect Addison Mizner, boxer "Alligator" Joe Frazier et al. Nobody could figure it, but Mahoney knew right away. He had a touch of the same disease.

Mahoney drove halfway across the state to the landmark Clewiston Inn on the underside of Lake Okeechobee and set up shop behind a glass of whiskey in the Everglades Lounge.

"Louie, another round."

"It's Pete," said the bartender, filling Mahoney's glass.

"Thanks, Louie."

The bartender walked away. Mahoney held the rocks glass in front of his mouth and idly rattled the cubes around in the sour mash, admiring the faded mural on the wall over the bar. Egrets, ibis, sawgrass.

Four guys walked in and grabbed stools. But another stayed out in the hall, examining the black-and-white photos on the wall of half-century-old ground breakings and sugar-queen pageants.

Mahoney picked up his glass and went out and stood next to the man, not looking at him. The man flicked a Zippo open and shut from nervous habit. Click-click.

"Nice photos," said Mahoney.

"Not bad," said the man. Click-click.

"I knew one other person who flicked a lighter like that," said Mahoney. "George Clooney in *Out of Sight*."

"I loved that movie! That's when I started carrying around the lighter," said the man. "They set most of the film right here in south Florida."

"Trivia footnote," said Mahoney. "Michael Keaton played the part of the same federal agent in that movie and Tarantino's *Jackie Brown*. Two completely different studios and directors. The only link was that they were both adapted from Elmore Leonard books containing that same agent."

"I could have shot Tarantino when he rewrote *Rum Punch* and moved it to California," said the man. "I was waiting for the Riviera Beach scenes. That's where I grew up."

"Riviera Beach? Me too!"

"I lived near Flagler Drive."

"Then we were practically neighbors!"

"Get outta town!"

"Name's Mahoney," said Mahoney, holding out his hand.

The man extended his own. "Serge."

They shook on it.

That's how Mahoney got in the gang. The others were suspicious, didn't want anything to do with him. What did they really know about the guy? But Serge was adamant—swore up and down vouching for Mahoney. He was one of his homeys.

Two days later, a cheap motel on the Tamiami Trail. They had widened the highway several times and tractor-trailers rattled the room. Their next caper was a hospital charity ball at C' d'Zan, the palatial winter estate of circus magnate John Ringling on the shore of Sarasota Bay. It was a costume ball.

The sun set. The crew was already dressed, sitting around a table loading weapons. The Marquis de Sade filled clips with bullets. Baby Face Nelson racked the slides on automatic pistols. Jesse James slammed a magazine home in a Mac-10. Dracula screwed a silencer on a Beretta. The headlights of a Kenworth swept across their faces as it thundered past, bullets dancing on the table.

"I don't like my costume," said Serge.

"Me neither," said Mahoney.

"I told you—it was all they had left," said Baby Face. "There was a big run on outfits for the ball tonight."

"Maybe I can make my own," said Serge.

"Too late," said Dracula, standing up and pumping a shotgun. "Let's hit it!"

They piled in a Cadillac and were quiet on the way over. Two retired couples in an Oldsmobile pulled up next to them at a stoplight. Dracula turned and nodded. The light changed. They went.

The party was in full swing when the gang arrived. Czar Nicholas was hitting on Joan of Arc at the punch bowl. Marie Antoinette and Kaiser Wilhelm were on the porch smoking. The gang mingled and made small talk with Louis XIV and Louis Pasteur. Except Serge and Mahoney; they were mollified by the Venetian and Turkish flair of the thirty-one-room manse and sauntered around the perimeter of the ballroom, inspecting stained glass, the cypress ceiling, the chandelier that used to hang in the Waldorf-Astoria.

Suddenly, Baby Face Nelson pulled out a tommy gun. "This is a stick up!"

A few people laughed and went back to their conversations.

"I'm serious!" yelled Baby Face.

They ignored him, refilling champagne flutes.

Baby Face finally had to pistol-whip Chiang Kai-shek to get their attention, and Dracula started going around the room with a pillowcase, collecting jewelry and wallets.

Unbeknownst to the gang, Mahoney had tipped off his superiors, and agents were staked out incognito.

"Drop it!" said J. Edgar Hoover, aiming a snub-nose at Baby Face.

Baby Face laughed.

Hoover fired a warning shot; Baby Face dropped it.

That was the signal for the other agents. John Wayne, Buffalo Bill and Zorro pulled guns on the other members of the gang, who quickly surrendered.

"This ain't all of them," said Hoover.

The agents scanned the room, overlooking the men in the Mr. Ed costume.

"What's going on?" Serge asked from in back.

"Hold on," said Mahoney. "My eye holes are off."

Mahoney shook around in the horse's head. "I can see now. Looks like a raid. I think—"

Mahoney suddenly felt the cold steel barrel of a revolver in his back.

"What are you doing?"

"You're a cop!" said Serge.

"What are you talking about?"

"Remember when I told you I lived on Flagler? That's in West Palm Beach, not Riviera. You would have known that if you *really* grew up there. Besides, no self-respecting criminal would ever have gotten into this costume. Put your hands up!"

"I can't."

"Right. Okay, start backing up, real slow."

Baby Face and Dracula were being handcuffed together when Buffalo Bill suddenly pointed across the ballroom. "There they are! They're getting away!"

The others turned and saw Mr. Ed backing out of the room.

John Wayne and Zorro aimed their pistols. "Freeze, motherfucker!"

"Stay where you are or he gets it!" said a muffled voice inside the horse.

"He's not joking!" said a different muffled voice.

"Who's in there?" asked Hoover.

"Agent Mahoney, Florida Department of Law Enforcement."

"Prove it!"

Mahoney stuck his gold state badge out the horse's mouth, then pulled it back.

"Okay," said Hoover. "Hold your fire, men."

Everyone watched tensely as the horse shuffled backward through the open doors and across the outdoor patio overlooking the bay. When the horse got to the edge of the patio, Serge cold-cocked Mahoney in the back of the head with his pistol butt.

The FBI agents saw the front half of Mr. Ed drop like a sack of cement, tearing away the zipper around the stomach, and the back half of the horse dove into Sarasota Bay. The agents sprinted across the patio and began firing into the night water, but it was too late. The business end of a horse suit floated in the moonlight . . .

MAHONEY FLOATED BACK to the present. ". . . And that was the last time I ever saw Serge."

"Okay! Okay!" said Ingersol. "I give up. Pack your bags."

"Tampa?"

"Tampa."

27

AFTER JIM DAVENPORT WAS FIRED, he encountered difficulty finding consulting work. Most of the big consulting companies had hired each other and recommended downsizing. Martha took a hard look at the family's financial situation and asked if she could give it a try.

Martha began interviewing and immediately landed a high-paying job at Consolidated Bank, which was aggressively hiring because they were critically understaffed due to recent layoffs.

But Jim never gave up. He kept lowering his salary expectations until he found a job on the night shift. Jim and Martha saw each other ten minutes each evening as they made the handoff.

Jim drove into work at sunset, went to his locker and put on his red apron. He pinned a plastic name tag to his pocket: ROBERT. They were still making his JIM tag, but regulations required him to wear something, so he used the tag left behind by an employee picked up on warrants from Tennessee. Jim's favorite part of the new job was the cheerful co-workers who befriended him at Sam's Club.

They began arriving shortly after Jim clocked in. There was Orville, a surviving member of Doolittle's Raiders, and Wilma, a former waitress from Tupelo who had pulled through three bad marriages with a gum-smacking, country-music outlook on life, and finally Satchel, who said he had pitched in the Negro Leagues, but nobody believed him.

"Hi, Robert," said Orville.

"Hi, Orville. It's Jim."

Orville and Satchel reloaded price guns and pushed open the swinging "employees only" doors that led to the sales floor. Wilma arrived and slipped into an apron covered with enamel pins representing years of service at Sam's Club, stock-car drivers and breeds of show dogs.

"Hi, Wilma."

"Hi, Robert."

"I'm Jim."

Wilma climbed into the driver's seat of a beeping forklift and burst through the swinging doors with a pallet of mustard jars the size of propane tanks.

Jim bent over and tied his shoes. The intercom came on: "Code Orange. Aisle one-twenty-three."

Jim grabbed a mop and headed through the swinging doors.

"Jim!"

Jim turned. "Serge! Coleman!"

"What are you doing here?"

"New job," said Jim. "And you?"

Serge pointed in his shopping cart at bottles of vitamins and herbal supplements.

"I'm on a diet, so I need essential minerals."

"You look great," said Jim. "You don't need to diet."

"I'm just doing it to prove I can. It's easy to criticize others when you haven't walked in their shoes . . . Check it out." Serge opened a crumpled paper bag for Jim to see inside.

"Old clothes?"

"The most precise scales in town are at the Publix supermarkets. I wear the same outfit every day when I weigh myself so I can get a consistent reading."

"Why is it all in the bag?"

"I just weighed the clothes on a digital scale at the post office so I can subtract it to get my naked weight. I can't exactly go in the supermarket naked. Actually I can, but, well, you know . . ."

Jim looked concerned.

"I have to lose fifteen pounds," said Serge. "Four days should about do it. Then it's roast pork and plantains for a week! Can't wait!"

"Don't hurt yourself," said Jim.

"You know my motto: Moderation in moderation. That's what the vitamins are for. If you're going to diet, then *diet*. No halfway stuff. It should be a Manhattan Project. If you're doing it right, you should always feel like you're about to pass out." Serge began grabbing bottles out of the shopping cart. "This is ginseng and this is your chromium picolinate, and you've got your ginkgo biloba for memory, so I don't forget to take all this stuff, and your St. John's wort, which combats obsessive-compulsive behavior—"

"So you don't go on extreme diets and vitamin binges?"

"Exactly."

Coleman pointed at the rack under the shopping cart. "I got a fifty-pound sack of beer nuts."

There was a crash.

Serge had passed out.

JIM AND MARTHA discussed it at length. She loved the Suburban, but the payments were a budget-buster. Before work the next day, Jim headed back to Tampa Bay Motors.

Rocco Silvertone was waiting in a golf cart when Jim got out of the Suburban.

"What can I do you for?"

"I bought this here a couple weeks back," said Jim. "There's been a change in our financial picture. I need to trade it in to lower my payments."

"I remember you," said Rocco. "You're the guy who wanted the total price—you didn't want to tell me how much you could pay a month."

Jim picked out another Aerostar with fifty thousand more miles than the one he had traded in. Rocco brought him into the finance office.

He typed up the contract. Jim inspected it and tapped a finger on the sheet. "What's this number? This four hundred dollars?"

"Oh, that's dealer prep. It's standard."

"That's four hundred dollars more than the price you gave me."

"So?"

"So it's not the price you gave me."

"That's okay," said Rocco. "It's standard."

Jim stared. Rocco forced a smile. He hated customers like Jim—the ones who could do math. Rocco motioned for Jim to take another look at the figure. "See? It's preprinted on the form. There's no problem."

Jim continued staring.

"Look, if it will ease your mind . . ." said Rocco, getting up and walking to a file cabinet. He brought back a bunch of blank forms. "See? They all have four hundred dollars preprinted on them."

"But they're your forms."

"Yeah?"

"You printed them."

"Now you understand," said Rocco, handing Jim a pen.

The head of the trade-in department walked in the office. He whispered in Rocco's ear.

Rocco looked up at Jim. "Did you know the horn on your Suburban doesn't work right?"

"Yes."

"Why didn't you tell us?" said Rocco. He began scratching out some numbers on the contract. "I can't give you what we offered if the horn doesn't work right. We'll have to take off a couple hundred . . . Hey, where are you going?"

JIM WAS LATE for work. He headed south on Dale Mabry Highway, stopping at a red light just before sunset. It was a Friday evening, and sexual expectations began to thicken across the city like a fog rolling in from the bay. Jim's body shook from the car stereos. Tampa's young adults in Galants, Mustangs, Corollas, Sentras, Supras and Wranglers. Most had something hanging from the rearview mirrors—compact discs, foreign flags, garter belts, big dice, Mardi Gras beads—to increase the likelihood of sex. Some had handcuffs hanging from the rearview to indicate the exotic brand of sex they were not getting.

Jim arrived at Sam's Club and clocked in.

"Man, Jim. You look awful," said Orville.

"Something bothering you?" asked Wilma.

"Don't look back," said Satchel. "Something may be gaining on ya."

"Thanks, guys," said Jim. "Just an off day."

Wilma removed one of her enamel pins and stuck it on Jim's pinless apron. "There. Feel better?"

Jim managed a sincere smile.

"Why don't you join us tonight?" said Orville.

"Join you where?"

"The crime watch," said Wilma. "This is our night. Every other Friday."

"You don't use guns, do you?"

"Oh no," said Satchel. "Just walkie-talkies. We're the eyes and ears of the police. It's loads of fun."

28

MEANWHILE, BACK AT THE RANCH, Coleman sat on the plaid couch with a beer in his hand.

Serge paced the living room. "This idleness is killing me! I've got to get out of here!" He went in the kitchen and checked the refrigerator—nothing he liked. He came back in the living room and resumed pacing. Coleman was still on the couch, facing the TV. Serge disappeared into his bedroom and changed his pants a few times, but nothing felt right. He marched into the kitchen and checked the refrigerator again. Still nothing.

Serge ran back in the living room. "Coleman! I can't take it!"

Coleman wasn't responsive, even for Coleman. He slouched into the loose couch cushions like gelatin.

"Coleman! What's wrong with you!" Serge then noticed the open prescription bottle on the coffee table.

"You got into my schizo medicine!"

No answer.

Serge buzzed around the house for an hour, trying on more pants, looking at his matchbook collection with a magnifying glass, sprinting the length of the hallway making dunk shots with a nerf basketball: "And here comes Jordan with the three-sixty, triple pump, over-the-shoulder, in-your-face, supergalactic mind-fucker! Eeeeee-yaaaaaaa!!!!!!"

Crash.

Coleman finally began to move as Serge climbed out of the Serge-shaped hole in the drywall.

"You okay?" said Coleman.

"Did I score?" asked Serge, shaking dust from his hair.

"I think so. I'm not sure. Those pills . . ."

"I know what you mean," said Serge. "I hate taking that shit."

"I thought they'd never wear off. That was fucked up!"

"Why would you do something so brainless?" said Serge.

"I got curious."

"Learn a lesson?"

"And how! It was like I spent six hours staring at the world through twelve inches of glass—a scary, unfamiliar land where my brain felt like molten plastic and my body refused to respond to the simplest command."

"That's why I stopped taking it."

"Oh, I'm not complaining," said Coleman. "I *liked* it."

Serge joined Coleman on the couch. Coleman grabbed the remote control and clicked on *The New Dating Game*.

"Weren't we supposed to rob someone tonight?" asked Coleman.

"Supposed to, but we needed Sharon for a decoy," said Serge. "She's nowhere to be found, as usual!"

"*Bachelor number three, if you could be any kind of cheese . . .*"

"Cool," said Coleman. "A night off."

"I can't stand the inactivity!"

"It's not so bad," said Coleman, balancing the beer on his stomach.

"I'm gonna explode if we don't get out of here!" Serge leaped off the couch. "I have no choice but to call it!"

"Night Tour?" asked Coleman.

"Night Tour!" said Serge.

"Righteous." Coleman climbed off the couch and rummaged through the fridge for a cold one for the road. "Will we be going by any place to eat?"

"I was thinking of Fat Guys."

"That's a buffet," said Coleman. "I better smoke a joint in the car so I can get my money's worth."

"If you eat enough, theoretically you can actually start *making* money."

"I'll bring two joints."

They jumped in the Barracuda, and Serge stuck a CD in the stereo and cranked it, *Spirit in the Sky.*

"Where first?" asked Coleman.

"Dale Mabry Highway. Tampa's spinal cord. We need to check the pulse of the night." They passed steak houses, lube shops, fern bars.

"I love main drags," said Serge. "They're so egalitarian. Biscayne Boulevard in Miami, U.S. 41 in Naples, A1A in Fort Lauderdale."

"Who's Dale Mabry, anyway?" asked Coleman.

"The most uttered name in Tampa, and maybe five people know who he was—local real estate man before he left to fight in World War One and later died in a 1922 blimp crash in Norfolk, Virginia."

Coleman pointed out the window. "Sure has a lot of strip clubs."

"We're known far and wide. You mention to any guy in America that you're from Tampa and he'll go, 'Oh, the Mons Venus.' It's our cash crop."

"Why?"

"Two reasons: quality and quantity. End of story. The clubs popped up like toadstools over the last couple decades because of city-council neglect. Now the mayor's trying to undo the damage through ruthless fiat. He just declared The War on Titty Bars."

"Sounds like another Vietnam," said Coleman. "Why now?"

"It's sweeps week. The man's no media fool. Every TV station in town has a giant video library of stock footage taken at discreet angles of strippers swinging around those poles. They're just drooling for an excuse to put that footage on the air under the pretext of being shocked and offended by the footage."

"This could hit us in the wallet," said Coleman. "Sharon buys a lot of our groceries with those lap dances."

"I know," said Serge. "That was the part of our portfolio I was counting on to keep us recession-proof. If the mayor succeeds, we may be forced to lower our moral code and start pimping Sharon as a Hooters waitress."

"What are his chances?"

"Damn good. He laid the groundwork last week by gathering a hundred of the city's most prominent clergy to view police videos that revealed exactly what kind of Sodom and Gomorrah we've become."

"Sharon told me she was in one of the videos."

"She was. It showed her sitting on stage with her legs apart, and some lucky gentleman who had paid ten dollars was working a remote control box, driving a Tonka truck with a dildo taped to the roof. The clergy was so horrified that they had to move the next day's viewing to a larger auditorium."

"Fat Guys is coming up," said Coleman. "Left lane."

Serge turned into the restaurant parking lot. They went inside and grabbed trays. Coleman was about to pick up an all-you-can-eat plate when Serge grabbed his arm. "The one-trip bowl is a better value."

"But the bowl is too small," said Coleman.

"And that's where they think they've got you, but don't fall into the trap." Serge reached for a bunch of celery sticks. "What you have to do is make yourself a bigger bowl. Watch carefully. First, you make a wrap-around cantilevered balcony with the celery. Then you mortar it in place with potato salad and anchor it all with the heavy stuff, pickles and hard-boiled eggs."

"Wow, now the bowl's huge."

"And perfectly legal."

"Where'd you learn that?"

"Watching the college kids. They're way out ahead in these areas."

Serge and Coleman slid their trays down the line until they got to the cashier. She stared at Coleman's tray an unusually long time, then at Coleman, then made change.

They picked up their trays and headed for a table.

"Why was she looking at me like that?" asked Coleman.

"Respect."

"Should I ask her out?"

"Absolutely. But be patient. You want to give a great first impression like that time to build in her mind."

They sat down at a table surrounded by families. Coleman looked at Serge's plate. Baked potato, french fries, potato soup, potato pancakes, ravioli and rigatoni.

"How's the diet coming?"

"Can't tell yet," said Serge.

"What are you on, the no-starch diet?"

"I was," said Serge. "But it wasn't working. Now I'm on the *all-*starch diet."

"Never heard of it."

"That's because nobody's done it before. Nobody's ever *dared.*"

"You're sort of like a pioneer?"

"I just want to participate in my times," said Serge, hammering the bottom of a ketchup bottle for the fries. "I'm riding the mood of my country."

"I thought it was about losing weight."

"The masses out there are lost," said Serge. "They're looking for something, anything. Right now they're following people who eat a bunch of crazy stuff. Like that doctor who came up with the all-protein diet. What kind of bullshit is that? Bacon and eggs and pork and hamburgers. The guy puts out a book that says eat all the wrong stuff, and now he's so rich he can go back to eating healthy."

"I think I've heard of that diet," said Coleman.

"I think you're *on* it."

Coleman picked up a buffalo wing. "Wow, I never thought of myself as a health nut."

"That's why you have to watch the news, to know where you stand at all times."

Coleman reached for one of Serge's french fries. Serge slapped his hand.

"Ouch!"

Serge pointed at the fries. "These have been counted. I'm taking notes."

"Notes?"

"If the diet works, they'll give me a book deal."

"They give you a book for eating fries?"

Serge speared a ravioli. "I've always wanted to be a writer."

"That sounds crazy," said Coleman.

"I don't make the rules. I just follow 'em. . . . Finish up. We'll hit the bookstore across the street. It'll help explain a lot of this."

They left their car at the restaurant and darted through traffic and into the giant new bookstore in town, Barnes & Borders.

"What do you think?"

Coleman looked concerned. "Everyone's sitting around reading. Why don't the store people get mad?"

"Something else that's changed," said Serge. "Nobody yells, 'What do you think this is, a library?' Now, you're *supposed* to sit and read. This is what I've been talking about. Everything's now the opposite. You weren't supposed to eat meat. Now, you are. You're supposed to read the magazines. Rob Lowe's working again . . ."

"Who can keep it all straight?" asked Coleman.

"It's nerve-racking, I tell you. No wonder people are going back to religion."

Serge led Coleman over to the health section and the display of books at the end of an aisle. *The Sugar-Busters Diet, The Carbohydrate Addicts Diet, Ten Days to a New You, Rediscover the Old You, Yoga a Go-Go, Natural Remedies That Can Kill You, Burn Fat Through Exercise, Prescription for Peak Performance, The Peak Performance Myth, Declare War on Love Handles, Surrender to Success, The Low-Expectations Revolution, Calcium Crackdown, Strong Colon for Public Speakers, Take a Pass on Bypass, Cooking Right 4 Unwanted Guests, The Complete Menopause Vacation Planner, Eat All You Want and Ignore Everyone, Time Out for a Breakdown, 101 Desserts for Multiple Personalities* and *Eliminate Stress Through Hysterical Screaming*.

"Look at how these are shelved. What a mess!" Serge began aligning books.

A customer mistook him for an employee.

"Can you help me find the self-help books?"

"No."

Serge and Coleman went over to the coffee shop. They grabbed magazines and a table by the window.

"This is a pretty nice setup," said Coleman.

"It's the new café society," said Serge. "Just like Paris."

Serge read *The New Republic*, and Coleman flipped a *High Times* open to a hotel-rating guide for a psilocybin tour of the Yucatán.

Serge stood up. "I need some coffee."

He went to the counter. A waif with a pierced tongue greeted him. "Mmgtgh skjhje?"

"What?"

"Mmgtgh skjhje?"

"What? I can't understand you . . . Holy God! You've got a piece of metal rammed through your tongue! Don't move—I'll get help! . . ."

The café manager stepped up. "Everything's fine. Can I get you something?"

Serge stared at the first woman a moment, then turned to the manager: "Coffee."

"Latte? Mocha? Café con leche?"

"Coffee."

"Chicory? Raspberry espresso? Frappuccino?"

"Coffee."

"Decaf almondine? Cinnamon Explosion? . . ."

"Never mind."

He walked back to the table.

"What the matter?" asked Coleman.

"They don't have any coffee. Let's get out of here."

They headed south through the Tampa night again, grooving on the moment. Traffic raced by on both sides. Sports cars, motorcycles, pizza-delivery trucks. Serge and Coleman smiled. This was their town. Serge began tapping the steering wheel and singing: *"Conjunction Junction, what's your function? . . ."*

Coleman: *"Hookin' up words and phrases and clauses . . ."*

Serge made a left into a grid-street neighborhood. It was a dark road, and he slowed the Barracuda to a crawl. The street was empty. He rolled down his window.

"You know what job I want?" said Coleman, pulling a joint from behind his ear and lighting it.

"I don't know. Guidance counselor?" Serge leaned across Coleman's lap and opened the glove compartment. He dug out a garage-door opener.

"You know how all those soul bands back in the seventies had some guy who would scream, *'Say what?'*"

Serge rolled by a house and pointed the remote control out his window and pressed the button. Nothing happened.

"That's the job I want," said Coleman. He took a double-toke and held it.

"What job is that?" asked Serge. He rolled by the next house and pressed the button again. Still nothing.

"I want the job of the guy who goes, '*Say what?*'"

"You're uniquely qualified," said Serge. He pointed the remote control and pressed again. Nothing.

Coleman exhaled a hit. "Check it out: *Say what?*"

Serge kept clicking the remote control without result.

"*Say what?*"

Serge looked both ways as he crossed a well-lit intersection.

"*Say what?*"

They continued into the darkness of the grid street on the other side.

"*Say what?*"

"Now it's annoying." Serge clicked the remote again.

"Sorry," said Coleman. He thought a second, took a hit. "If I can't get that job, I want the job of that tiny little fucker who screams on Sly and the Family Stone."

"I know his work," said Serge, clicking the remote again.

"I think there are several of 'em," said Coleman. "I've heard the same vocals on Kool and the Gang and the Edgar Winter Group, to name but a few."

"A cottage industry of James Brown midgets."

"Check this out: '*Yaaaaaaaaaaaaaaaaa-Hiiiiiiiiiiiiiiii!*'"

"Again, impressive."

Coleman grinned and nodded and took another hit. "That's why I really never worry about being unemployed. If push comes to shove, I always have that."

Serge clicked the remote. A garage door began rising. Serge stopped the car.

"This is the Eagle. We have lunar-module separation," said Serge. "Prepare for cabin depressurization and space walk."

"Roger," said Coleman. He grabbed Serge's flashlight and jumped from the car.

Serge soon saw a flashlight beam swooping around inside the garage. Then Coleman disappeared behind the parked car. The flashlight swooped across the ceiling. It was starting to take a long time. There were some noises, just a little at first, things dropping, pliers and screwdrivers. The flashlight went out. More noise. Serge could see Coleman's silhouette knocking over something, then hearing the crash, *then* reaching to try to catch it before it fell, only sending more things over, until Coleman built to his big *1812 Overture* finale, crashing into a set of metal garbage cans. One of the cans began rolling down the driveway. A light went on in the garage, and a man's voice: "What the hell's going on out there!"

Coleman came running down the driveway with something in his right hand. He stumbled and accidentally kicked the garbage can rolling ahead of him, sending it slamming into the side of the Barracuda. Serge stuck his head out the driver's window and looked down at the paint job.

The porch light went on, then a floodlight. Coleman jumped in the car. Serge hit the gas and sped off as a man in a bathrobe came out the front door with a shotgun.

They were three blocks away before Serge turned and saw what Coleman had taken from the garage.

"Electric pepper mill?"

"Is that what this is?" said Coleman.

"What the hell were you thinking?"

"It looked expensive in the dark."

"It's a piece of crap. It's for people with more money than imagination."

"We can always pawn it."

"It might bring five dollars on Crack Street, but that's it." Serge looked around the car. "Where's my flashlight?"

"I must have left it."

"Nice going, Rico Suave. That was my sentimental flashlight. Cost twenty-nine bucks." He pointed at the pepper mill: "We're losing ground."

Coleman pressed a button on the pepper mill; an electric motor began to whir. "Hey, it works." Coleman held the mill in front of Serge's face and pressed the button again. "See?"

"Get that fucking thing out of my face. I'm trying to drive."

Coleman removed it from Serge's face and began playing with it in his lap. "I'll bet I can use it to grind up dope."

Serge pulled out of the neighborhood and turned right on Gandy Boulevard. "There's the Seven-Eleven," he said. "It you want real coffee these days, forget the bookstores. This is where you have to go."

"I like those little creamers they have," said Coleman.

"Me too," said Serge, pulling into the parking lot. "The lavender ones are my favorite. I usually get about five of those and another five packs of sugars, dump it all in a piping-hot twenty-ounce Styrofoam cup, add a dozen ice cubes and chug the whole thing right at the cash register. After that, watch out! I once pulled back on the highway without my car."

Serge got out of the Barracuda and began taking pictures in the parking lot. He lowered the camera to check for a better angle. "This is a historic place."

"Historic Seven-Eleven?"

"Not the store. The location." He snapped more pictures. "The store didn't used to be here. They just built in on the corner. See what's wrapped around the back?"

"Yeah, an old motel nobody's staying at."

"Not just any motel," corrected Serge. "The Crosstown Inn. It's where Donald Segretti stayed."

"Who?"

"One of Nixon's henchmen. He stayed at the Crosstown when he was playing dirty tricks on the Democrats. Ever see *All the President's Men*?"

"No."

"Remember the scene where Dustin Hoffman and Robert Redford are going through Segretti's credit card receipts?"

"I didn't see the movie."

"If you put the VCR on pause, you can see a receipt for the Crosstown Inn." Serge turned and snapped more pictures, then lowered the camera. "If you watch an entire movie frame by frame, it's amazing what you'll find. That's what I do."

"Let's go in and get some beer."

"Hold on. I'm not done." Click, click. "It's stuck in a 1972 time warp! Can you feel it? Look at that old sign, the retro architecture of the office. I can just see Segretti checking in"—Serge started creeping around the parking lot—"looking over his shoulders, making calls from the pay phone, using code words like 'Condor' and 'The Package.'"

"You kinda like history, don't you?" said Coleman.

Serge straightened up. "Who doesn't? Let's get some coffee."

Serge pushed open both front doors of the 7-Eleven at once— Doc Holiday entering a saloon. He threw his arms out wide: "My people! I am home!"

The customers stopped and turned to see what the noise was about, then ignored him. They fell in three groups. Some were drunk. Others had been drunk. The rest would soon be drunk. That was it.

"What? No welcoming party?"

"Hi, Serge," said one of the clerks.

"What's shakin', Serge?" asked the woman in the deli.

"That's more like it," said Serge. "I could live in a convenience store. No fooling around. Everything's close to the bone."

"Beer," said Coleman, pointing at a stack of Bud twelve-packs.

"This place is like a proletariat terrarium. The salt of the earth."

"Beer."

"Okay. Go get your beer. I'll be at the coffee."

Serge grabbed a cup and picked up the coffeepot. He held it to his nose, sniffed and smiled. "February was a good month."

He filled his cup three-quarters, leaving room for creamers, sugar and ice. He went to the front counter and got in line. There were seven people ahead of him, six buying lottery tickets and one buying a lottery magazine.

Coleman arrived with a Budweiser suitcase in each hand and joined Serge in the back of the line. Serge twisted and fidgeted and stood on his tiptoes to see up to the counter. "What's the delay?"

The line bled down to the last customer in front of Serge, a middle-aged woman in jumbo sweatpants and a T-shirt with a rebel flag.

"What do you think about this Confederate flag controversy?" Coleman asked Serge.

"Sometimes people adopt fashions that say things about themselves they don't even realize they're revealing."

"What do you mean?" asked Coleman, munching a beef jerky and wearing a baseball cap that said, OFFICIAL PUSSY INSPECTOR.

"I'll explain later."

The woman in the sweatpants dropped a pile of candy bars on the counter and handed the clerk a lottery card.

The clerk stuck the card in the machine; a ticket popped out.

"Those are my lucky numbers," said the woman. "They're the birthdays of my cats."

"That so?" said the clerk. She handed her the ticket.

"Oh, what the hay!" she said. "I feel lucky. Give me a Quick Pick!"

The clerk gave her a Quick Pick.

The woman pointed down through the glass counter at the vibrant rolls of instant scratch-off tickets. Cowboy Cash, Lucky Seven, Gold Rush, Treasure Island. A strip of tickets with flying saucers grabbed her eye. "That a new game?"

"Which?"

"UFO Dough."

The clerk said yes.

"Give me one."

The clerk gave her one.

The woman leaned over the counter and rubbed the ticket with a quarter.

Serge spun around and grabbed Coleman by the shoulders. "Oh my God! She's scratching them off at the counter!"

"Easy," said Coleman.

The woman finished rubbing. "Fudge! I lost. Better give me another."

She scratched again with the quarter. No luck.

"Well, easy come, easy go." The woman began rummaging in a purse that was the extra-large size favored by refugees and klepto-maniacs. She eventually came up with a personalized checkbook imprinted with cats.

Serge turned and grabbed Coleman's shirt again. "Sweet Jesus! She's paying by check!"

"Hang in there," said Coleman.

The clerk bagged the candy bars. "You can use a check for this stuff, but you have to pay cash for the lottery tickets. State law."

"Oh, heavens," said the woman, beginning another excavation in her purse. She came up with a peanut butter jar. "How many pennies can you take?"

A fist slammed down on the counter. The startled woman jumped back and saw Serge.

"Bzzzzzzzzzzzz! That's our final buzzer. Time's up. You lose. Collect your shit and move along to extinction."

The woman was taken aback. "Well, I never! . . ."

"Pipe down, Chumley! I don't know what black hole of personal ambition you climbed out of, but it's now time to skee-daddle on back, you Crisco-based life-form."

The woman put a hand up to her open mouth, then ran out the door. Serge stepped up to the counter. He set the coffee down and opened his wallet.

"Dollar-six," said the cashier, blowing a bubble with her gum.

"Ever see the independent movie *Clerks*?" asked Serge, handing over exact change.

"No," said the clerk. "What's it about?"

"It's about your struggle, sister!" Serge held up a fist of solidarity.

Then he picked up the coffee and downed it all at once. He set the empty cup on the counter and gave a satisfied "Ahhhhhh," hydraulics venting pressure.

Coleman took a cautious step back. The clerk saw Coleman and took her own step back.

All was quiet for a moment. Then the tremors started, first in his legs, moving quickly up his body like the coyote after he eats ACME earthquake pills. When they reached his neck, the babbling started.

"*Al Lang, Jack Russell, Doak Campbell, Joker Marchant, Chain O'Lakes, Tropicana, Raymond James, Pro Player, O'Connell Center . . .*"

"What's he saying?" asked the clerk.

"He's naming Florida sports venues."

"*. . . Gulfstream, Brian Piccolo Park Velodrome . . .*"

"Why?" asked the clerk.

"Because he drank coffee. It makes his brain incontinent. The state's aquifers should be coming up next."

"... *Floridan, Biscayne, Chocoloskee, Hawthorn, Tampa Limestone* ..."

"Now the endangered flowers."

"... *Dingy Epidendrum, Delicate Ionopsis, Rose Pogonia, Yellow Rhexia, Teyrazygia* ..."

"The lighthouses ..."

"... *Jupiter Inlet, Rebecca Shoal, Sombrero Key, Fowey Rocks, Alligator Reef, Boca Grande—middle and south, Cape Saint George* ..."

"And the original Indians ..."

"... *Calusa, Tequesta, Tocobaga, Timucua, Apalachee* ..."

"Finally his favorite roadside attractions ..."

"... *Weeki Wachee, Tupperware Museum, defunct Xanadu home of the future, Alternate Highway 19 Chimp Farm, Pasco County Taxidermy Museum (with two-headed cow)* ..."

Serge stopped and jerked his head around in terror, screeching like a cornered animal. He bolted out the door. Coleman and the clerk ran to the window. Serge loped across the parking lot, arms swinging low to the ground. He ran out into the busy intersection. Drivers slammed on brakes and skidded sideways. Stopped cars filled the road at all angles. Serge jumped up on one of the hoods and screeched some more. He beat his chest with his fists before running across the intersection on the roofs of cars and disappearing into the night.

"Unbelievable," said the clerk. "He actually thinks he's a monkey."

"No," said Coleman. "He thinks he's an actor. He's doing a scene from *Altered States*. It's one of his favorites."

29

COLEMAN STOOD in the middle of a dark intersection in one of south Tampa's grid neighborhoods, giving his arms a rest. When feeling returned to his shoulders, he reached down and picked up the Budweiser suitcases at his feet. If only Serge hadn't run off with the car keys. He walked some more, but his arms tired quickly. Coleman set the cardboard boxes down again. When he did, the pepper mill in his back pocket began to whir. He reached and turned it off.

Coleman got an idea. He figured if he started drinking the beer, it wouldn't weigh as much. He put the boxes down again.

After sixteen blocks, Coleman had finished enough beer to consolidate the remaining cans into one suitcase. He took a rest near the Crosstown Expressway, smoking an emergency joint he kept in his shoe. Coleman saw a shadow near the top of the expressway embankment. He squinted at the dim form. Coleman guessed it was a woman because of the high heels and breasts, but of course that could mean any number of things. The tall figure climbed awkwardly over the concertina wire fencing off the highway from the adjacent neighborhood. She had a large, cumbersome object that took two arms to carry.

She started down the embankment. Something went wrong early. A heel got caught, and she went over. The woman and the object began tumbling separately until a ditch stopped them. Coleman ran over and helped her up, a streetwalker in red leather hot pants and halter top. He retrieved the large object from the ditch and handed it to her.

"Thanks."

"What is it?" asked Coleman.

"Meat smoker."

"I have a pepper mill." Coleman pulled it out of his back pocket and pressed a button. "It's electric."

"I'll bet I could use it to mix cocaine and baby laxative. Wanna trade?"

"Sure."

THEY WAVED GOOD-BYE. The prostitute went one way with the pepper mill, and Coleman went the other with the smoker. He had put the beer in the cooker's top compartment and lifted it by the handles.

Coleman headed into a dark neighborhood on another grid street. He went only one block before he had to set the smoker down. He was making poor time with the extra load and began to consider it a shit trade. He saw a pedestrian cross the street up ahead, carrying something, then disappear. Coleman picked up the smoker and went a block. He saw someone else on foot carrying something.

As Coleman continued on, the number of fellow pedestrians increased until it was steady flow on both sides of the street, everyone carrying something. Toaster oven, bug zapper, fax machine.

Coleman ran into a man at the corner of the fifth block. He coveted what the man had; the man eyed Coleman's smoker.

"Trade?" said Coleman.

"Deal."

The man went off in one direction with the meat smoker and Coleman in another, pedaling a three-wheeled senior citizen's bike with a ringer on the handlebars and a case of beer under the seat. He stood up to give the pedaling an extra oomph as he crossed the drainage crest of another intersection. Then he sat back down and coasted with no hands, drinking a beer and ringing the bell.

He reached the next intersection and more pedestrians poured in from side roads and congregated under a stretch of oaks. So that's it, thought Coleman. Crack Street.

Dealers worked brazenly on the curb. Business was so brisk it was spinning off support industry. Coleman recognized a man operating a floating pawnshop from the bed of a pickup. It was a prix fixe operation. Ten dollars for everything. CD player? Ten bucks. Laptop computer? Ten bucks. A line of people had formed behind the pickup with lawnmowers, rifles, microwaves and a pepper mill. Coleman was getting hungry. If only they had a sausage wagon or snow-cone cart. But it was no use even hoping. Coleman knew crackheads were like camels when it came to food and water. He pedaled on.

Seven blocks later, he stopped at a corner and saw fluorescent lights. A twenty-four-hour grocery. Coleman took a deep breath and leaned into the pedals again.

TWO PIZZA TRUCKS sped past the corner of San Clemente and San Obispo, where the local crime watch unit was keeping a lookout in Jim Davenport's Suburban.

"I told you this would be fun," said Satchel.

A car pulled up and a man got out on the passenger's side. "Is this the crime watch?"

"Yes it is," said Satchel. "You need anything?"

"Yeah." He stuck a gun in the window. "Your wallets and those walkie-talkies."

They sat for a while without speaking after that.

"Look on the bright side," said Satchel. "It can't get any worse."

Another car pulled up. A gun came in the window.

"Gimme the car."

"DOES ANYONE KNOW where we are?" asked Jim, standing in the middle of the street.

"I think we go that way," said Wilma.

"We just came from that way," said Jim.

"I thought it looked familiar," said Orville.

"How lost can we be?" said Satchel. "Let's just pick a direction and start walking."

They came to an overpass.

"The expressway," said Orville. "See? We're not lost."

"Why don't we grab a taxi?" asked Satchel.

"You see any taxis?" said Jim.

"We'll call one from a pay phone."

"You see any pay phones?"

"We'll find one if we keep walking."

A wino scurried to the expressway toll basket and stuck his arm down the hole. Dark forms milled about under the bridge. Up on the overpass, youths balanced concrete blocks on the railing, ready to drop on cars.

"Let's go the other way," said Jim.

They came to a dark intersection and looked both ways. A block to the right, a figure crossed the street on a large tricycle. To the left, a hooker pushed a gas grill on wheels. Ahead, some men hung back at the end of an alley, watching them.

"This way," said Orville.

At the next corner, a man sat at the base of a stop sign, drinking from a paper bag. He pointed at the four of them. "Y'all be bullshit! You know I'm right! Y'all be bullshit! . . ."

"This way," said Wilma.

They turned the corner and saw a boarded-up gas station. "A pay phone!" said Jim. He ran to it. The phone book was gone and the receiver had been torn out by the wires. A man in a Cadillac slowed as he passed, looked Wilma over, and sped up. The Caddy stopped a block ahead, helped a hooker put a gas grill in the trunk, and they drove off together.

"We're just going in circles," said Jim. "That's the same hooker."

"Let's go back this way," said Satchel. "At least the expressway was a landmark."

They passed the man at the stop sign again. "Y'all be bullshit *and* lost! Ha ha ha ha!"

They made a right.

Whoops. Crack Street. They made a left, past the floating pawnshop in the pickup.

"Look!" said Wilma, pointing at the back of the truck. "Our walkie-talkies!"

"Give those back to us!" said Satchel.

"Fuck yourself!"

"You better give them back! We're the crime watch!"

"Ooooo! Look at me, I'm shaking!"

"We're the eyes and ears of the police," Satchel warned him. "We'll report you."

"With what?"

"With our walkie . . ."

"Let's go," said Jim.

Three more blocks.

"I can see light from a sign," said Jim. "That means a store. And probably a pay phone."

He was right. A small twenty-four-hour grocery with a big tricycle out front. Jim saw a phone at the corner of the parking lot and headed for it.

A big-shouldered man in a sharkskin suit leaned against the hood of a black Mercedes parked next to the phone. Jim reached for the receiver.

"Don't touch that."

"But I need to use it," said Jim.

"I'm expecting a call."

"This is sort of an emergency. I need to call a taxi. Just be a second."

The man pulled back the right side of his jacket to reveal a shoulder holster.

"It's all yours." Jim walked quickly back to the others in front of the grocery.

"Did you call a taxi?" asked Wilma.

"I think it would be better to use the phone inside," said Jim. The crime watch headed for the the automatic front doors.

Behind them, stereos thumped in the passing traffic. It was now 3 A.M., the sexually desperate portion of the program. A man driving alone in a Datsun began wondering why his neon license plate frame and GAS, GRASS OR ASS bumper sticker weren't working. Those who not had sex the longest would soon begin pulling people out of cars and beating them.

Serge walked out the end of a grid street from a dark neighborhood and into the greenish fluorescent light outside a twenty-four-hour grocery store. A black Mercedes sat on the edge of the parking lot next to the pay phone. There was nobody in the car or near the phone. It began to ring. Serge answered it.

"*You got The Package?*"

"Yeah, I got The Package," said Serge. "Meet you at the Crosstown Inn."

"*Hey, that's not where we were supposed to meet.*"

"Plans have changed, Condor."

"*Condor? What the fuck are you talking about? Hey, you're not Vince!*"

"No, I'm not."

"*Who the hell are you?!*"

"Segretti."

"*Segretti? Who the fuck's Segretti?*"

"Segretti's calling the shots now. You want The Package, you come to the Crosstown!"

"*Fuck you! I'll kill you! I'll—*"

"Don't you threaten me!" said Serge, ripping the receiver out of the phone.

A large-framed man in a sharkskin suit came out of the grocery store unwrapping a pack of cigarettes and heading for the Mercedes. He saw Serge at the pay phone.

"That phone didn't ring, did it?" he asked Serge.

"Are you Vince?"

"Yeah. How'd you know?"

"I answered the phone a minute ago. Someone said they wanted to see Vince right away at the Crosstown Inn."

"That's not where we're supposed to meet."

"That's all I know," said Serge. "I'm just walking by and the phone rang, so I picked it up because that's the kind of guy I am."

"Something's not right here." Vince took a menacing step toward Serge.

Serge didn't flinch. "Damn straight something's not right. You'd think the V.A. hospital would know how to treat leprosy after all these years. You know why they can't? Because they're all androids. *I looked.*"

It was Serge's turn to take a step forward, and Vince backed up. "Get away from me, you crazy motherfucker!" Vince jumped in the Mercedes and took off.

"Is it my breath?" Serge cupped his hands over his mouth to check.

He began walking again, past the grocery store with the oversized tricycle parked out front. He came to the edge of the road, crossed it, and disappeared into the darkness of the grid streets.

Back inside the store, the crime watch stood in an ammonia haze near the registers. Number Six was open, the cashier going extra slow so she wouldn't break two-inch chartreuse nails. She had worked the graveyard shift for three years, but hadn't made the connection with her facial tattoos. The cast of *The Rocky Horror Picture Show* was in line at the register, buying beer, wine and over-the-counter remedies addressing all stages of digestion.

Jim walked up to the cashier. "I have to use the phone."

"There's a pay phone out front."

"It's in use. Can I make a call on the office phone?"

"Customers have to use the pay phone. Policy."

"But it's kind of an emergency—"

There was a rising grumble in the line at the register. Jim looked up; they were all staring daggers.

Jim walked back to the others.

"Will they let us use the phone?" asked Orville.

"It's best we find another . . ." Jim saw someone over by the milk. "I think I recognize that guy. He lives on my street."

Coleman stood at the dairy case and grabbed an aerosol can of whipped cream. He stuck the end in his mouth and sprayed. For some reason, regular aerosol doesn't work with whipped cream, and they have to use nitrous oxide instead. And, sitting on a grocery shelf, the laughing gas separates and rises to the top of the cream.

"You again!" yelled the night manager. "I told you to stay out of my whipped cream!"

Coleman dropped the can and stumbled. Sounds whooped and echoed in his head. He tried to take off running, but his equilibrium gyroscope was spinning on the wrong axis and he went sideways instead, plowing through an eight-foot promotional pyramid of Velveeta Lite.

"This time you're paying for it all!" said the manager, pointing at two dozen spent cans of whipped cream scattered in the bottom of the dairy case. The manager grabbed Coleman by the arm. "I want to see some green! Now!"

Coleman reached down the neck of his shirt and pulled out two fifties. He gave it to the manager, who slapped a cardboard box into Coleman's stomach and told him to pack up the empties, get the hell out of his store and never come back.

Jim waited until the manager had walked away. "Excuse me? Aren't you one of my neighbors?"

"I yam what I yam. Yug-gug-gug-gug-gug."

The crime watch stared.

"That's Popeye," said Coleman, filling his box with whipped cream cans.

"Do you think you can take us home?" asked Jim.

"Sure," said Coleman. "C'mon."

Jim stared at Coleman's chest. Something was wrong. But he was too discreet to say anything.

Not Satchel. "Hey! What's wrong with the man's tits?"

Coleman looked down at his chest. "Oh, that. It's much too dangerous to carry money around this town at night. You got to have a money belt. Except they were all out of money belts and I was drunk, so I got the money bra."

He pulled three hundred dollars out of his shirt as some kind of proof, then tucked it back.

"Why do you have so much cash on you?" asked Jim.

"You mean you don't carry bail money?"

"Not usually."

Coleman led them out the front door and stowed the box of whipped cream under his tricycle seat.

"I thought you had a car," said Jim.

"I did," said Coleman. "But I got in a wreck, and the insurance company refused to pay because I didn't have insurance."

"Look, the pay phone's free," said Wilma.

"Where'd the receiver go?" said Jim.

Coleman began pedaling down the street and the crime watch followed single file like baby ducks. He made a left, a right.

A pawnbroker in the back of a pickup waved. "Hey Coleman, what's the word?"

Coleman waved back. He went two more blocks. A man sat at

the base of a stop sign drinking from a paper sack. "Coleman! The Mac Daddy! Why you lettin' those people follow you around? That's bullshit stickin' to *your* ass! Ha ha ha ha!"

Coleman waved and pedaled on. He got to the expressway interchange and stopped. He yelled up at the kids on the overpass.

"It's me, Coleman. Don't drop no blocks. I'm comin' under."

"Okay, Coleman."

They went under the overpass.

SERGE CROSSED GANDY Boulevard on foot and reached the 7-Eleven just as the coffee wore off. He climbed back in the Barracuda and drove to the edge of the parking lot. He leaned out the window and took a last picture of the Crosstown Inn, where three sedans were parked at odd angles, people yelling, then gunshots. Serge pulled into traffic.

He sped north. Up ahead, something was going on at the side of the road. He hugged the center line and slowed as he passed a parade of pedestrians led by an adult tricycle. Serge pulled over in front of the trike and threw the keys to Coleman, who opened the trunk. Coleman put the tricycle inside, tied the lid down and climbed in the front seat next to Serge without speaking, as if this were a regularly scheduled bus stop.

Serge looked over his shoulder at the others. "You guys getting in?"

The crime watch got in, and the Barracuda drove off.

"Excellent Night Tour," said Coleman.

"Haven't had a bad one yet," said Serge.

30

THE BARRACUDA TURNED onto Triggerfish Lane and pulled up in front of Serge and Coleman's rental house. The crime watch crawled out of the car and thanked them for the lift.

Orville stopped on the sidewalk and pointed across the street. "Hey Jim, what's that in front of your house?"

"It looks like your stolen car," said Satchel.

"It *is* my stolen car."

"They must have dumped it in front of your place."

"What are the odds?" said Wilma. "This must be your lucky day!"

They walked up the driveway and went inside, and Jim immediately called the police for insurance documentation.

"I want to report a stolen car. . . . Yes, my wife called earlier in the week . . . No, that was a different stolen car . . . This one's my car . . . It's at my house right now . . . No, it was stolen somewhere else and brought here . . . I *know* it usually works the other way . . ."

Martha made coffee and opened a bag of Keeblers. Wilma, Orville and Satchel told and retold the evening's adventure as if it were the best thing that had ever happened to them. Then they called cabs.

Orville was watching for his taxi when he noticed something going on out the front window.

"Hey Jim, what's that guy doing out there?"

"Where?" said Jim.

Orville pointed out the window, and Jim came over and watched a police tow truck drive off with the Suburban.

JIM LAY IN bed on his stomach. Martha gave him a back massage.

"Don't get too down on yourself," she said. "You've had a pretty rough day."

"You wouldn't believe what I saw tonight. I may never be able to sleep again knowing what's going on out there after we go to bed."

"You need some TV. Always helps me sleep." Martha grabbed the remote from the nightstand and clicked on the set atop the dresser.

A studio audience applauded as a knockoff Regis and Kathy Lee hawked kitchen gadgets. A toll-free number crawled across the bottom of the screen.

"Unbelievable," said Jim. "People actually buy this stuff?"

"See? It's already taking your mind off it."

"I can't believe people are actually sitting in that audience."

"It's an infomercial," said Martha, kneading Jim's shoulders.

"I didn't even know this was going on."

"That's because you're never up at this hour."

"What normal person is?"

ACROSS THE STREET, Serge and Sharon were in their bedroom breaking lamps, throwing ashtrays, pulling knives and otherwise making love. Serge wrestled Sharon onto her back, her head pointed toward the foot of the bed. She struggled, but he restrained her without mercy, then penetrated. Again and again. Then he grabbed the remote and clicked on the TV set atop the dresser to watch a little tube during the dull parts.

"*Harder! Harder! Harder!*" Sharon yelled. "*Faster! Faster! Faster!*"

Her long, exquisite legs shot straight up in the air, and Serge grabbed her ankles and pushed all the way back, pinning them next to her ears.

"*Yes! Yes! Yes! Fuck me! Fuck me! Fuck me harder! I'm an animal! Fuck the dirty animal!*"

Serge thrust harder and changed channels until he found an infomercial. "Hey, that's that couple selling all those stupid kitchen gadgets. I bet half that stuff doesn't even work."

"Hurt me! Hurt me, you bad man!"

"What an incredible part of our culture," said Serge, maintaining rhythm. "Look at that studio audience. You want to know why the government is so awful? It's because these jelly-heads can vote."

"Oh God! Where's your flashlight? Put your flashlight in my butt!"

"I can't. Coleman dropped the fucking thing at a burglary. I *told* him it had sentimental value."

"Don't stop! Don't stop! Oh God, don't stop!"

"But where do they find the people to fill the studio audience? That's the part that baffles me. What kind of horrible sadness and broken lives do they come from that this travesty is an improvement?"

"I'm coming! I'm coming! Oh God, I'm coming!"

"They're just looking for approval. That's what it is. They need love, even it's fake and they have to buy a Cuisinart to get it. That's how badly damaged the family unit is in this country."

"I'm coming! Here it is! . . . Yi! Yi! Yi! Yi! Yi! Yi! Yi! Yi! Yi! Yi! Yi! Yi! . . ."

"Still, someone has to be calling in and buying this stuff, or they wouldn't keep purchasing these time slots. But who is their audience? Who is up at this ungodly hour buying this ridiculous shit?"

On the other side of the wall, Coleman was watching television with a beer in one hand and a phone in the other.

"Yes, I'd like to order the electric pepper mill."

31

YELLOW CRIME TAPE fluttered in a stairwell off Busch Boulevard. A sergeant from the Tampa Police Department was stationed in one of the upstairs units, guarding the crime scene. On the carpet was the chalk outline where a man in a silk Japanese robe had landed. The sergeant sat on the couch watching TV, squinting with his head cocked sideways, trying to make out a nipple on a scrambled channel. He lit the stub of a cigar and stuck the lighter in his pocket. There was a knock at the open door.

The sergeant looked up and saw a middle-aged man in rumpled slacks, pink shirt and tweed sports coat. He wore a fedora at a bygone angle. His black tie had hula dancers.

The man stepped inside and flashed a gold badge. "Agent Mahoney. Florida Department of Law Enforcement."

The sergeant stood up and turned off the TV. "No, I'm Sergeant Drysdale. I don't know any Agent Mahoney."

"No, *I'm* Mahoney."

"You should have said so."

Mahoney glared at the sergeant. "Obtuse bastard."

"Ambiguous son of a bitch."

"Let's start over," said Mahoney.

"Fine with me."

"What have we got here?"

"Neighbors got suspicious because of the naked woman bleeding and crying in the parking lot. Uniformed officers canvassed the place, found a man in a Kabuki robe shot to death in a crack den across the street from a theme park."

Mahoney shook his head ruefully. "If I had a nickel every time I heard that . . ."

". . . You'd have a lot of nickels."

"World's changing," said Mahoney. "I can remember when you could leave your front door unlocked."

"I can remember when the juvenile delinquents were the kids who toilet-papered the principal's house," said the sergeant.

"I can remember when convenience stores closed at eleven," said Mahoney. "Everyone was in bed at a decent hour."

"I can remember when you could walk the streets safe at night and not have to worry about being approached by an undercover cop posing as a hooker, and you feel sorry for her and give her cab money and then have to spend the next six months explaining it to internal affairs."

"It was a simpler time."

"Cab money was cab money. Nobody questioned it."

"You can't live in the past."

"You can't look back."

"You can't go home again."

"You can't tell me that girl looked fifteen in that dark theater."

Mahoney gestured toward the chalk outline. "What do your years on the street tell you?"

"The work of a joker. Some wise guy. A regular comedian. Thought he was real cute. Must have talked his way in because there were no signs of forced entry."

"Sounds like a smooth operator."

"Ice in his veins."

"A cool customer."

The sergeant pointed at the blood on the ceiling. "Then something went wrong. He got buggy and spooked."

"Then he went squirrelly."

"And wigged out," said the sergeant. "So he pulled his piece."

"You mean his rod?"

"No, his heater."

Mahoney looked down at the coffee table. There was an empty evidence baggie, *lighter* written in black grease pencil. Mahoney pointed at it. "Is that the lighter I got the fax about? That's the reason I'm here."

"What?" said the sergeant, then noticed the bag was empty. "Oh, sorry. Must have used it to light my cigar." The sergeant stretched out his leg to reach in a pocket and retrieve the lighter. "Here you go."

Mahoney put on a latex glove and accepted the lighter gingerly. "They didn't get up to the part about fingerprints at the academy before you graduated, right?"

"I already said I was sorry."

"Doesn't matter. I know whose this is."

"Really? How?"

"Orange Bowl. 1969. Super Bowl Three. I've seen this lighter before. I'll never forget it."

Mahoney picked up the evidence bag from the coffee table, dangled the lighter over it like a spider and dropped it in. He sealed the Ziploc and handed it to the sergeant.

"I'd like to get this processed for prints anyway, just in case you missed a spot."

"Sure thing," said the sergeant. "The lab boys are really backed up, but one of them owes me a favor. I'll call in some chits."

"One hand washes the other."

"Then we scratch each other's backs."

Mahoney headed for the door.

"Just one more question," said the sergeant.

Mahoney turned around. "What's that?"

"You stop someone for speeding and they just start unbuttoning their blouse. Now how is that *my* fault?"

32

JIM AND MARTHA ate instant waffles on the front porch of their bungalow.

"Morning!" Gladys walked up the steps with a straw basket of blackberry turnovers. "Tell me if these are any good."

The Davenports each took one.

Gladys looked around. "Where's your new car?"

"Stolen on the crime watch," said Jim.

Gladys took a seat on the swing. "I was on the crime watch once. Gave me a completely new perspective on the neighborhood."

"That's what I was telling Martha. It's like a human coral reef—at night an entirely different set of critters comes out."

"It can't be that bad," said Martha.

"You kidding?" said Gladys. "Do yourself a favor. Some weekend at three A.M., go to one of the twenty-four-hour supermarkets. It's like a zombie movie."

"I told you," said Jim.

"Remember the horrible student murders a few years back?" said Martha. "I had a friend who was on the police department at the time. He said as soon as it happened, the cops went to a filing cabinet and pulled out a 'usual suspects' list of like two hundred people. Some had no warrants or even records, but there had been instability indicators. The cops knew who they were, where they lived, and had no trouble believing any of them could snap. All these people living throughout the community, blending in. And that was a small town."

"I'd like to see the list for Tampa Bay," said Jim.

"No kidding," said Gladys. "We've got all kinds of odd circadian rhythms just on Triggerfish Lane alone. There's Mrs. Glasgow with her telescope, and Mr. Brinkley with his insomnia and his pogo stick. Mr. Renfroe told us the lights were burning late because he was up working on a children's novel until we found out he was really making pipe bombs. And of course there's Mrs. Anderson and her midnight Alsatian yodeling. Florida Power and Light told police that the Crumpets had tripled their energy consumption, and a search warrant turned up the grow lights in the rumpus room. Who am I forgetting? Oh, yes. Tommy Lexington, who never got married and lived with his mother until he was forty-five and was finally picked up at McDonald's covered with blood and eating a Happy Meal."

"Hey, Gladys," said Martha. "Didn't you tell me you've never even seen Mr. Oppenheimer?"

"Yeah?"

"Well, don't look now."

The automatic garage door slowly rose at the Oppenheimer place. Mr. Oppenheimer wheeled out his kit-built experimental aircraft.

"I'll be!" said Gladys. "He finally finished it. After twelve years."

"Is that thing safe?" said Martha.

The stared skeptically at the craft: a tiny transparent egg-shaped cockpit attached to a Delta wing and twin rotors on the tail. It was very light, and Mr. Oppenheimer towed it with a rope as he walked up the street and into the park at the end of Triggerfish. He opened the cockpit.

"Doesn't he need some kind of permit or FAA clearance?" asked Martha.

"Moot point," said Gladys. "My Jacuzzi has a better chance of getting airborne."

A Lincoln Navigator pulled up. The driver got out and slammed his door extra loud. He came up the Davenports' walkway.

"Heard you were fired," said Lance Boyle. "I'll pay top dollar for your house."

"Who the hell are you?" said Martha.

Gladys answered. "That's Lance Boyle, the guy I pointed out who owns all the rentals."

"Where did you hear my husband was fired!" demanded Martha.

Lance pointed at Gladys.

Gladys smiled and turned red. "I took your side when I told the story."

"We may sell some day, but not to a creep like you!" said Martha.

"Suit yourself," said Lance. "But the whole street's going rental. I just signed a lease with a couple of drug dealers for one of the places across the street. The longer you wait, the less your property's worth."

"No thanks to you!" said Gladys.

"I'm not breaking any laws."

An Audi pulled up across the street and two huge Rastafarians with waist-length dreadlocks got out. "Your new neighbors," said Lance. He set a business card on the porch railing. "If you change your mind . . ."

He drove away.

"What a jerk," said Gladys.

"Look!" said Martha, pointing down the street. "It's Mr. Oppenheimer! It's working! It's really working!"

"He's flying!" said Jim.

"I can't believe it!" said Gladys. "He's up! He's up! He's up! He's . . . in the power lines . . . Oooooooo. That didn't look good . . ."

OVER THE NEXT few days, the Davenports observed a steady stream of people driving up to the Rastafarians' house at all hours, walking to the door and leaving quickly.

Lance Boyle had been delighted when the Jamaicans answered his classified ad for the rental, but his glee faded when he discovered they were computer programmers instead of drug dealers. So Lance did the next best thing. He told everyone they were.

Jim and Martha were on their porch swing the following Monday when Lance parked across the street at 877 Triggerfish. He went up to his rental and took down the silk flag of sailboats hanging over the mailbox, replacing it with one that had a big marijuana leaf. Lance drove off as a VW microbus pulled up. Four Deadheads got out and knocked on the door. A Rastafarian answered. There was a sharp exchange.

"We're computer programmers! We don't sell drugs!" The door slammed.

The Deadheads left, and Coleman arrived. He knocked on the door.

It opened. Coleman began singing.

"I shot the sheriff!"

The door slammed.

Serge came running across the street with a baseball glove and stopped in front of the Davenports' porch. "Is Melvin home?"

"Yes," said Jim.

"No," said Martha.

Martha looked at Jim. "I mean, no," he said.

"Oh, okay," said Serge, and he ran back across the street. Coleman had just returned from the Rastafarians' pad and was sitting on the porch with a beer. Serge joined him with a *National Geographic*.

"Why'd you say Melvin wasn't home?" asked Jim.

"I don't want that man near our son."

"Why not?"

"Jim! There's something wrong with him! His roommates, too!"

Across the street, Serge was showing Coleman a *National Geographic* article about a tribe in Africa. "Check out how they make their necks really long with metal neck coils."

Coleman popped another beer. "We should get some neck coils."

"I have an idea."

They walked over to the hedge, and Serge pulled out a long garden hose, the collapsible flat kind full of pinholes that inflates with water to irrigate flower beds. Serge started wrapping it around his neck. "Okay. When I give the signal, turn on the water, and I'll have neck coils."

"Right," said Coleman, pushing his way through the hedge to the faucet.

"You're overreacting," Jim told Martha.

"They're dangerous!"

"Maybe to themselves."

"There's something weird about those men!"

"Maybe they're simple. Wouldn't you feel bad if you found out that was the case and you'd been talking like this?"

"They're not retarded—they're dangerous!"

Jim and Martha heard something across the street. Serge was flopping around the front yard, turning blue and fighting a garden hose wrapped around his throat like an anaconda. Coleman thrashed drunkenly in the bushes, trying to turn off the water.

Coleman finally cut the pressure, and the hose deflated. Serge unwrapped his neck and sat up, panting.

Jim turned to Martha. "I don't think you're supposed to use the word *retarded* anymore. It's offensive or something."

Coleman pointed across the street. "Are the Davenports looking at us?"

"Yeah, they are." Serge smiled and waved.

Jim waved back.

"Another close call," said Serge, feeling his neck. "I think God is trying to tell me something."

"Like what?"

"I think I'm going to try going straight."

"You?" Coleman laughed. "That's a hoot!"

"I'm serious."

"What brought this on?"

"We've been staying here a few weeks now, and I've been watching Jim over there. Talk about living on the edge. Guys like him don't get any glory. They've just quietly put away childish things and faced the relentless adult responsibility of taking care of others."

Coleman shook with the willies. "That's some scary shit!"

"No kidding," said Serge. "Jim's kinda like my hero now. I think I'll start hanging out with the guy and study him to see what his secret is."

"What about our financial situation? Looks like Sharon will be out of work for a while with the mayor closing the titty bars."

"We need a big score to make up ground in a hurry. I was thinking about kidnapping someone for ransom."

"I thought you were going to go straight."

"I think I can handle both," said Serge. "It'll be a full schedule, but that's what coffee's for."

"No, I mean isn't that a contradiction?" asked Coleman.

"You know the quote: 'A foolish consistency is the hobgoblin of little minds.'"

"Who said that?"

"Either Emerson or the Unabomber."

Sharon came out on the porch with some coke.

"Would you mind doing that in the house?" said Serge. "This is a family neighborhood."

Sharon made a face.

"He's trying to go straight," said Coleman.

"That'll be the day!" Sharon stomped back inside.

"And don't slam the—"

Sharon slammed the door.

A noise came up the street, a black '76 Chevy Laguna with Landau top and a stereo like a concussion drill. Across the top of the windshield in Goth script: NO FEAR. The young, shirtless man behind the wheel had a tattoo on his shoulder of a skull with a snake crawling through the eye sockets. He stopped in front of the Davenport residence and flicked a cigarette onto the lawn.

Debbie Davenport came out the front door and ran down the steps.

Jim stood up on the porch. "Debbie, come back here! I forbid you to—"

Debbie jumped in the car. Jim ran down from the porch, but the Laguna took off.

"See what I mean?" said Serge. "I feel for the American family. I don't know how Jim handles the pressure."

"Isn't there something we can do to help?" asked Coleman.

"You're right," said Serge. "We *should* do something."

"But what?"

"You know any couples with small kids?"

"No."

"People forget to invite them anywhere. We should try to get them out of the house and do something. Remind them what it's like to have fun."

"You really think that's what they want?"

"Of course! I'll bet they're just dying for me to come over and ask them. They're just too polite to bring it up themselves."

Martha pointed across the street. "Jim! He's coming back over here! Get rid of him!" She went in the house.

Jim stood on the porch talking politely with Serge. Martha peeked out through the curtains. They smiled and shook hands, and Jim came inside.

"What did he want?" asked Martha.

"He wants to do something with us."

"What do you mean, 'do something'?"

"A double date."

Martha cracked up. "You've got to be kidding me. Us and him and that woman? Can you image how funny that would be?"

"We'll find out Friday."

Martha stopped laughing. "You told him no, didn't you?"

Jim pulled out the phone book. "We still have a few days to find a baby-sitter."

"This isn't funny."

"Honey, they're making an overture to be good neighbors. We have to give them the benefit of the doubt. If we reject them, what does that say about us? What does it say about *our* commitment to the community? We forfeit any right to be treated well ourselves."

"Okay, we forfeit," said Martha. "I can live with that. Now, go over there and tell him we changed our minds."

"Honey, I can't just—"

"Do whatever you want, but I'm not going anywhere with that man."

33

AGENT MAHONEY ARRIVED AT the Little League field a few days after Coach Terrier's body was found. The pitcher's mound was still roped off by police tape. The sergeant guarding the scene recognized Mahoney.

"If it isn't my favorite state agent," said the sergeant. They shook hands. "I can remember when we didn't need parents or fancy uniforms to play the game."

"I can remember when aluminum was for beer cans, not baseball bats."

"I can remember breaking Miss DuBois's first-grade class window."

"We've all broken our share of windows."

"I had a crush on Miss DuBois. She wore these cute little berets that drove me wild."

"But that's not really the point, now, is it?"

"No, I just thought—"

"You thought wrong." Mahoney gazed wistfully over the left-field fence. "What do you got for me?"

The detective pulled a notepad from his pocket. When he did, several little berets fell out. The sergeant stared at them on the ground for a moment, then looked at Mahoney. "I'm getting help."

"I can remember back when you couldn't get help."

"I can remember when they weren't called diseases. They were hobbies."

"The world's changing."

"The mayor's closing down all the hobby shops."

Mahoney stared down at the pitcher's mound. "What a sick, pathetic bastard."

"Jesus! They're just little berets!"

"I mean the killer."

"Oh."

The radio in Mahoney's Crown Victoria cracked with static. "Mahoney! Come in!"

Mahoney reached in the window and grabbed the mike.

"Mahoney here."

"Where have you been?" asked Lieutenant Ingersol. "I've tried to reach you all morning."

"Sir, I found Serge's Super Bowl Three lighter at a murder scene, and now I'm at another murder scene. I think—"

"What did I tell you about this Serge thing? You're supposed to be on the McGraw case. You let the locals handle this! You're out of your jurisdiction! . . ."

"You're breaking up. I can't hear you."

"Don't give me that old trick!" said Ingersol. "Drop this Serge business right now! You're insubordinate! You're over the line! . . ."

Mahoney turned off the radio.

THERE WAS KNOCK at the door of 867 Triggerfish. Serge answered it wearing a chef's hat and eating a chicken salad sandwich.

It was Jim Davenport.

"Hey! Jim! What's up, buddy?"

Jim stepped inside. He looked troubled. "I have to talk to you about something."

"Sandwich?" asked Serge, showing Jim his own partially eaten one.

"No thanks. I—"

"Chicken salad," said Serge, pumping his eyebrows.

"Listen, I have to talk to you about our double date. Martha doesn't—"

"My special recipe," said Serge. "I'll give you half. Take a bite. You don't like it, you don't have to eat it."

"No, I—"

Serge tore his sandwich in two and handed Jim half and left the room.

Jim looked around uncomfortably. He glanced over at the couch and saw Coleman staring down, picking at something.

Serge came back in the room stirring a giant mixing bowl with a spatula. "Okay, you start with a bucket of KFC extra crispy. Debone and dice. Then mix with mayo and—here's the secret ingredient that puts it over the top—cashews!"

"Serge, I have to tell you something." Jim absentmindedly took a bite. "I came over here to—" He stopped and looked at the sandwich. "Say, that's not bad."

Serge pointed at the couch. "Have a seat."

"I can't stay."

Serge sat down and clicked on the TV with the remote. "Sit down. You'll hurt my feelings."

Jim sat tentatively on the edge of the sofa. Serge changed channels to *Deliverance* on TBS.

"Serge, listen—"

"I love *Deliverance*!" exclaimed Serge. "I'll make you a sandwich, and we'll watch the rest together. This is a good bonding movie."

"Serge—"

"Shhhhh!" said Serge. "Here's the Ned Beatty scene. Cracks me up every time."

"Damn it, Serge, I have to talk to you!"

Serge clicked off the TV. "Geez, Jim, I'm sorry. I didn't realize it was so important. What's the matter?"

"It's about Melvin—"

Serge stood up fast. "What's the matter with Melvin? He's okay, isn't he?"

"Melvin's fine—"

Serge sat back down. "Whew! You had me worried. He's a fine boy."

"Yes, he is."

"You should be proud."

"I am."

"Listen, Jim. I love that kid. I wish I had a son like that but, well, things never worked out. You tell me what the problem is. I'll do anything to help you. Just name it. Anything."

Jim hesitated and looked down.

Serge put his hand on Jim's shoulder. "What is it, Jim? You can tell me."

Jim looked up at Serge. "Martha doesn't think . . . *We* don't think we can go on that double date."

"I see."

"In fact, we would prefer it if you didn't come over anymore . . ."

Serge got up and went over to the window. He put his sandwich down on the sill. He stared outside silently with his hands in his pockets. He could hear songbirds. He picked up the sandwich and took a bite.

"I feel terrible about this," said Jim. "But we have kids, and you have . . . this *lifestyle*."

Serge turned and walked back to the couch. He put a hand on Jim's shoulder again. "Is that how you two feel?"

"That's how we feel."

Serge took another bite and nodded. He sat down on the coffee table facing Jim. "You know, Jim, Martha's a fine woman. You're a very lucky man."

"Thank you."

"And she's a great mother."

"I know."

"And a mother has to do what she thinks is in the best interests of her children. If she doesn't, she's not a good mother."

"I agree."

"So I understand completely. I'll stay away."

"Serge, I hope you don't take this—"

"No, no," said Serge, holding up a hand for Jim to stop. "No need to explain. Family comes first. I'm not going to interfere with that."

The screen door flung open and crashed into the wall. Sharon stood in the doorway backlit with bright sunlight, legs apart, hands on her hips like Superwoman. She wore cowboy boots, dark sunglasses, hot pants and the top half of a Corona T-shirt. No bra. Her flowing blond hair was untamed, and she was pissed off in a sexy way.

"Where's that shithead, Coleman! Wait till I get my hands on the little dickhead!"

"Sharon!" snapped Serge. "We have a guest!"

Jim stood and held out a hand to shake. Sharon looked at it like a turd. She walked by, flicking cigarette ash on the floor. "Who's this asshole?"

"Sharon!" Serge said. "This is one of our neighbors! Your manners!"

"Fuck manners! And fuck *him*!" Then to the room in general: "We got any liquor in this shithole?"

Serge snatched the sunglasses off her face and threw them against the wall.

"Hey! Those were my favorite shades!" She reached out and stuck him in the hand with her cigarette.

"Aaaaaauuuu!" Serge screamed. He looked at the burn mark, then backhanded her across the face, sending her tumbling into the kitchen. She got up and slapped him back. They began to struggle. A chair went over. Sharon broke free and Serge charged. She grabbed the hanging lamp and swung it, catching Serge in the forehead.

"Owwww!" Serge grabbed his head and staggered. Sharon went for the butcher's block. Serge reached for some utensils sticking out of a ceramic rooster. Sharon pulled a meat cleaver from the block and spun around, but Serge bonked her on top of the head with a soup ladle.

"Ouch!" She dropped the meat cleaver and grabbed the top of her head with both hands.

"You're dead now!" Serge hissed.

"Oh shit!" She ran down the hall into the bedroom and slammed the door.

Serge calmly walked down the hall after her and kicked the door open.

There was cursing, a tremendous crash and a woman's scream. More stuff breaking.

Jim looked with concern at Coleman and pointed down the hall. "Shouldn't we do something?"

"I think they want their privacy."

"What?"

"Listen," said Coleman.

Jim listened. They were still cursing and screaming. But Jim also began to make out bedsprings squeaking with a distantly familiar rhythm.

"Have a seat," said Coleman. "They'll only be a few minutes."

Jim awkwardly sat next to Coleman on the couch. Coleman clicked the remote control over to Jerry Springer and two obese women with mustaches fighting over the white supremacist who snaked their toilets.

The bedsprings got louder. Jim heard Sharon's voice down the hall again, rising in volume, her words falling into iambic pentameter with the squeaking coils: "Oh-God! Oh-God! Oh-God! Oh-God! Fuck-me! Fuck-me! Fuck-me! Fuck-me! . . ."

Sweat began to bead and trickle down Jim's temples. He looked out the corner of his eye at Coleman, who seemed oblivious as he watched TV. Jerry Springer grabbed his chin and looked on with pensive concern as a female Godzilla vs. Mothra hair-pulling contest got under way.

Sharon was now screaming at the top of her lungs.

"Don't-stop! Don't-stop! Don't-stop! Don't-stop! . . . Oh, my pussy! . . . My . . . wet . . . hot . . . snapping . . . pussy! . . . Yip-yip-yip-yip, Eeeeee-hawwwww!"

"Jesus!" screamed Jim, leaping off the couch. He looked at Coleman and pointed down the hall with a trembling arm. "I can't believe you're not hearing that!"

"Oh, I hear it all right," said a forlorn Coleman, listlessly pressing the channel-changer. "I wish I had a girlfriend."

Sharon's noisiness subsided, and Jim sat back down.

"I envy you married guys," said Coleman. "You probably get that every night."

It was quiet for a while. Serge finally came around the corner wearing only jogging shorts and holding a bath towel around his neck like a tennis star. Jim stood up.

"Oh, Jim, I'm so sorry. I completely forgot about you!"

Jim walked up to Serge bashfully. "Can I ask you something?"

"What is it, Jim?"

Jim tried to say something, but then looked down at the floor.

Serge leaned his head to look at Jim from a slightly different angle, then straightened back up. "You want to improve your love life with Martha?"

Jim nodded, still looking at the floor.

Serge put his arm around Jim's shoulders. "Step into my office. . . . Coleman, hold my calls. And bring Jim a beer."

Jim walked into Serge's bedroom. He stopped and stared. A seven-foot-tall, fifty-foot-long Mercator map of the world stretched all the way around the four walls.

"I put that up when I was working on my plans for global domination," said Serge. "But then I got distracted by Paleo-Indian archaeology." He pointed at the neat row of clovis-point arrowheads in a shadow box on his dresser. "I figure when I get back to world domination, I'll already have the map up."

Coleman came in and handed Jim a beer. Serge handed him a pad and pencil.

"You'll need to take notes." They sat down on the bed. "Okay, if you really want to please Martha, here's what you have to do . . ."

AN HOUR LATER, Serge and Jim shook hands on the front porch.

A '76 Laguna with chrome hubs screeched up in front of the Davenport residence, the stereo thumping about political disenfranchisement and bitches. Debbie and the shirtless driver got out and kissed.

"Hey!" Jim yelled at the driver. "I want to talk to you!"

Jim ran down from the porch as fast as he could, but the Laguna took off again. Jim walked back to Serge's house. "That guy's way too old for Debbie."

"You want me to take care of him?" said Serge. "I still got some of the baseball bats from coaching Little League. I know these guys—"

"No," said Jim. "I have to handle it myself. I'm her father."

"How old is Debbie now, anyway?" said Serge. "Sixteen?"

"Next week," said Jim. "I heard her talking on the phone with one of her friends. I think his name's Scorpion. He's twenty-two. And what was the deal with his underwear hanging out like that? Didn't he realize it was showing?"

"I think that's on purpose," said Serge.

"Really? That's what they're doing these days?" said Jim. He pointed inside Serge's open front door at Coleman bending over to go through some old albums.

"So Coleman does it on purpose, too?"

Serge shook his head. "That's not fashion. That's congenital."

34

JOHN MILTON held a can of spray paint in his right hand and looked up at the dripping red letters on the side of the new Consolidated Bank building: THE FIRST THING WE DO, LET'S KILL ALL THE CONSULTANTS.

He tossed the can in a trash bin and began walking south along Dale Mabry Highway. He passed a homeless man holding up a cardboard sign: WILL TAKE VERBAL ABUSE FOR FOOD.

"That's every job in America in a nutshell," said John.

"What?" said the man, but John kept walking. He was on a mission. Ever since the day John found Christ and the Antichrist rolling on the sidewalk, he had taken the Messiah's words to heart. He was on a quest, searching for The Messenger, the one who would *reveal all*. But John was getting discouraged. He started to think that maybe there was no messenger. He decided to take matters into his own hands.

That meant revenge. John came up with Plan A. That was the plan with the stun gun. In the meantime, John had started getting hungry. He had been walking all morning and was amazed at the kind of appetite dementia could whip up. Madness affects people different ways. In John's case, it made him crave chocolate malt balls. John began looking for a place that sold both stun guns and Whoppers.

He walked another half hour and went inside the Sam's Club near Gandy Boulevard. Ten minutes later, he strolled down aisle seventeen holding a stun gun in a clear plastic blister pack. He saw an employee.

"Where are the Milk Duds?" asked John.

"Aisle fifteen," said Jim Davenport.

John disappeared around the corner and came back. "Don't see 'em."

Jim put down his price gun.

They went to aisle fifteen. Jim pointed sharply upward, seventy feet above them on the steel-girder shelves. A forklift pallet of Milk Duds in ten-gallon cartons.

"We'll need the stairs," said Jim.

John waited as Jim left the aisle. Soon there was a squeaking sound, and Jim came back around the end of the aisle pushing a tall metal staircase with a revolving amber caution light. Jim rolled it into place and set the parking brake, then put on a hard hat and climbed to the top.

Jim put his hand to the side of his mouth and yelled down. "How many you need?"

"What?" John yelled.

"How many cartons you need?" Jim yelled louder.

"One! . . . No, two!"

Jim climbed down with twenty gallons of malt balls.

"Thanks," said John. He stopped and studied Jim's face. "Don't I know you?"

"Don't think so," said Jim. "I'm new in town."

"You look familiar," said John. "I was thinking it was from work, but I guess it couldn't be, since you work here."

"Where do you work?" asked Jim.

"I'm between jobs," said John. "Actually had a pretty good one until the company brought in the consultants."

"Don't get me started on the consulting business," said Jim.

"Bad experience?"

"Horrible. I was so naive. Then I learned the truth."

"They called me in on a Monday morning," said John. "What about you?"

"Friday afternoon."

"My boss said he had no choice but to fire me," John added. "Claimed the consultants were forcing his hand."

"He was lying."

"But that would be wrong."

"The company was the one who wanted to fire you in the first place. They told that to the consultants, who wrote a report recommending layoffs. Then someone from the company says, 'Hey, if it was up to me, I'd keep you on. You know I would.'"

"That's what they told me! Those exact words!"

"It's part of a script," said Jim. "They hand it out at a luncheon."

"But why would the consultants take the blame for something that's not their fault?"

"They're paid scapegoats," said Jim.

"Paid scapegoats?"

"It's this economy. There are all kinds of new jobs."

"Wow."

"That's not all," said Jim. "After an employee is dismissed, the company will start spreading vague hints about his mental stability."

"Why?"

"To discredit him in case he tries to talk to the others."

John stepped back and his face changed. He pointed at Jim and put his other hand over his mouth. "Oh my God! You're The Messenger!"

"The what?"

"You're the one I was supposed to find. The one who would *reveal all*."

"What are you talking about?"

But John fell silent, slowly taking steps backward. Then he turned and ran out of the store without paying, and the alarms went off.

JOHN MILTON RAN to a pay phone and dialed.

"This is Jerry, your account representative. How may I assist you today?"

"Jerry, it's me. John. John Milton."

"John!" Jerry whispered in alarm. It sounded like he was covering the phone with his hand. "Are you okay? There are some pretty strange stories circulating about you. They said you had gone . . ."

"Gone what?"

"... Mad."

John cringed. "He warned me this would happen."

"Who?"

"That's not important."

"John, I'm worried. Where are you?"

"I can't tell you right now. I have to ask you a big favor."

"Name it."

"Do you think you can get in the vice president's office without being seen?"

"Which one?"

"Number thirty-eight. The one with the inspirational poster."

"Of the rowing team?"

"That's the one. I need you to—"

"He took it down."

"Took what down?"

"The poster."

"That's not important."

"It was important enough for you to bring up."

"Forget about the poster. I need you to get in there and find the consultant's report."

"Don't have to."

"Why not?"

"They gave it to us. Everyone was getting really upset about the layoffs, a lot of tearful good-byes, so they passed out copies to prove it wasn't the company's fault."

"Meet me in an hour in the parking lot. Bring the report."

"An hour in the parking lot?"

"Right."

"What do you want me to do about the poster?"

"I don't care about the poster."

"Then what's this call about?"

"The consultant's report!"

"Oh! You want the report!"

"Of course I want the report!"

"When do you want it?"

"In an hour! In the parking lot!"

"You don't have to shout."

"Geez, Jerry! And you're one of the ones they kept!"

"You're the one who's crazy."

"See you in an hour."

JOHN WAITED ACROSS the street from Consolidated Bank. Jerry came down in a few minutes. He looked around to make sure he hadn't been followed, then ran across the street to Jim. He pulled the report from inside his jacket.

"Can you tell me what this is about?" asked Jerry.

"Shhhhh!" John flipped through the pages.

The report recommended laying off dozens of employees who should be given T-shirts with a flock of doves flying carefree in the sunshine over the word *Liberation*. Damocles Consulting had rewritten the report after the original author was let go. But, out of fairness, they had left his name on the report to receive proper credit.

John Milton came to last page and found the name. He memorized it.

". . . Jim Davenport. Jim Davenport. Jim Davenport . . ."

"Who's Jim Davenport?"

"The one who's going to pay."

35

MARTHA DAVENPORT'S PARENTS WERE STAYING the weekend, watching the kids.

"Can you zip me up?" she asked Jim in their bedroom.

"Sure thing." Jim slipped on his jacket and helped Martha with her new dress.

Jim sniffed. "Jasmine?"

Martha nodded. "When are you going to let me know where we're going?"

"I told you," said Jim. "It's a surprise."

"I'm so excited. This isn't like you."

"I'M NOT GOING to wear that fucking thing!" yelled Sharon.

"Wear it or so help me God!" said Serge. He stood in front of his bedroom mirror, straightening his tux.

"This stupid dress is bad enough!"

"It's just a corsage. It won't kill you to try to look nice."

"I don't know how it works."

"For the love of . . . !" Serge went over and pinned on Sharon's corsage. "Now hurry up. Your pumpkin's waiting."

MARTHA'S EXCITEMENT WAS getting the best of her as she and Jim sat in their living room, dressed and waiting.

"Give me a hint. Just a little one."

There was a knock at the door. Martha popped out of her seat and answered it. It was a chauffeur. A white stretch limo sat at the curb.

"Oh Jim!" She threw her arms around his neck and kissed him, then clung to his arm as they strolled down the walkway. The chauffeur opened the back door and Martha climbed in.

"You know Sharon," Serge said with a big smile, sitting in the opposite seat.

Martha looked back at Jim. "What's going on?"

"Don't worry. I've got it all planned."

The chauffeur closed the door.

THE DON CESAR Hotel opened in 1928 to much fanfare. The palatial resort combined Spanish architecture with Old World elegance on the Gulf of Mexico. Beach cabanas, poolside waiters. Presidents stayed there when they were in town. It was the finest hotel in Tampa Bay. You couldn't miss it. It was big, and it was pink.

Martha thawed to a mild frost as the limo crossed St. Petersburg for the gulf. She had to admit she'd never seen Serge and Sharon like this. Serge had a fresh haircut and close shave, almost respectable in the tuxedo. And Sharon—she almost looked *too* good. Serge had spent eight hundred on the strapless white number, and another three hundred on her makeover and hair. He tipped the team of stylists heavily and kept Sharon in the chair with small amounts of cocaine. Her blond mane now elegantly curled off her shoulders, a sprig of baby's breath over her right ear. She squirmed in her new dress like a Siamese cat in a wet suit.

The limo stopped, and the chauffeur opened the door. Martha gasped in delight.

"The Don Cesar! I've always wanted to come here!"

Bellmen open the doors, and the two couples strode inside. A man in tails played a grand piano in the cavernous Mediterranean lobby. Guests sipped cocktails and spritzers.

Jim led them through a door and up to the maître d' stand. "Davenport. Reservations for four."

"Right this way, sir."

He seated them in the dim blue light of the saltwater aquariums that constituted the walls.

Sharon immediately excused herself for the ladies' room.

Martha stood up. "I'll go with you."

Jim and Serge watched them leave.

"You've got quite a gal there," said Jim.

"You're joking, right?"

Jim didn't know what to say.

"That woman is a fucking nightmare," said Serge. "Any man is a fool to go within a hundred yards of her. She uses and abuses, thinks nothing of completely humiliating you in public, stomping your heart out and moving on to her next victim. She's stolen money from my wallet for her drug addiction, cracked my ribs with a tire iron and once tried to stab me to death when she was high on cocaine!"

"My God!" said Jim. "I didn't know! . . . Why are you still involved with her?"

Serge grinned sheepishly. "I think she's kinda cute."

Sharon lit a cigarette in the ladies' room and checked her eyes in the mirror. She took an airline miniature of Jack Daniel's from her purse.

"Want some?"

"No thanks," said Martha.

"Whatever." Sharon downed the bottle. She went in a stall and closed the door and began snorting.

Martha came back to the table alone.

"Something wrong?" asked Jim.

Martha leaned and whispered. "I'm not sure, but I think she's doing cocaine."

"I know," Jim whispered. "Serge just told me. It's a tragedy. He's trying to get her help."

Sharon came back to the table, now wearing sunglasses.

"Oh, great," said Serge. He grabbed her wrist under the table and leaned over. "Don't ruin this!"

"Let go!" She pulled away, and a glass of water went over. A waiter ran up with a towel.

Serge smiled at the Davenports. "Everything on the menu's good."

Sharon sniffled and played with her nose. "I'm going to the rest room."

"No, you're not!" said Serge.

Sharon stood up and Serge grabbed for her, but she jumped out of reach and took off. Serge held the large tassled menu in front of his face. He looked over the top at Jim and Martha. "Try the seafood." Then ducked back behind the menu.

The bread basket arrived, looking like a floral arrangement.

Sharon came back with the jitters and sat down. She saw Jim looking at her. "What the fuck are you staring at!"

Jim lowered his eyes and buttered a roll.

It went that way through each course, soup to nuts, Sharon popping up and down from the table, back and forth to the rest room. Serge was ordering another bottle of wine when he felt something in his lap. Sharon had slipped off one of her shoes and was rubbing his crotch with her foot. Serge kept a poker face. He folded the wine list and handed it to the steward. "Try to find something in those heavy rain years in Burgundy during the 1880s. Surprise me."

Sharon had a mischievous grin. She rubbed harder. Serge glanced to see if the Davenports were wise, but they were pointing at something in the aquarium.

"Stop it!" Serge whispered under his breath.

"Nope."

The Davenports eventually realized something was amiss. Serge had both hands in his lap, wrestling with something under the tablecloth.

"Stop it! Right now!"

Sharon shook her head and wiggled her toes.

Serge grabbed the ankle and pulled hard, and Sharon went down in her chair, grabbing china on the way.

Waiters arrived at the table again.

Sharon stood up, grabbed a glass of Chablis and threw it in Serge's face.

Serge smiled at the Davenports as the wine dripped down his nose. He ran his tongue around his mouth and smacked his lips. "Well-stated bouquet. Full-bodied yet uncomplicated."

The maître d' came over. He lowered his voice so only their table could hear. "I'm afraid I'm going to have to ask you to leave."

"But we haven't had dessert yet," said Serge.

The maître d' looked around the table. "You three may stay, but *she* has to leave."

"Oh, Sharon," said Serge. "Don't worry about her. Just a little feline distemper."

"I'm sorry. We don't serve people like her."

"Come again?" said Serge. "I didn't get that last part. For a second I thought you said, 'people like *her*.'"

The waiter didn't respond.

"She may be a little rough on Hints from Heloise, but she's still my date," said Serge, standing and folding his napkin. "And you have insulted my lady's honor."

Serge discreetly snapped his knee up. The maître d' doubled over with a groan, and Serge wrapped his arms around him, like he was helping. People at the other tables began staring.

"Nothing to worry about! Go back to your meals!" said Serge.

The maître d' tried to say something, so Serge kneed him again, producing a louder groan.

Everyone was looking now.

"Just a little food poisoning," said Serge. "You might want to lay off the seafood tonight and stick with the mad cow."

A chorus of forks went down in plates. Jim and Martha jumped to their feet.

"You don't want to try the chocolate mousse?" asked Serge.

"We have to leave."

The Davenports quickly headed for the entrance and the waiting limo. Serge caught up from behind and grabbed Jim's arm in the lobby. "I have to talk with you."

"This is out of control, Serge. I can't tell you how upset Martha is."

"That's what I want to talk to you about. Just take a second."

"I'll be right back," Jim told Martha. She gave him the eye.

Serge and Jim huddled by the grand piano.

"What is it?" Jim said, impatient as he'd ever been in his life.

"I'm really sorry about tonight," said Serge. "I don't know what I was thinking bringing Sharon. The whole thing was doomed right from the concept stage."

"Your heart was in the right place," said Jim. "Let's call it a night."

"I just had this fantasy," said Serge. "I was thinking maybe I could have what you have. A stable family and a normal life. Instead, look what I have to go home to. You have the ideal nuclear family. I have the fucking Chernobyl family. My domestic partner is a femme fatale Lucille Ball meets Nancy Spungeon by way of Squeaky Fromme, and we have de facto foster custody of a colicky man-child from the Island of Misfit Toys."

Serge pulled out a big roll of bills and began peeling off hundreds. "I'm going to make it up to you."

"That's not necessary."

"I absolutely insist."

Serge marched across the lobby and tossed money on the front desk. "We'd like the honeymoon suite."

Jim ran up from behind. "Serge, really, stop . . ."

"You want sparks in your marriage? Here's your sparks . . ." He jammed a couple more hundreds in Jim's breast pocket. "That's for the champagne." Then he put an arm around Jim's shoulder and whispered. When he was done he stepped back. "You can't miss."

"I don't know about that last part," said Jim. "I don't think she'll go for it."

"That's the most important facet of the plan," said Serge. "You can buy one in the gift shop. Trust me. I know women."

They walked back to Martha and Sharon.

"What's going on?" asked Martha.

Serge just grabbed Sharon by the wrist—"C'mon you!"—and yanked her out the front door toward the limo.

"Hey, that's our ride!" said Martha.

"Doesn't matter," said Jim. He held up the key to the honeymoon suite.

SHARON DID MORE coke in the limo on the way home.

Serge laid back in his seat and fiddled with some controls. "You ever think about having children?"

"Are you out of your mind!" said Sharon, sitting up with a rolled twenty-dollar-bill still hanging out her nose.

"I was thinking it might be kind of cool to settle down and maybe go straight for a while. I've been studying Jim . . ."

"Jim's a dork!" said Sharon, leaning over again.

"He's my new role model," said Serge. "Takes guts to walk in his shoes."

"And that's what you want?"

Serge turned on the tiny TV set installed in the bar and changed channels. "It does have a certain appeal. I wouldn't mind seeing what it's like."

"Boring! That's what it's like!"

"Maybe I *need* boring."

A HALF MOON reflected off the still Gulf of Mexico behind the Don Cesar. It was quiet in the honeymoon suite.

Martha sat at the edge of the bed on the verge of sobs. Jim sat next to her with his arm around her shoulders. He tried to console her, but Martha didn't seem to want to be touched. He took his arm away.

"A flashlight!" said Martha. "What on earth were you thinking!"

"I'm not sure."

"You had to be thinking something!"

"I guess I wanted to liven up the marriage."

"You certainly accomplished that. . . . But where did you ever get such a crazy idea?"

36

FOUR PAIRS OF EYES BLINKED IN THE DARKNESS.

Midnight in the retention pond. No sound except frogs and crickets.

"I thought we'd be rescued by now," said Eunice. "It's been five days."

"Nobody's coming," said Edith.

"They can't see us down here," said Ethel. "The weeds must be hiding us."

The E-Team had survived so far on the contents of four purses, and the floorboards were littered with wrappers from Life Savers, Altoids, chewing gum, Rolaids, SweeTarts, Motrin, Maalox, Necco wafers, Ricola cough drops and Beano. They had fashioned a condensate funnel from a rain hat and attached it to the cattails just outside the driver's window, channeling morning dew into a "World's Greatest Grandma" travel mug. The Buick's interior was hot and humid, and the women were down to their underwear.

A band of hobos camped in the woods on the side of the pond, and each night the woman could hear drunken revelry in the distance. They tried the horn, but it had shorted out in the water.

"Listen," said Eunice, "you can hear 'em again."

"Help! Help us!" yelled Ethel.

"They can't hear you."

"How long do you think we can last?" asked Edith, licking spearmint adhesive off a postage stamp.

"You'd be amazed," said Eunice. "Mrs. Natofsky spent nine days with a broken hip in her shower before they found her."

"How was she?"

"Dead."

"Great," said Edith. "Thanks for sharing that, Miss Sunshine . . ."

"The point is she lasted *eight* days."

Edith noticed Edna was the only one not talking. "What do you have in your mouth?"

"Nothing."

"You've got something."

"No I don't."

"Grab her!"

"No!"

Eunice and Ethel scrambled over the headrests from the front seat and joined Edith, who already had Edna's left arm twisted behind her back.

"Lemmo go! That hurts!"

"Check her mouth!" said Edith.

Edna clamped her jaw shut. Eunice and Ethel pried her lips apart with their fingers but weren't having much luck with the clenched teeth. Edith pulled back with a fist and slugged her in the stomach.

"Aaaaahhh!" yelled Edna. The others briefly saw a tiny white oval on the back of her tongue before it disappeared toward her larynx.

"Tic Tacs!" yelled Edith. "She's got Tic Tacs!"

The three woman tore through Edna's purse, finding something hidden in the lining. A plastic container with three pellets left.

"No!" said Edna. "I'm gonna die!"

"Survival of the fittest," said Edith, and she and the others chewed up their breath mints.

Edith felt something else in the lining and slowly extracted an unending string of perforated foil packs from the Trojan plant.

"Girl, you are living in a serious fantasy world."

"Just because you're a wet rag . . ."

They began wrestling.

"Knock it off!" said Eunice. "We have to save our strength."

Edith cleared her throat. "This is probably a bad time to bring this up, but there really is no good time. In situations like this people have to face it sooner or later. And it's getting to be later."

"Face what?"

"Cannibalism. How do you want to do this?"

"Shut up," said Edna.

"I'm serious. This is a practical matter."

"We've got a long time before we reach that point."

"Not as long as you think."

"I'm not sure I can take part," said Ethel. "It might be against my religion."

"You're Jewish. You just can't eat pork."

"I think this would be a little worse," said Ethel.

"I don't think that's it at all," said Edith.

"What are you talking about?" said Ethel.

"I think I know what it really is. We're not good enough for you."

"What!"

"Yes, it's all coming out now. The Chosen People . . ."

"You're crazy!"

"Ethel's right," said Eunice. "You're cracking up."

"No, no, no!" said Edith. "I know exactly what I'm saying. I think her meaning's perfectly clear."

"I can't believe what I'm hearing!" said Ethel. "You're mad because I won't eat you?"

"Look," said Edna. "If it'll make you happy, *I'll* eat you."

"You're Presbyterian," said Edith. "You'll eat anything."

"I don't think I want to talk about this anymore," said Ethel.

"I do!" snapped Edith.

"Ethel, for heaven's sake, tell her you'll eat her."

"I'm waiting," said Edith.

"This is the stupidest conversation I've ever had!" said Ethel.

"That's why I want it to end," said Eunice. "Just tell her and we can move on to another subject."

"This is crazy!"

"Tell her! C'mon. She tastes like chicken." Eunice clapped her hands quickly. "Let's go. Goy—the other white meat."

"This is nuts."

"I'm still waiting!"

"Okay, okay, I'll eat you."

"Like hell you will!"

There was a rustling in the cattails.

"What is it?" said Ethel.

"A moose?" said Eunice.

Dark forms broke through the reeds. There was crash on the hood of the car. Two men wrestled on the windshield, Christ and the Antichrist.

"We're saved!" said Edith.

The men pulled each other's hair and gouged eyes. They rolled off the hood and fell in the swamp water. The four women watched the tops of the cattails thrash in the moonlight as the wrestling moved farther and farther from their car until it was still and quiet again.

"Shit."

37

"I'M TELLING YOU, THERE'S NO WAY!" SAID SERGE.

"You're in denial," said Coleman. "Look at the obvious overtones."

Coleman pressed a button on the remote control, increasing the volume. Serge leaned forward on the couch for a better view. Coleman pointed with the remote. "See the way Race Bannon is looking at Dr. Quest? I'm telling you, they were getting it on!"

"You're reading things into it that aren't there. I can't accept it."

"I'm surprised at you," said Coleman. "After all you've said in support of gay rights."

"It's not that," said Serge. "Quest's and Bannon's sexual preferences are nobody's business but their own. I'm just saying it didn't happen. It would have been an office romance, and they were much too professional."

"Believe what you want," said Coleman. He picked up his beer and went out on the porch.

Serge followed. "Remember the Sargasso Sea episode? The mad scientist with the pterodactyl? And who can forget the giant mechanical spider that they fire on with tanks in the closing credits?"

"So?"

"So, if their judgment was clouded, they never would have gotten out of all those jams. You can't think clearly under those conditions if your lover is in peril."

Tires screeched in the distance. Serge and Coleman looked up the street. A '76 Chevy Laguna tore around the corner and down Triggerfish.

Serge stood up on the porch and yelled at the car. "Hey! Slow down! Kids play around here!"

"He didn't hear you," said Coleman.

The car pulled up in front of the Davenport residence and honked the horn.

Serge yelled again: "Go up to the door and knock like a human being!"

"Why are you so upset?" asked Coleman.

"The guy's pushing my buttons. And he's much too old to be going out with Debbie."

"That's Jim's business."

"I know," Serge said with resignation. "I promised I wouldn't interfere."

Debbie never came out of the house, and the Laguna took off up the street.

"What I'd like to do to him!" said Serge.

"Remember, you're going straight."

"I know, I know. What would Jim do in a situation like this?"

"Look," said Coleman. "He's turning around."

"Jim would have a talk with him." Serge stood up and nodded. "That's what I'll do."

"I think his name's Scorpion," said Coleman.

Serge jumped off the porch and ran down to the corner. He waited at the stop sign.

The Laguna screeched to a halt.

"Hi," said Serge. "Would you mind driving just a tad slower around here? We have a lot of children who play—"

The driver raised his middle finger. "Fuck off, pops!" He patched out.

Serge walked back to his porch.

"Did you talk to him?" asked Coleman.

"Yep."

"Well?"

"It's a start. You have to begin somewhere."

Coleman pointed. "He's coming back."

Serge ran down to the corner again.

"Excuse me, Mr. Scorpion," said Serge. "I was trying to point out that we have a lot of little kids—"

The driver flicked a cigarette at Serge and sped off.

Serge returned to the porch.

"How's it coming?" asked Coleman.

Serge was looking down at his chest. "He threw a cigarette at me."

"It made a burn mark."

Serge scratched the spot with his finger. "This was one of my best shirts."

There were more tire sounds up the street. They turned and looked.

"I can't believe it," said Serge. "He's coming back."

"And look. There's Jim right behind him."

"Maybe I can stop them both, and we can all sit down and have a civilized talk."

Jim Davenport was heading home from the grocery store in the Suburban when he pulled up at a stop sign behind a '76 Chevy Laguna. The Laguna turned left onto Triggerfish, and Jim turned left behind him. The horn honked.

Jim saw brake lights on the Chevy. The driver got out and ran back to the Suburban. "Don't you ever blow your fucking horn at me!"

"I wasn't—"

Before Jim could finish, the Laguna's driver had opened the door and pulled him into the street.

Serge and Coleman jumped to their feet: "Road rage!" They sprinted for the corner.

The driver was sitting on Jim's chest, delivering a flurry of punches.

"Hey! Get off him!"

Scorpion looked up and saw Serge and Coleman running down the street; he jumped in the Laguna and took off.

They got to Jim and sat him up. "Are you okay?"

He was not okay. His shirt was torn. Gravel filled his hair, and blood and mucus ran down his neck. His lower lip was split and both eyes were starting to swell.

"Let's get you to the house," said Serge.

They helped Jim up the porch and into the living room. Serge and Coleman ran around frantically for ice cubes, peroxide and Band-Aids.

Jim stared at the floor. Serge returned with a washcloth full of ice.

"Look up," said Serge.

Jim didn't look up.

"You'll have to look up."

Jim was breathing hard. "I don't want them to see me like this."

"Nobody's going to see you like anything," said Serge. "I'm going to fix you up like new."

"Are you kidding?" said Coleman. "With shiners like that?"

"Shut up, Coleman!"

Serge turned back to Jim. "I have to see where to put the ice."

Jim slowly raised his face. He looked worse than Serge had expected. He bundled up the ice and showed Jim how to hold it against his eyes.

Jim's lowed lip started to vibrate.

"No!" said Serge. "Don't! You better not!"

The vibrations increased.

"Stop it! Stop it right now! Don't you dare!"

Jim couldn't stop.

"I'm warning you! Stop it this second!"

Jim leaned forward and put his forehead down on Serge's shoulder and began shaking with quiet sobs.

Serge took a deep breath and put his arms around Jim's back and began patting him lightly. "There, there. It's going to be all right."

A HALF HOUR later, Serge tried to open the Davenports' front door as quietly as possible and sneak Jim inside, but Martha was waiting.

She screamed when she saw Jim's face. She ran up to Serge and began pounding him on the chest with her fists. Serge let her.

"What have you done to my husband! I never want to see you again! Get out of here!"

Serge opened his mouth to say something, but he changed his mind and left.

TWO A.M. Floor buffers hummed inside the twenty-four-hour Home Depot. Serge pushed his shopping cart down an empty aisle in the electrical department. He grabbed a box of security lights off the shelf.

A stock clerk came up. "Finding everything all right?"

"Got a question," said Serge.

"Shoot."

Serge held out the box. "Is this right? Only nineteen-ninety-five for a motion-detector floodlight?"

"The bulbs are extra," said the clerk.

Serge put two boxes in his shopping cart. "Where are the bulbs?"

"Aisle three."

"Glass cutters?"

"Two kinds. What kind of glass are you looking to cut?"

"Floodlight bulbs."

The clerk looked at Serge.

"Just tell me where both kinds are," said Serge.

"Aisles seven and eight."

"Gas cans?"

"Twelve."

"Orange vests for highway construction sites? Reflective signs?"

"Thirteen and fifteen."

THREE A.M. The driver of a Chevy Laguna flicked another cigarette out the window and bobbed his head to the stereo. A baffled expression appeared on his face. Something shiny in the road up ahead. He turned off the stereo and leaned over the steering wheel.

"What the hell?"

The driver hit his high beams. He thought he was seeing things. Someone was sitting in the middle of the road in a lawn chair. He wore an orange vest and held up a crossing-guard stop sign.

The Chevy rolled up slowly, and the man in the vest came around to the driver's window.

"What are you, some kind of lunatic!" said Scorpion.

"Yes," said Serge, sticking a forty-four Magnum in his face. "Now tuck in your fucking underwear."

FOUR A.M. Scorpion was standing in the middle of an aluminum shed in a darkened backyard. It was the shed behind the college rental, used to store tools to take care of the yard. Nobody had been in it for months.

Scorpion's wrists were bound tightly, and another rope stretched his arms up over his head and tied the wrists to an eye-bolt in the shed's ceiling. His mouth was duct-taped.

Serge sat cross-legged at the man's feet, tongue sticking out the corner of his mouth in concentration, wiring the motion detectors. He had one detector on each side of the man's feet, eighteen inches away, facing outward.

Serge looked up at Scorpion and smiled. "These new low-watt bulbs are incredible. The filaments will burn almost forever in the inert gases inside . . ."

Serge continued scratching away with the glass cutter until he had made a complete circle. Then he held the bulb upside-down over his head and tapped the circle lightly with the butt of the cutter. The round disk broke free.

"Of course, if the bulb's filament is exposed to the oxygen in the atmosphere, it'll sizzle and burn out in seconds." He screwed the modified bulbs into the motion detectors. Then he unwound the security lights' power cords and plugged them into the shed's utility socket.

Serge reached behind some plywood and pulled out a hula hoop. "You know who invented summer?"

Scorpion didn't move a muscle.

"The Wham-O Corporation."

Serge held the hula hoop in one hand and the gun in the other. "Step into this."

Scorpion lifted one leg, then the other. Serge raised the hoop up to the man's waist. He pressed the Magnum to his nose.

"If I give this thing a spin, do you think you can shoop-shoop hula hoop?"

Scorpion nodded.

"Marvelous. You seem a lot more cooperative than when I talked to you before. I knew I had caught you on a bad day. That's my motto: Don't be quick to judge others."

Serge gave the hula hoop a healthy spin, and the man began moving his hips.

"Hey, you're a natural! You should see some of the kids around here with these things. You'd think they had them in the womb. . . . Oh, but I already told you about all the kids we have playing around here. Remember? When I was saying how cars really should go slow? And while we're on the topic, Debbie's way too young for you. What's the matter with women your own age?"

The hoop continued rotating, and Serge continued pointing the gun.

"Let's see how long you can keep that thing going," said Serge. "I remember when I was a kid, the neighborhood record was like two hours."

Serge grabbed a metal five-gallon gas can and slowly poured the contents across the shed's concrete floor.

"If the hula hoop falls, the motion detector will pick it up and turn on the floodlights. But they'll only be on a moment. That's how long it'll take for the filaments to ignite the gasoline vapor. It's the vapor you gotta watch out for, you know. The stuff explodes like you wouldn't believe."

Serge sniffed the air.

"In fact, it's starting to smell pretty powerful in here right now. I better get going. By the way, concrete is porous, so there's a slight chance that if you can keep the hoop going long enough, the gasoline will seep in and the fumes dissipate. It'll take hours, but it's theoretically possible. And I wouldn't try to kick the detectors out of the way because that will set them off instantly. . . . Well, toodles!"

38

THE MCGRAW BROTHERS ran out of the Florida National Bank in Clearwater with $2,375 in a fast but sloppy heist. The bank had a double set of entrance doors with locks that could be activated by any of the tellers. As the McGraws fled, one of the tellers hit her lock button, trapping Ed between the doors.

He banged on the glass for his brothers to come back.

They were halfway across the parking lot when they heard the racket. They turned and saw Ed pull a large pistol, preparing to blast his way out.

"He can't be that stupid," said Rufus McGraw.

Ed fired a quick burst from the automatic pistol. But the glass was bulletproof, and bullets began ricocheting and whizzing back and forth, the rest of the McGraws watching in amazement as their younger brother was slowly cut down in a hail of his own gunfire.

AGENT MAHONEY ARRIVED in south Tampa just before noon. The crime scene was fresh. He could smell Serge.

A sergeant was guarding the scene. Mahoney walked up and pulled a toothpick from his mouth.

"If it isn't my favorite state agent," said the sarge. "We have to stop meeting like this."

Mahoney didn't like small talk. He didn't like the sergeant. He didn't like this whole stinking case. He stared down at a chalk out-line on the still-smoldering ground. "What have we got here?"

"Aluminum shed flattened in some type of explosion," said the sergeant. "The corrugated roof was found on the next block. Pieces of melted hula hoop everywhere."

"He was here. I can feel him."

"Who?" said the sergeant.

"Serge."

"Never heard of him."

"He never heard of you."

"I guess that makes us even."

"What do you have behind your back?"

"Nothing."

"Yes you do. You're hiding something."

"Nonsense."

"Your hands are behind your back."

"No they're not."

"Yes they are. Look!"

"Don't be silly."

"Let me see!"

"No!"

Mahoney reached his arms around the sergeant, and they struggled briefly. Mahoney snatched something from the sergeant's left hand. A ruby red stiletto pump high heel.

"You sure have a lot of hobbies, sergeant."

"Tried building eighteenth-century schooners out of Popsicle sticks. Didn't do it for me."

"Hobbies are funny that way."

Mahoney reached through his car window for The Good Book, and flipped to the back.

"What's with the Bible?" asked the sergeant. "Daily inspiration? Comfort at grisly crime scenes?"

"No. I've been getting into the Book of Revelations," said Mahoney. "And it's all coming true. We're entering The End Times. The signs are all around us. The nations of Gog and Magog. The cashless society. Soon they'll be tattooing a UPC code on your nuts . . ."

"I'll call in sick that day."

". . . After that, it gets strange. The raging battle between Christ and the Antichrist. Seven-eyed beasts. The blood of the Lamb.

Demons and archangels fighting in the sky. Born-again people rap-tured right out of moving vehicles, improving the quality of their driving. And finally, total Armageddon."

"I didn't know you were religious."

"I'm not. I'm looking at it as a major law-enforcement headache. We can barely handle the crowd at the Gasparilla Parade."

"Armageddon," said the sergeant, shaking his head. "Try get-ting any backup *that* night."

"There are going to be a lot of battlefield promotions," said Mahoney. "Why not me?"

The radio in Mahoney's Crown Victoria began to squawk. Mahoney reached in the window and grabbed the mike.

"Mahoney here."

"You son of a bitch!" said Lieutenant Ingersol. "Where are you?"

"I'm—"

"Never mind! I know you're looking for Serge. You get back on the McGraw case right now. They just robbed Florida National in Clearwater. Ed McGraw's dead."

"Clearwater is in striking distance of Tampa," said Mahoney. "You have to let me warn the Davenports!"

"We're too close," said Ingersol. "We're about to tighten the noose. Now drop this Serge thing and get over to the bank."

"Sir, I think I can find both Serge and the McGraws—"

"Forget it!" yelled Ingersol.

"Lieutenant, you're breaking up."

". . . Mahoney, you're a loose cannon! You've gone rogue! . . ."

Mahoney changed the radio to easy-listening jazz.

39

H. AMBROSE TARRINGTON III awoke the next morning to the sound of a woodpecker tapping on a dead cabbage palm outside his window. Ambrose didn't know it yet, but this was going to be the day that would change his life forever. Before it was all over, he'd make the national news and get married on the *Today* show.

Ambrose polished off his Pop-Tarts, put on a three-piece suit and inspected himself in a full-length mirror. Then he packed swim trunks and a Polaroid camera in his briefcase and headed out the front door of 918 Triggerfish. He walked three blocks to a cement bench advertising bail bonds, sat down and waited for the Number Eight.

ROCCO SILVERTONE jumped to his feet in the showroom of Tampa Bay Motors.

"He's back!"

"Who's back?" asked Vic.

"I didn't think this chance came twice in a lifetime!"

Rocco ran to the door to greet Ambrose Tarrington III. They shook hands and exchanged business cards.

"I'd like to drive the Rolls again," said Ambrose.

"But I thought the color didn't match your house."

"Changed my mind," said Ambrose. "I'll paint the house."

They took the golf cart out to the luxury cars. Ambrose and

Rocco got in the Rolls and drove a mile up and down Dale Mabry Highway.

"Rides like a dream, don't she?" said Rocco. "A real cream puff."

Ambrose pulled back into the dealership. "Don't like it."

Rocco felt like he had taken a gunshot. He had been on top of the world, and in an instant he was back at the bottom again. "What is it? I can probably fix it. The leather? Is it the leather? Gas mileage? I'll take off the catalytic converter—"

Ambrose pointed. "I want one of those."

Rocco turned and saw a snow-white Ferrari F50.

My God, he thought, that costs more than the Rolls. He became light-headed from the rapid swings of fortune and steadied himself against a Saab.

"You all right?" asked Ambrose.

Rocco nodded. "Wait here." He zipped back to showroom and grabbed the Ferrari's keys off the pegboard. He returned and opened the driver's door. Ambrose climbed down into the Ferrari. There was a pair of brown, open-knuckled driving gloves on the dash. Ambrose slid them on.

"Let me switch the dealer tags from the Rolls," said Rocco.

Ambrose turned on the car, put it in gear and gunned the engine until the tachometer was pegged.

"Okay, forget the tags." Rocco jumped in as Ambrose bolted off the lot.

Ambrose quickly ran through first gear, then second and third, agile coordination of clutch and shift. Rocco leaned over. "Maybe you should be a little easier—"

Ambrose grabbed the mahogany shift knob with the trademark gold stallion crest, jerked it into fourth and let her unwind. The G-force pasted Rocco into his seat as the Ferrari split Tampa like the Bonneville salt flats. Ambrose let off the fuel and coasted seven blocks.

Rocco's color returned. "She's got some pickup, eh?"

"But how does she handle in a turn?"

"I don't think you should—aaaaaaauuuuuuuu!"

Ambrose held the wheel left, against the edge of the centrifugal envelope, executing a perfect bullwhip half-spin. After the U-turn, he spun the wheel back to twelve o'clock, straightened her out.

Rocco opened his eyes. They were still alive.

"I love it," said Ambrose.

Time for the kill, thought Rocco. He sized Ambrose up as an ethnic joke man.

"A priest and a rabbi walk into a bar—"

"Ethnic jokes are the last refuge of a bankrupt intellect."

Rocco was knocked off balance. "Even the Mexican jokes?"

"Especially the Mexican jokes."

Rocco panicked. Those were his funniest jokes. What now? He thought a second.

"How about faggots?" asked Rocco. "I can tell butt-burglar jokes, right? They're not an ethnic group. And *everybody* hates them . . ."

Ambrose pulled the Ferrari off the road. He turned and stared at Rocco.

"You want me to get out?"

Ambrose nodded.

It was a long, lonely walk back to the dealership. Rocco kept telling himself it would all work out. He had broken the rules, but the rules were for losers like John Milton. Nobody ever made it to the top without risks. He'd walk right in the owner's office and tell him that. Surely he'd understand. Of course he's not going to understand! Are you insane?

Rocco made a big walking loop to avoid being spotted. He slipped inside the ice cream hut across the street from Tampa Bay Motors, where he could stake out the dealership until Ambrose returned.

"Chocolate smoothie, waffle cone, extra nuts."

AMBROSE DROVE OVER to Bayshore and put the Ferrari through the paces. He raced up the circular drive of the biggest mansion on Bayshore and got out with a Polaroid camera and snapped a picture.

A butler came to the door shaking a fireplace poker. "I thought I told you to stay out of here!"

Ambrose jumped back in the car and shot out of the driveway, speeding across the peninsula, looking for something to eat. He pulled into a shopping-center parking lot and entered the drive-through for Wendy's, home of the ninety-nine-cent menu.

40

SERGE CALLED A MEETING.

Coleman sat on the couch.

"Fuck this stupidness," said Sharon.

Serge pointed. "Sit down."

"You guys can play house. I'm going out," said Sharon. She headed for the door.

"I said, sit down!" Serge grabbed her and threw her on the couch.

Sharon folded her arms and frowned. "I'm not going to listen."

Serge paced in front of the couch, tapping his clipboard with a pencil.

"We've got cash-flow problems. I blew too much money on our night out with the Davenports. And I misjudged the electric bill. That means no more coke."

That got their attention.

"It gets worse," said Serge. He turned up the volume on the TV.

It was a local newscast. A bunch of people sat at a long desk with microphones and nameplates.

"That's the Tampa City Council," said Serge. "They're meeting on the lap-dance ban. There goes Sharon's income."

"They can't do that!" said Sharon.

"They just did," said Serge. "Better dust off those nursing textbooks."

The TV station cut from the city council to extended stock footage of a stripper swinging around a pole.

"Shocking!" said the anchorman, shaking his head in disgust. "Can we see that again?"

Serge turned down the volume and resumed pacing. "I've been doing some figuring. With our current reserves, we have about a week until two of us will have to kill the other and harvest their organs for the black market."

Coleman began to perspire. He knew Serge and Sharon were sleeping together, and that could mean a voting bloc. He raised his hand.

"We have a question in back?" said Serge.

"There's got to be another way!" said Coleman.

"There is, my fine hookah-sucking friend. It's time we put my kidnapping plan into motion."

"Kidnapping?" said Sharon. "You have to be kidding!"

Serge flipped a page over on his clipboard, revealing a story-board. Coleman and Sharon saw three stick figures running around with guns, another stick figure with a sack over his head and other crude pencil drawings of telephones, getaway cars and bags of money with dollar signs on the side. Then Serge got a little carried away and there were lots of dotted lines for bullets flying through the air and cars exploding and stick figures lying around with X's for eyes and their heads chopped off.

"Don't worry about those last pictures," said Serge. "That's the worst-case scenario. Had to consider everything."

Serge flipped to another page.

"What's that?" asked Sharon.

"Chronology of historic kidnappings. The Lindbergh baby, Frank Sinatra Junior, Patty Hearst and of course the big one in Florida, Barbara Jane Mackle, daughter of Miami developer snatched December 17, 1968. Survived more than three days underground in a coffin equipped with a ventilation fan. Wrote a best-seller, *Eighty-three Hours Till Dawn*. Reader's Digest condensed it."

"What's that got to do with us?"

"This could be a two-fer," said Serge. "I want a book deal."

"What about your diet book?" asked Coleman.

"That was last week. I have no idea what I was thinking."

"That's the stupidest plan I've ever heard!" said Sharon.

"Is not!"

"Is so!" said Sharon. "And you haven't said who we're gonna grab."

"Whom," said Serge.

"What?"

"Whom to grab."

"That's what I said."

Serge closed his eyes hard, silently counted to ten, then opened them. He looked at his watch. "We have to start getting ready. It's almost time."

"I'm not going anywhere!" said Sharon.

Serge pulled a tiny baggie of coke out of his pocket and dangled it in front of her.

The three sat around the kitchen table. It was covered with bullets, clips, pistols and brass knuckles. The stereo played "Helter Skelter" with extra bass.

Sharon pressed nine-millimeter rounds into a clip, then did some blow. She rammed the clip home in the butt of the Beretta and smiled wickedly with a cigarette clenched in the corner of her mouth. "I'm really gonna fuckin' enjoy this!"

Coleman tried on the brass knuckles and hit himself on the jaw to see how it felt. "Ow!"

Serge used a speed-loader on his .357. This was Serge at his finest, before a job. Distilled focus, fluid movements—loading weapons and packing gym bags with clothes and rope. His lucky untucked floral shirt gave him the elegance of a stalking cougar before the strike. Lanky, quick, chilling.

"... *Tell me, tell me, tell me the answer. You may be a lover, but you ain't no dancer* ..."

Serge stood up. "Let's rock!"

SHARON WANTED TO kill something right away, but Serge told her to be patient. Coleman was content in the backseat with his *Cracked* magazine. They found their mark by midmorning and began a loose tail.

"What are we waiting for!" said Sharon, powder across her upper lip, waving her gun.

"The right moment," said Serge. "This is delicate stuff. We have to make a surgical strike."

The target pulled into a parking lot and rolled to a stop. Serge eased the Barracuda in from behind. "Okay, remember: timing, precision and stealth."

Sharon and Coleman jumped out yelling and waving guns.

"Open the fucking door!" screamed Sharon, banging on the window.

"This is a kidnapping!" shouted Coleman.

"Open the door right now or I'll blow your fucking head off!"

"Resistance is futile!" yelled Coleman.

Sharon stepped back and aimed her pistol. "Die, motherfucker!"

Serge walked up and snatched the gun from her hands—"Gimme that before you hurt someone!"—and opened the unlocked door of the Ferrari F50 in the Wendy's drive-through. "Would you mind coming with us?"

They climbed back in the Barracuda as the Wendy's people phoned the police.

Serge floored it and raced to the side of the parking lot for a quick getaway on Interstate 275. But when he got to the edge of the lot, there was no exit. Just a cement curb along a strip of Bermuda grass.

"Damn! It's one of *those* parking lots!" said Serge, cutting the wheel.

"What kind is that?" asked Coleman.

"The new kind that doesn't let you out where you want to go. Instead it deliberately channels you to some place you don't want to be at all. Hold on!"

Serge accelerated toward a free-standing building in the front of the parking lot. "We'll exit at Miami Subs."

But when Serge got to the restaurant, he saw another long curb with no opening.

"We can't get through! Miami Subs is connected to the next shopping center, and it won't let us in unless we enter from the highway!"

"But how do we get to the highway?" asked Coleman.

"Who the fuck knows?" said Serge, slapping the dash. "What the hell do they want from us?"

Serge turned the wheel again, making a skidding one-eighty on open asphalt, and headed back.

Witnesses had begun gathering outside the Wendy's to exchange accounts of the abduction. Latecomers arrived and wanted the story repeated. Employees were still on the phone with police.

Someone pointed. "They're coming back!"

Everyone pressed against the side of the Wendy's as the Barracuda blew by.

"We were just here!" said Sharon.

"Hello, Cleveland!" said Coleman.

"Shut up! I can't think with all this chatter!"

"What about over there?" said Coleman, pointing to a string of palm-tree islands. "There must be a break."

"I see it!" said Serge. He raced over to the islands, searching for an opening.

"Look. A new store," said Coleman. "*The High Seas*. Paraphernalia and nautical gifts. I'll have to come back."

Serge got to the end of the palm-tree islands without finding a break. Instead, a concrete abutment jutted from the left, shunting the Barracuda back to the shopping center.

Serge banged his head on the steering wheel. "What kind of satanic parking lot is this!"

People pressed against Wendy's again as Serge made another pass.

41

JOHN MILTON HAD DECIDED THAT HE WAS INVISIBLE. That's what his days on the streets of Tampa had taught him. That's how people treated all street crazies, looking right through them. John liked being invisible. It opened up options.

John walked down a Dumpster alley, talking and gesturing. He came out from behind a shopping center and started across the parking lot. There was a large gathering of people outside the Wendy's. John walked right through them until he came to a white Ferrari with the driver's door open and keys in the ignition. John began to hear police sirens in the distance. God told him to get in the car.

ROCCO SILVERTONE FINISHED his second smoothie cone and wiped his hands with a napkin. What could be taking Ambrose so long? He balled up the napkin and made a jump shot off the side of the wastebasket.

When he looked up, he saw a white Ferrari coming down the street.

"Finally."

He walked to the edge of the road. The Ferrari didn't stop— didn't even slow. Rocco looked in the window as it went by.

"Oh, no."

Rocco waited for a break in traffic and sprinted across the street to the dealership. He ran in the sales office, pulled Ambrose's business card from his wallet and got on the phone.

Vic showed up in the doorway. "What's up, Rocco?"

Rocco ran around the desk, grabbed Vic by the arm and jerked him into the office. He slammed the door.

"Rocco, what's going on?"

SERGE PULLED THE Barracuda off the highway and into the grid streets. Coleman and Sharon got out their respective stashes.

Coleman and Sharon did drugs like an algebra equation. If Coleman has a hundred dollars of Panama Red and starts smoking at three o'clock, and Sharon has two hundred dollars of Peruvian Marching Dust and begins vacuuming at four o'clock, at what time will they drive Serge absolutely batshit?

Sharon snorted up an amazing amount of coke in the front seat of the Barracuda. She raised her head, her eyes not working in tandem. "When do I get to shoot the little bastard? I could get off on that!"

"We're not shooting anyone," said Serge. "That's the whole point. We gotta get some money for him."

Serge glanced over his shoulder at Coleman. "Found his wallet yet?"

"Hold on," said Coleman, patting Ambrose down. ". . . I got it!"

"What's inside?"

"Hey! There's no money!"

"We're not looking for money this time. Any ID?"

Coleman peeled the billfold apart. "Here's a business card."

"What's it say?"

"Tarrington Import . . . H. Ambrose Tarrington the Third, President and CEO."

"I knew it!" said Serge. "I knew he had to be somebody important! I've seen him all over Tampa driving fancy cars. . . . Anything else on the card?"

"Says they have offices in Tampa, New York City and Beverly Hills."

Serge smacked the seat. "Jackpot! I'll bet they'll pay anything to get him back alive. Not that they care about him. But stock prices tumble when a corporation is decapitated. It could mean a billion off the Dow, take down the whole industrial thirty . . ."

"What the fuck are you talking about!" screamed Sharon, waving her gun at Serge. "Nothing can be simple with you! You have to complicate it with all your bullshit! When do we get the coke?"

"What coke?" asked Serge.

"That's what we're here for! The big coke score!"

"What are you talking about?"

"That was the plan! We grab the guy and he takes us to the coke!"

"Sharon, you're fucked up. Come back to us. This is just like the time you started seeing rats and chiggers on your skin."

Sharon scratched her head rapidly like a spider monkey. "No coke? Where did I get that from?"

Coleman lit a joint and took a deep drag. "Sharon, you have to learn to handle your drugs a little better. . . . Ooo, shit! I dropped it. Where'd it go?"

Ambrose picked the joint off the carpet and handed it back to Coleman.

"Thanks."

Serge looked in the rearview. "Did you burn something again in here? You know I love this car!"

Serge then checked Ambrose in the mirror. "You don't look so good, Ambrose. You okay? You're not going to stroke out on us, are you? Tell me if you are . . ."

Ambrose yawned. "No, I just usually take a nap about this time."

Serge smiled in the mirror. "That's what I like. Someone who can handle pressure. My two partners are falling apart, but Ambrose is solid as a rock. Ambrose, this your first time?"

Ambrose nodded.

"You're doing great. Keep it up." Serge tossed a cell phone over his shoulder to Coleman. "Time to make the call."

"Which number should I use?"

"The New York office. That's where the decision-makers will be."

Coleman punched up the two-one-two area code.

"Remember to use the voice scrambler I gave you," said Serge.

"Right," said Coleman. He reached under the seat and pulled out a Dixie cup and put it over his mouth. He pressed the bottom of the cup against the phone.

Sharon looked at Coleman, then Serge. "You've got to be joking."

"Shhhhhhhhh! He's making the call!" snapped Serge. "They'll recognize your voice. You don't have a scrambler."

Serge handed Coleman a scrap of paper with the script he'd written. Coleman took the phone away from his ear. "It's an answering machine."

"Read it anyway," said Serge.

Coleman put the Dixie cup back over his mouth and began reading. "We have Insert Name Here . . ."

"Ambrose!" said Serge.

"We have Insert Name Here Ambrose. Do not call the authorities. Put ten million dollars in small, marked bills . . ."

"Unmarked!"

". . . correction, unmarked bills in a duffel bag and await further instructions. This is the Simian Liberation Army."

Coleman hung up. He popped a beer and poured it in the scrambler.

Serge stopped the car and turned around.

"What?" said Coleman. "What are you looking at me like that for?"

"What the hell was that last part?"

"What last part?"

"The Liberation Army. That wasn't on the script."

"Oh yeah," said Coleman, smiling proudly. "I added that myself. I found it in your history papers. Pretty cool, eh?"

"Symbionese."

"What?"

"It's Symbionese, not Simeon. You've made us into some kind of radical animal-rights brigade."

Coleman chugged the beer. "I thought you'd like it."

Serge turned back around and resumed driving. "Next time I read the note."

"Fine," said Coleman. "I didn't ask to read any note."

"But I'm driving. I can't do everything. I need some help in here . . . Sharon, what the fuck are you doing?"

Sharon was taking off her clothes as fast as she could. "Things are crawling on me! Get 'em off!"

Serge turned to their hostage. "Ambrose. *Ambrose!* . . . Coleman, he's dead! We killed him!"

Serge reached back and shook Ambrose, and he woke up.

"Jesus, Ambrose! You scared the shit out of me!"

"Sorry."

"Ambrose, you're a maniac!" said Serge. "The rest of us are all jumpy, and *we've* got the guns. But you're back there catching some winks. You are stone cold, my man!"

ROCCO SILVERTONE GOT a busy signal in New York. He sat at his desk with Ambrose's business card in his hand. He hung up and tried again.

"You really think John stole the Ferrari?" asked Vic.

"I don't think—I know! I saw him driving it!"

"But what did he do with the old man?"

"I don't know," said Rocco. "That's what I'm trying to find out."

"Maybe we should tell the boss?"

Rocco reached across the desk and grabbed Vic by the arm. "No! We can't say anything! I wasn't supposed to get out of the car." He let go of Vic. "I have to figure out a way to handle this without anyone finding out."

"Good luck."

Rocco dialed the New York number on Ambrose's card again. This time he got through.

"Shoot," Rocco said under his breath. "Answering machine."

He hung up and tried to think.

"CHECK IT OUT," said Coleman, pulling a driver's license from Ambrose's wallet. "He lives on Triggerfish Lane. Don't we live on Triggerfish Lane, too?"

"Can't be the same one," said Serge. "Let me see that."

Coleman passed the license forward.

Serge looked at his license. His rubbed his eyes and held the license closer. He looked up and hit the gas.

The Barracuda whipped around the corner of Triggerfish Lane and skidded to a stop in front of a tiny house with *918* over the door. Serge double-checked the license. 918.

He looked at Ambrose. "Tell me this isn't your home."

Ambrose stared down and nodded.

"Would you mind explaining what the hell's going on?"

Ambrose looked away, out the window.

"I'm talking to you!" yelled Serge. "We've gone through a lot of trouble for you! Now what's the story?"

Ambrose wouldn't look at him.

"That wasn't your Ferrari, was it?" said Serge.

Ambrose shook his head.

"The other cars. None of them yours?"

He shook his head again.

"Then what gives?"

Ambrose mumbled.

"Louder," said Serge. "I can't hear you."

"Test drives," said Ambrose.

Serge started punching the roof of the car. "Dammit! Dammit! Dammit! Dammit! . . ." His knuckles started to bleed and he stopped. He turned back to Ambrose. "Would you just tell me why?"

Ambrose hung his head.

"Look at me when I'm talking to you! I asked you a question!"

Ambrose looked up.

"Well?"

Ambrose's voice was barely a whisper. "I was lonely." A tear started down his cheek.

"No! Not that! Anything but that!"

More tears.

"Stop it! Stop it right now!"

It only got worse.

Serge kneeled backward in his seat, grabbed Ambrose by the shoulders and shook him. "What have I ever done to you! What is it you want from me!"

"Can I stay with you?"

"No! No, you can't stay with me!" Serge reached over and opened Ambrose's door. "Get out right now! You're free to go!"

"I promise I won't make any false moves."

"Didn't you hear me? Go!"

Ambrose looked down and the tears started again.

"Okay, okay! You can stay! But only briefly. Very temporarily. Just until I can figure out what to do, so don't get all attached or anything."

Ambrose raised his head and smiled.

Coleman took a hit on his joint and tapped Serge's shoulder. "Does this mean his company won't pay the ransom?"

"Oh no. They're going to double the amount."

Coleman grinned. "Really?"

Serge faced forward and gripped the steering wheel. "All right. What's done is done. Can't get paralyzed by this. Have to do damage assessment . . ." Serge's brain time-lapsed through the last hour. ". . . The Ferrari! Dammit! We had a three-hundred-thousand-dollar car! Ohhhhhhh—this nightmare just won't end! . . . Okay, keep going. Don't get hung up on that SAT question. What else? . . . The ransom demand . . ."

Serge turned back to Coleman. "We have to get that ransom message off the voice mail. It's evidence. Those things have retrieval codes." He turned to Ambrose. "What is it?"

"Eleven."

"Coleman, dial the number again, punch in eleven and follow the instructions to erase messages."

Coleman dialed. He tapped Serge's shoulder again. "I'm getting a busy signal."

"Who could be calling?" said Serge.

42

Dammit, I'm still getting a recording," said Rocco.

"Are there any other menu options?" asked Vic.

"It says if you don't want voice mail and need to speak to someone right away, hit one. I've been hitting one but nobody answers!" Rocco began banging away in frustration at the number one. There was a click on the line and a new recording. "Hold on," said Rocco. "I'm getting something."

It was a robotic voice: "You . . . have . . . one . . . new . . . voice mail . . . message." Then a beep and another voice. "We have Insert Name Here . . ."

"What is it?" asked Vic.

"Shhhhh!"

Rocco listened to the entire message, then quietly hung up.

"Rocco, you look like you've seen a ghost!"

"It's a kidnapping," said Rocco. "It's John."

"John's been kidnapped?"

"No, the old man's been kidnapped. John's the kidnapper!"

"You recognized his voice?"

"No. He was using a scrambler."

"You have to call the police!"

"I told you—this can't get out."

"What are you going to do?"

Rocco thought a second, then nodded to himself. "His company. Maybe I can work through them. I've got information they need, and big corporations always like to keep kidnappings quiet." He dialed again.

"But there's nobody there," said Vic.

"I'll leave a message."

"Maybe they'll give you a reward."

The recording started and Rocco waved for Vic to keep it down. The machine told Rocco to wait for the beep. Rocco waited.

Beep.

"Hello, this is Rocco Silvertone in Tampa, Florida. I understand your president, Ambrose Tarrington the Third, has been kidnapped. I have some important information you may be able to use . . ."

"Remember to ask about a reward," whispered Vic. Rocco pushed him away.

". . . I think I know who the kidnapper might be, and I may even be able to help you locate Mr. Tarrington . . ."

Vic held up a piece of paper with *REWARD* in big letters.

". . . I'm not seeking anything for myself, but any gratitude you might wish to show my favorite charity, I'd be happy to handle the delivery . . ."

Rocco left his phone number and hung up.

"I'M STILL GETTING a busy signal," said Coleman, hanging up.

"Try again," said Serge.

Coleman dialed again. "I'm getting through this time."

"Remember to hit eleven," said Serge.

Coleman pressed one-one. He heard his ransom demand begin to replay, then followed the instruction to erase it. He was just about to hang up when another message started. He listened and began to shake.

"Coleman. What's wrong?"

"They're on to us!"

"Who is?"

"Rocco Silvertone. He says he knows who we are!"

"Who the hell's Rocco Silvertone?"

"I can't go to prison!" His hands trembled as he lit another joint.

"Nobody's going to prison," said Serge. "Now who's Rocco Silvertone?"

Coleman handed him the phone. "Listen to the message."

Serge dialed again and pressed eleven and listened. He closed the phone. "Who on earth is Rocco Silvertone?"

"I know," said Ambrose.

He told Serge all about the most successful salesman at Tampa Bay Motors.

Serge popped a stick of gum in his mouth. "As if the plot isn't thick enough!"

Coleman took another deep hit and tapped Serge on the shoulder again.

"What is it?"

"Remember the two Darrins in *Bewitched*?"

"Yeah?"

"Their names were Dick Sargent and Dick York."

"Your point?"

"Don't you see? Dick Sargent. Dick York. *Sergeant York*!"

"So . . . ?"

"So it makes you wonder."

"Uh, yeah, Coleman. It makes me wonder all right. I'm going to turn back around now and start driving again. But please feel free to report in with any more bulletins as they become available."

Coleman nodded and took another hit.

Serge made a left. Before they knew it, they were back on Triggerfish Lane. Serge pulled up in front of Ambrose's house.

"Well, here she is! Home sweet home!" said Serge.

Ambrose didn't move.

"I told you when this started it was only temporary. We have to go our separate ways. Fly high, oh freebird, yeah! . . . Come on, Ambrose, get out of the car."

Ambrose began moving slowly. He took off his wristwatch and held it out to Serge.

"Ambrose, really, that's not necessary."

He kept holding it out to Serge.

"Okay, if you insist." Serge took the watch and looked at it. "Nice Rolex."

"It's a fake," said Ambrose.

"The thought that counts."

"Sure I can't stay?"

"No, I—" Serge looked at the watch again. "Holy cow! Look at the time! Today's Friday, right?"

"What is it?" asked Coleman.

"I've got a commencement address to deliver at the University of South Florida! The dean asked me back when I was teaching there this summer."

"Ha!" Sharon laughed. "You're no teacher!"

"Can't you let me have my little dreams?"

"What about Ambrose?" asked Coleman.

"I guess he's coming. I can't argue with him now. I have to think of the students."

THE DEAN WAS onstage in a cold sweat, checking his real Rolex.

Serge turned the Barracuda off Fowler Avenue and blew through the security gate. The floor of the Sun Dome was already a sea of gowns when Serge hopped a curb and parked on a downed handicapped sign.

"You go ahead," said Coleman. "We'll catch up."

Serge took off on foot.

The dean was wiping his forehead with a handkerchief when Serge bounded up the stairs and slapped him on the shoulder. "Sorry I'm late, teach." He ran out onstage.

The audience quieted as Serge walked up to the podium. He tapped the microphone.

"Has anyone heard that Jerry Springer now has a place in Sarasota?"

A few people nodded.

"I mention this because I'm still waiting for Tonya Harding to move down here and make it a clean sweep. I'm going through withdrawal because I haven't heard anything about her since she beat that guy in the head with a hubcap at a hoedown. And what about the poor guy? I don't think there's any better time to sit down for that little heart-to-heart with yourself. 'Good morning. This is your wake-up call. It's from Darwin.' But that's just one person's tiny drama, meaningless except in the bigger picture, which is trying to isolate the exact moment we turned into Trash Nation, and nearest I can tell, it was one second after Nancy Kerrigan took a telescoping blackjack to the knee. Now there was a cute little soap opera. What an absolutely fascinating underwater view into the Kmart inflatable backyard American gene pool. I have a dirty little confession. I loved it! We may have learned everything we needed to know about life in kindergarten. But you know what? We can learn everything we need to know about the incredibly rude, selfish, infantile country we've become by observing the human spokes revolving around the Tonya Harding sociocultural axis. The Greeks reveled in Homeric tragicomedies; the English lived out Shakespearean dramas. But we, America, are the cast of the Kerrigan farce. Is it any wonder we've thrown manners, compassion and respect out the window? We've become one big, self-absorbed nation holding up an ice skate, pointing at a broken lace and blubbering our eyes out. We don't know our neighbors anymore. We have no shame, no consideration, no sense of duty or sacrifice. Need more metaphors? We won't go the extra mile, meet anyone halfway, and if, somehow, somewhere, anything at all goes wrong in our pathetic daily wanderings, if some random misfortune drops at our feet and splatters like a Taco Supreme, we don't commence to tidying up the floor and getting on with our lives. We start making a litigious radar sweep of the room, seeing if there's anyone in recrimination range, some entitlement cadet to whom we can construct a Bridge-over-the-River-Kwai blame-path of tortured logic and sheer, reality-sculpting self-deception. Maybe they handled a taco once, maybe even made tacos. Maybe they could have warned you—yes, they knew all about that treacherously viscous emulsion of grease and sour cream on wax wrapper. They deliberately chose not to say anything as they saw it slipping out of your hand in Peckinpah slow motion while you were trying to eat, talk on the phone and log on to eBay at the same time. Well, here's a news flash for you. Believe it or not, the blacks and the gays and the Jews did not drop your taco. You dropped the fucking taco, my friend! It doesn't make you a bad person. It doesn't even mean it's your fault. What it does mean is that this cosmic slapstick we call life has just elected you the shmuck who has to go get the mop. So go get the goddamn mop already! Don't just stand there staring down, reliving the lunch-that-could-have-been and trying to figure out how affirmative action did this to you. That's just the way life is. It can be exquisite, cruel, frequently wacky, but above all utterly, *utterly* random. Those twin imposters in the bell-fringed jester hats, Justice and Fairness—they aren't constants of the natural order like entropy or the periodic table. They're completely alien notions to the way things happen out there in the human rain forest. Justice and Fairness are the things *we're* supposed to contribute back to the world for giving us the gift of life—not birthrights we should expect and demand every second of the day. What do you say we drop the intellectual cowardice? There is no fate, and there is no safety net. I'm not saying God doesn't exist. *I* believe in God. But he's not a micromanager, so stop asking Him to drop the crisis in Rwanda and help you find your wallet. Life is a long, lonely journey down a day-in-day-out lard-trail of dropped tacos. Mop it up, not for yourself, but for the guy behind you who's too busy trying not to drop his own tacos to make sure he doesn't slip and fall on your mistakes. So *don't* speed and weave in traffic; other people have babies in their cars. *Don't* litter. *Don't* begrudge the poor because they have a fucking food stamp. *Don't* be rude to overwhelmed minimum-wage sales clerks, especially teenagers—they have that job because they don't have a clue. You didn't either at that age. Be understanding with them. Share your clues. Remember that your sense of humor is inversely proportional to your intolerance. Stop and think on Veterans Day. And don't forget to vote. That is, unless you send money to TV preachers, have more than a passing interest in alien abduction or recently purchased a fish on a wall plaque that sings 'Don't Worry, Be Happy.' In that case, the polls are a scary place! Under every ballot box is a trapdoor chute to an extraterrestrial escape pod filled with dental tools and squeaking, masturbating little green men from the Devil Star. In conclusion, Class of Ninety-seven, keep your chins up, grab your mops and get in the game. You don't have to make a pile of money or change society. Just clean up after yourselves without complaining. And, above all, please stop and appreciate the days when the tacos don't fall, and give heartfelt thanks to whomever you pray to. . . . You've been a fine audience!"

Serge stepped back from the microphone, and a loud cheer rose from the crowd. Mortarboards filled the air, students hugged each other, parents snapped a thousand Instamatics. Serge ran over to the dean and slapped him on the shoulder again. "Well, I'm outta here."

43

THE FOURTH OF JULY WAS COMING.

You could feel it in the neighborhoods, gathering steam. Kids selling lemonade, parents barbecuing, the Tampa Bay baseball team mathematically eliminated ... Ambrose was still hanging around after two weeks, and Serge had long since stopped trying to ditch him. Serge refused to admit it, but the little bugger was growing on him. Ambrose was ready at a moment's notice to go check out some arcane historic site with Serge, and he became a dependable pinch hitter when Coleman was too fucked up to leave the house.

"Right up there! See that window?" said Serge, pointing at the former Fort Harrison Hotel in Clearwater. "That's the room where Keith Richards wrote 'Satisfaction' while the Stones were on tour in sixty-five."

"Cool!" said Ambrose.

"Don't get the idea I'm starting to like you or anything," said Serge. "Hey! Want to go to the Museum of Science and Industry? They have a new IMAX movie on the space shuttle!"

"What are we waiting for?"

Ambrose sat and cheered between Serge and Coleman at a minor league game, drank a beer between them at The Press Box, had a roast beef sandwich between them at the Tahitian Inn lunch counter. On the third of July, the three sat on the porch eating Serge's secret Cuban recipe for calamari.

"This is great," Ambrose said with his mouth full.

"See, Coleman? Finally, someone who appreciates a gourmet meal!"

"I like your cooking," said Coleman.

"You always ruin my *boliche mechado* with ketchup."

"My body tells me it needs ketchup."

"What's Jim doing over there?" asked Serge.

Across the street, Jim Davenport tacked up red-white-and-blue banners along the porch soffits with a staple gun.

"Looks like he's getting ready for a Fourth of July party," said Ambrose.

"I haven't heard about any party," said Serge.

"Jim is Serge's role model," Coleman told Ambrose.

"Jim's one of the unsung heroes," explained Serge. "He quietly goes about holding our society together without thanks or fanfare."

"What does he do?" asked Ambrose. "Work on the bomb squad? In the emergency room?"

"He's a parent."

"Have you told him how you feel?" asked Ambrose.

"Not in so many words."

"Then you should go over there."

"See if he's having a party," said Coleman. "I love parties."

Serge stood up. But just then, Jim stapled the last banner in place and went inside. Serge sat back down. "Now he's inside. You can just show up if they're out on the porch. But you have to pick your spots if people are inside. It's one of those invisible borders of courtesy. I'd hate to be annoying."

"Maybe he needs help with the party," said Ambrose. "You could volunteer to pitch in, then it would justify the intrusion."

"You've got something there," said Serge. "But I want to bring something over."

"We have most of that bag of Dunkin' Donuts left in the fridge," said Coleman.

"But you took a bite out of every one of them and put 'em back," said Serge.

"I couldn't tell the kind of jelly from the outside," said Coleman. "Just cut the bite marks off with a knife."

"Isn't it kind of late in the day to be eating doughnuts?" asked Ambrose.

"Every time is doughnut time," said Coleman.

MARTHA DAVENPORT WAS standing by the window. "He's coming over here again!"

"I'll get rid of him," said Jim.

"No! Remember what happened last time? Don't answer the door! Maybe he'll just go away."

A knock. "Hello? Anybody home?"

"He knows we're here," whispered Jim.

"Maybe he'll take the hint."

"This is embarrassing. We've already stopped hanging out on the porch 'cause of this."

"I know you're in there!" Serge said cheerfully.

"I have to answer the door. We look silly."

"He's looking in the window! He's spotted us!"

Jim turned to see Serge smiling and waving through the window, holding up a Dunkin' Donuts bag and pointing at it. Jim smiled painfully and waved back.

"Now I feel stupid," said Jim, walking toward the door.

"Don't mention the party!"

"There are streamers all over the place. He already knows there's a party."

"Don't invite him. And if he asks, say he can't come."

"How do I do that?"

"Say anything you want. If he shows up, I'm leaving."

Jim opened the door a crack and slipped out onto the porch.

Serge tried to look around him into the house, but the door closed. "What were you doing? Hiding in there?"

Jim turned red. "What's up?"

"Looks like you're going to have a party. I must have been away when you handed out invitations. I'd love to help any way I can."

"No, everything's taken care of. Actually it's not really a *party* party. It's just going to be an intimate little gathering of immediate relatives—"

"That's great!" said Serge. "I'll get to meet all your kin!"

"What I'm trying to say is—"

Serge held out a paper bag. "Doughnut?"

"No, look Serge—"

"They're still good."

"Serge, Martha and I—"

"You'll hurt my feelings." Serge opened the bag so Jim could see inside.

"Okay, I'll take a doughnut." He pulled one out. The right third had been sliced off.

"I had to cut out Coleman's bite marks."

Jim put the doughnut back.

"Don't blame you," said Serge. "God only knows where he's been."

"Serge, there's something very important I have to say. You can't—"

"Wait," said Serge. "I want to go first. I've got some big news. Sharon and I are engaged! We're going to get married and have kids, just like you!"

"Serge! Congratulations!"

"Isn't it great? After we went out to dinner the other night and I saw what a wonderful marriage you and Martha have, it really got me thinking. It all started making sense. So I decided to marry Sharon and raise a family."

"Really? When?"

"Well, I have to tell her first. And then I have to convince her to have kids, because she doesn't want any. And of course she'll have to give up the cocaine. And the stripping. But right after that!"

It sounded shaky to Jim.

"I want to have what you have," said Serge. "It's these last few weeks living across the street from you, seeing what an incredible thing a family is. You must be a very proud man. I was telling Coleman, you're my new hero. I've decided to model my life after yours."

Jim blushed.

"Okay, now your turn," said Serge. "What was it you wanted to tell me?"

"We're having a Fourth of July party. Would you like to come?"

"Great! I'll bring my fiancée!"

LANCE BOYLE ASSIDUOUSLY waxed his gold Lincoln Navigator. He had gone over the whole vehicle four times now with a hirsute rag and had been working on this one particular spot on the door for the last hour. He checked his watch. Still time for some more buffing before his appointment with the new renters.

Lance pulled out his nitroglycerin container and snorted. Nothing happened.

"What? Empty?" He held it up to his eyeball. "How could I have gone through all that speed? I better slow down. I need to exercise some discipline. I have to get some more right now."

Lance jumped in the Navigator and took off.

He pulled his appointment book out of the glove compartment as he drove across the center line. Cars honked. Lance made a left on red. He opened the book on the steering wheel. Two o'clock: Turn over keys to new tenants renting the home of the late Jack Terrier. The three brothers had unnerved Lance the moment they walked in his office. They propped their boots up on Lance's desk and put out their Pancho Villa cigars on his restored wooden floor. They called themselves the Snyders. The smallest one had this horrible scar that deeply cleaved his left cheek. The middle one had a milky right eye and black gums. The biggest one had tattoos across his knuckles. *H-A-T-E* and *H-A-T-E*. They were the worst applicants he had ever seen. They were perfect.

Lance checked his watch again—still a few minutes before they were due to arrive. He dropped in at the college rental and knocked.

"Coming, dude."

Bernie opened the door.

Lance's eyes were ostrich eggs. "Haveanymorespeed?"

"Man, you are toasted!"

"Haveanyornot?"

"Maybe you should drink a beer instead."

"Iwantspeed."

"Your call," said Bernie. He turned and yelled. "Waste-oid! Got any crank left over from finals?"

Lance walked across the street, covering his nose, tooting up. He stopped in front of the Davenports' porch and sniffled.

"Readytosellyourhouse?"

"What?" said Jim.

"Readytosell?"

"We already told you!" said Martha. "We're not selling. And even if we were, it wouldn't be to the likes of you!"

Lance sniffled and pointed across the street. "Newtenants."

"What?"

"Newtenants. Don'tyouunderstandEnglish?"

"I'm sure we'll get along fine," said Jim.

"Ifyouchangeyourmind," said Lance, placing another business card on the porch railing.

A brown Cutlass pulled up across the street, and Lance went to meet it.

"What was wrong with him?" said Martha.

"Probably too much coffee."

"Coffee doesn't do that. He wasn't blinking."

Jim and Martha looked back across the street. Three huge, frightening men got out of the Cutlass.

"I don't like the looks of this," said Martha.

"Me neither."

"Let's go inside."

Lance turned over the keys to his new tenants and climbed back in the Navigator. He had had it with unreasonable people like the Davenports. Fair was fair, but they were standing in his way. He had done some checking, totally illegal but incredibly easy. He found out that Consolidated Bank held the mortgage on their house. They were paid up but consistently late, seven to ten days a month. Lance also learned some other things. He called Consolidated Bank and told the loan officer that he was Jim Davenport and had lost his job and tried to trade in his car for a cheaper one, but the loan got kicked back. Now, he said, he couldn't afford the house and wanted a way out of the mortgage. The loan officer said he'd call him right back. Lance gave him his cell-phone number.

The loan officer did some checking, totally illegal but incredibly easy. Jim Davenport had indeed lost his job and applied for a loan to trade down his car, but for some reason it had never gone through. The guy's in bad shape, he thought. But the officer had taken three defaults already this summer and his keys to the executive washroom hung in the balance. He called Lance back and said he was sure they could work something out. Lance said it looked bleak.

"Let's meet."

"Great," said Lance. "I'll come to your office."

"No, I'll come to your home. Tomorrow."

Lance panicked. "But it's a holiday! It's the Fourth!"

"Not a problem. Anything for a customer. Because we have babies, too."

They set the meeting for 4 P.M. on Independence Day.

Lance hung up. Shit, he thought. I never even considered he might come out to the house. Now I'm screwed! Why did I think this idiotic plan would work? It's all because of this stupid speed I've been taking. I need some more.

He tapped out the rest and did it, then got a brainstorm. He picked up his cell phone and called Insult-to-Injury Process Servers.

". . . The address is eight-eighty-eight Triggerfish . . . Yes, Elvis will be fine . . ."

THE COLLEGE STUDENTS POUTED on the front porch of their rental.

"There's nothing to do," said Chip. "We don't have any money. We don't have any dope . . ."

"This sucks," said Waste-oid, chin in his hands.

Bernie looked around. "Want to drive out in the county and tip cows?"

"We did that last night," said Frankie.

"Why don't we go out there and look for 'shrooms instead?" said Waste-oid.

"I'm tired of mushrooms," said Bernie.

"I'm not!" said Waste-oid.

"What's the point?" said Bernie. "Remember the last time you did 'shrooms and spent half the night in your closet?"

"Don't make fun. There was a big storm with lots of thunder. It was very upsetting."

"Is that why you puked?"

"No. I didn't boil the 'shrooms long enough to get the toxins out when I made the tea. For about two hours it was like there were all these little knives trying to stab their way out of my stomach."

"What happened?"

"Tried to get my mind off it by focusing on something else. I started staring at that painting of the lion we have in the living room. But then the lion came alive and looked like it was going to jump off the wall and I began screaming, and the knives in my stomach got worse. Then the thunder and lightning started and I barricaded myself in the closet."

"Then you threw up and fell asleep in your own vomit?"

"Right."

"So why on earth do you want to go back and get some more?"

"Because 'shrooms are the best!"

The front door opened and Siddhartha the solipsistic student walked out and punched Waste-oid in the shoulder.

"Ow! That hurt!"

"No it didn't. You're only a figment that I control. I can make you do anything I want. I can make you say 'Ow' again."

"What?"

Siddhartha hit him again.

"Ow!"

Siddhartha walked back in the house.

The front door opened again and Bill the Elder came out.

"They said on TV it's the Fourth of July tomorrow."

"Wow," said Waste-oid. "July already?"

"We need to buy fireworks," said Bill.

"We don't have any money," said Bernie.

"Let's collect aluminum cans," said Chip.

"Let's pick 'shrooms and sell them," said Waste-oid.

"I know," said Chip. "Let's sell our textbooks!"

"I don't know where mine are," said Waste-oid.

A BLUE SIERRA cruised north on rain-slick Dale Mabry Highway, Bernie in the driver's seat, red afro pressed against the roof. They passed the strip clubs and car dealerships and stopped at a light.

A Camaro full of University of Tampa women pulled up on the left.

Waste-oid leaned out the window and put the tips of his thumb and index finger to his lips. "Hey pretty things, wanna get high?"

The women laughed and peeled out when the light turned green.

"What's wrong with you?" said Bernie, putting the Sierra in gear.

"What do you mean?"

"You're always embarrassing us. It's the same thing every time. 'You wanna get high? You wanna get high?' . . ."

"What's the matter with that?"

"What's the matter is this isn't 1973 and you're not in Grand Funk Railroad."

"The babes love it."

"No they don't. You have never gotten laid with that. Not once!"

"Yes I have!"

"When?"

"Well, it was Christmas break. You weren't around."

"That's what I thought."

"There it is!" said Chip.

A giant hot-air balloon stood in front of a red circus tent. A man in a gorilla suit waved cars into a dirt parking lot under a banner: INDEPENDENCE DAY FIREWORKS BONANZA BLOWOUT!

A chain-smoking ex-carny was on a portable phone when the students arrived. "Gotta go. Some live ones just walked in." He hung up and stubbed out a Camel on a box of bottle rockets.

The students began pawing the cellophane on some Roman candles.

"I can tell you fellas know quality," said the salesman. "Those are the best Roman candles in the world. Direct from China."

The students walked through the tent in awe: Black Cats, M-80s, stink bombs.

"Take your time. I'll be right over here." The salesman went back to the register and lit another Camel.

The students finished browsing. The salesman was staring down at a magazine and heard them whispering. "You ask him!" "No, *you* ask him!"

The salesman looked up. "Got a question?"

Bernie glanced around to make sure nobody was listening. He leaned over the counter. "Got anything *special*?"

"Oh, right." The salesman winked. "The *special* stuff. Follow me."

He led the students to the "employees only" area of the tent and pulled back the curtain. He produced a box from under a table. The students gathered around. He began opening the box with slow drama, then stopped and closed the flaps. "You sure you're cool? For all I know you could be cops. How do I know you're not The Man?"

"I'll show you my penis," said Waste-oid.

"What!"

"You idiot!" said Bernie. "That's how you prove you're not a cop to prostitutes!"

"Oh."

Bernie turned back to the salesman. "We're not cops."

"You know what? I believe you. Because I like you guys."

He stepped away from the box and gestured toward it. The students approached and cautiously opened the cardboard flaps.

"Oh, man!"

"I've heard about these!"

"Those are the professional models," said the salesman. "Thousand-foot tricolored whistling air bursts. Same ones the city launches from barges in the bay."

"We gotta have 'em!"

"I'm only allowed to sell to licensed fireworks handlers."

The students hung their heads.

"You *are* licensed fireworks handlers, aren't you?"

The students didn't answer.

The salesman slowly repeated the question and nodded. "You *are* licensed fireworks handlers?"

"Oh, that's right. We are."

"Good. That'll be three hundred dollars."

"We don't have three hundred dollars."

"What do you got?"

"Textbooks. They're in the car."

"Same as cash in here. Go get 'em. I'll wait."

The students returned with armloads of books, and the salesman worked quickly with a calculator, tossing the books on top of the giant pile of textbooks already behind the register.

"Nice doing business with you," said the salesman. He chain-lit another Camel and threw the old one over his shoulder.

AGENT MAHONEY SAT at the bar in a tweed jacket and black fedora. He was on an island in the bay. The bar was called Yeoman's Road.

"Another one, Louie," he told the bartender.

The bartender poured whiskey. "My name's not Louie."

"It should be," said Mahoney. He swiveled on his stool and pointed out the front window. "What's the deal with the weird red phone booth, Louie?"

"It's a British phone booth."

"What's it doing here?"

"This is a British pub."

"Are we in Britain?"

"No."

"Then I don't like the idea."

Mahoney pulled out a pack of Chesterfields, stuck his finger in the opening, then took his finger out and looked in the hole. Empty. Damn. He crumped the pack and got off the stool. "I gonna get some smokes at the machine. Don't let anyone take my spot. The night's still young, Louie, and full of irony."

"It's Rich."

"It certainly is."

Mahoney walked up to the silver machine and pulled hard on the Chesterfield knob. He bent down and grabbed the cigarettes from the tray and began smacking the end of the pack in his palm on his way back to the bar.

A stranger was waiting.

"Who's this mug, Louie?"

"Says his name's Blaine," replied the bartender, wiping a beer mug.

"Blaine Crease," said Blaine, extended a hand.

Mahoney looked down at it skeptically, then back at the stranger.

"I don't like you, Blaine."

"Fine. We don't have to be friends. I have a business proposition—"

"Mickey."

"What?"

"I might like you if your name was Mickey. You look like a Mickey. Or a Floyd. Blaine—that's the name of some guy who drinks peach schnapps."

Blaine looked at the bartender, who shrugged and walked away.

"I understand you're looking for some bad dudes," said Blaine.

"Who wants to know?"

"I'm a TV reporter for Florida Cable News. I can help. I'm the host of *Florida's Most Wanted*."

"You connected with *America's Most Wanted*?"

"Only if you call stealing the name being connected."

"Where do I fit in? Better yet, where do *you* fit in?"

"We can team up. You feed me information. Or disinformation—doesn't matter to me. I'll put a segment on the air and we flush 'em out into the open. You just give me the exclusive when it's all over. What do you say?"

Mahoney took off his fedora, pulled a sawbuck out of the lining and tucked it under an ashtray. He put his hat back on and turned to Blaine. "Where's the action in this town?"

THE SUN SET on the third day of July.

John Milton walked down the street, waving his arms and talking to himself, repeating the same thing over and over. He had just called the phone company, asking for the address of one Jim Davenport, the name he had found on the back page of the consultant's report that had gotten him fired from Consolidated Bank.

"... *Eight-eighty-eight Triggerfish Lane. Eight-eighty-eight Triggerfish Lane. Eight-eighty-eight Triggerfish Lane* ..."

John turned left on Triggerfish and began looking at house numbers. When he got to 888, there were a bunch of people on the porch. John hadn't expected that. He decided to come back when there was less of a crowd.

Jim Davenport looked off the porch at the man walking briskly down the sidewalk.

"That guy looks familiar. Where have I seen him?"

"Why is he trying to hide his face?" asked Martha.

"Where do you want these?" Gladys asked with an armful of Statue of Liberty mosquito candles.

"Put them around the railing," said Martha. "What am I forgetting? I know I'm forgetting something."

"Will you relax?" said Jim. "You're like this every time before you entertain."

Martha couldn't relax. She'd worked herself silly getting ready for the big July Fourth costume party tomorrow. She couldn't stop the checklist from looping through her head. Hamburgers, hot dogs, charcoal, marshmallows, American flag paper plates, Declaration of Independence napkins . . .

Across the street, the college students were making their own preparations. They had located some stale hash cookies and decided to pool all of their fireworks purchases and construct a single multistage rocketship held together with masking tape and hallucinogenic optimism. Its construction was conceived, directed and overseen by the students' next-door neighbor, Serge A. Storms, who was paying particular attention to the scale and authenticity of the Saturn V replica. His assistant was a short old man wearing Serge's nifty silver NASA jacket, his hands barely poking out the ends of the sleeves.

"Vehicle Assembly Building, Level Twelve, report in," said Serge.

"Roger, control," said Ambrose. "Stage coupling confirmed." Then they did a secret NASA handshake that Serge had invented.

The students finally had to stop building when the rocket reached the living room ceiling. Serge said good night and advised the students not to stay up too late.

"Tomorrow's the big day!"

45

THE SUN ROSE IN A WARM, clear sky the morning of July Fourth.

John Milton got out of bed at Splendid Acres and went in the kitchen and ate a piece of dry toast. *"Eight-eighty-eight Triggerfish, Eight-eighty-eight Triggerfish . . ."* He watched seven hours of talk shows, then grabbed his stun gun and headed out the door to the apartment building parking lot, where he removed the protective tarp concealing a white Ferrari F50.

SERGE'S EYES FLEW open when the beam of sunlight hit his pillow. He checked the date on his diver's watch. July Fourth.

"Yessssss!" Serge threw back the covers and jumped out of bed. It was his favorite day of the year.

He stuck a Springsteen CD in the stereo and got to work. Serge was running around the house with a feather duster when Coleman and Sharon stumbled down the hallway.

"Why's the stereo so fucking loud at this hour?" said Sharon.

". . . Born in the U.S.A.! I was born in the U.S.A.! . . ."

"It's Independence Day!" said Serge. "Look alive. We got a full schedule!"

"I'm not doin' shit today!" Sharon plopped down at the kitchen table and lit a cigarette. Coleman got a beer from the fridge.

"Oh, yes you are!" said Serge. "You think freedom is free? A lot of blood was spilled so we can live like this!"

Coleman held his beer at arm's length and admired it. "You mean they fought for my right to party?"

"Exactly."

"How can we show our appreciation?"

"By barbecuing."

"I can't believe what I'm listening to," said Sharon. "You're a couple of boobs. I'm going back to bed."

"No, you're not," said Serge.

She began walking toward the bedroom. "Oh, yes I am!"

Serge followed.

Sharon took off running. "Get away from me, you freak!"

Serge chased her down the hall. "The redcoats are coming!"

THE ZUCKERMANS OF Sarasota pulled into the Davenports' driveway in a late-model Cadillac Seville.

Jim and Martha came down off the porch.

"God, I hate this," Martha said through an artificial smile.

"They're *your* parents," Jim said through his own smile.

Everyone hugged.

"You look thin," Mrs. Zuckerman told Jim. "Martha, have you been feeding him?"

"Don't start."

"What? So shoot me for caring."

"Mom!"

Melvin came running out of the house. "Grandpa! Grandma!"

"You still sure you want to take them for the weekend?" asked Martha, installing Nicole's safety seat in the Caddy.

"Are you kidding? I could take the little darlings for a year." Mrs. Zuckerman looked around. "Where's Debbie?"

"I'll get her," said Jim. He went inside.

He found Debbie on the couch, sullen.

"You need to get out there," said Jim.

"I'm not going," said Debbie.

"Why not?"

"Sarasota sucks. And their house smells bizarre."

Jim just looked at her. It was his hurt look. Debbie could fight like cats and dogs with her mother, but not her dad.

"Stop looking at me like that!"

"Like what?"

"Okay, I'll go!"

Jim returned to the driveway. "She'll be out in a minute."

Debbie finally came out the front door with a scowl. She had stringy black hair, black clothes and black lipstick.

"My little angel!" said Mrs. Zuckerman.

Jim and Martha waved at the departing Cadillac, then went back inside and continued preparing for the big block party.

There was a knock at the front door.

"I'll get it, honey."

Jim opened the door.

It was Elvis. At the curb sat a white van with a magnetic sign on the side. Elvis handed Jim an eviction notice. He put his head down and pointed at the sky.

"*Vivaaaaaaaa, Las Vegas! Vivaaaaaa . . .*"

Jim closed the door.

Martha walked into the room opening a box of red, white and blue plastic forks. "Who was that, dear?"

"I don't understand it," said Jim. "We're paid up."

Through the door: "*Thank you. Thank you very much.*" Then a van started up and drove away.

"There must be a mistake," said Martha.

Jim turned the notice over. It said in big red letters that the appeals deadline was today at 4 P.M., and they both had to appear in person at the bank.

"But it's a holiday," said Martha. "They're closed."

"Something fishy is going on," said Jim.

Martha grabbed her purse. "Let's get to the bottom of this."

LANCE BOYLE WAS parked across the street in his gold Navigator, snorting speed and staking out the Davenport residence. He saw Elvis deliver the fake eviction notice he'd printed up on his computer, then saw Jim and Martha drive off for their bogus meeting at the bank.

When they were out of sight, Lance climbed down from the Navigator and walked across the street. He took a seat on the Davenports' porch swing and waited.

He swung nervously and whistled and checked his watch. He

started to worry that the loan officer he had talked to on the phone the day before would be late, and maybe the Davenports would return early after finding the bank closed. Just then, a car slowly turned the corner. A snow-white Ferrari F50. It stopped in front of the Davenports'.

"Wow! The bankers must be doing pretty good!" said Lance. He got off the swing and trotted down from the porch.

John Milton got out of the Ferrari. ". . . *Eight-eighty-eight Trig-gerfish. Eight-eighty-eight Triggerfish. Eight-eighty-eight Trigger-fish* . . ." He met Lance in the middle of the lawn.

"Are you Jim Davenport?"

"Yes, I am," Lance said with a big smile. He put out a hand to shake.

John stuck out his own hand, but it had a stun gun in it, and he jolted Lance in the chest.

John went back and stood next to the Ferrari with his hands on his hips, casual, as if Lance weren't flopping around on the lawn behind him. So far, so good, John thought. He pulled out a piece of paper. It was *Plan A*. He crossed out Jim Davenport's name at the top of the page, then looked at the next name. Rocco Silvertone, who was due back at the dealership after dinner.

John started getting back in the Ferrari when he realized a flaw in *Plan A*. If he pulled into the dealership in the Ferrari, Rocco would recognize it, and he'd lose the element of surprise. He closed the Ferrari's door and walked over to Lance, twitching in the grass. He reached in Lance's pocket and pulled out some keys. They said *Lincoln*. John turned and saw the Navigator. He got in and drove to the end of Triggerfish, and stopped to let four pedestrians cross the street.

Serge, Coleman, Sharon and Ambrose strolled single file across Triggerfish Lane in the crosswalk, a tropical *Abbey Road*. Coleman was barefoot. A Lincoln Navigator made a left behind them and drove away.

"Serge, you're such a dipshit!" said Sharon.

"I'm warning you, woman! Get off my case!"

"Hey!" yelled Coleman, pointing up the street. "The Ferrari!"

Everyone except Sharon began running to the stolen car dumped in front of the Davenport residence.

"The keys are still in it," said Coleman.

"There's a guy flopping around on the lawn," said Ambrose.

"That can't be helped," said Serge. "Get in."

Serge took the driver's seat, and Ambrose sat in Coleman's lap on the passenger side. "There's no room for you," Serge told Sharon. She gave them the finger and headed back to the house.

Lance slowly came out of his seizure. He pushed himself up into the sitting position, shook his head to clear the fog and saw the Ferrari pulling away.

"Man!" he said. "The banks are getting *rough*!"

VIC PACED THE showroom at Tampa Bay Motors. He stared at Rocco's office door. It was locked. Loyalty was one thing, but a man's life was at stake and Rocco's judgment was beginning to give off a bad odor. Vic decided to call the police. He picked up the phone.

CORRESPONDENT BLAINE CREASE burst breathlessly into the office of the news director at Florida Cable News. He said he had to go on the air right away.

"Slow down. What's this all about?"

Crease told him.

"I don't know," said the director. "Where'd the tip come from?"

"A police officer trying to nail the weather girl."

"We get more stories that way," said the director. "Details?"

Crease said a local captain of industry was being ransomed, and the victim's corporate headquarters in New York wasn't answering their phones. Crease had tried calling the number himself without luck. The company must be trying to avoid the cops and media. A briefcase was probably changing hands in Tampa right now.

"It's airtight," said Crease.

"Check the computer files," said the news director.

"Do I have to?"

"We don't even know if this Ambrose guy even exists, let alone if he has any money."

A few minutes later, Crease ran back in the news director's office out of breath again. "Nothing in the computers. Now can I go on the air?"

"Of course not!" said the director. "Nothing in the computers is a red flag. That means there might be a hole in your story."

"So *that's* what that means."

"You sure there was nothing?" said the director. "Not even a charity ball grip-and-grin?"

Crease shook his head.

"Go back further," said the director. "Check the hard files."

Crease thought all this fact-checking was getting ridiculous, so he lateraled it to a nineteen-year-old intern named Sinbad, who came back in an hour, unable to find any files at all.

"Where are the old files?" Crease yelled across the newsroom. He got a group shot of puzzled expressions.

"Ask Bartholomew," said one of the reporters, pointing over toward the oldest member of the staff.

"Hey, Bartholomew!" yelled Crease. "You know where the old files are?"

Bartholomew said he'd been forced to hide the files to prevent them from being thrown out by people who didn't give a hoot about the profession.

"I can't tell you how many times they've been *this close* to being trashed. With all the turnover, there's no institutional knowledge anymore!"

"But what good are they if they're hidden?" asked Crease.

"When was the last time you looked anything up?"

Crease was growing tired of Bartholomew's stupid questions. "Where are they?"

"Will you promise not to let anything happen to them?"

Blaine nodded like he was dealing with a child. Bartholomew told them which closet. Crease and Sinbad ran down the hall, opened a janitor's storeroom and began unsealing dusty cardboard boxes.

Luck was on their side. It was in the third box: a file marked *Tarrington* containing a single, fragile newspaper clipping.

"We've got it!" Blaine yelled. He started reading the yellowed clip on Ambrose.

Maintenance workers came by with a rolling bin. "Got any-thing to throw out?"

Blaine looked up, distracted. "What? Oh, yeah. Get rid of these old boxes."

He ran back to the studio and burst in the director's office.

"We got it!"

"How solid?" asked the director.

"Bedrock!" said Blaine. He proudly handed over the clipping with a smiling photo of a much-younger Ambrose. "It's from 1978. It's the only thing we got. Ambrose Tarrington the Third, wealthy owner of a chain of duty-free shops, just elected secretary of Tampa's chamber of commerce."

"Sounds legit. Run with it."

46

INSIDE 887 TRIGGERFISH, all was quiet. The three surviving McGraw brothers sat motionless on the couch watching a cuckoo clock. Weapons cradled in their laps. Bandoliers across their chests. Passing a bottle of George Dickel.

A small wooden bird popped out four times.

"One more hour," said Rufus McGraw.

"THAT'S THE STRANGEST THING," Martha said as they pulled back in their driveway after finding the bank closed.

"I'm going to straighten this out first thing next week," said Jim.

"Look at the time!" said Martha. "The guests will be arriving any minute!"

Sure enough, a car pulled up. Paul Revere and Betsy Ross got out.

After that, the guests came in bunches down both sides of the sidewalk. Ben Franklin and his kite, John Hancock with a giant inflatable novelty pen, Nathan Hale with a rope around his neck. Dolley Madison brought cupcakes.

Lance Boyle came uninvited, but nobody recognized him. His face and hair were painted silver, and he wore a giant papier-mâché Liberty Bell over a hoop-skirt frame.

"We don't have enough food," said Martha.

"Will you relax?" said Jim. He reached up and adjusted Martha's George Washington wig. "You've done a great job. Now it's time to enjoy yourself."

More guests arrived in chronological order. John Adams, Thomas Jefferson, Andrew Jackson, Eli Whitney and his cotton gin. The Robinsons and their two children came as Mount Rushmore. Lewis and Clark apologized for being late, but they had trouble finding the house.

The party picked up.

Martha and Jim pulled furniture out of the way in the living room and turned on some music. Guests filled the makeshift dance floor. Indians with tea boxes, John Paul Jones, Crispus Attucks. Benedict Arnold thumbed through the CDs and stuck "Back in the U.S.S.R." in the stereo. Everyone booed.

"See?" Jim said in his stovepipe hat. "The party's a success. Will you stop running around?"

"You better start the grill." She ran to check something in the oven.

Jim went out on the patio. Aaron Burr and Alexander Hamilton were dueling it out at horseshoes. The Wright Brothers played badminton. Jim squirted lighter fluid in the barbecue and lit the coals. General Sherman came over and told him the fire wasn't big enough.

Martha ran around dumping ashtrays. Ulysses S. Grant spiked the punch bowl. Uncle Sam was in the bathroom snooping through the Davenports' medicine cabinet.

Gladys Plant came up the walkway dressed as George Washington. Martha greeted her.

"I brought a cherry pie," said Gladys. She noticed something wrong on Martha's face. "What's the matter?"

"You're wearing the same thing I am."

The burgers were ready. Jim rang a dinner triangle, and everyone came inside and ate. Martha ran around collecting greasy paper plates and crumpled napkins.

"We forgot the games," Martha told Jim. "They're going to get bored."

"Will you stop?" said Jim.

"Better put some more burgers on," said Martha. She ran into the master bedroom closet and pulled down an old Milton Bradley box. She returned to the living room and unfolded a large plastic mat with colored circles.

"Anyone for Twister?"

Suddenly, the front door crashed open and three huge men with guns charged into the room.

"Nobody move!"

"I can't place the costumes," said Thomas Edison.

"Shut up!" yelled Rufus McGraw, slamming Edison in the head with his shotgun stock.

Everyone went silent.

"Where is he?"

Nobody answered.

Rufus racked his shotgun. "I said, where is he?"

"Who?" said Gladys Plant.

"Jim Davenport!"

"Jim who?" said Gladys.

"Don't play stupid!" said Rufus, pointing the shotgun at her. He yelled over his shoulder to his brothers: "Check all the rooms!"

Lance Boyle was sneaking some more crank in the bathroom, then headed back out to the party. His Liberty Bell got wedged in the doorway, and he struggled briefly and pulled free. He turned the corner and saw what was happening. He was delighted.

Rufus was covering the guests with his shotgun when he noticed the Liberty Bell shuffling sideways along the wall toward him.

"What the fuck?"

Lance slid up next to Rufus.

"Psssst!" said Lance. "It's me!"

"Who?"

"Your landlord."

"So?"

"So this is great!"

"What are you, high?"

"Yes . . . When I asked you to annoy the neighbors, I never expected this."

"Don't mention it," said Rufus. "Anything else you might like us to do?"

"Tell them to take off their clothes."

Rufus just stared at Lance.

"Once they've all seen each other naked, there's no way they can still live on the same street together. Can you imagine how uncomfortable it will be? They'll have to move out!"

Rufus broke up laughing. "You're one sick motherfucker! I like you!" He turned back to the guests in the living room. "Listen up! We have a request from one of your local landlords . . ."

"Shhhh! Don't tell them it's me!"

". . . Everyone take off your pants!"

Nobody moved.

"Now!" Rufus shouted, smacking Amelia Earhart with his gun barrel.

Everyone took off their pants.

"Psssssst!" whispered Lance.

"What is it now?"

"Why just their pants?"

"Because it's funnier!"

Lance looked around the room at the history of the United States naked from the waste down.

"I see what you mean." Lance got out his nitro capsule and did another toot.

"Any more requests?" Rufus asked sarcastically.

"Make 'em play Twister."

THOMAS JEFFERSON, JOHN Adams and Andrew Jackson were tangled and bent in unnatural directions.

Rufus spun the game wheel. "Left hand, blue!"

"I can't reach it," said Jefferson.

Rufus picked up his shotgun. Jefferson reached it.

"I found him!" said Sly McGraw. He shoved Jim Davenport into the room. "He was out back flipping burgers."

"Jim!" yelled Martha, running to him.

"So this is the shit-sucker who killed our brother," said Rufus. He walked up and stuck the shotgun in Jim stomach. "Say goodbye, shit-sucker."

"Someone's here!" said Willie McGraw, peeking out the window. "They're coming up the steps!"

Rufus pointed the shotgun around the room. "Nobody make a sound. Just act like everything's normal." He turned to his brothers. "Quick! Hide behind the door!"

They heard voices outside as the late-arriving guests came up the steps.

"We should have gotten in the costumes first," said Coleman. "Everyone else will already be dressed. I hate to stick out."

"We're late as it is," said Serge. He nodded down toward the costume box he was carrying. "We'll put it on in the bathroom right after we go through our proper social graces with the hosts."

"But Ambrose got to put his on already," said Coleman, pointing at J. Paul Getty.

The McGraws bunched together behind the Davenports' front door. Everyone was silent. They heard steps on the porch. Then a knock. Rufus motioned for Jim to answer.

"Door's open. Come in."

"Sorry we're late—" Serge stopped and looked around the room. "Have you all lost your fucking minds!"

"Man!" said Coleman. "And I thought *I* partied."

The front door slowly creaked closed behind them, and Serge turned around.

"Who are you?" said Serge.

"Shut up!" yelled Rufus, pointing with his shotgun. "What's in the box?"

"My costume. Want to see?"

"No!"

"It's pretty cool."

Rufus motioned with his gun. "Over there with the others. And take off your pants."

Serge began unzipping his trousers. "Of course you know, this means war."

Rufus sat back down in the chair by the door and picked up a bottle of sour mash he'd taken from Jim's liquor cabinet. "I'm gonna really enjoy this! . . . Hey! Did I say you could stop playing Twister?"

Serge walked over to the wall. Sly McGraw, the Gentleman Bandit, covered him with a Mauser.

"Good evening," said Sly.

"Evening," said Serge.

"How do you like this neighborhood?" asked Sly.

"It's great. Nice park, good schools nearby, roads in decent shape, but mainly it's the neighbors."

"That's important," said Sly. "I might come back here and settle down."

"Good choice," said Serge. "Nowadays you gotta be real careful where you live. Florida's getting pretty scummy. We're cursed by good fortune. Great weather, beautiful beaches, booming growth. But it's a completely transient culture. Pick any street; almost nobody grew up there, and most will be gone in a few years. They appear to be neighborhoods, but they're just collections of houses"—Serge put his hands together and interlaced his fingers—"There's no fabric."

"I respectfully disagree," said Sly. "Florida doesn't have any copyright on this problem. It's going on all over the country. I've seen the same thing across the Midwest all the way into New England. Parents aren't doing their job anymore. That's where the problem is. They let the entertainment industry raise their kids. Don't even get me started on that."

"You're right about the parents, but that doesn't change the truth about Florida," said Serge. "We have a special confluence of economic and social factors that are killing the roots of the communities."

"Towns are falling apart everywhere," said Sly. "It's the New Selfishness. There's no shame anymore. It's not any worse here."

"Again, I must dissent," said Serge. "What I'm talking about is purely a function of demographic trends. It's getting really strange out there."

"Okay, if we're limiting it to a kind of tropical diaspora, then I have to give you that. What I'm saying is the pathologies exist everywhere. Florida has no monopoly on truly bizarre and freakish crimes. That's anecdotal, not empirical."

"What? Like forcing people to play half-naked Twister at gunpoint?"

"I knew you were going to use that."

"Will you two shut up over there!" yelled Rufus. "This ain't a coffee klatch!"

Coleman walked over and turned on the TV.

"What are you doing?" asked Rufus.

Coleman pointed at the set. "Watching some tube."

"Do you *see* what I have in my hands here?"

Coleman nodded.

"Turn it off!"

Coleman reached for the set again, then stopped. "Hey! It's Ambrose!"

Everyone looked. The face on the TV belonged to the guest dressed as J. Paul Getty. The picture was almost twenty years old, but it was unmistakable. The image on TV switched to Blaine Crease, standing in front of the biggest house on Bayshore Boulevard. Crease dramatically explained the abduction, spinning a tale of mind-bending wealth and corporate intrigue involving Ambrose Tarrington III, whose net worth Crease randomly fabricated at sixty million dollars.

"Sixty million!" said Rufus.

"Sixty million!" said Ambrose.

On television, Crease walked down the mansion's driveway talking to the camera.

"While Ambrose had been a regular on the chamber of commerce luncheon circuit back in the seventies, little is known about him in recent years, except that he lived out a bizarre and reclusive Howard Hughes existence behind the walls of this Bayshore mansion . . ."

The butler came out the front door and yelled for Crease to get off the property.

". . . But even this opulence couldn't protect him from ruthless kidnappers . . . Stay tuned for Florida's Most Wanted. *. . . Back to you, Jacqueline."*

Rufus looked at his brothers. "Screw this caper. We're grabbing the old dude here. He's worth a fortune!"

Sly pointed at the TV. "Rufus! Look! We're on television!"

Florida's Most Wanted opened with a compelling segment about a trio of southbound desperados. Mug shots of Rufus, Willie and Sly McGraw appeared over the gang's new nickname, "Three Dog Night."

"How'd we get a nickname!" said Sly. "That's so not fair!"

The crimes of the McGraw brothers were depicted by a trio of actors, two of whom were improvisational players from an L.A. troupe, and the third an original member of Three Dog Night trying to break into theater.

47

TELEPHONE TECHNICIANS HAD just finished wiring ten additional temporary lines in the studios of Florida Cable News. Agent Mahoney sat poised with a support crew of local detectives and police officers ready to handle the anticipated flood of phone calls.

The TV show began. Mahoney stood at a wall map with a box of pushpins.

Florida's Most Wanted was on the air no more than a minute when all lines lit up. Nine callers placed the gang in a south Tampa neighborhood. The tenth said that he was saddened his favorite band had turned to crime and that "One Is the Loneliest Number" had always made him cry.

The police officers manning the phones called out locations as the tips came in; Mahoney inserted pushpins for each address. He stood back from the map. "That's enough. We've got a fix." Mahoney grabbed his hat and ran out the door.

He raced south without his siren or lights. His police radio came on.

"Mahoney, you son of a bitch!" said Lieutenant Ingersol. "You wait for backup!"

"No time."

"I'll have your badge!"

Mahoney turned off the radio and cut his headlights. He eased around the corner at the dark end of Triggerfish Lane. Cars were parked all over the road outside the Davenport place. Mahoney pulled óver four doors down. He reached in his jacket for his shoulder holster and crept along a hedge.

"Rufus," said Sly. "Someone's creeping around outside. . . . Now he's coming up the steps."

Rufus swung his shotgun around the room. "Everyone act natural!"

The McGraws hid behind the door again.

Mahoney crept silently across the porch with his gun drawn. He tried the doorknob. Unlocked. He turned it slowly, then pushed it open with a light creak.

In the middle of the room were three nineteenth-century American presidents playing Twister without pants.

"Not again," said Mahoney.

He stepped into the house, then felt a gun barrel in his back.

"Drop it," said Rufus.

Mahoney dropped it.

"Get over there with the others. Take off your pants."

"You'll never get away with this," said Mahoney. "Cops are going to be swarming all over this place."

Rufus laughed.

Mahoney took his place against the wall with the other hostages. The person next to him looked familiar.

"Serge?"

"Mahoney?"

"Last time I saw you, we were in a horse suit and you had a gun on me."

"Nothing personal."

"It'll be nothing personal when I put you away for good. Don't think I'm going to go easy on you because we're experiencing this common adversity together."

"Wouldn't have it any other way."

"So, got any ideas how to get out of this?"

"Matter of fact I do. All we need is one little opportunity. A single moment when they're distracted. Then this is what we do . . ." Serge leaned and whispered.

"You two! Stop talking!" said Rufus. "Doesn't anybody see I have a gun?" He walked into the middle of the room and addressed the group as a whole. "Okay, here's the deal. We're taking Ambrose with us. Anyone calls the police in the first half hour—we know where you live and we'll be back. . . . But before we go, there's a little matter that I have to settle with an old friend."

Rufus walked up to Jim Davenport. He popped open the cylinder of his revolver and dumped all the bullets in his other hand. He put one bullet back in the chamber and slammed it closed. Rufus spun the cylinder and pointed the pistol between Jim's eyes. He pulled the trigger.

Click.

Rufus laughed and spun the cylinder again.

THE COLLEGE STUDENTS had waited patiently for sundown. Now they carefully lifted their Saturn V replica onto a dolly and wheeled it out the front door.

"On three!" said Bernie, gripping one of the fins. "One, two, three!"

The students heaved together and lifted the rocket off the dolly and set it down on the front porch/launch pad.

"This is going to be so great!" said Waste-oid. He knelt next to the fuse and flicked a Bic. The fuse began to sparkle.

"Run!"

They all ran except Siddhartha the solipsistic student, who remained next to the rocket, watching it curiously.

The other students dove over a hedge and stuck their heads back up.

"Sid! Watch out!" yelled Bernie.

Siddhartha didn't move. "Don't worry. It can't hurt me."

The fuse was almost down to the solid-fuel booster. The rocket the students had assembled was quite impressive. And heavy. Too heavy, in fact, for the first stage, and one of the cardboard fins slowly began to buckle.

"What's happening?" Bernie yelled to Siddhartha.

"I think it's tipping over."

"Do something!" Bernie yelled.

"No, I won't interfere. It doesn't matter anyway."

The fuse burned into the rocket fuel a split second before it fell over completely, and it took off like a Sidewinder missile.

"I DON'T LIKE these odds," said Rufus. He put all the bullets back in the gun and pointed the pistol at Jim again. "This is for Skag. Nice knowin' ya."

He cocked the hammer back with his thumb.

There was a tremendous whoosh outside the house.

Rufus turned. "What the—"

The front window crashed, spraying glass, and everyone shielded their eyes. When they looked again, a Saturn V rocket was lodged in a human Liberty Bell, shooting sparks. The papier-mâché caught on fire and Lance began screaming.

"I'm really starting to get pissed off!" said Rufus.

The second stage ignited with massive thrust, pushing Lance across the room. Rufus opened the door at the last second, and the Liberty Bell ran out onto the front lawn.

A gash opened in the side of the papier-mâché, and the rocket shifted inside the bell, sending thrust off at an angle and spinning Lance across the lawn like a top. Everyone ran to the windows.

The third stage ignited, and the extra thrust caused the Liberty Bell to pitch up on its side. It began rolling and took off down the street at high speed, the rotation creating a Doppler effect in Lance's screaming.

At the intersection, the third stage burned down to its core pyrotechnic charge, and Lance exploded in a flaring six-point starburst of blue, green and magenta. Seconds later, all that was left of him were twinkling little tracers fluttering to the ground.

The college students looked at each other.

"Hide!"

They ran inside and got in a closet.

"Un-fucking-believable!" said Rufus. He turned back around. "Show's over. Everyone get away from the windows . . . Hey! This isn't everyone. Who's missing?"

Rufus looked at Willie and Sly.

"We were watching the fireworks."

"Dammit!" said Rufus. "Search the house!"

"WHAT'S GOING ON?" asked Serge.

"I can't see," said Mahoney. "Hold on a second. Let me adjust this thing. There we go. We need to come up a little on our right."

"What's our range?"

"Fifteen feet and closing. Get ready. On my mark . . ."

Jim Davenport stepped into the middle of the room. "I'd like you to leave now."

Rufus almost didn't notice, Jim was so quiet-spoken. "Huh? Did you say something?"

"I would like you to leave my house now."

Rufus began laughing. "Oh, you would?"

Jim nodded. "Please leave."

Martha whispered urgently behind him: "Jim! What are you doing?"

"Hey guys!" Rufus yelled to Willie and Sly. "The wimp's throwing us out of his house!"

"My husband's not a wimp!" yelled Martha.

Rufus leered. "You got some fire. I'm gonna enjoy that later, right after I settle the score for my brother."

"Last chance," said Jim. "Leave or else."

Rufus broke up laughing again. "So tell me, why do you want us to leave?"

"Because you're scumbags, and this is where my family lives."

Rufus's amusement tapered off.

Time was slowing down for Jim. It was like he was outside his body watching it all from the ceiling. He heard the words coming out of his own mouth like a tape recorder on dying batteries. It was as if a part of his brain that had always stayed behind a locked door was now in control. Jim saw himself begin to walk toward Rufus.

"My patience has run out," said Jim. "I can handle you being a loser and stupid and rude, but not all three at the same time."

Rufus stopped laughing and raised his gun. "You're in a serious rush to die, you little worm!"

"No!" Martha screamed.

Sly pointed across the room.

"I don't remember that costume."

"You're right," said Willie. "There wasn't any buffalo at the party."

The buffalo began to charge.

"Rufus! Watch out!"

"What—"

Too late. Mahoney and Serge nailed Rufus in the back. He tumbled over a coffee table, and his gun went flying. Rufus came up on the other side of the table mad as hell, yelling to his brothers. "Shoot the buffalo! Shoot the buffalo!"

Jim Davenport was approaching the speed of light. Time slowed, mass expanded, sound went dead. He saw Willie and Sly turn in slow motion and level pistols at the buffalo. He looked down and saw Rufus's loose gun skittering across the wood floor, taking forever. He dove for it.

Willie and Sly began firing at the buffalo. They hit it in the head, and the bison slammed against the wall. They continued firing, striking it again in the midsection and flank. The buffalo slumped in the corner.

Jim rolled on the floor, picking up the pistol. He continued the roll, onto his back, aiming at Willie and Sly. Jim was no trick shot—he didn't know guns at all. It was big and heavy and foreign in his hand. And he was still rolling fast as his pistol arm swept across the room. All he had was himself—a lifetime of discipline, circumspection and clarity. He would have only one chance, and he took an extra millisecond to aim and compensate for his roll, like a twisting basketball player adjusting during hang time at the top of a jump shot, then releasing just as he starts coming down.

Willie and Sly looked at their chests in disbelief. They touched their shirts. What the hell is this? Blood? They fell over.

Jim came up on his knees and instinctively fired behind the coffee table, the last place he had seen Rufus. But no Rufus.

Instead, Jim killed a grandfather clock. Time speeded back up to normal, and the sound came back on. People were screaming and crying and running in all directions. Everyone raced over to the buffalo and unzipped the costume. They pulled the back end off. Serge stood up and looked himself over.

"I can't believe I wasn't hit."

He looked down at the front end of the buffalo, lying there. "Mahoney!"

Jim and Serge grabbed the buffalo head and pulled it off. There was a lot of blood. Mahoney wasn't moving.

Serge lifted Mahoney's head. "Talk to me, buddy."

Mahoney opened his eyes. "Damn, that hurts!"

He sat up grimacing and grabbed his bloody right arm. "What about the McGraws?"

"Willie and Sly are dead," said Serge.

Gladys Plant stepped up next to Jim. "Wow, you've killed again. According to the experts, one more time and that technically makes you a serial killer."

"Serge," said Jim, "Rufus got away."

Serge looked around the living room. "Where's Ambrose?"

They heard tires squeal outside and ran to the window. The Ferrari took off down the street.

"He's got Ambrose!" yelled Coleman.

Serge ran for the front door, then hesitated and looked back in indecision.

"I'll be all right," said Mahoney. "Go save Ambrose. I'll catch up."

Serge nodded and opened the door.

"Serge!" yelled Mahoney.

Serge turned around.

"This doesn't change anything. I'm still gonna get ya."

48

IT WAS A MOONLESS EVENING. Approaching storm clouds from the east made the sky prematurely dark. It began to rain. A barge was moored in Tampa Bay; city workers in plastic ponchos set up a row of mortar launchers and went over safety checklists. The mist and clouds trapped the light from the city, creating an eerie yellow dome. Along Dale Mabry Highway, neon from steakhouses, sports bars and dance clubs reflected off the moist cars. Traffic was backed up from the three-day weekend.

Agent Mahoney slapped a bandage on his bad wing and jumped in the Crown Vic. He radioed a bulletin on the Ferrari, and immediately got reports of a car matching the description speeding north on Mabry. A police helicopter lifted off.

John Milton was approaching Tampa Bay Motors in Lance's gold Navigator. He spotted Rocco Silvertone standing outside the showroom, looking for customers. John slowed and pulled in the side entrance. He got out of the car, held the stun gun at his side and approached.

A snow-white Ferrari zoomed past the dealership.

"I can't believe it!" yelled Rocco. He jumped in his Corvette and sped after it.

"Nuts!" John ran back to the Navigator and took off after Rocco.

Vehicles moved in packs between the traffic signals up and down Dale Mabry. A red light stopped sixty cars in three lanes at the intersection with MLK Boulevard, across from the stadium. The Ferrari with Rufus and Ambrose sat in the pole position.

Serge and Coleman were six rows back in the Barracuda. Rocco
Silvertone gunned his Corvette in the middle of row fourteen.
John Milton was in the Navigator at the end of row seventeen,
and Agent Mahoney brought up the rear in row twenty. The rest
of the field was Tampa's standard nightly issue of young adults
flowing together in a sexually charged amoeban steel river of Sat-
urns, Mustangs and Corollas. Curbside homeless men with cardboard lies worked the intersections. The police helicopter hovered,
its search beam sweeping across the wet pavement for a Ferrari.
The rain came down harder, and the first bolt of lightning flew.

The light turned green; sixty cars began moving. The Ferrari got
a jump on the pack, but Serge slipped around a Camaro and
began gaining in the breakdown lane. Then Mahoney made his
move, squeezing by two carloads of teenagers driving abreast in
the left lanes, yelling to each other, trying to have sex. Everyone
accelerated to top speed, then braked and bunched together again
at the next red light. Tempers simmered through the long left-turn
cycles. Squatters sat under umbrellas at the four corners of the
intersection, selling used cassette tapes, broken wristwatches, two-
dollar rhinestone sunglasses and thoroughbred ferrets.

The light turned green. Everyone accelerated. The road opened
up and traffic spread out. Rufus got the Ferrari up to a hundred.
He looked in the rearview. Everyone was way back. Then something caught his peripheral vision. Two pizza trucks passed on
the left, continued accelerating and disappeared over the next
overpass.

There was an explosion. Rufus ducked. "What the hell?"

Ambrose pointed out the windshield. "The fireworks are starting."

"Fireworks!" said Coleman, hitting a joint. "Green, yellow,
pink, blue . . ."

Serge saw an opening and went for it. A Subaru driver on a cell
phone drifted left and forced a Sentra into a row of orange rubber
construction cones, and Serge used the opening left by the Subaru
to force them both into the construction area so he could pass.
The Sentra and Subaru rubbed sides, then diverged. The Subaru
caromed off a bus-stop rain shelter and wedged under a semi full
of Posturepedics. The Sentra spun out in the intersection, hit a

curb sideways and rolled, scattering a squadron of homeless men on the corner, cardboard signs Frisbeeing into the air as they dove for cover, knocking over ferret cages. The ferrets escaped northbound as the Sentra continued rolling and slammed into a Florida Power cherry picker, sending the crane arm spinning. The electrician leaped from the basket *F Troop*–style before it smashed into a transformer, which blew with a bang and a shower of sparks. All the traffic lights went out, and twenty blocks of Dale Mabry lost electricity. The police were in the middle of raiding the Red Snapper strip club during a surprise Tet Offensive of the mayor's War on Titty Bars when the power went. The strippers used the cover of darkness to make a run for it, and they came pouring out of the club, kicking off heels and sprinting south. The stampede of dancers was at full gallop when they were met in a Blockbuster Video parking lot by oncoming waves of terrified, scampering ferrets. The strippers shrieked and scattered like a billiard break. A motorist swerved to avoid the naked women spilling into traffic, and he locked up his wheels in the rain, jumping a curb and sliding into a gas pump. The man ran from the wrecked car as gasoline gushed across the concrete.

Mahoney was three blocks back when the hundred-foot firemushroom went up from the gas station. Traffic was snarled. Smoke filled the air. Sirens wailed. Helicopters swooped with search beams. More transformers began blowing in sequence down the highway like a string of firecrackers. Hysterical people ran crying everywhere. Some of the ferrets became separated and stood on their hind legs, looking for a familiar face. Looters hit the beer coolers at the burning gas station. Frantic strippers banged on the Crown Victoria, breasts pressed against the windshield: "For the love of God, take me with you!" Mahoney looked up at the elevated pedestrian bridge over the highway for the Yankees spring training complex, where Christ and the Antichrist waged fierce hand-to-hand combat against a backdrop of lightning and fireworks. Mahoney looked over at the Bible sitting on his passenger seat and laid a reverential hand on the cover. "So it begins in Tampa." Mahoney pulled out of traffic, popped his blackwall tires up onto the cement median, and floored the Crown Victoria straight into the Jaws of the Apocalypse.

The Ferrari was now all alone, a half mile ahead of everyone. Rufus sped up the next overpass, watching the bedlam unfolding in his rearview mirror. "Yes! We made it!"

He was still watching the mirror as he crested the overpass. He finally looked forward again. "Uh-oh."

The pavement ahead was covered with flares, stop sticks and pepperoni, where two overturned pizza-delivery trucks with punctured tires were engulfed in flames in front of a police roadblock.

Rufus hit the brakes, and the Ferrari went into a slow counterclockwise spin down the incline. It angled off the overpass and punched through the guardrail, sailing thirty feet before crashing into the embankment nosefirst and flipping out into the retention pond, landing upside down on top of a late-model Buick already stuck in the water. The force of the crash blew out all the windows in the Buick and collapsed the roof down to the headrests, still a good six inches above the heads of the four elderly women trapped inside.

Eunice pointed out the slit that used to be the passenger window. "An arm!"

"Pull it!" said Edith.

Eunice pulled it. It fell off.

It belonged to Rufus. He was dead.

There was a thud from above, followed by an "Ouch!"

Ambrose had pushed away his deflated airbag and hit the release latch on the seat belt. He fell to the roof.

"Someone's still alive up there," said Edith. She leaned toward the crack where her window used to be, just as Ambrose's upside-down head hung over the edge of the Buick.

"Stud-muffin!" said Edith.

"Uh-oh," said Ambrose.

Another voice: "I'll save you!"

It was Rocco Silvertone, sloshing through swamp water. "Hold on, Ambrose! Help's coming!"

Rocco broke through the edge of the cattails. He grabbed Ambrose under the armpits and pulled him the rest of the way out of the Ferrari, then carried him piggyback off through the reeds toward the highway.

"Hey! What about us?" said Edith.

It was quiet again.

"Shit."

ROCCO REACHED THE top of the embankment with Ambrose on his back. He stepped over the twisted guardrail and carefully lowered Ambrose to the ground. More cars arrived and screeched to a halt. Doors slammed.

Serge and Coleman jumped from the Barracuda and began running toward their little friend. "Ambrose! Are you okay?"

"Hold it right there!" ordered Rocco, seizing Ambrose around the neck with a thick forearm. He leaned to Ambrose's ear. "Who are those guys?"

"Oh, it's okay," said Ambrose. "They're my kidnappers."

"The kidnappers!" yelled Rocco. He pointed at Serge and Coleman. "Don't come any closer!"

Rocco wrapped his other arm around Ambrose's chest and lifted him off the ground. He began slowly backing up with Ambrose in front of him—not as a human shield, but more like a valuable prize that nobody was going to take away from him. "Stay where you are! I'm warning you!"

Agent Mahoney skidded up in his Crown Victoria. He jumped out and flashed his badge at Rocco. "Let him go!"

The police came running from the roadblock. Rocco pointed at Serge and Coleman. "They're the kidnappers! Get 'em!"

The police pulled their guns on Rocco.

"Not me, you idiots! *They're* the kidnappers! I'm the one who saved him!"

"Just stay calm," said Mahoney. "Nobody's going to get hurt." Mahoney saw someone quietly circling around behind Rocco, but he didn't give it away.

Rocco tightened his grip on Ambrose. "What's the matter with you!" he yelled at the cops. "The real kidnappers are standing right there! Arrest 'em before they get away!"

"Everything's going to be just fine."

Rocco heard another voice behind his left ear.

"Flipper was a dolphin." Then: *Zzzzzttt!*

Rocco flopped around the street from the stun gun. The police pounced and cuffed him. Ambrose went running toward Serge and Coleman, who met him halfway.

Serge grabbed the little guy by the shoulders and looked him over. "You okay, buddy?"

Ambrose nodded that he was.

The three turned for the Barracuda, but Serge suddenly stopped when he saw Mahoney standing there with his .38 by his side.

"Where can a poor shlub get some decent fried chicken in this town?" asked Mahoney. "And I want a side order of history. Local funk. A real joint."

"That would be Palios Brothers on MacDill Avenue," said Serge.

"This one's on the house," said Mahoney, holstering his pistol. "But it still doesn't change anything. Some day I'm gonna nail you. . . . Now get the hell out of here before I change my mind!"

Serge gave a quick salute, and they ran for the Barracuda.

Epilogue

And that's the story.

Thirty seconds to airtime. One of the hospitality ladies is pinning an EDITH name tag on me like I'm in kindergarten. They say they can't tell us apart.

We can hear the TV audience applauding now. It's time. They're leading us down the hall. They pull open the curtains. Here we go again.

"GOOD EVENING. I'M *Bill Maher and welcome to a special expanded edition of* Politically Incorrect. *By now you've probably all heard what happened down in Tampa, Florida, the third best place to live in the United States . . ."*

(Audience laughter)

". . . It's the story of a neighborhood's decay. Wild parties, kidnappings, drunkenness, fast cars, deviant parlor games. So I guess next year they'll be ranked number two . . ."

(Audience laughter)

"Let's all give a big hand as we meet the meet the neighbors we've reunited. The Davenports. It was their home that was invaded. They've since gone into real estate speculation, bought up all the vacant properties on the street and made a killing . . ."

(Applause)

"Jim and Martha, welcome . . ."

"Thanks, Bill. Martha and I would like to dispel some of the rumors . . ."

"Meet Ambrose Tarrington III, the kidnap victim. A millionaire in the eighties who went bust and now has a six-million-dollar movie deal. He's since gotten remarried—nudge-nudge—and is here tonight with his new wife, Edith Grabowski, and her brides-maids, the E-Team."

"Thanks, Bill. I—"

"Hey Edith, how's the sex life?"

"Better than yours."

"What a live wire! . . . Next is John Milton, now a highly sought-after workplace expert. John, I understand you were the consultant behind the recent demolition of the Consolidated Bank Building. Nice to have you."

"Thanks."

"Nothing else to say?"

"Well, I was going to point out—"

"I direct your attention to the television set on the side of the stage, where Rocco Silvertone is with us live from prison, where he is serving a life term for kidnapping . . ."

"We're going to appeal."

"But what about the evidence? The thinly veiled ransom message you left on that answering machine?"

"I can explain—"

"We also have with us the five college students who were renting across the street. They've since dropped out of school, opened up a chain of voyeur dorms on the Internet, gone public and retired. Is this where the institution of the neighborhood is going? We'll all just stay inside and watch each other on computers?"

"We hope so."

"Finally, we have Agent Mahoney, who cracked the case wide open. I understand your boss wasn't exactly grateful and gave you your walking papers. But you were quickly snatched up by the Metro-Dade Police Department, so the story has a happy end-ing. . . . Agent Mahoney, we'll start with you. What the hell kind of crazy neighborhood was this?"

"No different from a million others in Florida."

"So they're all like this? Is that some kind of indictment? . . . Jesse Jackson?"

"The real question is how do we come together and heal . . ."

"C'mon! Aren't we all getting just a little too touchy! . . . Carrot Top? Your thoughts?"

"I think this is a slippery slope . . ."

"Then what does that say about us as a people? Or does it say anything at all? . . . Howie Mandel?"

"Everyone's got an agenda now. You can't say anything without stepping on toes."

"Does anybody have a problem with that? . . . Penn and Teller?"

"We don't have a problem with that."

"Do we even need neighborhoods anymore? . . . Jewel?"

"We have to draw the line somewhere . . ."

"Oh, come on! . . . Jimmy Breslin?"

"I remember in the summer the whole neighborhood would sit outside the Fifty-sixth Precinct and open up the fire hydrants . . ."

"So the answer is mob rule? . . . Ice Cube?"

"I think there's a double standard here . . ."

"Hasn't the neighborhood been a myth for a while now, anyway? . . . Michael Douglas?"

"I disagree. When I was growing up, my father—"

"Mike, come on! Sex addict? Give me a break!"

"That was uncalled for."

"Anybody got a problem with that? . . . David Crosby?"

"Sorry, I wasn't paying attention."

"Hold on. We have a phone call. It's someone we've been trying to get in touch with for a while . . . Serge, what's going on?"

"Same old same old. Trying to find this dentist who owes us some money."

"Serge, I understand you're a big advocate of family neighborhoods. You've heard what the celebrities have said. Are they even in the ballpark?"

"Fuck celebrities."

(Audience gasp)

"Well (chuckle), that's why we call it Politically Incorrect. . . . So what's your take? Are neighborhoods a thing of the past?"

"It's anyone's ball game right now. The parents have home-field advantage, but the numbers are with the pinheads."

"I guess I know who you're pulling for."

"Whom."

"(Chuckle) *Maybe we should call this 'Grammatically Incorrect.'*"

(Audience laughter, building to applause)

"My hat's off to 'em. I considered starting a family myself, but I had to admit that I'm just not made of the same Right Stuff alloys like Jim and Martha."

(Gunfire and squealing tires in the background)

"Why do you say that?"

"I've watched them up close. It's a nerve-shattering daily routine raising a family with all the bozos running around today."

"You couldn't handle it?"

(Screaming, shattering glass)

"No way. You have to have balls of steel for that kind of work."

"Well put."

(Sirens, "Freeze! Police!" More gunfire)

"Bill, gotta run."

Click.

8/04   14   5/03
6/09   21   4/08
3/14   (30) 11/12
2/16   (32) 12/15